BLOOD HEIR

NEW YORK TIMES AND USA TODAY BESTSELLING AUTHOR

JASINDA WILDER

To Megan,

Thank you for your friendship over the past 10 years.

This one's for you!

BLOOD of HEIR

Chapter 1

"REMIND ME AGAIN WHY YOU PICKED LA?" I tug the seatbelt away from my chest and settle it more comfortably between my breasts. "At least I had a few friends in Sedona. Everyone here is a spoiled brat."

Mom sighs, brushing her long, pin-straight, glossy auburn hair over one shoulder. "Maeve, I told you. I got transferred."

"You worked for that company for less than a year. Why would they transfer you?"

"I impressed my boss, I guess, and they needed someone to take over the office here. It means a raise, plus the condo paid for by the company, and a company car." She glances at me, frowning. "We've been here for four months, and you're a month into school—you don't have *any* friends?"

"The condo is nice and the car is nice…for you. And sure, you bought some new outfits and that's cool, too. But Mom, you don't get it. I don't even have my own car. Everyone at school who can drive has, at minimum, a BMW or Mercedes. Their own. Not their parents', *theirs*. Their purses are Gucci, Chanel, YSL, and more than a few girls even have Birkins." I lift my purse off my lap. "I have a five-year-old Coach."

"Maeve—" Mom starts.

"You know I don't care about that stuff, Mom. That's not my point. I'm not telling you to go buy me a Birkin. The point is, they judge me for not having it. I'm not cool enough. I'm not blonde enough. My boobs aren't fake enough. And if I went and got all those things, it'd be something else, because I just…don't…*fit*."

Mom makes a face at me. "Girls in high school are getting boob jobs?"

I snort. "There's a girl who's a freshman who's talking about how she's trying to get her dad to get her one. I'm not sure she's even done growing her own actual boobs yet." I roll my eyes. "So yes, quite a few of the girls in my senior class have fake boobs."

Mom's eyes cut to me—to my slender build and my B-cup-on-a-good-day breasts. "You're beautiful, Maeve. You don't need bigger boobs to be beautiful."

I thunk my head against the window. "I *know* Mom. You're missing the point. I don't *want* a boob job. I don't *care*. The point is that I *hate* LA. Hate it. I get it if we can't go back to Sedona, I just…"

"You'd rather move again than stay here?" Mom's tone is shocked.

I groan and shake my head. "No. Maybe. I don't know." I watch the suburbs roll by—there's the giant house with the golden gates blocking the circular drive, which means we're close to the school. "No, I guess not. If you're asking me, I'll just suffer it out here and graduate. One school my whole senior year would be cool, even if I'm lonely and un-popular and have no friends and hate every single thing about Los Angeles."

Mom is quiet for a while, then sighs. "I'm sorry, Maeve. I know…I know I've put you through a lot, mov-ing around the way we have."

I snort, but say nothing; "moving around the way we have" is code for "we've moved at least once a year every year of my entire life, and some years we've moved twice, and my sophomore year we moved three times." All for work, or so Mom says. I'm not sure I believe her, but there's no arguing with her. If I bring it up, if I try to push the topic, she just shuts down and refuses to answer. She won't ignore me, she never yells back, and she doesn't engage.

We drive the rest of the way to the school in silence. She pulls into the drop-off line—in which I'm the only se-nior. The vice principal, Mr. Singleton, strides over to our car. Mr. Singleton is tall, Black, handsome, and a student body favorite staff member. He's funny, charming, under-standing, and seems to know just about everyone in the school, which should be impossible, considering there are a couple of thousand kids.

Mr. Singleton has a thing for my Mom. He clips his walkie-talkie to the hip pocket of his khaki chinos, smooths his wildly colorful tie down his chest—he's famous for his collection of bright, almost offensively colorful ties, and the graduating class gives him a new one at graduation, or so goes the tradition.

He leans into my open door before I can slide out. "Eliza, hey." He shoots her his toothy white grin. "Good morning, so far?"

"Sure is, Tom," Mom says, giving him a shy smile in return. "You?"

Mr. Singleton's smile widens, brightens. "Oh you know, can't complain. Not that I would even if I could. Gotta stay positive for these kids."

"You're a wonderful example of positivity for them, Tom." Mom lets her hair fall in a curtain across her face between her gaze and his, and rolls her shoulder. "Well, I should go. Better not be late."

Mr. Singleton backs away, letting me out. "Well, I hope I see you around, Eliza. Have a good day."

"You too." I duck and wave at Mom. "Bye, Mom. Love you. See you later."

"Love you too, honey. Have a good day at school."

He closes the door and turns to me as I drape my purse across my torso and shoulder my backpack. "Your mom is something else, Maeve. You know that?"

I barely restrain an eye roll. "Yeah, she sure is."

He claps me on the shoulder. "See you later, Maeve."

I just nod and head inside.

God, men. They fall all over my mom everywhere we go. In every school I've ever been to, at least one of the male faculty develops an intense crush on her. More than once, they've been married. Mom never seems to acknowledge their crush and certainly never encourages them to act on it.

And I get it. She's tall, she's slender but still curvy. Her eyes are so pale blue they're almost white, startlingly bright and intense. Her hair is long and glossy and perfect, and in the right light, almost glows reddish. She's quiet, shy, and intelligent.

And I'm a near clone to her, in appearance and personality. Except where Mom seems to have some sort of internal magnetism that draws people to her…I don't. And where Mom is ethereally graceful in every movement, I'm clumsy and prone to tripping over my feet—it's an affliction, really.

My balance is fine, my hand-eye coordination is fine…my feet just seem to refuse to cooperate with my brain, sometimes. I've even had doctors look at me for it, but they just say it's a phase and I'll grow out of it. So far, I haven't. And I'm eighteen, almost nineteen. I'm starting to despair that I never will grow out of it. I'll just be clumsy my whole life.

School is dreadful. Boring. Stupid. In some classes, like English and history, I've already covered the material. Others, like calculus and physics, they're teaching new material I've not covered yet or they're teaching it in a different way than I'm used to. I sit alone at lunch. The Material Girls follow me from lunch to physics; that's my internal nickname for the gaggle of the most popular girls in the school—the mean girls. The ones who drive Porsches and carry Birkins, the ones whose fathers are CEOs and celebrities and plastic surgeons to A-listers. They follow me and stage-whisper about my white Converse shoes, on which I've doodled abstract designs in black Sharpie. Or about my ugly, fake-leather, five-year-old Coach purse that wasn't even good when it was new. Or about how I don't even wear makeup. And god, could I at least put on a bra?

I don't bother responding. I like my shoes—doodling on them gets me through boring classes. I wouldn't mind a nicer, newer purse, but this one is fine and I'm not ever going to be part of their clique, even if I wanted to, even if I had the most expensive Birkin on the planet. I hate makeup and refuse to wear clown paint on my face in some ridiculous, patriarchal notion of attracting the attention of men—most of whom aren't even going to pay attention to my face in the first place. They're going to be staring at my chest. And speaking of which—I don't wear bras because I don't need to, for one, and they're uncomfortable and constrictive, for another, and also, I just don't care if my boobs are saggy or whatever when I'm older. So you can see the outlines of my nipples. Oh, the horror. Whatever shall you do?

God.

Snobby, judgmental bitches.

I hate LA. Have I mentioned that, yet?

I suffer through physics, languish through AP History, doze through Literature of the Western World From Chaucer through the Modern Era, and then finally I can leave the sunless, noisy, prison that is high school. Mom works late, so I have to take the bus. With the freshman and sophomores.

I put in my earbuds and work on homework; I'm the last stop, which means I get the majority of my homework done by the time I'm home. The condo is quiet, tomb-like. There's very little by way of personalization—Mom never bothers with nonsense like decorating. There are a few framed photos of her and me throughout the years, but that's about it. The walls are bare. The furniture isn't even ours—we don't own furniture, we always rent fully furnished condos or apartments. It means when Mom is ready to pick up and go, again, all we need to do is shove our clothing into a handful of suitcases and box up stuff from the kitchen and bathrooms. We can be packed and on the road in under three hours, max. Usually, less.

There's not even a TV—we both have laptops, and neither of us is into TV. The one unnecessary thing we lug around with us everywhere is our books: we have a lot of books. Several heavy crates of them, which Mom always displays in a handful of ancient red and black plastic crates, the kind with holes in them, from way back in the day. They all stack openings out in three rows of four high, and they're filled to the brim and double-stacked with dog-eared paperbacks of all genres, but mostly romance and historical fiction.

I finish my homework, stream some reality TV on my laptop, and then make myself dinner—frozen burritos slathered liberally with sour cream and melted cheese, with a side of nachos, by which I mean corn chips with more cheese melted on top. More Netflix. Thumb through social media—I'm a lurker who never posts; most of my contacts on social media are people from previous schools, which I suppose is a form of self-torture, seeing as I'll never actually encounter any of them again. It's a way of pretending I have a social life, perhaps. Lame, I guess.

I quickly tire of social media and go back to my favorite secret indulgence: Real Housewives. I love the arguing, the drunken fights in exotic locales, the over-the-top craziness. It makes me feel something like normal.

I must doze off, because I wake up, instantly and

abruptly—I'm on the couch. My laptop fell off my lap and onto the floor beside me; the battery died, so the screen is black and silent.

The condo is dark.

Mom never came home.

I swallow worry as I get up and pad across the living room to the short hallway, peek into her room. Dark. The bed is tidily made, as always, with neat corners and perfectly fluffed pillows. The bathroom is dark. There's nowhere else she could be; the condo is two bedrooms, two bathrooms, the living room, and the kitchen.

I dig my phone out of my purse; no missed calls, no unread messages.

I call her—it goes to voicemail: "Hi, you've reached Eliza Sparrow. Sorry I missed your call. Leave a message and I'll get back to you as soon as I can."

"Mom? Where are you? It's…" I trail off, glance at the time on my phone screen, "four thirty in the morning and you're not home. I'm worried. Call me ASAP."

It's not like her. She's always home on time. If she's going to be somewhere else, she tells me. She does go on dates occasionally, but she always tells me first, and she always drops me a pin to wherever they're going for dinner, and when she'll be home. Usually, she texts me updates every couple of hours. She's never stayed out all night, not once in my whole life.

I try the "Find My" app, but all it does is spin, and show "location not found." Which means her phone must be dead.

I know even if I called the police, they wouldn't take it seriously for another twenty-four hours, at least. Although, that may be TV bullshit. I don't know.

How am I supposed to get to school? I'm not on the bus pickup route since Mom always takes me to school.

I manage to pass the hours until things start to open: I take a shower, blow-dry and brush my hair, then braid it in an elaborate, time-consuming, intricate series of braids. My phone is on the sink, and I check it obsessively.

At seven, I call her again. Straight to voicemail; leave another message, this one verging on angry.

Last time, it rang, at least.

I have her work number, but no one is there till eight-thirty.

I skip school. Try to read ahead in the book assigned for Lit, but I have to reread each paragraph ten times, and eventually give up.

I call Mom again at seven-thirty, leave a third message, this one equal parts and angry and scared.

Again at 7:45.

I quit leaving messages after the third one.

I pace the condo obsessively. Just for something to do until her office opens, I scrub the counters, sweep the kitchen, and vacuum every room. I make my bed. Pace some more.

Finally, it's eight thirty, and I call her office.

"Hello, McCaffery Accounting, how may I help you?" A pleasant female voice, of indeterminate age.

"Hi, this is Maeve Sparrow, Eliza's daughter? I, um. I was wondering if she's been into work yet today." I try to keep the panic out of my voice.

"Maeve? Hi, honey. Um, no, Eliza's not in yet. In fact, it's rather unusual, she's always very punctual."

"What time did she leave, yesterday, do you know?"

"Is something wrong?"

I swallow hard. "I, um. She never came home last night. I'm sure it's…" I can't bring myself to say it's nothing, because in my gut, I know it's not.

"She left when she usually does, honey, right at six-thirty."

"Did she seem…I dunno. Normal?"

A pause. "She did seem a little stressed out, now that you mention it. She spent the last hour or so of the day on her phone, texting someone. Which is kind of unusual for Eliza."

"Do you know who?" I ask.

"No, I'm sorry, I don't."

"Do you…I don't suppose you know if there's anywhere she'd go?"

A kind, worried sigh. "No, I'm sorry. Have you tried calling the area hospitals?"

"I guess I'll do that next. Thanks." I don't wait for her to hang up or say goodbye, I just end the call.

I search nearby hospitals. The one closest to her work doesn't have a patient under Mom's name, nor any Jane Does. Same for the hospital closest to our house. I'm on hold with the third hospital, farther away but nearer the interstate, when there's a knock at the door.

Panic, fear, and dread swirl inside me like a thick, black, heavy sludge, settling deep in my gut like an acidic bowling ball. I hesitate at the door, hand trembling as I reach for the knob. There's another knock, firm and authoritative—this is silly, perhaps, but it just *feels* like a policeman's knock.

I open the door, and the bowling ball in my belly explodes into shrapnel of horrible knowledge; on the other side of the threshold is a uniformed police officer.

"Maeve Sparrow?" His voice is quiet, smooth, and even. Overtones of professional composure, with subtle notes of compassion.

"Y-yes?"

"I'm Officer James Hawthorne. May I come in?"

I scan him—the uniform looks right. The utility belt has all the usual things—yellow-handled taser on one side, service pistol on the other, handcuffs, and all the other stuff I'm not sure of. His badge is shiny, proclaiming his name, with the badge number.

I step back and lead the way into the living room, sitting on the edge of the couch. Officer Hawthorne sits on the loveseat kitty-corner to me. For a moment, he just sits, as if looking for the right words.

He's young and improbably hot—it's an absurd, inappropriate thought, but it's there. His features are perfectly symmetrical, his jawline square and strong, clean-shaven with nary a hint of stubble. Blue eyes, blond hair still neatly combed even as he holds his hat on his thighs. His uniform doesn't quite hide his bulging biceps and broad shoulders.

I shouldn't find him attractive, but I do.

Almost worrisomely so.

Something in my gut shivers, something in my bones hums at his presence. A sort of buzzing. Physical, yet undefinable. I've never felt it before.

He addresses me with a heavy, sorrowful tone. "Ms. Sparrow, I'm sorry to be the one to tell you this, but, there was a car accident yesterday evening, on the interstate. Your mother was involved. And, I'm afraid she's...I'm afraid your mother has passed away."

"If the accident was last night, why am I just being notified now?" I ask.

He doesn't quite hide a wince. "The accident was…well, there's no polite way to put it, Ms. Sparrow, it was quite bad. Semi versus car. It took medical staff some time to, um, identify your mother's…remains. They had to use dental records."

I swallow hard. "They know it was her?"

He nods. "I'm afraid so. The driver of the semi is still in critical condition, and your mother was the only other victim involved."

"Do I…do I need to come identify her or anything?" I'm trying to think of what happens on TV.

He shakes his head. "No, that's not…no. I believe they have some of her personal effects, whatever they were able to recover from the scene of the accident. Which wasn't much. As I said, it was…it was quite a violent crash. There wasn't much left of her car."

"Um." I shake my head. "What—what do I do?"

"Do you have any family you can contact?"

"No." I feel tears pooling in my eyes, but I think I'm in shock more than anything. "How do I get to the hospital?"

He checks his watch, then smiles at me. It's a complicated smile—professional, compassionate, and composed. "I can take you and bring you back, if you like."

"That—I would appreciate it."

The ride to the hospital is silent. I ride up front, in the passenger seat of his cruiser. Under other circumstances, I might be curious, even a little excited. Not now. Not like this. His radio crackles a few times, and a call comes through, at one point; he answers it in crisp, clear, brief tones, using professional lingo and codes.

He parks under the portico at the main entrance and leaves the cruiser running, but locks the doors. He guides me through the maze of the hospital corridors, from one elevator to another, across wings, past gurneys, and pairs of doctors and squadrons of nurses. Eventually, we come to a quiet little sub-office far underground, in a back corner. A male nurse is acting as a receptionist in color-coded scrubs. He takes my name and Mom's name. Nods, leaves—after a few minutes, he comes back with a large plastic bag. I see Mom's purse—scorched, battered, ripped; her cell phone, mangled until it's barely recognizable. There's a handful of individual purse contents pooled at the bottom of the plastic bag: lipstick, a package of antibacterial wipes, hand sanitizer, her favorite lotion.

I take the bag of effects, and thank the receptionist; Officer Hawthorne waited outside the little office.

He drives me home. Walks me to my door.

"Officer Hawthorne?" I ask as he turns to leave. "What do I do now?"

He opens his mouth to respond, but his radio squawks with a call—his eyes widen and he responds to the call as he jogs away, with an apologetic glance at me over his shoulder.

I guess I'm on my own.

Inside the condo, I close the door. Lock it behind me. And then…just stand there.

It doesn't seem real. Doesn't seem possible.

What do I do now?

CHAPTER 2

J EXPECT SOMEONE TO CALL ME, OR SHOW up. I feel like there should be some sort of arrangements I have to make, right? In the movies, when someone dies, there are "arrangements" to be made.

I'm an eighteen-year-old high school student. I've never paid a bill. Mom's wallet, supposedly, was never found at the scene of the accident, so I don't even have her cards or anything. How do I access her bank accounts? How do I buy food? What about rent? There are no child services because I'm eighteen, I assume. Did she have a will? What would she have to leave me in a will anyway?

I call the school and tell them there was a

family emergency—I can't bring myself to say the words. I tell them I need a bus pickup.

School.

How am I supposed to go to school?

I keep expecting her to walk through the door, but she never does. She's just...gone.

The next day, I sleep through my alarm.

I sleep until my eyes literally won't stay closed anymore, and even then, I can't make myself get out of bed.

Eventually, I have to pee.

And once I've peed, I have some vague notion that I should eat—cereal tastes like cardboard, but I choke it down anyway.

The silence is what does it, eventually.

The empty condo.

Mom's room, the bed still made. Her phone charger cord trailing over her bedside table, the end hanging limp.

It's the silence.

I can't fall asleep that night and end up staying awake until the next day, bingeing some documentary on Hulu.

I don't bother with food.

I dress in Mom's clothes. They smell like her.

Her best jeans—they always look so good on her, fitting her like a second skin. On me, they just seem too tight. Constrictive. I can barely move. But yet, I don't take them off. They're hers. I wear her blouse, a black sleeveless button-down. My Converse; I couldn't handle her shoes, since they're all heels. I even wear a bra—my own. I stand in front of her mirror in her bathroom and think about putting on her makeup, but I can't bring myself to do it. I do use her brush, for about three strokes through my hair, and then I look at the brush, with strands of her hair still in it.

I leave my hair down, loose around my shoulders.

I'm early for the bus, at the new stop, a couple of blocks away.

I listen to Mom's favorite band, an acoustic duo.

I drift through the day, barely hearing anything. I think I may have had a test in history, but I don't remember taking it.

The Material Girls trail me from lunch to physics again, and the sound of their voices and the usual parade of ridiculous insults rake down my spine like knives on a blackboard. Usually, I can tune them out. Today, I can't.

I whirl on them, fury and agony blazing inside me, radiating from my very pores. I can't even summon words, I just stalk toward them, so charged with the emotions churning inside me that I feel like I'm on fire, like something inside me is going to catch fire and snap.

I don't know what they see in me, in my eyes, but they stumble to a halt, fear in their eyes, stammering apologies, and then they turn and flee.

In physics, I ignore the teacher entirely and doodle on my shoes. When he calls on me, I just stare at him; he must see something in my eyes, because he trails off mid-question, and turns his attention to someone else.

I skip my last class, sit outside behind the gym and wonder why I haven't cried yet.

Except for the pooling of almost-tears with Officer Hawthorne, I haven't shed one tear.

Maybe I'm still in shock.

When the bell rings at the end of the day, I drift to the bus. Sit at the back, earbuds in, staring at the ceiling. I don't even care if I'm in public, on a bus full of freshmen and sophomores—I will myself to cry for my mother.

I can't.

It doesn't seem real, or true. When I get home, I walk through the door and I have a moment of expectation, where I look around, expecting to see Mom on the couch, or at the kitchen counter, embarrassed at the silly mixup.

She's not there.

She's not anywhere.

And I can't cry.

I make it through a whole week. It's a blur, honestly. Faces, voices, bus rides.

The cupboards and refrigerator are getting thin.

Shouldn't there be…someone? Some official "they" to make sure I deal with…things?

Yet there's no one. Just me, alone in the condo. Alone at school.

Did Mom have a mother or father? It's another thing she never spoke of. I always just assumed they were estranged.

I search her room—I find an envelope full of 100s in the bottom of her underwear drawer, at the back, hidden behind old underwear she never wears but doesn't throw away; I count $5000.

There's jewelry, but nothing special. No keepsakes, no heirlooms. No lockbox in her closet. No safe deposit box key. No shoebox full of old letters or photographs. Just her clothes, her shoes, her makeup, her basic personal belongings—but nothing to say *who she was.*

Who was she?

She loved Penny & Sparrow, and Johnnyswim, and

Drew Holcomb and the Neighbors. She liked Dateline murder mysteries and standup comedy specials. She hated onions and loved avocados. She dressed somewhere between a mom and a fashionable younger woman: fitted jeans, T-shirts and blouses, blazers, slacks, and skirts. Nothing crazy sexy, but not frumpy either. She went on dates fairly regularly, but I never met any of the men, and as far as I am aware, never went to their houses and certainly never brought them here. At least, not when I was here. Her favorite color was forest green. She could peel a clementine in one long spiral.

I have her eyes.

I have her everything—her body type, her hair, her shy, quiet mannerisms.

I don't have her grace, or her mysterious ability to draw the attention of every man around her without ever seeming to try, or even really noticing. She wasn't showy or flashy or loud. People just…noticed her.

People wanted to do things for her. Women, too. Cashiers, bankers, and gas station attendants. One time, we ran out of gas and she convinced the clerk to give us gas for free. I don't know how.

But…who was she? Where did she grow up? Who were her parents?

How old was she? I don't even know that.

How do I know so little about my own mother?

Another week passes, and something is building up inside my chest. Weight, and pressure.

Grief, I think.

I just don't know what to do with it.

I've stood beneath the shower spray thinking of her and missing her and wanting her back, but I can't cry.

I'm going through the motions at school, and I'm sure my grades are suffering, but I can't summon the energy to care.

The thing in my chest grows. It feels almost hot, and dense. Sometimes, it chokes off my breath, and makes my eyes water, my head spin…

But I still can't get it out.

I'm alone.

Ten at night. I'm listlessly watching Dateline, for Mom, even though I hate these stupid murder shows.

There's a knock at the door. It's firm, three sharp raps.

I shut my laptop and set it on the coffee table. I turn on a light since I was in the dark.

On the other side of the door is a man just into middle age. Tall, lean, sharp-featured. Very, very handsome. His hair is dark, not quite black, clean cut. He's wearing clean dark blue jeans, a white button-down with an open collar, and a thin black leather jacket. The jacket looks expensive. His boots are well-worn western boots; there's dirt on the toes and heel, old and dried.

Everything about him screams law enforcement.

"Can I help you?" I ask, poking my head through the cracked-open door.

"Are you Maeve Sparrow?"

"Yes."

He pulls his wallet out of his jacket's inside pocket,

and I see the butt of a pistol. He flips open his wallet, showing me a badge and a license. "My name is Detective Andreas Burke."

"Andreas?"

He shrugs, smirking self-consciously. "Family name. I go by Andy." He doesn't look like an Andy. He looks like an Andreas. "May I come in, please?"

"Are you with the LAPD?"

He shakes his head. "No, I'm not. I'm from Michigan. A tiny little town up on the northern shores of the lower peninsula called Elk Rivers."

"Is this about my mother?"

He nods. "It is."

I blink, confused. "Um, sure." I open the door the rest of the way and step aside to allow him in. He takes a seat on the couch, in almost exactly the same place Officer Hawthorne sat. "How can I help you, Detective Burke?"

"Andy, please." He stares at me. "You look *so* much like Eliza."

My eyes widen. "You knew Mom?"

He nods. "I did." He blinks a few times, jaw tightening briefly. "I knew her quite well, as a matter of fact." A bark of laughter.

"I'm sorry, Detective, but I'm not sure what's funny."

He shakes his head. "Nothing's funny, Maeve. It's just…I'm your father. I was engaged to your mother. To Eliza."

My head spins, dizziness rippling through me. "Excuse me?"

He pulls his phone from his back pocket, unlocks it, scrolls with his thumb a few times, taps, and then turns the phone to me. "Look."

It's him, with Mom. Neither of them looks much different, perhaps a little younger. She's tucked under his arm, her head resting against his chest, a hand on his belly. His arm is slung over her shoulder with his hand resting possessively on her hip. They look…in love. Happy. There's no way to tell when or where the photo was taken since all that's visible in the background is a brick wall.

"Who took this?" I ask.

"A…friend. Someone no longer with us." He sighs. "Swipe right—there are two more photos."

I move my thumb from right to left. The next photo was taken by the same person, in the same place, moments after the previous one. Andreas—Andy—is laughing, eyes crinkled, white teeth flashing. He's tickling Mom, who is trying to get away while laughing as well. I've never seen Mom look that way. That carefree, that happy.

The next photo is just Mom. She's leaning against a huge pine tree, wearing a tiny sleeveless white sundress—her legs are long and bare, her arms bare. No bra, hair loose and tangled and drifting across her face. She's pulling it away from her mouth, not smiling. Her eyes, though… they communicate desire, and love, and humor. Her feet are bare, one foot propped up against the tree behind her.

"I took that one about a month before she disappeared." His voice is thick, low.

"Disappeared?" I ask, looking up at him. "What do you mean, she disappeared?"

He lifts one shoulder, accepting his phone back. "I mean, I woke up one morning, and she was gone. Packed her clothes in a suitcase, took all her toiletries, a framed photo of us, and about half the cash we'd been saving. She left a note." He pauses, then quotes. "'Andreas, my love. I'm sorry. One day I hope you'll forgive me.'" He shakes his head. "That's it. No reason. I never saw her again."

"She loved you, you loved her, but she just…left?" I ask. "Why?"

He shrugs. "I never knew. Not until four days ago, when I received an anonymous email telling me that Eliza Sparrow had been killed in a car accident, and was survived by her daughter, who has no other family."

I watch him carefully—something isn't adding up. "How does that lead you to think you're my father?"

"It's the only thing that would make any sense. I was about to leave for the police academy at the time. We'd been…arguing, I guess, about our future. Where we would go if we did get married. She wanted to wait until I was done at the academy to get married. She didn't want to hold me back from my future—she knew all I ever wanted was to be a cop, a detective. She was worried if we got married we'd…it'd hold me back. I didn't care. I loved her. I wanted to be her husband. I wanted it all with her."

"And then she came up pregnant and decided…what? To leave without warning, without telling you she was pregnant? Without even giving you an option?" I frown, shake my head.

He doesn't answer for a while. "Maeve. I…I loved your mother. I never stopped. Even after she left. There've been other women, of course, but…nothing that's lasted, because there's never been anyone who could compare with Eliza." He looks away from me, seeing the past, I think. "But your mother wasn't perfect. She was…flighty. Easily spooked. She never wanted to stay in one place for long, you know? Like, she couldn't sit still. She changed apartments every few months, never took out a lease, only rented month to month. Before we got together, she moved around the country—even lived in Europe for a few years. She lived in Paris, Berlin, Vienna, Prague, Budapest, Norway, Finland, Iceland. She was just…nomadic. And I…I wanted to be a cop. Which meant staying in one place. And having a baby with me? Let alone getting married? It scared her. So yeah, she left. With you. And never told me."

I shoot to my feet and pace away from him to the window. "My whole life, I've never lived anywhere longer than six months. I've been to five elementary schools, two middle schools, and six high schools."

"Sounds like Eliza." He stays where he is, on the couch. "I know it can't be easy to hear this. And I'm sure you have questions."

"Why are you here, Detective Burke?" I turn around, back to the window, and meet his dark, impenetrable gaze. "What do you want from me?"

He smiles—it's kind, friendly. "I want you to come with me. Live with me."

"In Michigan?"

He nods. "Yes. There's a good high school so you can finish out your senior year. It's not far from malls and movie theaters. There's lots to do. I don't know what you're into, but…" he trails off, shrugging, lifting his hands palms up.

"I just met you five minutes ago."

He nods. "I know. I don't expect you to, like, call me Dad or anything. We'd just be friends. Roommates, sort of. But…Maeve, you're alone here. I'm just offering you…a place to be, where you're not alone. I can help take care of you until you graduate and figure out what you want to do."

I turn away. My eyes burn, my throat burns. "I never saw her body. There was no funeral. I don't…I don't know what to do. I don't know how to pay rent. I don't…" I shake my head. "I don't know what to do."

"I know. And that's why I'm here." I hear the couch shift as he stands up, and I hear his steps, feel him behind me.

He touches my shoulder—a frisson of something sharp and wild moves through my gut at his touch. It's a strange, intense, and scary reaction to a simple touch.

"I might be wrong. Maybe I'm not your father. Without a paternity test, there's no way to know for sure. But honestly, I don't really care. I loved your mom, and I think part of me always has and always will. You're part of her. And I know she'd want you taken care of. She wouldn't want you to be alone. If you want, I can just stay for a few days and help you figure out arrangements for your mom, and try to set you up here on your own. You'd need a job, and probably a different condo. Unless your mom bought this one, there's no way you'd be able to afford this place on the kind of income you'd make as an eighteen-year-old."

"It's provided by her job," I say. "I've been half expecting someone to come tell me I have to leave. But….there's been no one. No one's told me anything. A police officer showed up, told me Mom had been killed, brought me to the hospital to get what was left of her effects after the wreck, brought me back here…and then nothing. From anyone. Till you."

He frowns. "That's not how these things are supposed to work."

I shrug. "I don't know—I don't know how anything is supposed to work." My throat aches and my words come out hoarse—like they've been scorched by the heat in my esophagus. "All I know is Mom never came home from work one day, and now I'm alone."

"And that's why I'm here," he repeats. "You're not alone anymore."

"I don't know you."

"That's okay. We can get to know each other. It'll be awkward at times, I'm sure. But it's gotta be better than what you're facing here, alone, right?"

I turn and look at him—all I see in his dark eyes is compassion. I see no deceit, no subterfuge. "Michigan?"

He nods. "Yup. Way up north. There are beaches, hiking trails, horse riding, there's skiing or snowboarding in the winter. It's not LA, but it's not the boonies, either." He laughs. "Well, the town where I live, Elk Rivers…it's pretty quiet. Very small, the kind of place where everyone knows everyone. But it's not far from Traverse City, which is… not metropolitan, but it's not nothing, either."

"I've never seen snow," I tell him.

He blinks, and then laughs. "What?"

I nod. "We've always lived in hot, sunny places. LA, Sedona, Phoenix, New Orleans, Miami, Ft. Lauderdale, San Francisco, Santa Fe. We lived in Nashville for a few months, when I was…eleven? I think it sort of snowed, once, but it didn't stick, and by the time school got out, it was raining again."

He laughs. "Well, I guess we'll have to get you a winter wardrobe, huh? We can cross that bridge when we come to it. For now, we just handle today. How's Michigan sound, Maeve?"

I try to smile. Almost manage it. "I guess it's better than being here alone. So…sure. I'm in."

He nods, slaps his thighs. "Well, I have a hotel not far

from here. I'll come by tomorrow morning and we can figure out our next steps."

"I guess I shouldn't go to school, huh?"

He shakes his head. "Nah, you're transferring. I'm not your guardian, but you're eighteen, right?" He waves a hand. "We'll figure it out. You don't have to worry about a thing, okay? Just get some sleep. We'll take this one step at a time."

It's an awkward moment, then. He's my dad, supposedly. Am I supposed to hug him? Shake his hand? Call him Andy?

He gives my shoulder a rough, friendly squeeze. "I'll see you tomorrow, kiddo."

"Um, okay. Bye?" It comes out like a question.

He doesn't seem to mind. He heads for the door, then pauses, digs his wallet out and tosses a business card on the kitchen counter. "That's my cell on there. You need anything, you call, okay? Day or night, no matter what it is."

"Thanks."

He just nods and takes his leave.

I'm alone again.

This is all happening so fast. I have a father? Mom wouldn't tell me a single thing about my dad. Just that it was history, and not a history she cared to discuss. I had her, and that's what mattered.

Am I allowed to be angry at her? For keeping the truth about my father from me? For keeping him out of my life? For moving me around so frequently?

For dying?

Am I a bad daughter for not being able to cry for her?

I eventually fall asleep, and when I do, I dream of Detective Andreas Burke. His eyes, watching me, smiling at me—in the dream, his eyes seem to glow, almost. The dark rings around his pupils are backlit, brown and amber and golden, warm light from within. His features are sharper, more angular…not quite normal. Something off, something different. There's something off about his ears, but in the way of dreams, before I can figure it out, the dream shifts.

I see Mom.

She's wearing creased white business slacks, a pale blue sleeveless button-down blouse, and a matching white blazer with the sleeves pushed up to her elbows—the outfit she was wearing the day she…the last time I saw her. Her feet are bare. Her face is in shadow. Her eyes glow like Andy's—her eyes are pale blue, almost white, and they glow incandescent, like miniature versions of those LED light rings social media influencers use for recording videos.

"*Maeve, honey.*" Her voice is faint, distant, and echoing. "*I love you.*"

"*Mom?*" My voice is loud in my dream-ears, yet mine also echoes, as if we're in a large, empty room.

There's nothing around us. Just blackness. Darkness. Shadows.

"*Andreas…*" It's a whisper, faint, shivering with emotion. "*…Good.*"

"*Mom? Come back. Please.*" I hear the tremble in my voice. I want to reach for her, but I don't have hands. I don't have anything, I'm not a person, I'm just a ball of nothingness, aching for my mother.

"*Maeve…You're not you, yet.*" This is stronger, clearer.

Yet, my vision of her is fading. Shadows consume her. Writhing tendrils of darkness curl around her thighs, winding up around her hips, over her shoulders, and into her hair.

"*No!*" I cry. "*Let her go!*"

"*You're not you, yet.*" Faint, now.

All I can see of Mom is a bare foot, the nails painted pale pink, chipped—the way her toes looked in life, the day she didn't come home. A hand. Her nose. Those glowing white rings that are her eyes—the rings fade. The light in them dims.

My soul aches. I want to reach for her, pull her out of the grip of the shadows. I want to cry, but I can't. I want to scream, but I have no mouth. There is no me, only the darkness and my lonely heart, and my mother, vanishing into nothingness.

"*Maeve...*"

I wake up with a start.

I'm alone, in my bed. It's dawn.

Usually, when I remember my dreams, I only remember scraps and pieces, vague impressions that fade as the day wears on.

This dream, I remember every single instant. Every word. Every feeling.

Even as I wake up, it feels more real than reality.

One detail in particular stands out: in the dream, mom's ears curved back into delicate, arched, pointed tips. In life, she had tiny round little ears.

I don't understand.

"Mom?" I whisper into the silence of my bedroom. Nothing.

I pad into the kitchen and pick up Detective Burke's business card. Hold it in my hands and stare down at the ten digits of his phone number.

There's only one real choice, though. I don't know how to be alone. I'm not an adult. Maybe I should be—maybe in another era I would be. But I'm not. I'm a girl in high school.

I call him; he answers on the third ring. "Detective Burke?"

His laugh is warm and kind. "Call me Andy, or Andreas, if you must. Your mom always called me Andreas, never Andy. She thought it didn't suit me."

"Fine. Andreas, then." I swallow hard. "I'll go to Michigan with you."

He sighs in relief. "Good—good. I'll be by with breakfast in a few minutes. You drink coffee?"

"Yes."

"You like donuts?"

I actually laugh. "Who *doesn't* like donuts?"

"Good answer. I'll see you in twenty minutes."

I laugh again. "This is LA, Andreas. I'll see you in an hour."

It's thirty minutes, and he arrives with two huge paper cups of coffee and a dozen assorted donuts.

He bumps me with his shoulder, a friendly, masculine gesture—I feel that odd frisson of energy again.

I think of my dream.

His ears are normal, round like anyone else's. His eyes don't glow.

Maybe I'm going crazy. Can grief make you hallucinate?

Chapter 3

Michigan feels like a totally different country. It's like nowhere I've ever been before—it's closest to Tennessee.

We're in his truck—a huge black beast of a thing, old, maybe even a classic, but inside it's all red quilted leather and a shiny new touchscreen radio, with big knobby tires. I had to literally climb up into it. It's splattered with dried mud. There are thick, heavy, muddy chains in the bed and a chrome brush guard with a heavy-duty winch.

We flew from LA to some tiny local airport. Cherry something, maybe. And then we drove past fast food places and car dealerships and banks and microscopic strip malls with yoga studios and organic grocery stores. Past hotels with a crescent of bay beyond them. Then it all opens up, no more hotels, no more restaurants, just the bay, miles of water with a strip of land jutting out into it, and then open water beyond. After a while, the bay is occluded by trees lining both sides of the two-lane highway. Pines, fir, and spruce, with some deciduous mixed in. Thick, so thick you can barely see past the first row of trees. There's an occasional break for a driveway and mailbox, and sometimes a sign proclaiming the name of the property. Cutesy names like "Wave Break Inn" or "Clark's Cove."

We've been driving for nearly forty-five minutes when the forest on our right—the side where the water is, I think—thins, and then gives way to a gas station with a big convenience store-like mart attached to it. Then a stop-light blinking yellow for us and red for the traffic coming perpendicular. There's a bridge over a churning, fast-moving river, and an antique wooden sign framing the bridge: "Welcome to Elk Rivers" is painted on it in white letters. We turn and cross the bridge into Elk Rivers. The river itself curves and follows the road on our left; there are old-timey, false-front, Old West-ish sort of buildings lining the road on both sides. Those on the left butt right up to the river, and between the buildings I catch glimpses of a boardwalk running at the base of the buildings along the river, with short piers jutting out into the water, small boats tied up here and there.

Behind the buildings on the right is an open field, with a thin rim of trees hiding the field from the road; it's a park, I realize. Benches line the perimeter, and an old man tosses a frisbee for a golden retriever. A younger couple lounges on a blanket, chatting. The field transitions to a fenced-in basketball court, with a large white gazebo on the other side of the court. Beyond the gazebo, the parking lot, and beyond that a thick stand of trees looping back around to line the edges of the park.

There are a few cars in the lot. A middle-aged couple sits at a picnic table under the gazebo, and three men play basketball on the court.

People stroll the sidewalk along Main Street, singles, couples, and a few larger groups. There are tourist gift shops, clothing stores, a book store, a breakfast-and-lunch restaurant, a pizza parlor, a bar, a photography shop, a locally-owned pharmacy, and a general store. Most of the restaurants are on the river, and they all seem to have back porches with tables overlooking the river.

The river leads to the lake, opening up into a wide harbor with a pier of rocks as a wave break off in the distance, marked by colored lights. Where the river opens to the harbor and the larger waters of the lake, there are even older buildings on either side of the river—faded gray clapboard buildings with wide walkways suspended over the river. Beneath is the river itself, with jetties on both sides and stairways leading up to the boardwalks. The boats here are larger, which means the water must be pretty deep—these are deep-water fishing boats, I think.

Main Street curves left at the end of the little village, with a long stretch of white sandy beach on the right. A parking lot cuts between the beach and Main Street with the spaces open to the road. The beach must be almost half a mile from the edge of the older fishing village area to where I see trees cutting across the vista. There's a blocky hut-like building—bathrooms, with an outdoor shower for rinsing off. Benches are scattered here and there through-out the beach, planted right into the sand. The parking lot nearer the village transitions to sidewalk, so tourists can park at the beach and walk into town.

Across from the beach is a neighborhood, the houses all fairly small and close together with narrow strips of lawn between and little postage stamp front yards; all the houses have deep front porches. The houses all look old, historic, even. Main Street—or what was Main Street and is now Wapiti Way—continues straight, lined on both sides with houses. The lake curves away, and the road goes straight, so the neighborhood is built up along the shore. I imag-ine most of the houses along the shoreline, here, are fairly expensive. Evenly spaced cross streets lead into the neigh-borhoods, most of them named after trees or forest ani-mals, with the occasional Native American word thrown in here and there.

Andreas drives slowly through the village, waving to people he knows now and then. Once we're out of the downtown area, he picks up speed. Wapiti Way becomes a two-lane road after a couple of miles of residential sprawl, lined once more with trees on both sides. On the right, a few miles from town, the trees abruptly fall away, giv-ing way to the school complex. The high school, middle school, and elementary school are all clustered together in a four-square arrangement, with the administration build-ing as the fourth side. Around the buildings are athletic fields—baseball diamonds, a soccer pitch, a football sta-dium, tennis courts, and open fields to function as prac-tice areas. Beyond the trees lining the school complex, the air has that open feel, telling you the lake isn't far. I spy trails leading through the woods, which I assume lead to the shore.

Back into dense forest, and now Wapiti Way narrows once more, with regularly-spaced driveways on both sides cutting through the woods. The road curves right, angling toward the shoreline. We go a mile or so farther, and then I see the water glittering in the distance, framed by trees. The road dead-ends at the water, I realize.

Andreas pulls into a driveway on the left, almost to the end of the road. The driveway is a narrow dirt-lined tunnel between towering pines whose tops wave in the wind. Here, the forest is open, old-growth, cathedral-like, with nothing between the trees but a carpet of pine needles, and shadows. A squirrel scampers between the aisles of pines, pausing to sit on its haunches with little paws clutched together, watching us pass. Farther along, I see the clearing open up.

Andreas elbows me, points out his window—I gasp. A huge doe with a smaller fawn stands in the trees not twenty feet from the driveway, wide dark eyes watching us.

"They get that close?" I ask.

He nods. "There's no hunting allowed anywhere near Elk Rivers—the closest place to hunt is another ten miles north. Around here, they'll come right up to the backyard."

"Why is it called Elk Rivers, plural? Is there more than one river?"

He shakes his head. "I dunno. The local lore isn't clear on the subject. Some stories claim there used to be another river that somehow vanished—how a whole river can vanish, I don't know. Others say it was just a misunderstanding between the white settlers and the local tribes, way back in the day." He laughs. "There've been several attempts to vote a change, to call it Elk River, singular, but it always fails. It's Elk Rivers, and that's that, to the local folks."

We leave the shade of the forest and pull into the sunlit clearing—his house is a small two-story cottage, with a screened-in front porch. An American flag ripples in a gentle breeze, mounted next to the screen door of the porch. Two cracked, tilted steps lead up to the porch. Off to the right of the house sits a small pole barn or garage, painted a faded, peeling green. The doors are open, revealing a small orange tractor, a tarp-covered vehicle, an older motorcycle with a toolbox on the ground nearby, and various other items back in the shadows which I can't make out. The vertical plank siding of the cottage itself was once a pale blue, I think, almost the color of Mom's eyes—my eyes; now, it's more an off-white, faded with age. The roof is shingled in weathered gray cedar shakes, with bright, vivid blue shutters on either side of the dormer windows.

"Home sweet home," Andreas says, parking at an angle to the house.

There's no front yard, to speak of, just a circle of dirt in front of the house and garage. Between the house and garage, I can see an expanse of green lawn, recently mowed. Then, more trees.

My stuff is in the bed of his truck—three suitcases and a duffel bag. Andreas claims he'll handle everything in LA. On the flight here, he mentioned having a memorial service for Mom, but I couldn't answer. I don't think I've really accepted that she's...

See? I can't even think the word.

I keep waiting for my phone to ring.

Andreas shuts off the truck and hops out, closing the door with a loud slam. I'm alone in the cab, in the silence. I feel the truck shift as he leans in and heaves out my belongings.

I hear a screen door creak...slam.

My vision clouds, goes hazy. My eyes burn.

Emotions are a tangle in my chest, my mind a whirlwind of chaotic thoughts. Memories of Mom. Road trips from town to town, city to city. Missing her. Anger that she left. Confusion at the story Andreas told—how could she have taken me away from my father? How could she have never once spoken his name, if she loved him? Fear of being in a new place; I've lived in new places all my life. Every six months at most, I'm in a new place. But this is different. I always had Mom. She always landed us somewhere cozy. We had a tradition: whenever we arrived in a new city, the first thing we'd do is find the nearest pizza place; if the pizza was good, we were good. If the pizza was bad, keep going.

Now, I'm in a new place, but...no Mom.

Just me and Detective Andreas Burke, possibly my father.

I sit in the silent cab for a few more minutes. Andreas seems to realize I need a minute, and brings my bags in, leaves the inner front door open, and just...leaves me be.

I guess I live in Michigan, now.

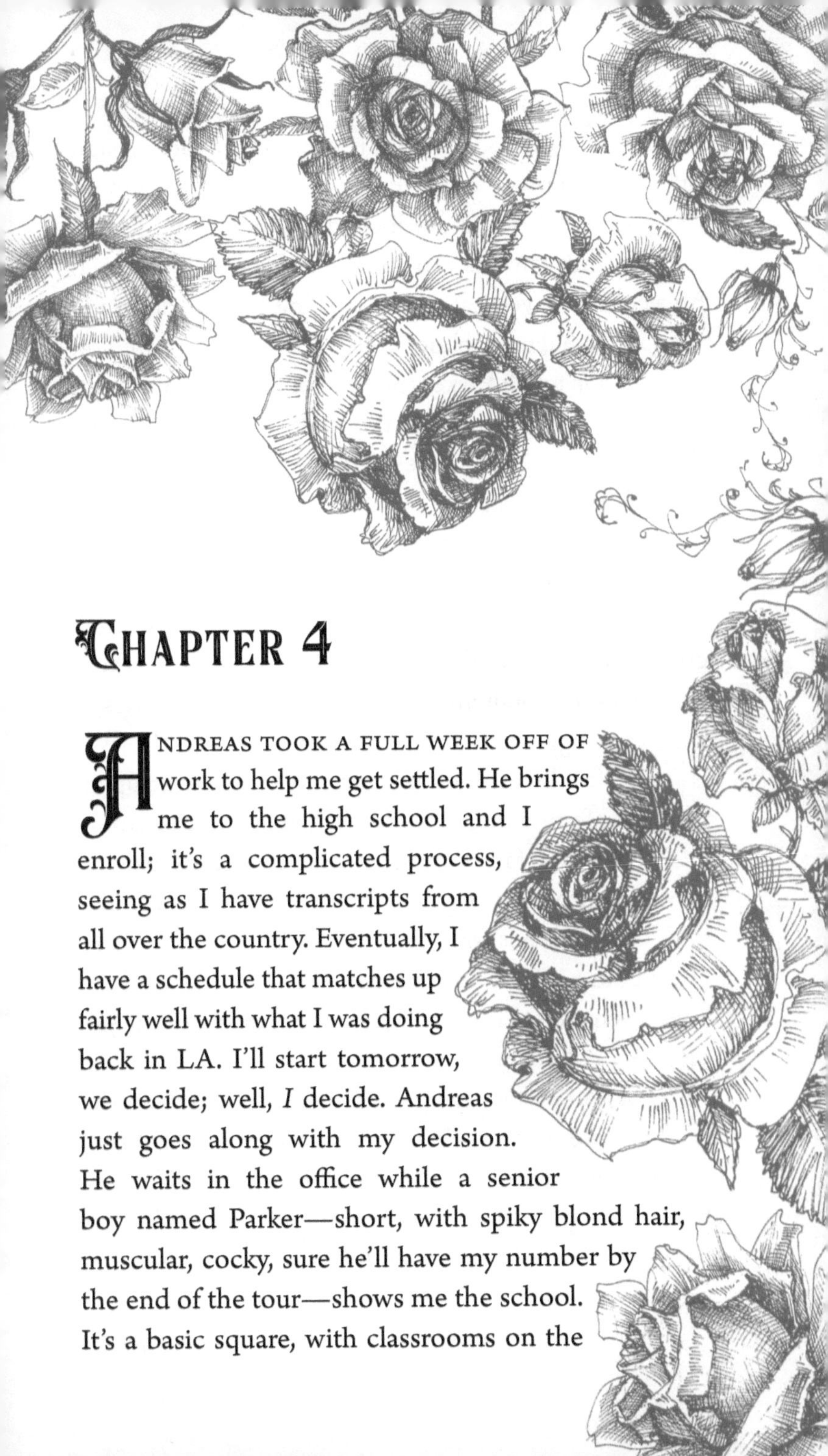

CHAPTER 4

ANDREAS TOOK A FULL WEEK OFF OF work to help me get settled. He brings me to the high school and I enroll; it's a complicated process, seeing as I have transcripts from all over the country. Eventually, I have a schedule that matches up fairly well with what I was doing back in LA. I'll start tomorrow, we decide; well, *I* decide. Andreas just goes along with my decision. He waits in the office while a senior boy named Parker—short, with spiky blond hair, muscular, cocky, sure he'll have my number by the end of the tour—shows me the school. It's a basic square, with classrooms on the outside, a gym, pool, weight room, supply rooms, staff offices and a break room, cafeteria, and auditorium on the inside. All doors are locked during school hours, juniors and seniors can leave campus during lunch break, park in your assigned parking spot…yada yada yada, same old new school bullshit. I've done it a million times. I don't give Parker the time of day—can't give off desperate new girl vibes to the cocky kid who probably thinks he's the king of the school. Maybe he is. I guess I'll find out tomorrow.

Enrolled and toured, we take Andreas' truck into town. He parks at the beach end of town and follows a path around behind one of the buildings, down a set of old, rickety wooden steps to the riverside boardwalk. Here, there are more shops built into the backsides of the buildings—which are bigger than they look from the street; the river is several feet below the street level. We come to an open-fronted cafe smelling of freshly baked bread, cinnamon, and coffee. The fare is pastry heavy: croissants, pain au chocolat, turnovers, bagels, muffins, pot pies, and the like.

"The coffee is roasted in-house," Andreas tells me. "Best coffee in a hundred miles. I also recommend the pain au chocolate if you've got a sweet tooth, or the pot pie if you're hungry."

I pause—is he paying? I still have some of the cash I found in Mom's room. What's the etiquette, here? I scan the chalkboard menu; the items are handwritten and embellished with elaborate nature-themed artwork ranging from elk and bear and whitetail deer to squirrels and salmon and eagles.

"Order whatever you want, Maeve." He bumps me

with his shoulder, which I realize is his way of offering casual affection and breaking the awkwardness. "I've got it."

I get a coffee and a pot pie, and he gets a coffee and a chocolate chip muffin the size of my skull.

There are little bistro tables at the edge of the cafe and the boardwalk, and we sit, facing each other.

For a while, we eat and sip coffee in awkward silence.

"So." He breaks a piece of muffin off. "You need some fall and winter clothes. Hoodies, sweaters, warm socks, boots, a coat or two, a hat, gloves, and a scarf. There are some good shops here in town, but to be honest they're a little pricey and sort of touristy. Do you have a license?"

I nod. "Yeah, I do."

"I've got a car you can drive. It's not new, not by a long shot, but it's…" he laughs, tips his head to the side. "Well, it's a classic. I think it's cool, but you may hate it. I can keep an eye out for something else if you don't like it, but for now, it'll get you to school and wherever."

"What is it?" I ask.

"An eighty-seven Subaru Brat."

"A what?"

He laughs. "They're kinda unique. You know what an El Camino is?"

I tip my head side to side. "I think? A car that's a truck, right?"

He nods. "Right. This is like that, but smaller. Two doors, with a tiny bed. Most people, including me, put jump seats in it. Mine is kitted out as a Baja—a dune runner."

I shake my head. "I have no idea what you're talking about."

He chuckles. "Don't worry about it. The point is, it's

yours for as long as you want it. It was a weekend project for me, and now it's done but I rarely drive it."

"Will it break down on me?" I ask. "Because I can drive a car, but that's it. I know how to put gas in it, and that's as far as my mechanical knowledge goes."

"Nah, it's a great little car. The motor and transmission were both professionally rebuilt. It won't break down on you. I won't go so far as to promise, but I'm confident. I've been wrenching a long time." His grin is confident. "So. We finish lunch, you can check out the shops here, or go down into town to the mall. Or you can skip it and go another day. It's warm enough now, but in a week or two, it's gonna start cooling off real fast, so don't put off shopping for warmer clothing too long."

"How much colder cold will it get?" I'm in jeans, Converse, and a T-shirt, and I wish I had a hoodie or something—there's a sharp chill in the air.

"Oh, we're into fall now. You'll see it drop down into the fifties during the day before long, and colder at night. Another month or so, and it'll be in the forties, most likely. It usually snows in November, and we're usually covered in snow come December."

"Awesome," I mutter.

He chuckles again; that weird buzz in my chest is ever-present, around him, I've just learned to tune it out. "I thought you wanted to see snow."

"I said I never had, not that I *wanted* to." I eye him, smirking. "There's a difference, you know."

He shrugs, nods. "I guess so. But one way or another, snow is coming. It was a pretty cool summer, never got over eighty-five. I'd give it a month and a half before you see flakes in the air, and not long after that before it starts accumulating."

We go back up to the street level, and I find a little shop that sells a variety of touristy sort of clothes and gear. I pick a navy blue sweatshirt with Elk Rivers emblazoned on it in gold lettering—I buy larger than I need, so I swim in it. It's thick, the inside so soft it feels almost like fur. I also buy a beanie, heather gray with a rolled-up rim bearing a patch with the logo of some local conservation fundraising committee or something—the logo is a river leading to the lake, with a stylized sun on the horizon. I pull my hair out of the ponytail and put the beanie on over my hair.

As Andreas and I leave the shop, an old pickup rumbles past. The engine is loud, the muffler rattling. It's not as souped-up and fancy as Andreas's—just a brown old truck, with rust on the rim of the wheel wells and spotting the chrome bumper.

The next moment seems to stretch out like taffy.

The driver turns his head to look at me—he's wearing mirrored aviator sunglasses, but I feel his gaze on me like a palpable thing. The truck rolls past seemingly in slow motion.

The driver is the most beautiful human being I've ever seen. My heart stops. My mouth goes dry, my tongue sticks to the roof of my mouth.

His features are hard, rugged, hewn from marble by the hand of Michelangelo himself. He's about my age. His hair is longish, artfully messy, strands draping over his eyes and temples, down his cheekbone, curling at his collar. Dark, almost black but not quite.

The window is open, his hand dangling down. His fingers are long and strong. His skin is pale, almost like ivory, as if he doesn't get enough sun. Music wafts to me from the speakers—the rough, snarling, churning, screeching cacophony of heavy metal.

His gaze never leaves me, his head pivoting to track me as he passes.

He's not alone in the truck—two more young men are with him, but I barely register their existence. I only see *him*.

My chest vibrates, almost violently—as if I've put my hand on a speaker stack at a concert. My gut twists, leaps. My skin seems too tight. The hum isn't just in my chest, it's all through my body. My *hair* seems to vibrate. It feels like there should be a sound with the humming inside me—a roar, a snarl, a shout, a voice, a scream, something. Instead, the silent rattling of my bones.

It's like when I met Officer Hawthorne, or when I'm around Andreas, except a million times stronger.

I *feel* his eyes on me. I feel them on my face, on my neck, on my hands, on my thighs.

An eternity curls around us, framing us together in this moment, me and this boy.

And then his truck is past me, turning onto the highway—the moment is broken.

I'm breathless.

I don't know who he is, but somewhere in my gut, where the humming originated, it feels like I *do* know him.

I will.

I *have* to.

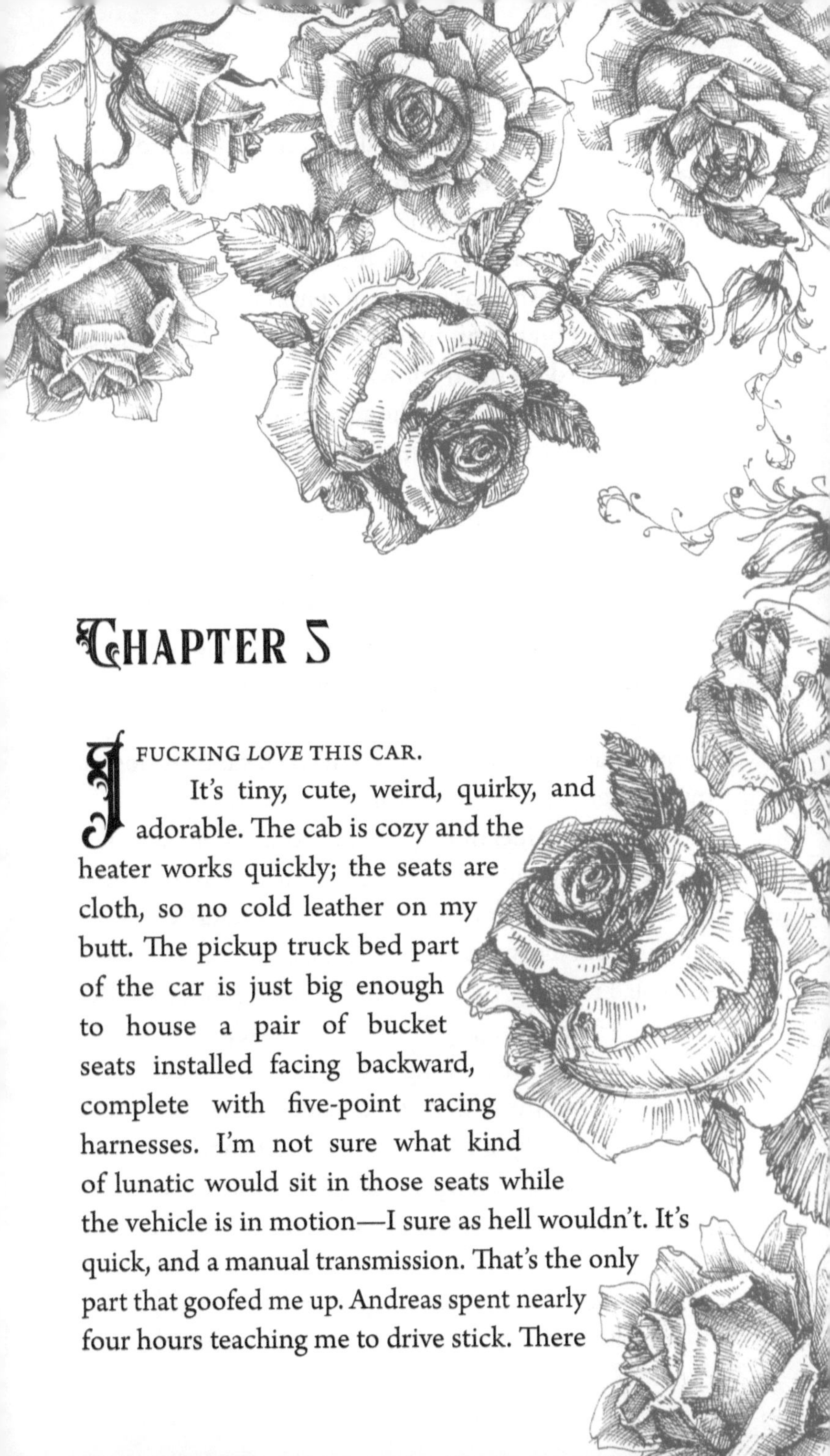

Chapter 5

FUCKING *LOVE* THIS CAR.

It's tiny, cute, weird, quirky, and adorable. The cab is cozy and the heater works quickly; the seats are cloth, so no cold leather on my butt. The pickup truck bed part of the car is just big enough to house a pair of bucket seats installed facing backward, complete with five-point racing harnesses. I'm not sure what kind of lunatic would sit in those seats while the vehicle is in motion—I sure as hell wouldn't. It's quick, and a manual transmission. That's the only part that goofed me up. Andreas spent nearly four hours teaching me to drive stick. There was a lot of lurching and stalling and wince-inducing grinding of gears, but I finally got the hang of it. And honestly? I like it—it's fun.

The Subaru Brat is glossy black, with knobby off-road tires and what Andreas calls a suspension lift and level kit, meaning it's higher off the ground than normal. There's a brush guard on the front with an LED light bar in the spaces between the bars of the guard, and another light bar on the roof, as well as two small, square LED light boxes installed at the rear corners of the bed, facing backward. The interior is mostly stock, with black-and-gray plaid cloth seats, rubber mats on the floor, plastic knobs for A/C and heat control…the only modern amenity inside is the new touchscreen radio faceplate with wireless Bluetooth.

I feel cool driving it. And more importantly, it's *my* car. No more getting dropped off like a little kid. My eyes burn, because the cost of having my own car is the loss of my mother. I'd take her back in a heartbeat.

I honestly feel numb, where Mom is concerned. It worries me. I should be grieving. I should be locked in my room, unable to function. Yet inside my soul? Crickets. Nothing. I'm just void, blank. I mean, I miss her. I miss her like hell. I'm angry. I get choked up thinking about her. But true grief? Crippling, agonizing grief? Nada.

I wonder what's wrong with me.

I pull into the parking lot outside the high school—my spot, since I'm a transfer, is near the back. Which is fine, I don't mind walking. I'm early, so I sit with the engine idling, heater blasting, and sip my coffee, watching some kids get dropped off and others arriving in their cars. Most cars disgorge two, three, or four people. To my relief, there's not one luxury car on the lot, even when it's less than ten minutes from the first bell. It's mostly pickup trucks of varying ages, from as old as my Brat to brand new. There are a lot of compact SUVs, a few older, hand-me-down full-size SUVs, a few sedans and hatchbacks, and a small handful of older muscle cars.

My car fits right in.

The kids, as they filter into the school, are also dressed…normally. Jeans, hoodies, sweaters, fleeces, joggers, leggings. No "fashion", not like at that godawful LA school, where everyone acted like every day was New York Fashion Week.

My black Lululemon leggings, gray zip-up fleece, and ever-present doodled-on Converse will fit in just fine. I also don't see any purses more expensive than the one LV I saw a girl carrying, and that one looked handed down.

I shut off the engine, lock the doors behind me, and toss my keys in my purse, sliding my backpack onto my shoulders. Deep breath.

It's just a new school, Sparrow, you've done this a hundred times. No big deal.

Except something feels different.

I'm not ready to acknowledge that the difference is *him.*

The guy from the truck, yesterday. Something about him. I can still feel his gaze on me like a physical touch. I can still feel the whole body buzz—like grabbing a live wire.

I find my first class easily. No one pays me any attention—the teacher only mentions in passing that I'm a new student. No standing in front of the class introducing myself, thank god. I hate that shit.

Next class, more of the same. Parker, my tour guide

from yesterday, is in this class—Mythology, an easy-A blow-off class, judging by the number of athletes wearing ERHS football or basketball hoodies. He flirts with me as we work in pairs on a worksheet about Demeter and Persephone. I ignore the flirting and force him to keep focused on the work.

Finally, Parker tosses his pencil on the desk in irritation. "You're a tough nut to crack, huh?"

I pencil in the last answer, suppressing a sigh. "I have a strict rule about jocks—I don't date them."

"Who said anything about dating?" He leans toward me, giving me what I assume is his Panty-Melter 500 grin. "I just want to take you to dinner and show you Lookout Point." His smirk is suggestive—as if I can't figure out what he means by showing me Lookout Point.

"No thanks." I stare at him, the dead, blank stare that always seems to ward off guys like this overconfident douchebag.

He blinks, waiting for more—for a comeback, or a snarky comment. I give him nothing, just the "no thanks" and the stare. "Damn, shot down. All right, Sparrow. But I'll get you around. You'll see."

"Don't hold your breath, Parker," I tell him.

The bell rings, and I gather my purse and backpack and leave without a backward glance. I hear laughter and raucous teasing as his friends rib him for getting shot down by the new girl.

It's warm in the school, so I take off my new gray beanie and pull my hair back into a ponytail as I head to third hour. Calculus, my old nemesis. I feel him before I even enter the classroom—my chest starts to tingle the moment the door is in view. By the time I'm walking through, my hands are trembling and my skin feels too tight on my bones. Then, I see him.

Folded into a desk that's two sizes too small for his build, he's wearing black jeans, gray lightweight sneakers, and a thin maroon wool sweater. His almost-black hair is loose and wild, tangled and messy but clean. It drapes over his face, tickling his sharp cheekbones. He's wearing those aviators again. His muscles bulge the sleeves of the sweater, his shoulders are broad and his thighs powerful in the jeans.

He turns his head ever so slightly, and I feel his gaze lance into me, prickling my skin like needles. The humming and the vibration in my chest and the tightness of my skin are almost unbearable.

I want, in equal measure, to run away and to be as close to him as I can.

The bell is about to ring, and the only open seat is in front of him. With no choice, I take the seat, slipping into it quietly, hoping this teacher will follow the pattern and not make a fuss about me. I do my best to ignore the catalytic presence of the boy behind me, even though I feel him like a black hole pulling at me.

The Calc teacher is a short, pudgy little man wearing a sweater vest over a button down, pleated khakis, penny loafers, and a pinched, unpleasant expression. His hair grows in a Picard-like U around the back of his skull. His voice, as he addresses the class, is nasally and droning.

Not to be judgmental, but…kill me now. I can tell how this class is going to be.

Hell.

He goes through roll call and pauses when he gets to

my name in the S's. "Sparrow—Maeve." He finds me with his eyes. "A transfer. Today is your first day, yes?"

I nod.

"Will you please stand up, state your name for the class, and tell us three interesting facts about yourself?"

Oh for fuck's sake.

I glare at him, but he glares right back—and authority is on his side, so I stand up, begrudgingly. "Um. My name is Maeve Sparrow. I've been to thirteen schools since kindergarten. Um. I like to read. And um…I don't know. I've never owned a television."

The teacher nods curtly. "Very good." He consults his roster. "Where were we? Sparrow—Stanley, Alicia, present…" his eyes go to Mr. Aviators, behind me. "Taylor, Caspian, present."

Caspian Taylor? His name is *Caspian*?

Dear lord. How apropos.

"In today's class we'll be covering…" The teacher—Mr. O'Hara—has finished roll and he's off, droning on about finding the limit of a function; this is stuff I did in fact cover in LA, so I should be okay. I expect the teacher to tell Caspian to remove the sunglasses because he's just that kind of teacher, but he doesn't.

There's a brief lecture, and then Mr. O'Hara starts scribbling sample equations on the dry-erase board with a handful of markers, black, red, and blue, using different colors for various elements of the equations and where most students go wrong.

Behind me, Caspian doesn't seem to move.

Other students around me take notes, sniffle, shuffle their feet, adjust position, scratch their ears… Caspian, from what I can hear, does none of this.

The bell rings, after an eternity—we have a huge number of problems to do for homework, yippee. The other students all packed up before the bell rang, which means I'm one of the last ones out the door.

Caspian is the last. And he seems to be staring at me, watching me pack up. I try to not look at him. To ignore him. But finally, as I'm shouldering my bags, I look into my reflection in his sunglasses.

"Hi." I hold out my hand. "I'm Maeve."

He ignores my hand. "Caspian." His voice is deep for a high school student, low, quiet, and silky.

Seductive…

And menacing.

"None of the teachers make you take those off?" I ask, jutting my chin at him.

"No." He stands up in a slow, languid motion. "I have a genetic condition—extremely light-sensitive eyes."

"Oh."

He's so much taller than me. Six-three? Six-four? He towers over me, six inches between us. He's so utterly still I'm not sure he's even breathing. Then, he leans toward me, almost imperceptibly, and I see his nostrils flare. I hear the soft inhalation of breath—a long, slow scenting of the air.

Of *me*.

The corners of his jaw tighten, and some dark energy fills the space between us—anger? Menace. Threat. My heart pounds, and every instinct inside me is screaming at me to *run*.

Run from this person.

I don't. I can't.

I'm frozen in place. I smell him—a complex barrage of scents: woodsmoke, cologne, and something else I can't place. Musky, coppery.

His skin is pale; he radiates cold.

The hum, the buzz, the manic energy cascading through me—his proximity makes it intolerable, and intoxicating. My hands shake. My legs shake. Heat billows through me, centered in my belly, low.

Neither of us speaks.

"A-*hem*." Mr. O'hara raps on his desk with a marker. "Get to class you two. Have your staring contest on your own time."

With that same liquid, languid movement, Caspian weaves around me and is gone. I take a moment to suck in a breath—my lungs burn, and I realize I hadn't been breathing the entire time. I push down how shaken I am by the encounter and hustle out of class.

I'm late for fourth hour, but fortunately I'm not called on to embarrass myself in front of everyone. I head to lunch after fourth hour—the cafeteria is packed and bustling. Cliques and friend groups sit together at their chosen tables, with other tables reserved by some unspoken agreement for loners like me.

Caspian is nowhere to be seen.

Fifth hour is Lit, my favorite class, usually. This is no exception—the instructor is a beautiful woman in her thirties with fine blond hair, wearing a gypsy skirt and a peasant blouse. She talks with passion about the book they've been reading—*The Book Thief*. I've read it, and I still have my essays on it saved to my laptop; I can probably tweak and reuse them.

On the way to sixth hour, I pass Caspian in the hall.

His skin is less pale, warmer, ruddier. His gaze follows me as we pass, and electricity crackles between us. I refuse to look over my shoulder, even though I desperately want to; I reach my classroom, and I can't help but pause outside, letting the flow of stragglers part around me.

He's standing in the middle of the hallway like a boulder in a stream. Hands at his sides, fists clenched. His chin lifts, nose tilting to the air, as if he's scenting me again, from fifty feet away.

I'm the first to turn away, entering the room and attempting to put him out of my mind for the duration of History class.

I fail miserably.

The schedule is broken into A days and B days—today is an A day, which means my last hour is Spanish, one of my two electives. Caspian is in this class as well, but his seat is across the room from me. The teacher, an elderly woman with silvering black hair, teaches the entire class in Spanish—not just fluent, but a native Spanish speaker. I've taken Spanish since middle school, so I'm decently proficient. Or so I thought. This is Spanish 2, which means everyone should be roughly capable—yet when Mrs. Hernandez calls on students to answer questions, in Spanish of course, many of them can't seem to get even the most basic pronunciations or conjugations right.

Except for Caspian. He's fluent and even has a natural-sounding accent. He speaks low, quiet, barely above a whisper, yet somehow, across the room, I can hear him perfectly.

My whole being vibrates the whole period. Even when I'm not looking at him, I *feel* him.

The next day is B day—my last hour is gym class.

I *hate* gym. I'm the least athletic, least coordinated person on the planet—nine times out of ten, I'll trip over my own feet or simply trip on nothing at all, or I'll try to run and end up lurching awkwardly, as if my brain doesn't know how to provide the correct amount of power input.

There's a sub today, which means dodgeball.

Fuck me.

I stay toward the back on my side, hiding behind the other, braver, more coordinated kids. Which includes Caspian, of course. He's dressed in black gym shorts, a bank sleeveless shirt, and old, battered, well-worn running shoes. He moves like a panther, lithe and agile, and never seems to hurry. There's no running, no sudden dives out of the way, yet no one seems able to come even close to hitting him. He catches the red bouncy balls easily— once, he catches two at the same time, one in each hand, and then catches a third by pinching it between the balls in his hands. Like it's nothing at all.

I, meanwhile, lurch, duck, dive, and waggle around like a lame duck, my braid flopping around and whacking me in the face. I hit my knees more than once, and I've soon got reddening abrasions on my kneecaps.

The other team is mostly the jocks, so our side, even with Caspian's otherworldly ability, is quickly decimated. In fact, with ten minutes left in the period, it's down to Caspian, another boy, and me. The other boy is tall and lanky, quick but snazzy and not quite graceful. His skill, however, is his arm—he whips his throws sidearm, the balls whizzing audibly, whanging off the stacked bleachers with loud echoes when he misses, which isn't often. He's either a quarterback or pitcher, with that arm. He and Caspian work together, then, in unspoken coordination. Caspian provides defense, blocking incoming throws and scooping up loose balls which he feeds to the other kid—Adam.

Between them, they run interference, and I seem to escape unnoticed.

Until Parker, on the other side with his jock buddies, sees me.

The grin on his face is not kind.

He edges closer to his buddies, murmuring to them with his eyes lasered on me.

And then it begins—the shift in their tactic. No longer are they trying to hit Adam or Caspian, they're going for me. Their throws are brutally hard, curving toward me with blazing speed, whistling past me, thudding off the wall behind me or glancing off the floor.

Caspian quickly catches on and adjusts. Intercepts, blocks, and returns fire with pinpoint accuracy.

And that's when I realize that for his freakish skills, he's been *holding back.*

Adam picks off two more jocks, and then he's out, leaving Caspian and me. The rest of the class watches from the sidelines as if this is a pitched Friday night football game against our rival school. Me and Caspian against Parker and three of his buddies.

The throws come hard and fast, and more than one nearly takes off my head, should they have hit. Somehow, they never do. And then it happens—I move to duck a ball, angling to the side. Only, my legs provide far too much power and I go flying, hitting the gym floor with a loud smack. My elbow hits hard, the skin breaking. I roll to the side, knowing Parker and the gang won't show mercy, even though I'm visibly hurt, clutching my elbow.

A ball hits the floor next to my face, the wind of its impact fluttering my hair. Another skates over my nose, the rough red rubber skinning the tip. And then Caspian is there, blocking a throw, a second, a third, catching a fourth. One out—three to go.

The sub seems oblivious to the fact that I'm bleeding, and doesn't whistle a stoppage.

Caspian sidearms a ball, deflects an incoming shot, scoops up a loose ball rolling past—another out.

He's standing over me. He glances down at me side-long. "Stay down, Sparrow." It's a low, growled order.

The next moment seems impossible. Parker and his remaining friend have taken opposite ends of their side, each clutching three balls. Their tactic is obvious—fire off throws as fast as possible from either direction, forcing Caspian to choose a direction, leaving me open to the other.

It works.

Or, it should have.

Instead of catching or deflecting, Caspian seems to shunt the balls aside with the flat of his palm, redirecting them like a martial artist. He moves unhurriedly, yet he's always in perfect position, never a stumble, never a hasty pivot. And then Parker and the other kid are out of balls, and Caspian takes advantage.

He outs the other kid first with a pair of throws—one low, causing him to leap, and then another while he's in the air and can't dodge. Then it's just him and Parker.

Parker is livid. Sweaty and red. The charm is gone, leaving behind what I knew lurked beneath all the while—ugly, competitive asshole vindictiveness.

Caspian is toying with him. Waiting to the last minute to dodge. Making impossible deflections. Redirecting instead of catching to force the out.

Finally, Parker scrambles for a loose ball, trips to one knee—and Caspian nails him in the ear.

"Headshot! Doesn't count!" Parker snaps. "Headshots don't count."

"I was aiming for your chest. It's not my fault you tripped."Caspian's voice is level, even, and calm, in stark contrast to Parker's out-of-breath outrage. Caspian isn't winded or sweating.

The sub blows the whistle. "The point goes to Caspian. It was an accidental headshot. A team wins."

Our side cheers and Parker storms off for the locker room, elbowing off his friends with a torrid stream of curses.

I snicker from my place on the ground. "Imagine getting that worked up over gym class dodgeball."

Caspian reaches down to help me up—I've been cupping my bleeding elbow, and I unthinkingly reach for him with that hand. He recoils sharply at the sight of my bloody palm, hissing.

"Oh, crap, I'm sorry." I scramble to my feet. "It's no big deal, really. I'm just uncoordinated." I try to laugh. "Not a fan of blood, huh?"

His lip quirks as if in a burst of amusement, and then his lips press together. "Something like that." He's inscrutable behind those aviators—he didn't take them off even for gym class. "You should see the nurse. Get a Band-Aid."

I roll my eyes. "Yeah, right." I don't want to leave. Don't want to be out of his presence, even though I hum, ache, buzz, feeling too tight in my skin, too hot, too flushed. "Thanks for, you know…playing the hero. You should have just let me get out."

"Can't let leeches like Parker Landry get away with their bullshit." His jaw pulses. "He'd have taken your head off with some of those throws. He was gunning for you."

"I shot him down in second hour, and I get the impression he doesn't take no for an answer very well."

"People like him don't tend to." The bell rings, yet Caspian doesn't move. "Get a Band-Aid, Sparrow."

He says my last name not like most people do, like "Yo, Sparrow!" but as if he's referring to the small winged bird that is my namesake as a nickname for me.

I pull my hand away from my elbow—it *is* getting a bit messy. "Yeah, I should get this cleaned up."

His nostrils flare. The pink tip of his tongue slides along his lips, there and gone. "Yes. You should." This is through clenched teeth. I can't see his eyes, but I'd bet money they're narrowed at me.

As if I've done something wrong, offended him, pissed him off.

He turns away, moving stiffly, and then once he's a few steps away, he seems to relax, rolling his shoulders as if to loosen tension.

Weird.

He was paler again, I realize. Colder. Moodier. We didn't get a chance to talk during any of our other classes together, but he seemed more normal right after lunch.

Maybe he's diabetic and gets cranky before lunch.

I clean up in the locker room, dabbing at my elbow

with wet paper towels until it stops bleeding. By the time I'm changed, I'm the last one in the locker room, and the school has emptied.

My car is by itself at the back of the parking lot—except for a shiny new red pickup with tinted windows and way too much chrome; stickers on the back window proclaim the driver to be ERHS varsity football, basketball, and track.

Parker.

He's waiting for me.

I groan audibly, and then gird myself, internally. Ignore him—that's the ticket. I unlock the doors—by inserting an actual key into an actual lock and turning, how adorably archaic is that?

"Yo, Sparrow."

See?

Ignore.

I toss my backpack onto the footwell of the passenger side and my purse onto the seat.

"Maeve, I'm *talking* to you," Parker snaps.

I glare at him—the kind of glare that would peel the skin off his bones, if a look could do such a thing. "What, *Landry?*"

"Stay away from Caspian Taylor." His voice is hard, angry. "Trust me on this one. I'm doing you a favor. He's a freak. He and his brothers are trouble. I'm telling you— you're new in town, and you need to know. Stay away from him. He's bad news."

I don't answer, just hold the fuck-off stare until he holds up his hands in an "I surrender" gesture. "Okay, then, fine. But don't say you weren't warned." He pulls away with a souped-up rumble and a squeal of tires.

On the drive home, I consider Parker's warning. It's one I should heed—a small, quiet inner voice tells me as much. He terrifies me on multiple levels.

His display in gym class today was casual magnificence. I'm not sure anyone could do what he did, yet he made it seem easy as breathing.

His very presence affects me, physically.

I should heed Parker's warning and stay away from Caspian.

But I know I won't.

I'm drawn to him, like a fly into a spider's web.

CHAPTER 6

I'M DREAMING.

I'm back in that black void space. Instead of Mom or Andreas, however...

Caspian.

Shadows cling to him like shreds of black gossamer. He doesn't have his aviators on, here. I almost wish he did: his eyes are black pools in his face. No whites, no iris, no pupils. Feral, alien, and hungry. He faces me in the shadow space, floating in nothingness. Does he see me?

I can't tell.

I can't speak; I have no mouth. No voice.

There's no me—only a spark of awareness floating in a vast universe of darkness.

He sees me. Bares a mouthful of sharp white teeth—his eyeteeth are longer than the rest and needle-sharp.

Fangs.

Caspian bares those fangs to me and hisses. No, not a hiss. A snarl. Throaty, animal.

Suddenly, he's inches from me. Towering over me. Staring down at me with those pools of nothingness where his eyes should be.

You should not be here, little Sparrow. His voice is thick, dark, inhuman. **Wake up.**

I don't want to. It doesn't come out audibly.

You do not belong here. He responds as if he heard me. **Wake up.**

Who are you?

A bad dream. One you'd do well to forget.

His nose draws along my temple. I feel the cool rush of air as he inhales my scent. This close, he radiates such cold it feels almost like heat—burning, sharp, intense.

Wake up, he whispers, his breath an icy wind on my ear. **Wake up, little Sparrow.**

I jerk awake. I'm sweating, the sheets sticking to my skin. I'm panting. My ear burns where his breath blew. I remember it vividly. It seemed *real.*

Realer than reality—which makes no sense, I know, but that's the feeling banging around in my skull.

There's a knock on my door. "Maeve?" It's Andreas.

I pull the blanket up to my throat as I sit up—I've sweated through my thin white sleep shirt, and I don't want to give my new guardian an eyeful. "Yes?"

The knob twists, and he steps into the opening as he pushes the door inward. "You okay?"

I frown. "Um, yeah?"

"I thought I heard you."

I don't think I yelled out. "Um. Yeah, I'm okay. Just a weird dream, I guess. Don't really remember."

Lies. I remember every single moment more vividly than I remember my own past.

"Oh. Okay. Well, I have a call. I gotta go."

It's still dark out—the alarm clock on my nightstand reads 4:35 am. "Everything okay?"

He tips his head to one side. "I wouldn't be on a call-out at four-thirty in the morning if it was, Maeve. I'm a detective." A shrug. "It's the job, though. Nothing for you to worry about. Elk Rivers is a safe community. You've got my numbers if you need anything, yeah?"

I nod. "Yeah. I'm good. Thanks, Andreas."

He pats the door twice. "All right, well, have a good day."

I lie back down after he closes the door, but I know I'm up, now. A few minutes later, I hear the screen door creak open, but he closes it quietly rather than letting it bang closed; considerate of him. Then his truck rumbles to life, the sound fading as he pulls away down the driveway.

Once he's gone, I get up. Turn on the lamp on my bedside and regard my new room. It's fairly large, one of the largest bedrooms I've ever had. The floors are old wooden planks original to the house, with a thick pile rug under the queen bed. Wrought iron frame with an elaborate headboard and footboard. The bedside table is a small black cabinet with two drawers, not new but not old either. The roof is low and pitched—this is the second floor, taking

up most of the upper story. The dormer window features
a window seat with a thick, comfortable cushion, and the
window looks out over the roof of the first story. I could
probably climb out onto the roof if I wanted to.

The room is painted a soft, warm, pale green, comforting, soothing. There's a small closet, a tall bureau, and
an antique roll-top desk. Across the hall is a bathroom,
recently redone in white subway tiles with black metal
accents—clean, modern, simple. A pedestal sink, round
black-framed mirror, and a shower-tub combo with a
sliding glass door. Between the sink and the wall is a tall,
narrow, open-fronted, floor-to-ceiling black cabinet for
storage, featuring neat stacks of washcloths, hand towels,
and bath towels, each taking up a shelf from the bottom
up, leaving several of the upper shelves free for my use. I've
sorted my bathroom supplies into the shelves, and I take
a long, hot shower, braid my hair, and dress in jeans, my
new hoodie, and my new beanie.

Down in the kitchen, Andreas has left half a pot of
coffee on for me. The main floor, like the upstairs bathroom, is freshly remodeled in a timeless modern style—
original hardwood floors, walls painted a flat white, with
a white ceiling and attractive dark wooden beams. A few
walls have been taken out, making the interior open plan.
The kitchen is a mix of open-front and closed cabinets in a
muted navy blue, with an island featuring a butcher block
countertop, cabinets on three sides and an overhang for
four stools on the fourth. There's a round table with four
chairs between the kitchen and living room, which is parti-
tioned off by a heavy black leather sectional in an L-shape,
deep and comfortable looking, facing a river stone hearth
with a flat-screen TV mounted above it.

All in all, the cottage is attractive, cozy, and homey.

I feel comfortable here, even alone.

The one weird thing is there are no photographs. No real evidence of Andreas, the person. In the living room there's a floor-to-ceiling bookshelf along one whole wall, and I pour myself a cup of coffee, fix it the way I like it, and wander over to the shelf, pursuing the titles. *Frankenstein, Dracula, the Complete Works of Lord Byron,* several titles by Jules Verne, some twenty or so titles I don't recognize—paperbacks, dog-eared, their cover art making them sci-fi from the forties and fifties. Fantasy titles. Histories and biographies—The American Civil War, the Revolutionary War, Benjamin Franklin, Roosevelt (both of them), Napoleon, Patton, The War of 1812, biographies on historical figures I've only heard of and some whom I haven't; there are works on various philosophies, on Islam, Judaism, and Buddhism; there's more poetry—Rainer Maria Rilke, Walt Whitman, Ezra Pound, Robert Frost, TS Eliot, e. e. cummings, and translations of poetry by authors from all over the globe and across history.

It's a stunning collection. What's more, many of the tomes appear old, some seem to be original, possibly even rare and valuable.

I pick one of the less rare-looking poetry translations and sit with it and my coffee in the big, deep, overstuffed chair cornered facing the fireplace, with a standing floor lamp behind it. I'm soon lost in the flow of words, and my coffee goes cold, untouched.

I take a sip and splutter. "God, gross."

I dump it out and refill it, sipping the black, bitter liquid as I look out the window into Andreas's backyard. It's still well before dawn, the sky just lightening into gray.

Frost whitens the lawn. The trees framing the rear of the property stand like silver-gilded sentries, guarding the shadows beyond.

You do not belong here. I hear Caspian's words from my dream rattling in my skull, almost audibly.

I'm not sure what possesses me. I'm not usually a brave person.

There's a heavy tan Carhartt jacket hanging on a hook by the back door. I shove my feet into my Converse and shrug into the jacket, pulling the hood up over my head as I step out the back door. I don't know what it is drawing me toward those trees, but something is. A silent siren song.

Outside, the cold is sharp, with a hard dryness to the air that stings my cheeks and the tip of my nose, and sends ice crackling down my throat with every breath. A few small hard white flakes swirl in the air, sparse, drifting. It's dull gray out here, not quite light. Enough to see my feet, to see the frosted grass.

The mug in my hand is hot, the steam skirling upward in a thick, drifting plume. I clutch it with both hands and take a sip. My feet carry me across the lawn—it's big, expansive, more of a field than a backyard.

A bird flutters overhead.

My heart pounds.

You do not belong here.

My skin prickles, tightening around my bones. My stomach twists into a knot. That weird, inescapable hum starts in my veins, in my blood.

He's here.

I cross the lawn to the edge of the trees but stop short of going in. I take a fortifying sip of hot coffee. The coffee is real. The coffee is here, it's now. It reminds me that I'm awake.

Yet I feel like I'm back in that dreamspace, that I'm nothing but a spark of identity in an endless gulf of shadows. The forest is silent. Still sleeping? Or frightened into silence by the presence that's making my skin tight and my blood hum.

With a gulp, cursing myself mentally for a fool, I step into the woods. Into the tree line, into the shadows.

A pace.

Two.

Six.

Darkness writhes around me; my pulse thuds dully in my ears; tree trunks are dim columns of shadow around me. I turn and look over my shoulder—the yard is a haze of lighter gray, half a dozen steps into the trees.

I dare go no further. I have no clue how vast this forest might be, and I'm no woodswoman.

I smell him—a tangy, coppery, almost familiar scent. A rush of icy wind trickles down my neck. The thud of my pulse becomes a tympanic hammering—fear, adrenaline, excitement, dread, all intermixed until they're indecipherable from each other. Fight-or-flight response wars in my skull, but neither takes over. I'm frozen in place.

"The woods are no place for delicate little sparrows." His voice is midnight silk whispering over my skin; close—behind me.

"I…"

What? I what? What reason drew me out here?

He did. But I can't tell him that.

You do not belong here. His dream-voice shudders in my skull.

I feel the hood of my borrowed coat being pulled back, drooping down between my shoulders, letting in a blast of cold air.

I feel more than hear the pull of his nose inhaling my scent. "You smell…" another scenting sniff, and this time, I feel his nose brush my hair just behind my ear. "Like honeysuckle. And…" a third pull of scent. "Sunlight."

"I smell like sunlight?"

I turn, shaking all over, but he's not there. Only the swirling dregs of a chill wind remain where he was. "Caspian?"

My braid is lifted from along my spine; it's still wet. Another long inhalation. "Berries."

"It's my…my conditioner." I turn again, abruptly, swiftly.

Nothing. Only that hint of cold where he was.

"Caspian?" My voice is unnaturally high and breathy with nerves. "Where are you?"

"Here."

Shadows resolve into a pale, marble face a foot in front of me. His lips are crimson against his cold white skin.

"You also smell like sadness, Maeve Sparrow." Here, alone, just the two of us, his tone and manner of speech are slow and formal. Not like the lazy modernity of the way he talks at school.

My thighs tremble, shivering against each other. My belly twists. The hum is so violent in my blood that it nearly hurts. My breath comes in quick, sharp pants.

He's closer.

"Why are you sad?" His eyes are dark, but there are whites to them—they aren't the black pools I saw in the dream. They still pierce and intrude and delve. They see too much.

"My mom died. It's why I'm here." I haven't spoken of it since it happened. I've barely spoken of it to Andreas.

"How?"

"Car accident."

"And he—" he turns his head to glance in the direction of the clearing, and the house, "is your father?"

"I think so."

A wry, arch tone tinges his voice. "You think so? Don't you know?"

"It's complicated."

"Families always are."

"Parker Landry…" I'm not sure why I'm telling him this. "He confronted me after school yesterday."

"And?" His voice is hard as concrete. He does *not* like Parker.

"He warned me away from you. He said you and your brothers are troublemakers. He said you're bad news."

"Are you going to listen to him?" His gaze bores into me, in the slowly lightening gloom of a forest dawn.

"Probably not. He's a dick—I don't listen to dicks."

A bark of laughter, although I'm not sure it reaches his eyes. "He is a dick. But not a big one. He's a small, shriveled, pathetic dick."

I cackle. "You kicked his ass in dodgeball."

"He thinks far too highly of himself. But not without reason. His family is important in this town. They go back to the first settlers in this area." He pauses. "But he *is* right, just not in the sense he means."

"He's right?" I ask.

A dip of his chin, dark eyes lancing into mine. "You should stay away from me."

"Why?"

A silence. "You just should. For your own good."

I frown. "Can't I decide that for myself?"

"Of course. But you would be wise to stay away from me."

"Parker Landry would like that."

"I'm not saying it for his benefit."

"Well, I'm not sure I can." It's an honest statement—perhaps too honest.

"No? Why not?"

I shake my head, swallow hard. "I don't know. You scare me, but you also…" I trail off.

"I also what?"

"I don't know. I just don't think I can stay away from you." I'm still clutching the mug of coffee, and there's still a hint of warmth in the ceramic against my palms. I take a sip—lukewarm, but tolerable. "I'm not sure I want to, even if I could."

"I don't want you to. But you really, really should. It's safest."

"Safest? Are you dangerous?"

"Yes."

I swallow hard. The buzzing of my blood is at a manic frenzy, wanting him nearer, needing him closer. Demanding more of whatever it is in him that I'm reacting to so powerfully.

"Dangerous to me?"

A long pause. "The truth, in this case, is a complicated, slippery thing."

"I don't know what that means." I step closer to him. "Are you going to hurt me?"

A wind blows, cutting across the back of my neck and ears like a sharp blade. I shiver.

"You should go into your house, Maeve. You'll catch a chill."

"But Caspian—"

"I'll see you at school, Maeve Sparrow." His voice is a few feet away; there's no sound of footsteps.

He's gone. His scent is gone, the heavy weight of his presence absent. More telling, the buzzing in my blood has quieted.

He never answered my last question. Which should tell me everything I need to know.

I turn and leave the woods, feeling a lightening of my spirit as I emerge into the salmon-pink of daybreak.

I know I should stay away from him.

I also know I'm not going to.

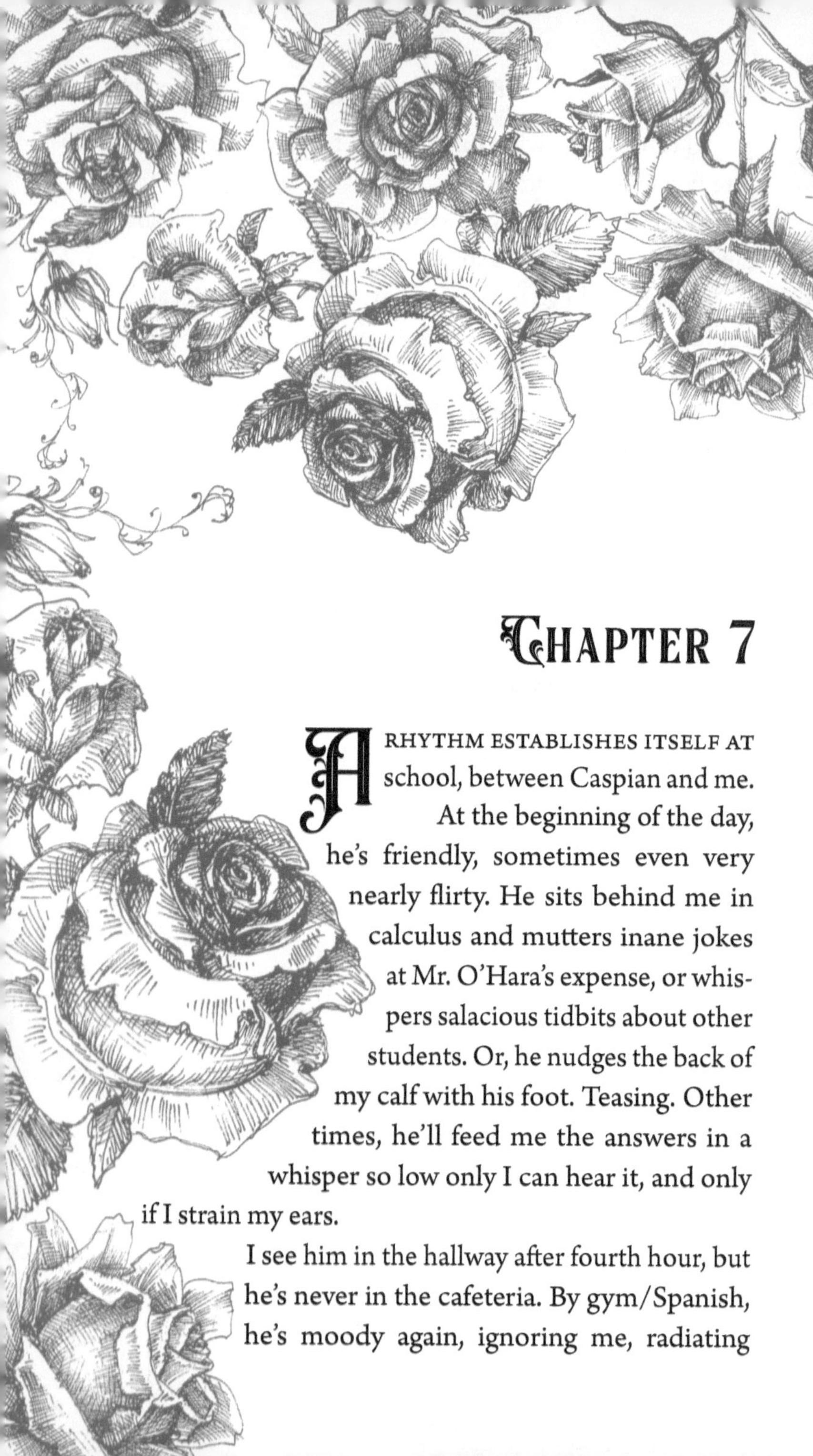

CHAPTER 7

A RHYTHM ESTABLISHES ITSELF AT school, between Caspian and me. At the beginning of the day, he's friendly, sometimes even very nearly flirty. He sits behind me in calculus and mutters inane jokes at Mr. O'Hara's expense, or whispers salacious tidbits about other students. Or, he nudges the back of my calf with his foot. Teasing. Other times, he'll feed me the answers in a whisper so low only I can hear it, and only if I strain my ears.

I see him in the hallway after fourth hour, but he's never in the cafeteria. By gym/Spanish, he's moody again, ignoring me, radiating fuck-off energy. His skin, warmer and rosier early in the day, is pale again by the end of the day. His mood matches his skin—cold.

He vanishes after school, and I never see his truck entering or leaving the parking lot.

He's an enigma.

I sometimes wonder if that morning in the forest was a dream.

We never reference it in school, and I feel silly for thinking it might have been real. But what if it wasn't? I'd feel even sillier asking him about it if I'd dreamed it.

I doubt my sanity, the more I think about it.

How he appeared out of nowhere. How I was drawn out there as by a string connected to my belly button…

The way he moved without sound, barely even stirring the air. The way he seems to be obsessed with my scent.

His reaction to my bloody elbow, that day in gym class.

Yet…what keeps bouncing around my mind is how he never answered my question—will he hurt me? Does that mean he could?

He *did* say he was dangerous.

The days pass in this rhythm. I don't go into the woods again. Andreas and I have our own patterns—he works early and comes home late, and he usually brings home carryout from one of the local restaurants. Burgers and fries, chicken tenders, pasta, pizza. In return, I make sure the main floor stays tidy. He never asks me to, but Mom always made it clear keeping the house neat was a team effort since we both live there.

After we eat, Andreas and I both read. Occasionally, he drinks some kind of whiskey from a glass decanter he keeps in a cabinet in the living room. The fireplace is gas, and with it getting colder every day, he often turns the fire on. Sometimes, we talk about what we're reading. Other times, we just read in companionable silence.

He never asks me questions about school, or if I have friends, or about how I'm feeling. He's there—in a real, solid, dependable way. It's comforting, honestly. I don't feel like he's my *dad*, and I'm not even one hundred percent sure he's my father, but he *is* a reliable adult figure when I need one.

I'm lulled into a sense of security by the easy rhythms—coffee with Andreas in the morning, friendly, flirty Caspian in calculus, lunch alone usually, though I am developing a few school friendships with some other girls from other classes, then more Caspian at the end of the day, though he mostly tends to brood and ignore me, doing the bare minimum in class, speaking rarely, and always, always wearing his mirrored aviators. The only time I've ever seen him without them on is that morning in the forest, which I'm starting to think I imagined or dreamed.

Then, one snowy day in early December, everything changes.

It's a half day—a teacher in-service thing. Everyone was excited all day because apparently it's the first real snow we've gotten, and half the school had plans to go to the nearby ski hill. As I was getting into my car, a good eighty percent of the kids were milling around their cars, putting on snow pants and chunky boots, shrugging into layer after layer of warm clothing, tucking mittens and gloves and hats into coat pockets, checking skis and poles and snowboards.

I've never been skiing and I don't plan to start—my lack of coordination makes that a highly dangerous activity. I slipped and fell in the parking lot on the way to my car, for god's sake. Strapping slippery sticks to my feet and sliding down a perfectly good hill? On purpose? In the snow?

Hell no.

I sit in my car and let it warm up—I've learned the engine is a little temperamental and likes a good five minutes to warm up before it behaves itself. The heater, however, works almost too well, blasting out desert-level heat within minutes.

When the engine has had time to get its shit together, I head out of school. Never having driven in snow before, I'm very careful. Other more experienced drivers frequently get pissy with me, since I'm going half the speed limit, but hey, I'd rather get there alive and un-wrecked, thank you. Go around, if you're in that much of a hurry.

Intending to spend the afternoon shopping, I head out of the village and follow my phone's GPS directions to the mall; a little more than halfway there, the engine starts acting weird. Sputtering, coughing, making the car lurch. I check the fuel gauge—more than half a tank. The temperature gauge reads halfway, which I assume is normal.

Shit.

Traffic is light, but it's frigid outside, and I really don't want to be stuck out here. Andreas would come get me, I'm sure, but I don't want to bother him while he's out solving murders or whatever it is he does all day.

"Come on, baby," I murmur. "Don't take a shit on me now."

Sputter, cough.

"No, no, *no!*"

And then it cuts out, giving one last weak cough before going quiet. I manage to guide her off the road and onto the shoulder before it rolls to a stop.

Silence.

"Well shit." I rest my forehead against the steering wheel. I put on the emergency flashers, and then pull out my phone. A moment's hesitation, and then I call Andreas.

It rings a few times, and then goes to voicemail—call declined.

Instead of leaving a message, I text him:

Sorry to bother you, but the Brat just died on the side of the road.

A moment later, my phone pings with his response:

Shoot, sorry kiddo. I'm in the middle of an investigation and I can't leave. Send me your location and I'll get a wrecker there ASAP.

I give the message a thumbs up, and then rest my head against the headrest, groaning out loud. "So much for a fun afternoon," I grumble.

Closing my eyes, I settle in to wait.

I'm not sure how long passes, only that it grows steadily colder without the engine to run the heater. I start to shiver.

A knock on my window startles me so badly I scream and then burst into laughter when I see Caspian on the other side. He's wearing a black beanie over his hair, just the ends showing, curling around his neck. His ever-present aviators are on his face, and he has a black hoodie on, the hood tugged up over his head—snow skirls in thick flakes around him.

I roll down my window a crack. "Hey."

"Car trouble?" His silky dark voice caresses over me, sends shivers through me—the hum takes up immediately, almost like I'm a cat purring.

"Yep." I smile at him. "Andreas is sending a tow truck."

"I can drive you." He jerks his head in the direction of his truck, idling on the shoulder behind mine. "No sense sitting in a cold car by yourself."

A shiver goes through me at the prospect of being in a vehicle alone with Caspian. "Okay. That'd be great. Thanks." I pull the keys out of the ignition, grab my bags, and exit the car.

He leads the way to his truck—I can't help but admire the way the boy wears jeans. They fit him just right, faded, well-worn, cupping his backside in a way that has my pulse hammering a little harder than it should.

He opens the passenger door for me—it's a big step up and in, and he waits for me to climb in and get settled before closing the door behind me. The interior is toasty warm, a pleasant contrast to the cold interior of my poor, dead Brat. It smells good, too; woodsmoke, cologne, and that indefinable scent of old trucks with plush, velvety up-holstery. Caspian's truck interior is all original, with analog controls and dials. The radio is playing softly, something classical, a symphony I recognize but couldn't name.

Red plush seats, red headliner and plastic dash—a lot of red.

He's in beside me, and suddenly the scent of Caspian wreathes around me. He's in a good mood—his cheeks are flushed, his skin ruddy and almost warm. As he pulls the column-mounted shifter into drive, he turns the radio down till the strains of the symphony are almost inaudible;

a check of traffic, and then the engine rattles and roars as he accelerates into the roadway.

"So. Where were you going?" He asks.

"The mall. I was gonna look for a new coat."

There's an armrest between us, a fold-down type with a cupholder built into it. I wish I dared to put it up and slide over to sit closer to him.

"I can take you."

I look at him. "I wouldn't want to interrupt your plans."

He shrugs, gives me a smile. "No real plans. Stirling and Fin are both working, so I'm on my own for the day. Spending it with you sounds fun to me."

"Those are your brothers?"

He nods. "They are. Fin is next, and Stirling is the oldest." A glance at me. "What about you? Any siblings?"

I shake my head. "Nope. Just me."

"How are you doing?" He pauses. "For real, I mean. With the passing of your mother."

I freeze, barely breathing. I told him that in the forest that morning I've become half-convinced I'd imagined. "I, um. I don't know."

"You don't know how you're doing?" He frowns. "I mean, are you coping?"

I shake my head. "Not really, to be honest. I'm…I'm numb. It's hard to think about her. It still doesn't feel real. I…" I look away, out the window. "I can't cry," I whisper. "Sometimes I think I'm broken. It makes me feel like I'm—like, did I not love her enough because I'm not crying?"

It feels weirdly cathartic to admit that out loud. I don't know why I feel comfortable saying it to Caspian when I don't really know him at all. But then, do I really know Andreas any better?

"Grief is a weird thing," Caspian says. "It's entirely personal. There's no wrong way to experience it."

"You've lost someone?" I ask, looking at him.

He nods, his features blank, smooth, expressionless. "Yes. I have."

Clearly, no further inquiry is invited.

"I'm sorry," I say. "It sucks."

He looks at me. "Yes. It does."

We sit in companionable silence—the scenery outside has transitioned from snow-clad trees to open fields, rural and expansive. Cows graze, fields lay fallow and tilled in even rows, and silos rise like aborted rockets. Dirt roads cut across the fields, bisecting them here and there. A huge truck with a green and yellow flasher on top whizzes past—it has a massive plow on its belly, angled toward the shoulder, and a little spinner just above the rear bumper scattering salt. The noise of it is deafening and abrupt, and I give a little squeak of surprise.

Caspian chuckles. "Plow truck. Typical around here, this time of year."

We approach an intersection—the light turns red as we approach, so Caspian brakes to a stop. Idly, I examine the businesses on the corners: a gas station, a Mcdonald's, a KFC, and a former gas station turned into a donut shop. The light turns green. Caspian waits a moment, looks for oncoming traffic, and then accelerates into the intersection.

There's no warning. I'm looking at Caspian, about to say something, I don't even know what. Some inanity about snow, maybe.

Then the world tilts. There's a deafening crash, glass

shattering, metal screaming. A moment of silence, and then another tremendous impact—another instant of silence, momentum spinning us the other way. Another crash. I'm jerked in a million different directions at once.

Then I feel the nausea of being airborne. A fragment of an instant—the blacktop of the road flashing past the shattered windshield.

Something cracks against my skull, and the world goes dark.

CHAPTER 8

GRAY SKY.

A flake of snow drifts, twists, tilts. I can see the shape of it—the crystalline structure. It settles on my nose, a sharp point of cold.

Everything hurts.

What happened?

The wreck.

Where's Caspian? It hurts to move.

"Cas—Caspian?" My voice is a hoarse croak.

"Don't move, miss." A stern, authoritative male voice. "You were in a car accident. You've hit your head."

"My…my friend. Where is he?" I try to lift my head, but a firm yet gentle pair of hands prevents me.

"Who are you talking about? You weren't alone in the car?" A face appears above me—older, rough and rugged, buzzed salt-and-pepper hair, a neat, short goatee.

"No. No. I wasn't driving. Caspian was driving. My friend. Caspian Taylor."

Lights flash—blue and red, white and red. Something rattles—an ambulance stretcher.

I'm lying on something cold and wet—the ground, snow. I blink. Another snowflake touches my cheek.

"There's no one else here, miss. When we arrived, you were lying here." I hear the puzzlement in his voice. "How did you get here? There's no way you were thrown this far from the wreck with barely a scratch on you."

"I…I don't know. I don't remember."

Male voices murmur a few feet away. A radio crackles. I hear something about someone fleeing the scene. I hope I didn't get him in trouble. But…where is he? Why did he leave?

"We were T-boned." I feel myself being lifted, carefully moved onto the stretcher, and then I'm going up. "It wasn't Caspian's fault. They ran the red. They hit us."

I'm dizzy. The world is blurry. I see a face at my feet, I squint, and I can make out a female figure in EMT blues. Young, pretty, serious. Dark hair.

"I think I have a concussion."

"I think you're lucky to be alive." This is the male EMT at my head. "I honestly don't know how you survived. How you made it out of that vehicle in the first place is a miracle." A pause. "You don't remember?"

"No, I…I remember the initial impact. We were hit

several times, and then I think we were rolling? I hit my head, and…" I shake my head, but it hurts and I groan. "I don't know."

"It's okay. Just relax."

The wheels bump as the stretcher goes over the curb, and then the wheels rattle across the blacktop. I smell smoke—we pass the ruin of Caspian's truck. It's mangled beyond all recognition—it's a flattened, twisted, smoking hulk of metal. Nothing, and I mean nothing, could have survived in that thing.

How did I get out of the car? How did I survive?

Where is Caspian?

Andreas fusses with the blankets, frowning. "Are you sure you don't need anything?"

I spent a full day at the hospital, under observation. Aside from the concussion, I have a few bruises here and there, and some cuts from the glass shattering. The doctors can't figure it out. No broken bones, nothing but a concussion, and not even a very severe one.

The word everyone is using is "miraculous."

I still can't remember anything after the initial crash. And I still haven't seen or heard from Caspian. Police questioned me, wanting to know why he would leave the scene. They have questions for him. All I can tell them is that I don't know where he lives, and I don't have his phone number…in fact, all I really know about him is his name and that he has two brothers, Stirling and Fin.

Odd. It feels like I know him far better than that, but in truth, I know next to nothing about him.

"I'm fine, Andreas," I assure him. "I don't even really have a headache anymore."

"Well, until the dizziness is gone, you're staying in bed." He sets my laptop on my lap.

"I'm fine. I swear, Andreas. You don't need to fuss over me." I open the laptop but don't log in. "You can go to work. I'll be fine on my own."

"You almost died, Maeve." He regards me with a serious look. "I'm taking the day off."

I shake my head, grab his wrist. "Andy." I intentionally use the shorter nickname he prefers. "Please, just go. You took yesterday off, you don't need to stay home today. I'll rest, I'll stay in bed as much as possible, I promise."

He's barely left my side since showing up at the hospital in a panic—apparently, one of the responding police officers knows Andreas and knew he'd taken me in, and called Andreas to let him know about the accident.

He had some sharp words about Caspian, and I know there's going to be a lot of questions if and when he ever shows up again.

And honestly? I have my own questions. Probably not the same ones the cops are going to have, though.

Andreas spends another few minutes with me, making sure I know there's food in the fridge and the pantry, and I can always order pizza to be delivered and reminds me about forty times to rest and to stay in bed as much as possible, and if I get dizzy or the headache comes back to call him.

Finally, he leaves, and it's kind of a relief. I mean, it feels good to have someone worrying about me. But also, a little suffocating. He woke me up every hour all night long, asked me my name and who the president is and what year it is…he even slept sitting up in a chair at the foot of my bed.

Makes me feel taken care of, but it's nice to have a minute alone to process everything.

Once I'm alone, my mind goes into overdrive.

What happened? Why did Caspian leave me?

Where is he?

Why can't I grieve for my mother? I feel scared—like, am I broken? I haven't cried. Not once. I miss her—when I think about the fact that she's gone forever, I start to panic, and I just…shut down. I think I'm almost avoiding thinking about her at all. I know she's gone, but part of me still wants to think she'll show up. That there's been some mixup.

I feel myself going into a tailspin—missing Mom, wanting her back. I think about my favorite memories with her. Going to Cedar Point the summer I turned thirteen and we went on every ride, some of them several times. Disney World the summer I turned fifteen. Going to honky tonks in Nashville last year. Hiking in Yosemite.

All the hours in the car, crisscrossing the country. Bickering about the perfect road trip playlist, and how we'd always end up alternating her playlists and mine. Stocking up the back seat with cases of Coke and sacks of powdered donuts and beef jerky and bags of peanut M&Ms.

I can see her in my mind, smiling and laughing at some dumb joke, one hand on the steering wheel and the other out the open window, tilting her hand up and down in the wind. She'd turn the music up obnoxiously loud, open all the windows, and sing at the top of her lungs. She'd only ever show that side of herself to me—around everyone else, she was quiet, withdrawn, introverted. With me, she could be loud and silly.

My eyes burn. My heart cracks, twists. I want my mother back.

But I can't cry. The grief is there, the tears are there, but it's like there's this wall up around me, not allowing anything in or out.

I purposely think of Mom for hours, like probing a sore tooth with my tongue.

No tears.

Just heartache.

Eventually, it hurts too much, and I go back to putting her out of my mind. I turn on a reality show and binge an entire season.

At some point, I fall asleep.

CHAPTER 9

I'M IN THE TRUCK WITH CASPIAN. I'M dreaming. I'm me, I'm in my body, but I can't move. I can't do anything but experience it all over again.

I see him in profile—sharp, vulpine features, aviators hiding his eyes. Hair protruding under the edge of his black beanie. Clean-shaven, but so clean it's as if he doesn't even have facial hair at all. Not a hint of stubble. Weird that I never noticed that until now.

Shock and alarm suffuse his features.

It's not happening in slow-motion—instead, it's like I'm able to catalog each individual second like a photograph.

It happens so fast there's no way he could

have avoided it. Even in the weird taffy-like stretching of time in dream-logic, it happens in a single instant. The car plows into the driver's side. Glass shatters. I watch pieces of glass hit his face, but instead of cutting him as they did me, they just…bounce off.

They leave no mark. No blood. No cuts.

The first impact sends us skidding in a circle through the intersection—I can make out the Golden Arches in a smear of color spinning past. Then another car hits our back end, sending us the other way. A third impact on the front left quarter panel. The redirection of momentum sends us rolling airborne.

My hair drifts up as we go inverted.

My comprehension of time distorts further.

Caspian, in the driver's seat, looks at me. Fear and worry and panic contort his beautiful face. He yanks at his seatbelt—plastic shatters and the nylon material shreds as he literally rips the seatbelt off of himself. He does the same for mine, tearing it away as if it were made of tissue paper.

This happens in less time than it takes me to blink once.

He grabs me by the arm and yanks me out of my seat and into his embrace.

We're still airborne, twisting in midair. We're about to hit the ground again, the first impact with the earth after going airborne. A fragment of time has elapsed—five seconds, maybe?

He twists in place, his arms wrapping around me—one around my head, the other around my torso. They feel like iron bands—cold and hard.

We hit the ground. He takes the force of the impact on his own body, protecting me. It's impossible. It's just a dream. This isn't what happened.

Right?

The metal roof of the car crumples, molding around the shape of his sheltering arms as if his body is an immovable object. Indestructible.

Another fragment of an instant.

We're airborne again, in the process of spinning, rotating on our axis. Earth, sky. Earth, sky. One rotation, two. Three. McDonald's. Marathon gas station sign. KFC. Gray sky. A snowflake drifts across my frame of view.

I hear and feel his feet smash against the floor of the truck. His fist crunches upward, punching through the metal as easily as if through cardboard. He rips the metal apart with both hands, creating an opening in the roof.

Another rotation, still airborne.

His arms banded around me, he leaps. Through the roof, skyward. Away from the spinning vehicle.

I'm not entirely certain of the next sequence of events, even in the weird clarity of the dream. We hit the ground, and my head knocks against the road.

I'm still dreaming.

We're motionless. I hear my heart beating unnaturally loudly.

Caspian moves with exquisite gentility, depositing me on the grass. I feel something icy touch my cheek, a tender ghostly caress. So cold it burns. It burns. Beyond cold—it's the perfect frigidity of absolute zero.

"You're safe now, little sparrow." It's not even a whisper—it's a breath.

The touch vanishes, leaving, surely, a scar in its place. A slight whoosh, a whirl of colder air.

I wake up.

Chapter 10

MY CHEEK BURNS WHERE CASPIAN touched me, in my dream. I rise from my bed and go into the bathroom, moving a little unsteadily. I look at my reflection in the mirror, leaning close.

I gasp.

My heart crashes in my chest, thudding painfully against my ribcage.

There, on my left cheekbone… am I imagining it? I have to be.

There's a slight shimmer. Not like glitter, but like…ice. Like frost. Where he touched me.

A thought occurs—I peel off my shirt and twist my back toward the mirror, craning my neck to see.

On my lower back, on the right side, are five circular bruises…as if fingertips had dug in, impossibly strong, impossibly hard fingers.

Not absolute evidence, necessarily, but it makes it harder to deny that what I saw in my dream is what really happened.

I mean, how else can you explain it? I shouldn't be here. I should be dead. He should be dead—the first impact of the car T-boning us hit directly on the driver's side door. It should have killed him.

How else could I have gotten clear of the car? Andreas showed me a photograph his friend sent him of Caspian's truck after the wreck; it was a mangled ruin, barely recognizable as a vehicle. Nothing could have survived inside that.

Yet here I am.

My cheek is…frostbit? I don't know. It's numb to the touch, and it burns. Did I just not notice it, earlier? Am I experiencing things in my dreams that are…real?

What does that mean for the dream I had about Mom? She had, like, elf ears. Except, where Legolas's ears are pointed upward from the tip, hers were pointed more backward, elongated and pointed from the back side rather than the top.

She spoke to me…

Was that really her? Do I have, like, premonitory dreams?

What about Andreas? In that dream, he had pointy ears too. And I know he doesn't. I'd have noticed that.

And I dreamed about Caspian—those eyes. In the forest, they weren't totally black like that, but they still weren't…normal eyes. They were too black, too…I don't know. Alien? Animal, almost. Not human.

Was that real? Or was that another dream?

God, I'm confused.

I put my shirt back on and get into bed—my head swims, a little, after moving around. Put the reality show back on and start the next season. But my mind isn't on the show.

It's on Caspian.

The mystery of him. Those fangs in the dream. His reaction to my blood, in gym class.

I can't think the word which my subconscious offers up for what Caspian is, or could be.

That's crazy. They don't exist. Edward, Lestat, Dracula… they're just fictional characters. Made up.

But there've been stories and legends for centuries, maybe even thousands of years. Could those legends and myths and stories be based on some kind of truth?

I must have hit my head harder than I thought, to be considering it.

Andreas comes home late, visibly exhausted and stressed. He checks on me, and goes right to bed, skipping dinner.

In the morning, he tries to insist I stay home another day, but I refuse.

"Maeve, you experienced a significant trauma. You had a concussion." He stands in front of me in the kitchen, blocking my path to the door and his truck. "One more day."

I cross my arms over my chest and shake my head—carefully. "Andy, if I have to stay here in bed one more day, I'll go crazy. I'm fine, I promise."

He says nothing. Crosses his arms.

"Please? I spent the whole day in the hospital and all

day here yesterday. I barely got out of bed. I'm okay. Achy, like, I definitely won't forget what happened, but I can't just lay in bed and stew on it. I have to keep moving."

He growls. "No headache?"

"Nope." This is mostly true. It comes and goes, but it's not bad.

"You're not dizzy?"

"No, not really. I get a little woozy if I stand up too fast, but I'll take it easy." I show him my phone. "If I start to not feel good, I'll call you, and I'll come home. I swear."

"No playing tough."

"Promise."

He sighs. Waves a hand. "Fine." A frown. "Wait, your car. In all the craziness of the accident, I forgot all about it. I meant to call a tow truck, but then my captain came in with the new case and I never did. Which means your car is still broken down on the side of the road."

"Caspian can bring me home. Assuming he shows up and has something else to drive."

He scowls at me. "That boy has some explaining to do. I'm not sure I want you associating with him anymore."

I just lift an eyebrow at him.

He holds up both hands. "I guess I can't really make that call, huh?"

"No. I'm eighteen, almost nineteen. And I'd like to know why he vanished too, but…the accident wasn't his fault. I'm not mad at him, and you shouldn't be either."

"Leaving the scene of an accident is a crime, Maeve. It's suspicious."

I nod. "I know. But I'm going to give him the benefit of the doubt, and I'm going to ask him."

He plants his hands on his hips and hangs his head,

then looks at me. "Just…be smart, okay? If you have a feeling that something isn't right, listen to it." He blows out another breath. "All right. I'll drop you off, but we have to go."

At school, it's obvious everyone has heard about the accident—I get asked what happened about a hundred times, at least. The principal tells me if I need to go home early, to just let him know and it'll be excused.

No one asks about Caspian.

He's not in class.

My heart drops out of my chest with disappointment as I realize he's not here at all. I need to see him. I need to talk to him—hear his explanation.

School ends, and I'm desperately glad; I'm exhausted, my head is starting to hurt, and I'm feeling a little unsteady on my feet. I need to be home, and I need to lie down.

I'm standing outside the school by the parking lot, trying to decide how to get home. Andreas seems to be the only option.

I'm working on a text to him when I hear a vehicle pull to a stop in front of me.

"Maeve." Caspian's sleek, midnight voice washes over me.

My head snaps up. He's in a different truck. This one is newer than the one that was wrecked, but not by much— it's from the eighties, maybe, although I don't much about cars. This one is gray with a red stripe on the hood, with a long bed and a two-door cab. Normal tires, no lift, nothing fancy. He's wearing a red sweater, cable-knit, thick and chunky, offsetting his pale skin and dark hair. Aviators, of course.

He has a small square bandage on his head, at an angle up near his left temple.

I don't know what to say, now that he's here.

The buzz kicks to life at his presence, making my chest hum, my bones rattle, my blood sing.

He jerks his head at the passenger seat. "Get in. Fin is meeting us at your car."

I round the hood without a word, climb in, and buckle up. This truck's engine is well-maintained, idling with a healthy, muscular grumble. "Nice truck."

He shrugs. "Bought it from a friend of Fin's."

"Surprised you didn't get a new truck, like actually new."

"I like old things." He pulls out of the parking lot and heads for the road out of town.

A long silence. Finally, I can't hold it in anymore. "Why'd you leave after the wreck?"

He doesn't answer.

"Caspian?"

"It's hard to explain."

I look at him; he's impossible to read, his smooth, hard features expressionless. "I think you owe me some kind of explanation. I woke up alone on the side of the road."

He glances at me, then back at the road. "I know. I'm sorry."

Silence.

"So?"

Another look at me. A frown mars his features; even frowning, he's so beautiful it almost hurts to look at him. "Maeve, I…" a sigh of frustration. "I can't explain it. Not in a way that would make any sense to you."

"You could try."

"You wouldn't believe me."

"You'd be surprised what I might believe." I turn away from him and lift my shirt to show him the bruises on my back. "How'd I get these, Caspian?"

His frown deepens, becoming a scowl, his jaw hardening. "I don't know, Maeve. It was a seriously intense wreck. Who knows?"

"Quit bullshitting me, Caspian," I say, dropping my shirt and turning back to him. "Those are fingerprints. Your fingerprints."

We come to a stoplight and he takes the opportunity to look at me. "What are you suggesting?"

"I had a dream."

He's puzzled by the non sequitur. "What?"

"About you. About the accident."

He gazes at me—inscrutable behind those glasses. Those damn glasses. I want to see his eyes. "Maeve—"

"You did something impossible, in the dream. You got me out of the car while it was midair."

His jaw flexes, ticks, and pulses. "That does sound impossible. Dreams are weird, though, right?"

"Yeah, I'd think so too. Except in the dream, you had your arms around me. And the way you were holding me in the dream, it would put your fingers exactly where I have the bruises." I stare at my reflection in the glasses. "And then there's that morning in the forest. I almost thought I'd dreamed that too, but I didn't, did I?" The light turns green, and after thoroughly checking traffic in all directions, he accelerates away. "You said you were dangerous. You said I should stay away from you."

He shakes his head. "I'm not sure what you want me to say."

"Honestly, me either. But I'd settle for the truth."

"What if you learn the truth and you wish you hadn't?"

"You're not answering."

"I don't remember what happened, Maeve. It all happened so fast." This is delivered flat, stilted.

He doesn't expect me to believe him. And I don't.

I huff, angry. "So you're just not going to answer me? You're not going to tell me the truth?"

He shakes his head. "No."

"Have you had lunch?"

He glances my way. "What?"

"Lunch. Have you had lunch yet?"

He rolls a shoulder. "Um, not yet. Why?"

"Because you're always cranky right before lunch and then you come back in a better mood."

"My blood sugar," he says. "It gets low, makes me moody."

"Where do you go? You're never in the cafeteria."

"Juniors and seniors can leave campus. I go home for lunch." I feel like this is the truth, just not all of it; I could leave too, but I don't.

We reach my car, then. There's an orange sticker on the window. In front of it, a massive old pickup, glossy black, huge tires, lifted, dual exhaust pipes protruding from the bed of the truck behind the cab. Attached to the truck is a flatbed trailer, and a burly young man wearing dirty, faded jeans, heavy boots, and a white T-shirt is in the act of hauling a winch from the front of the trailer toward my car. He's huge—Caspian's height but built like a bull. Huge, round shoulders, heavy with muscle, thick arms stretching the sleeves of the T-shirt. He looks like he could bend horseshoes with his bare hands. His hair is the brown of a grizzly's fur, short and thick, messy. His skin is as pale as Caspian's, but his has the ruddy tint to it that Caspian gets after lunch. He's wearing a pair of polarized Wayfarers.

Caspian pulls over behind my Brat and puts the truck

in park. I get out after him and we head up to where Fin is bent over, connecting the winch hook to my car. He finishes connecting it, straightens, and brushes his palms on his jeans. He grins as he sees Caspian, but the grin fades, his jaw tightening when he sees me—I'm not sure if it's distrust or dislike. It's there and gone quickly, but I definitely saw it.

"Fin," Caspian says, approaching the end of the trailer. "Thanks for coming."

"No worries, Cas." He lifts his chin at me in a distinctly masculine greeting. "Phineas Taylor. Call me Fin."

"Maeve Sparrow." I offer him a bright, friendly smile. "Thank you for helping with my car, Fin."

His smile in return is friendly enough. "Nah, nothin' to it." He darts his chin at the car. "What'd it do?"

"It started, like, coughing and sputtering, and then it just died."

He smirks at me. "Sorry, gotta ask. Does it have gas?"

I roll my eyes. "Yes. I put gas in it myself just the other day."

"Yeah, well, gotta ask." He does something to the box housing the winch motor, and it starts grinding away, hauling the car up the gate ramp of the trailer. "You'd be surprised how often people bring cars in for silly things like that. They just don't realize, you know?"

"You're a mechanic, then?"

He nods. "Yup. I own a little shop just outside of Elk Rivers."

"Entrepreneur, huh?"

He shrugs. "I worked there in high school, and after I graduated. The owner was retiring, so I had Alistair hook me up with a loan, and voila, I'm a business owner. Pretty nice working for yourself."

"Alistair?" I ask.

Caspian leans on the side of the trailer, on the opposite side from Fin. "Our guardian. Father figure, sort of. He adopted us—me, Stirling, and Fin."

"But you don't call him Dad?"

Fin shakes his head. "Nah. We were all older when he took us in, and it just seemed weird."

"I understand that. My mom recently…um." I swallow hard. "She uh…she passed away not long ago, and my…I guess he's my dad, but I don't really think of him as Dad—he showed up and took me in. He's just Andreas, although he's trying to get me to call him Andy."

"Sorry for your loss," Fin says. "How recent?"

"Just a few weeks ago."

He winces. "Damn, girl. Sucks. Sorry to hear it."

I nod. "Yeah, thanks. It's been…it hasn't been easy."

"No, it never is." His expression shuts down; like Caspian, he has his own trauma in his past. He extends a hand to me. "Keys?"

I fish them from my purse and toss them to him. He catches them and turns away.

The winch finishes hauling the car up onto the trailer, and Fin grabs a tangle of yellow straps out of the bed of his truck and begins connecting them to the trailer and the car, securing it in place.

The hum in my chest is disconcertingly powerful—distracting, almost an ache. My teeth almost chatter in my jaw, so strong is the buzz in my belly. It's more powerful than ever, with Fin and Caspian.

After a few minutes of ratcheting the straps taut at all

four corners, Fin secures the gate and pats the side of the trailer. "All set. Let's roll, gang."

His truck is a single cab, meaning I'm going to have to sit in between Caspian and Fin. I'm worried about being in proximity to them both—I may well combust, or my bones will rattle right out of my skin.

Caspian opens the door for me—it's high, which means there's no graceful way to climb in. I just have to heave myself in, which gives Caspian a nice view of my ass.

I can feel him staring.

I find I don't mind—the hum in my chest doesn't either; the longer he stares, the more my cheeks heat, and the more the hum turns into a purr. It approves of Caspian's attention.

Heat billows in my chest, in my cheeks. Between my thighs.

God. What's wrong with me?

The inside of the truck is warm and smells of old tobacco and motor oil. Caspian slides in next to me, and then Fin is behind the wheel, and now. . .

Oh god.

This is going to be tricky. It's not just a hum, now that I'm wedged between the two men. The quarters are close—their thighs brush mine, their elbows and shoulders. I smell them—woodsmoke, cologne, and that coppery tang.

My whole being is on fire, a vibration so powerful it takes my breath away. Heat flames in my face, flushing my skin till it tingles, prickles, wraps too tightly around my bones. An emptiness yawns inside me—a need for. . .something. I don't know what. Just a need. A hunger.

I fiddle with my fingers, pluck at my jeans, at the strings

of my hoodie. It's hard to pull in a breath—the purr in my chest and the heat and the need are too much.

Neither of them is speaking, and the radio is off.

I become abruptly aware of the tension—it crackles in the cab, so thick it could be sliced away like meat off the bone. To my left, Fin's fist creaks on the steering wheel. To my right, Caspian isn't moving, not at all; he's not breathing, not blinking, not twitching, sniffling, scratching, nothing. Motionless, exactly like a statue carved from marble.

For that matter, other than his eyes roaming the road and his hand subtly tilting this way and that to keep the truck on the road, Fin is as motionless as Caspian.

Unnaturally so.

Perhaps "preternaturally" is a better word. Or supernatural? I'm not a hundred percent certain of the difference. All I know is that their absolute motionlessness is not normal human behavior at all.

My breathing gradually speeds until I'm almost hyperventilating. Who are they? What are they? Who or what have I gotten into a truck with?

The answer has been bubbling around in my subconscious for a while, now.

"Breathe, Maeve," Caspian's deep, dark voice crashes through my thoughts. "Breathe in. Deep. Slow."

I suck in a breath and realize as I do so that I've gone from hyperventilating to not breathing at all.

"There you go." I turn to look at him but only see his jawline and sharp high cheekbones and my reflection in his eyes. "You need to breathe."

Fin turns his head to look at Caspian, and I know they're sharing a significant moment over my head.

"We're almost there," Fin says.

Despite being so much larger than Caspian, his voice isn't quite as deep and yet is much rougher, raspier, and harsher. His speech patterns, also, are less formal. I want to say less educated sounding, but that doesn't feel quite right. Just…more informal.

We're coasting slowly through downtown Elk Rivers; those students who aren't at the ski hill are downtown, shopping, hitting up the general store for candy bars, sodas, and slices of pizzas. As our truck slides through the throngs of students crossing the road in herds, groups, and clumps, I feel eyes on me. Watching me. Staring at me, sandwiched between the two Taylor boys.

Assessing. Judging.

"Hope you didn't have designs on class president or prom queen," Fin remarks. "Being seen with us ain't exactly good for your popularity."

I huff a sarcastic laugh. "I couldn't possibly care less. I just want to graduate and be done with high school."

"What's next, after you get your diploma?" Fin asks. His jaw is clenched, clipping off his words—he sounds casual and friendly, at the surface level, but I can tell the tension still has him tightly gripped.

I shake my head. "Not a clue. Community college maybe. Or a gap year."

That seems to have exhausted his attempt at friendly chitchat, for we lapse back into a tense, awkward, uncomfortable silence.

Through downtown, past the beach, and to the very end of Wapiti Way, passing the driveway to Andreas's house— my house, I suppose, to the very last driveway on the left. Except, it's not really a driveway—it's more of an unnamed secondary road; on either side of the entrance from Wapiti

Way are matching signs, black backgrounds with large red letters outlined in white:

KEEP OUT

NO TRESPASSING

PRIVATE PROPERTY

It winds seemingly at random through the dense, park-like forest; here, the cathedral-like quality is heightened, the trees close together and having grown in what I suspect may be artificial rows. No underbrush at all, just the towering pines, and the fresh blanket of powdery white snow.

I can almost hear the hush beyond the windows.

"Can you stop and let me out, for a minute?" I ask, on impulse.

Fin brakes to a smooth stop, the tires crunching in the snow. Caspian exits, holding the door for me. I slide out of the truck and hop to the ground—into snow up to my ankles. Thank god one of the first things Andreas made me buy was a pair of calf-height fur-lined boots with rubber lowers, so my feet stay dry and warm.

Neither Fin nor Caspian asks me what I'm doing as I walk away from the truck and into the shadowy narthex of the forest beyond the path. Fin shuts the motor off, and now the silence is complete.

It's a thick, enveloping blanket, the quiet. It wraps around me, constricting, dense, all-consuming. High above, the tips of the pines sway in a breeze not felt down here. The snow descends in fat, lilting, sparse nodules. The cold is sharp and hard, biting my skin where it's exposed—cheeks, forehead, nose, throat.

I crunch through the snow until I feel alone, and then I close my eyes, and I just...

Listen.

The nothingness is absolute. Not a bird chirping, not a car rumbling, not a horn honking or a dog barking or a person laughing. I've never experienced such near-absolute quiet.

The only sound is the breathing of the forest—a soft, quiet, almost imperceptible soughing.

I feel him, smell his coppery tang sharp in my nostrils, feel the purr in my chest that I get whenever I'm within ten feet of him.

I don't look at him. "Do something weird for me, would you?"

A pause, then a chuckle. "Sure."

"Back up slowly till I say stop."

"Okay."

I keep my eyes closed. His feet somehow make no sound in the snow. No crunching, no squeaking, nothing. The only way I know he's doing as I asked is that I feel the hum in my blood fading. Then, it's almost gone, receding to the faint vibration you'd feel from a laptop fan as the machine rests on your thighs.

I open my eyes and turn: Caspian is a good twenty feet away, on the other side of the path—his crimson sweater stands out bright against the pure white of the snow, as does his dark hair and faded jeans.

I smile at him. "Thanks. Just... experimenting."

I turn back around—in the time it takes me to suck in a full breath, I feel him at my back again, close enough that the purr is violent, arresting, distracting. No human can move that fast, that silently. He's just—there. No evidence of movement.

"Cas." This is Fin's voice, a low growled warning. More of a scold, really.

"You feel my presence, don't you?" It's phrased as a question, but his tone makes it a statement of fact.

I nod.

"How so?"

I place my palm flat against my chest over my coat—the center of my chest, not my heart, neither physical nor metaphorical. "Here. It's…a hum. A buzz? Like a purr." I swallow hard as I speak the truth that sounds insane as I put it to voice, here in the cold air between us. "The closer you are, the louder it is. Not louder—I don't think it's… well, it's real, but I don't know if it's physical. Like, anatomical. I don't know."

"Do you feel it around Fin?"

I nod. "Yes. Not as strongly, but I do."

A silent, pulsing pause—I can almost feel Caspian and Fin exchanging glances, reflective sunglasses aimed at each other.

"What does it mean?" I ask.

"I don't know," Caspian says.

"Liar," I whisper.

He doesn't respond to my accusation. "Come on. Let's go. Fin can probably fix your car in a few minutes."

"Why did you leave your truck back there?" It's something that popped into my head a few minutes ago, and I can't figure out the answer.

Other than to think he just wants to be near me…or to be the shield between me and Fin, as if he doesn't trust Fin around me. Or vice versa, perhaps.

"I'll get it later."

Again, not an answer to the question.

I turn and face him—he's inches behind me. I stare up

at him. My reflection gazes down at me from his mirrored lenses. "I hate these," I murmur, reaching up.

He tilts his head away. "Don't."

"I've seen your eyes before." I reach again, and he leans away again, but not as much.

"It was dark, then. It's too bright, now. The light will hurt my eyes."

"Is that the truth?" I ask. "Or is that a convenient excuse?"

He doesn't answer. Doesn't move.

I reach further, my fingers touching the cold metal arms of the glasses. The air is cold, snowflakes dancing around us; his glasses are cold from the air, icy against my ungloved fingertips.

He is colder yet.

Arctic, subzero cold radiates from him. He's pale, almost bloodless—his skin could camouflage in the snow. The red of his sweater seems redder yet against his ivory flesh.

"Cas." Fin again. "No."

I ignore Fin—Caspian ignores Fin.

I pull his glasses from his face—I almost drop them, a gasp hissing past my lips. His eyes are black, pupil-less, whites-less. Narrowed to slits, they fix on me like lasers. His jaw tightens, teeth grinding. A moment, then. Frozen, utterly silent, my heart not beating, my breath lodged in my lungs.

Then, he growls—a feral, predatory, animal sound emanating from his chest, a ripping snarl. He snatches the glasses from my hand in a movement too fast to track—they're in my hand one instant, and on his face the next. There's not even a blur to mark the action.

He turns away.

Marches toward the truck in a stiff, angry gait completely unlike his usual fluid grace.

Fin catches him with his body, stepping in front of Caspian at the last second—their bodies meet with an audible crunch, as if two marble statues had collided. I hear their voices murmuring low—rough, angry whispers.

Caspian shoves Fin hard—the larger male staggers backward, heels skidding in the snow before he rights himself—Caspian stalks away down the lane, head ducked with his chin tucked against his chest, hands shoved into his jeans pockets. He stomps away a few feet, stops, and turns back to look at me. I feel his eyes on me.

I blink. Once.

And he's gone.

"Fuckin' goddammit, Cas," I hear Fin grumble. "Fuckin' moron." He turns to regard me. I feel like an insect beneath his palpable but unseen eyes—an insect being considered for dinner by a nearby lizard. "Come on, then. Let's go."

I head for the truck but stop with my hand on the passenger door handle. "Is it much farther?"

He tosses his head in an impatient negative. "Nah. Quarter mile, maybe."

"I'll walk."

His mouth tightens in a frown. "It's cold. You'll freeze."

I zip up my jacket the rest of the way, tug my hood up, fish my thick wool mittens from my jacket pockets and put them on. "I'm good."

"Sure you don't want to ride?"

"You don't want to be alone with me in that truck, that's what I'm sure of." As soon as I say it, I know it's the truth.

He stares at me another moment, then nods. "Suit yourself."

I step back from the truck and follow Caspian's footprints. I come to where he'd stopped—beyond this point, nothing. No tracks.

I march onward. Fifty feet, maybe? I find a single footprint. A left foot. Deep, as if the landing was heavy with momentum.

Another fifty feet—a right bootprint.

A thought occurs to me. I look up: splotches of snow dot the tree trunks here and there…exactly as if left there by a foot. In other places, the horizontal branches have bare spots on them absent of the snow that coats them an inch thick everywhere else. Almost like a pair of hands had gripped there for an instant before swinging onward.

Well—at least I know he can't actually vanish.

I just…I can't explain in any kind of rational way the factors that are building up in my subconscious. Because I know exactly what Caspian is…it's just not possible.

Or, I didn't think it was. Clearly, however, there are things I don't know about the world I live in.

Chapter 11

C ASPIAN IS WAITING FOR ME AT THE end of the lane where it opens into the clearing. He turns his head at my arrival, glancing my way over his shoulder.

"Are you okay now?" I ask.

He doesn't answer my question. "Alistair is home. Stirling is not. You can come in until Fin has your car fixed."

He looks in the direction of the house: it's a huge, sprawling Victorian with a third-story turret spiking upward from the left corner; pointed gables with the windows trimmed in what seems to be delicate lace march across the front fascia, the roof shingled in arched cedar shakes. The siding is creamy ivory, the roof an aged gray. A deep porch wraps around the right side of the house from the front door, disappearing around the rear of the house.

An old green Land Rover is parked at an angle in front of the house—the kind of thing you see in nature documentaries set in Africa, although this one features a full roof with bubbles of glass over the rear tires and a snorkel running from the hood and sticking up over the driver's door. It's battered, dented, and scratched, the paint faded, but the tires are new; despite the falling snow, the white roof and the hood with its mounted spare tire are both clear, indicating it's been driven recently.

"Come. Alistair waits."

He strides away at a normal pace, and I walk beside him. The house perches on a hill in the clearing; behind the house, the land slopes sharply upward, thickly forested; here the forest is newer rather than old growth, with thick underbrush making it nearly impassable, if not totally. The clearing is wide enough that should a tree fall, it wouldn't strike the house. The tree line is stark, the shadows beyond dark and thick.

The lake must be close—I swear I smell water, although I know the Great Lakes are freshwater rather than salt. I can't explain it, I just know I smell water. I glance to my right, and the air above the trees has that weird indefinable quality that makes me feel like the beach is that way. I scent the air, and again I smell water.

Weird.

We reach the house and the steps leading up to the front porch; my legs betray me, providing too much impetus, and I trip forward, catching myself on the wooden stairs.

Slivers spike my palms, and I hiss in pain. "Damn it. Stupid legs."

Caspian glances at me, his jaw tight. "Are you all right?"

I nod. "Fine. Just some slivers. I'll need some tweezers."

"You trip quite frequently."

I roll my eyes. "I know. Lifelong curse. No one can explain it. I even had an MRI once, but my brain is normal. I just…I'm not clumsy like I don't drop things, and I don't knock things over, I just…" I shake my head and shrug. "I don't know how to explain it. It's like…my brain short-circuits randomly, while I'm walking or running or climbing stairs, and I just…fall. It's almost like my brain forgets how much energy I need to go up the steps or something. I'm used to it by now. It's just annoying."

He opens the front door for me, holding the glass storm door open and pushing the heavy, intricately carved wooden main door open with an ominous squeak of old hinges. I step through and into an eclectic mixture of old-world design ethos and modern amenities. The floors are dark wood, original and old—worn smooth and faded, with high traffic areas more faded yet. There are handwoven rugs here and there—in front of the door in the foyer, a long runner leading from the foyer to the kitchen at the rear of the house.

The original layout is long gone but still detectable—once, when the house was first built, there would have been a narrow hallway as you enter, with a steep narrow flight of stairs leading up; a sitting room would be on your right—a formal parlor; on the left, a formal living room; at the end of the hallway, the kitchen, and to the right of the kitchen would be the formal dining room separated by walls, communicating with the parlor. On the left of the kitchen, a back door leads to the wraparound porch.

Now, nearly all the unnecessary walls have been removed. The stairs float up to the second level, with a graceful curving banister with dark wood to match the floors; storage is built into the backside of the staircase. The living room left of the front door wraps around to the kitchen, continuing to the dining room and from there to the parlor on the right of the front door, where a more formal set of dark leather couches and chairs face an antique grand piano angled toward the semicircular window seat. The living room is less formal, with a deep, comfortable, worn camel-colored suede sectional and a pair of wide, deep armchairs with matching ottomans facing a massive fireplace, in which a roaring fire crackles merrily. I can't see much of the kitchen from here, but it appears to be more mixtures of modern and old. Except for a couple of supporting pillars in key places, the whole main floor is open; it's spacious but not cavernous, and the arrangement of couches, chairs, end tables, and several curio cabinets with collections of antiques creates a cozy, homey feel.

A man of medium height and build stands facing the fire, hands clasped behind his back, head bowed in thought. His nut-brown hair is cut in a timeless style, cropped nearly to the skin on the sides and clipped short on top, swept back and to the side; he turns to face me, and I'm struck, as several times before with other people, that he is stunningly, almost otherworldly handsome, in a sharp-featured, vulpine sort of way. He wears a dark brown tweed suit, three pieces, with tan patches on the elbows and the vest a lighter shade than the blazer. A maroon bowtie with white polka dots adorns his neck, and he wears fine patent leather brogues.

He may well have stepped out of history at any point in the previous hundred and fifty years. Yet, on him, it looks natural, and I can't fathom this man wearing anything else. And damn me if he isn't smoking a briar pipe; the smoke curls lazily up from the bowl, sweet-smelling.

He's as clean-jawed as Fin and Caspian both are—not a single hint of stubble anywhere, only a short rectangle of sideburns ending in a clean cut.

His skin has the same ivory and marble appearance as Fin and Caspian, but his is ruddy, tinted with life.

He smiles at me, a blinding, brilliant grin of white teeth. "Miss Maeve Sparrow. Welcome, welcome." His voice is stentorian, with a crisp British accent; he didn't just step out of history, he stepped off the set of Downton Abbey. "My name is Alistair. How wonderful to have you in our home."

The purr—or, as it's beginning to form in my mind: The Purr—is already humming away vigorously inside me, kicks up into mad overdrive. It makes my hands tremble, and my breath shakes in my throat. Caspian shuffles closer behind me; vaguely, I'm aware of Fin parking the truck and joining us in the foyer.

Three of them. My thighs press together, heat boiling in my belly, in my throat, behind my eyes, in my chest...

Between my thighs.

That yawning, aching void within me threatens to swallow me whole from the inside out.

Alistair's kind, intelligent, warm eyes—dark, dark brown, more black than anything, yet with normal whites and pupils—narrow with astute suspicion. His nostrils flare.

His eyes cut to Fin. "Will you put the kettle on for tea, Phineas? Thank you." Then to Caspian. "Fetch the tweezers from the powder room, if you please, Caspian. There's a little basket beneath the sink, I believe. They should be in there."

Both men—I realize that they are not boys, no more than I'm merely a girl—move to do as their bid. There's no question who's in charge here. The moment they're gone, Alistair's kindly professor demeanor vanishes, his eyes harden—blackness swallowing the whites.

I blink, and he's inches from me. The cold he radiates is less intense than from Caspian. His presence brings with it a waft of coppery tang.

"What are you playing at, child?" His voice is pitched low, for my ears only. Hard. Brutal. Menacing.

I swallow hard. "I…I'm not—I'm sorry. What are you talking about? I'm not playing at anything."

Fear pounds thick in my blood, tasting of things that lurk in the shadows as you creep down the stairs at midnight, of the eyes gleaming in the primordial darkness beyond the firelight.

He leans closer. The copper tang assaults my nostrils, acrid, sweet, thick, rich, almost oily. It's not unpleasant, but the scent makes the pulsing of terror in my veins a mad boiling desperation.

Cold as he sniffs the side of my throat…his nose brushing my skin—icicles from where his skin touches mine.

"What *are* you, Maeve Sparrow?" His voice slithers in my ear.

"I'm just…I'm me. I-I-I…I don't know. Please." I'm not sure what I'm begging for, but I'm begging for something.

He stares down at me, eyes pools of blackness, empty voids which pierce my soul and dredge up all my most secret nightmares. "It can't be. It simply can't."

"What can't be?" I whisper the question.

"You." He sniffs me again. "You are an impossibility, child."

He appears no older than forty-five at most. Yet the aura which chokes the air around him is ancient: old parchment moldering away in a forgotten corner of a library; dust gathering on a high shelf, where many-legged things go to die; flickering torchlight and oil lamps and fireplaces with guttering coals.

Staring up at him, I feel like a day-old gazelle fawn looking into the eyes of a hungry lion, his pelt scarred from innumerable battles, grizzled, hungry, for whom I am no more than a midday snack.

Somewhere, there's a high-pitched whistle: a kettle come to boil.

It snaps the moment, shatters it into shards which soon dissolve.

Alistair turns on a heel and takes two large, normal-paced steps toward the fireplace. Pauses, then turns back to me, puzzlement still on his face. He blinks, twice, and the black pools are stained by gray, which fades to white.

The black fades into a dark burnt brown, and the menacing cold and the ancient, primordial terror recede into the corners of the room like shadows retreating before a high-held candle.

Once more, he's a genial professor with a tweed suit, a

briar pipe, and endlessly kind eyes, gesturing at the couch. "Please, Miss Sparrow. Sit, sit. Phineas will be in shortly with tea."

Knees knocking, I gingerly sit on the edge of the couch. Alistair sits in the wide-armed, high-backed red velvet chair nearest the fire, puffs on his pipe until the cherry glows orange and smokes billows to the ceiling, swarming around the room in a cloud of cloying sweetness.

"So. Tell me about yourself, Miss Sparrow."

As if nothing happened.

"Um." I hate talking about myself. I never know what to say. Truth spurts out of me, unbidden as if tugged free from my gut by an invisible hook and line. "My mom died not even a month ago. I'm living with a near stranger. This is the first time I've experienced a real winter with actual snow."

A nod, a puff on the pipe. "The loss of one's mother, especially so young…" he tuts, a cluck of his tongue that somehow manages to *not* sound condescending. "Awful. Simply awful. My condolences."

Another truth is yanked out of me. Is Alistair somehow doing this? It's monstrous and insane to consider, but I have no other explanation for why I would say something so personal to a man I've just met as what comes next from my lips.

"I don't know how to mourn her." I close my mouth and clench my jaws together, but words seep past them anyway, muffled and tight. "I think I'm broken. I can't cry. I won't let myself remember her."

The compassion on his face somehow soothes the ache in my heart, just a little. "Often, one must achieve a certain distance from the event of loss before the heart and the soul are capable of true grief. All too often, the pain of loss itself is mistaken for grief, and the tears which frequently—but not always—accompany a loss are mistaken for grief. They are not, however. Grief is… a process." He hooks one knee over the other, gesturing with the pipe, sending arabesques of smoke pluming around him. "Child, just because you cannot cry does not mean you will not grieve, and it most certainly does not mean you do not love her. Notice, if you will, that I use the present tense. *Love*—not the past tense, *loved*. She may be gone from this plane, but I assure you, she lives on within you, and your love for her will not die. Not ever. It will simply…take a new shape, that's all."

"Why can't I cry?"

A roll of a shoulder. "Oh, many reasons. Most frequently, I believe, it is simply shock." He looks at me, direct and intent. "Was it a sudden loss? I would imagine so."

"Yes. Very sudden." I swallow hard. "I…I never saw her body. There wasn't a funeral. She just…a police officer came to the condo and told me she was gone. That was it. I collected a little bag of her stuff, and…" I shake my head. "It still doesn't feel real. But I know my mother—she wouldn't abandon me. I'm all she had, and she's all I had. And I…" I close my eyes and duck my head. "Maybe this sounds crazy or whatever, but I just…I *feel* it. That she's gone. Deep down, I know she is, even if my…my mind, my higher self, my emotions may not."

"That is not crazy at all, Maeve. Not at all." A tense pause, his gaze searching me, probing. "Tell me—have you dreamed of her, since her passing?"

My head snaps up, my eyes narrowing on him in suspicion. "Yes. I…yeah. It was…it was the most vivid, most realistic dream I've ever had. Well…up to that point, at least. I've had a few similar dreams since."

He holds my gaze, his expression carefully blank. "I think it is not lost on you, Maeve Sparrow, that there is more to this life and this world than may initially meet the eye."

I do not look away. "Does that mean the dreams are… real?"

He looks away, puffs at his pipe. "Without inquiring more closely into the exact nature of the dreams, I fear I cannot say for certain. And *real* is often an…insufficient term. But I would think yes, to a degree, your dreams are quite likely more than merely your subconscious spinning away the detritus of your day, as most mortal dreams tend to be."

At that moment, Phineas glides into the room from the kitchen, bearing a silver tea service, set with a silver teapot, four fine china teacups, with milk in a tiny jar and a bowl of sugar cubes. It's a proper British tea—although I have a vague idea that true high tea comes with little cakes or sandwiches or something. Or maybe I've simply watched too many movies.

Caspian arrives from somewhere, bearing a pair of tweezers in one hand.

A couple of things flash across my mind.

One, both Fin and Caspian are flushed, their skin tinted with life.

Two, Alistair's casual, almost missed use of the word "mortal." As opposed to immortal?

The Purr goes into overdrive as Fin sets the tea service on the table in front of the sectional. His huge, powerful hands seem entirely too large for the delicate silver, like bear paws performing a task for which they are unsuited.

Caspian sits on the couch, next to me but not precisely near me. The humming chasm inside me stretches toward him, and my body responds outside my conscious control, shifting me closer to him.

"Caspian, please remove the sunglasses." Alistair says this as a scold, oft-repeated. "They are unnecessary in our home."

Begrudgingly, Caspian slides them from his face, folds the arms, and places them on the coffee table.

Alistair pours tea, glancing askance at me. "How do you take it, my dear?"

I shrug. "I've never been much of a tea person. But I like my coffee with a splash of cream and just a little sugar."

Alistair puts a couple drops of cream in the tea, then a single cube of sugar, and hands me the teacup and saucer.

I take a tentative sip, and then my eyes go wide, shocked. "Ohmygod, this is great!"

Alistair snorts, a sarcastic, derisive noise. "We English have done tea for centuries, Miss Sparrow. Of course it's good."

"But this is Michigan," I point out.

An eyebrow arches. "Surely it hasn't escaped you that I am, in fact, English?"

I laugh. "No, I noticed."

A shrug, an elegant sweep of his hand. "I didn't forget how to prepare a proper tea when I came here, my dear. And of course, I would teach the boys." He fixes the other two differently—no cream or sugar for Fin, and one sugar, no cream for Caspian. "I hear you're quite the anomaly at the high school," he says to me.

I frown. "Am I? I'm the new girl and it's a small school, but I'm not sure I feel like an anomaly."

Alistair glances at Caspian, then at me. "Hmm. Caspian says all the students discuss you."

Caspian's eyes, as they fix on me, are "normal"…meaning with whites and pupils. "I don't know that Maeve quite grasps her own appeal. Especially on the opposite sex."

I snort, shake my head. "You're crazy. Except for Parker—and ew, no—no one has so much as looked at me."

A bemused smirk from Caspian. "That's because all the others are too intimidated by you. And Parker is an arrogant ass with more swagger than sense."

"You don't like him, do you?" I say this with a laugh, knowing the answer quite well.

"That's far too tame a phrase," Caspian says, his tone dry. "I would snap his bones like twigs and feed him to the hogs. Such things are frowned upon, however, so I force myself to refrain."

"Which hogs?" I ask.

Caspian answers without missing a beat. "There's a farm north a ways. He has hogs. Big ones. Mean ones. They'd devour a person and leave not a trace."

Alistair shakes his head. "Caspian. Be civil."

Fin just growls a laugh. "I've met Parker Landry." He tosses back the entire teacup's contents in one go. "If anyone deserves to be fed to Allen Baker's hogs, it's him. That kid is a jackass."

"Let's go back to how *all* the boys at the high school are intimidated by me. I'm not sure that can be true." I sip my tea, glancing at Alistair. "Honestly, I may like this more than coffee. It's smoother. Not as bitter."

"I can teach you how to prepare tea the English way—the *proper* way. Not that…that barbaric…*nonsense* you Americans call tea."

I have questions. If he's…like Caspian, why does he feel so strongly about tea?

I put that aside, for now. I have larger questions which need answering.

Fin stands up—the same lithe, liquid, sinuous movement as Caspian. "Gonna get your car fixed. I took a peek before I came in and I think it's just a loose hose. Shouldn't take more than a few minutes."

My palm stings. I hold it up toward Caspian, showing him the multitude of dark dots that are the slivers in my palm. "Could I, um…use those tweezers?"

Caspian frowns, then glances at the utensils in his hands. "Well…shit. I'm sorry, Maeve." He holds out his empty hand. "Let me see."

I extend my hand to him; he holds my hand palm up against his. Unusually for him, his flesh is almost warm—like the hands of someone who's been outside in the winter cold, rather than so inhumanly to touch him burns my skin. He doesn't hunch over, doesn't squint, doesn't hesitate. His precision with the tweezers is, like everything about him, abnormally precise, perfect. In a matter of moments, he has all the slivers removed.

He doesn't let go of my hand.

The contact makes my heart pound as if I've just sprinted up the steps of a stadium. Every part of me tingles; my skin is too tight, my breathing is shaky.

Just from him holding my hand in the most utilitarian, practical way possible.

This is pathetic.

The Purr is so violent in my chest that it's hard to focus on him, on Alistair watching us with hawklike fascination.

Tiny droplets of blood bead on my palm—so small I'd

normally not even have bothered to wipe them off on my jeans. Yet I feel Caspian's attention laser in on those minuscule beads of crimson—I glance at him. His eyes narrow. The whites recede—not totally, but a telltale erasure of whites being subtly and gradually swallowed by blackness.

Abruptly, he flips my palm upside down on his thigh, pressing hard. "All set."

"Thank you," I whisper, shaking—shaken.

I sneak a look at Alistair. He clenches his pipe in his jaws at an angle, teeth grinding, the bowl dipping and bobbing. His eyes, normal, flick from me to Caspian and back.

"Well." He slaps his thighs with his palms, speaking around his pipe. "Maeve, I have work I must do before my class this evening. A pleasure to meet you. Come by any time."

I hesitate. Do I mention the weird scene before Fin and Caspian showed up? "Uh. Yeah. Great to meet you too, Alastair. Thanks for having me, and um…I guess I'll see you later."

He nods, snatches up his teacup and saucer in one hand with a smooth, fluid, intensely graceful movement, and seems to almost float out of the room, his gait liquid—you could balance his teacup on his head and not a single drop would spill.

We're alone, Caspian and me.

"Did he say anything?" Caspian asks.

"Who, Alistair?"

Caspian nods. Looks at me sidelong. "Anything… unusual."

I opt for honesty. "Yes, he did. He, um. The moment you left, his eyes went like…like yours do, sometimes. All black, and scary? He seemed angry at me. Like, *what do you think you're doing, girl?"* I do my lowest, deepest, growliest voice. Which isn't at all like Alistair's smooth, crisp voice. "And then he seemed confused by me. He smelled me." I shrug. "I'm not sure what to make of it. You guys are all…"

Caspian's eyes fix on me, raptly waiting for me to finish the sentence.

"Unusual."

He smirks. "Unusual. Yes, that is one word for us."

At that moment, the front door slams open, loud, violent, and abrupt. I jump a foot off the couch, squeaking in shock, and clap a hand over my chest.

The individual who appears in the doorway is very tall, taller than Fin even, lean and hard, without a spare ounce of flesh or muscle or fat on his body. His features, like the rest of his family, are superhumanly perfect, symmetrical, sharp, angular. His eyes are dark blue, cerulean shading toward nearly violet, set deep in his face. His hair is dark, dirty blond, pulled back into a neat ponytail. Like the others as well, there's not a hint of facial hair, not even stubble. He's dressed in gray chinos in a slim fit and pressed, black leather dress boots, a white button down, sharply creased and perfectly white; a bright crimson handknit wool scarf is coiled loosely around his neck. The button-down is open three buttons, showing a wedge of ivory skin; a necklace hangs in the opening, a platinum cross glittering with diamonds.

The whole effect is of elegant European refinement—his bearing is definitively masculine yet cultured and sophisticated.

If he is what I think they are, then popular fiction has some serious explaining to do.

He's angry.

At me.

CHAPTER 12

I RISE FROM MY SEAT, MOVING SLOWLY and carefully. Take a ginger step in his direction. "You must be Stirling."

He ignores me. Looks at Caspian. "Why is she here?"

Caspian's voice is smooth and unruffled. "Her car broke down. Fin is fixing it."

Stirling's jaw pulses. Those dark blue eyes narrow on me. His nostrils flare. "She's injured?"

I show him my palm. "I tripped on the stairs. Got a few slivers. Nothing to worry about. Caspian pulled them out."

"Did he." It's a flat, hard statement.

Distaste, or maybe just antisocial dislike, emanates from him.

"As soon as Fin is done with my car, I'll be going."

Caspian's cold hand descends to rest on my thigh—the placement more than friendly, yet less than intimate. "You don't need to. Stirling is often rather out of sorts when he comes home." His tone is firm, not inviting argument. "There are leftovers. You're not yourself when you're hungry."

The corner of Stirling's mouth quirks at the inside joke—which I recognize as a reference to a candy bar commercial. "Leftovers. Yum." Sarcasm drips from the two words.

He ghosts past me, his stride panther-smooth, yet there's a hint of recalcitrance to his gait and his posture as if he resents being joked out of his bad mood.

I hear a fridge open and close. A microwave door. The soft, faint hum of a microwave.

The Purr is manic—Fin is just outside, Caspian is *touching* me, Alistair is somewhere in this house, and now Stirling is here as well.

It's too much.

The reaching, hungry void inside me doesn't know what to do, what to want.

The sensation is familiar yet alien—it feels like… like sexual need. Yet *more*. Far, far more. It's like sexual need except instead of mere desire, mere attraction, it's a need that borders on a physical requirement to survive. Like being at the bottom of a pool, knowing if you don't reach the surface *now*, you'll die. It's that intense of a need.

Yet it's also not *merely* sexual.

I'm not a virgin. I've had a couple…I hesitate to call them boyfriends, yet they were more than what most of my generation would call a "hookup." I'm by no means experienced. I'm just not innocent, not lily white virginal.

It's a kind of need I can't quantify, can't explain even in my own mind.

I *need* Caspian.

The need is more muted with the others—Fin, Stirling, and Alistair. It's there, but it's not life or death. Which is to say, it's still infinitely more intense than anything I've ever felt in my life.

The desperation I feel for Caspian? Human language cannot encapsulate or express the feeling.

Not even close.

It makes me feel crazed, manic. I shake with it.

I bolt abruptly for the front door. "I need air."

Stirling appears, lounging against the side of the stairs. He holds an opaque white plastic pouch in one hand and a matching opaque white plastic straw between his lips. His cheeks hollow as he sucks the contents of the pouch. "I was rude." This is to me. "I apologize. I had a stressful day at the college."

"You're a professor?"

He smiles, shakes his head. His tongue, vividly red, slides over his lips. "No. I'm a TA. Economics and history, specifically the intersection of the two. I'm working on my doctoral dissertation."

He looks to be a few years older than the other brothers, putting him in his mid-twenties, to Fin's early twenties and Caspian's late teens.

In appearance, anyway.

The Purr makes it hard to think. Stirling crosses the room, and I feel Caspian tense beside me. I smell pennies. Stirling takes a long draw from the juice pouch—because it's juice. Just juice. Or maybe a weird way of consuming soup…tomato soup, judging by the red stain on his tongue and lips.

"Stirling." Caspian's voice contains a note of warning.

He stops a foot away from me—the sweet coppery tang in the air stings my nose and makes my stomach twist even as my saliva glands begin to work overtime, filling my mouth. I can't breathe. Stirling *towers*, his lean build whipcord hard, razor sharp. His dark blue eyes swim in pools of darkness—expanding, billowing black.

He's closer. Inches.

His scent is everywhere—a hint of cedar, woodsmoke, copper. I stare up into his eyes and I couldn't move if I wanted to.

And I'm not sure I want to.

His hand, the empty one, lifts from his side and drifts to my cheek. Touches—cold but not burningly so; the ivory has taken on a pinkish hint of life. "So lovely."

"Stirling." Caspian's voice is almost a growl. "Don't."

The darkness in his eyes threatens to swallow me whole. Consume me. Drown me. Pulling me in, hypnotizing me. "Such pale eyes." His do not move, but I feel them probing me, threatening to dredge up my secrets. "A blue so pale they're almost white. I've never seen eyes like yours before."

"I have my mother's eyes." A common statement for me—people always comment on my eyes.

"Didn't she need them?" He says this with a coy smirk.

His touch, just the tip of his middle finger to my cheekbone, aches. Burns. Sears. Draws me closer—I feel my feet wanting to creep me forward.

Caspian smacks Stirling's hand away with a sound like two boulders crashing together. "I said *don't*."

Stirling grins at Caspian. "*You* brought her here, brother." A wink at me. "What did you think would happen?"

And then he turns and swaggers away—a liquid swagger, if such a term makes any sense. He sucks at the juice pouch noisily, with that crackling slurp of the straw end seeking the dregs.

Caspian's arm curls around my shoulders protectively…possessively. "Don't mind Stirling. He's… moody."

I burst out laughing. "You guys take moody to a whole new level. For real. I thought he hated me when he first showed up. And then…*that*?" I wave a hand behind me as we exit the house and clomp onto the porch. "That's mercurial times, like, a bazillion."

Caspian is angrily silent. We lean against the porch railing and watch Fin bent into the open hood of my car, one thick arm extend, working as he turns a wrench.

I elbow Caspian's rib, and it feels like nudging a brick wall. "Hey, quit brooding."

"Stirling can be an asshole."

"He was just…flirting." I wonder, in a hidden recess of my mind, why I'm defending Stirling.

Caspian glances down at me, clearly wondering the

same thing. "You have a warped comprehension of flirting, then, Maeve."

"Maybe I do." I shrug. "But I'm not upset about Stirling doing…whatever *you* want to call it, if you don't like the word flirting for it. Better that than glaring death daggers at me, at any rate."

Caspian just stares at me for a long moment. "Most people aren't comfortable around my family."

"I'm not most people. You guys are…fascinating."

"You aren't frightened?" He stares at me, and I realize I'm not sure I've ever seen him blink. "Of us? Of… me?"

I take a page from his playbook, opting to not answer directly. "That morning in the forest. That really happened, didn't it?"

"Yes." It's a murmur, reluctant.

I swallow hard, my next question sticking in my esophagus. I clear my throat, and feel the words on my tongue, against my teeth. "Do you ever dream of me?"

He continues to stare, but I feel his interest, his focus, his attention…narrowing. Sharpening. "Dream? Of you?" A pause. "Why do you ask?"

"Because I dreamed of Mom after she…after she passed. And Andreas." My turn to let a silence writhe up between us, brief but fraught. "Of you."

"You dream of me?"

I nod. Hold his gaze without blinking, without moving. "Alistair, during that conversation, he said my dreams may not be….normal. That they may be…more real than those of most…*mortals*."

"He said that? He used that word, *mortals*?"

"Yes, he did."

Silence again.

"What do you see in your dreams of me, Maeve?" It's an edged, dangerous question.

"You. But…different." I hesitate. "Your eyes. Your…teeth."

He exhales slowly, looking away for a long time—perhaps a full minute before he returns his eyes to mine. "Be wary of such dreams, Maeve. Do not linger in those black, empty places."

"Caspian, I…." I shake my head. "It's not like I have any control over them. They're just dreams. Right?"

He touches a cold finger to the corner of my jaw, beneath my right earlobe, and traces a hot, burning line across the edge of my jaw, to the tip of my chin. My skin *burns* where he touched me. Aches. Tingles.

"Be wary," he repeats. "Things are not always as they seem." Another long pause, this one as if weighing what to say. "You may have more control than you think. And if you find you do—do not linger, Maeve."

The echoing metallic slam of a car hood closing makes me jump, breaking the shivering tableau between Caspian and me.

Fin puts one foot on the bottom step, wiping his hands on his jeans. "All set. No biggie."

"What was wrong?" I ask.

He laughs, giving me a teasing grin. "If I told you, would you know what I'm talking about?"

I roll my eyes and laugh. "No. Shut up."

"Then you're all set." He tosses me my keys, and I catch them.

"Thank you, Phineas."

He wrinkles his nose, shakes his head. "Call me Fin.

Only Alistair uses my whole, actual name." He moves up the stairs and stops even with me, shoulder to shoulder, him facing the house and me the stairs; his nose crinkles, sniffs, and he leans into me. Sniffs again—close, his nose nearly touching the side of my neck. "*Fuck*, you smell good." Another long inhalation. "Sunlight and honeysuckle."

Exactly the same words Caspian used in the woods.

The Purr likes this: him, and Caspian. Almost as much as it liked Stirling and Caspian. Or, it *doesn't* like it—the vibrating and humming in my chest is so strong it's hard to tell.

I wonder if they can hear it, or feel it.

I don't dare ask. Or try to explain the feeling, for that matter. They'll think I'm nuts, probably.

And, honestly? Maybe I am.

Fin shakes his head, like a lion shaking away a fly. "See ya 'round, Sparrow."

I can't tell if he's saying my name like Caspian does, like a nickname, or just using my last name to informalize and create distance.

He's inside, then, and once more it's just me and Caspian. Surreptitiously, I sniff myself—my hair, my shoulder.

Caspian laughs. "I doubt you'll catch the scent he did."

"How do I smell like sunlight? Honeysuckle I get, even though I don't use anything honeysuckle scented."

The laughter fades, and his eyes are nearly swallowed by darkness. "I couldn't possibly begin to explain it, Maeve. Only that you have a scent like…like nothing

I've ever smelled. It's intoxicating. It explains the behavior of my family, if it doesn't quite excuse it."

He guides me down the stairs—ready to catch me if I fall, I realize. Opens my door for me. "I'll see you soon."

"You want a ride to your car?" I ask.

I'm hoping he'll say yes. I don't want to leave him. I don't want to leave this house. These strange, frightening, intense, fascinating, addicting men.

He shakes his head. "No. You'd better go." He gestures at the lane. "You're just at the end, turn right, and then the next right."

"You're sure? I don't mind."

He smiles at me. "Alistair will take me, later. He teaches history at the university, and it's on his way."

I hesitate. "You owe me answers, Caspian."

He nods. "I know."

"You're not going to give them to me right now, are you?"

He shakes his head. "No, I'm not. I can't."

I sigh. "I'm getting pretty annoyed with the cagey bullshit, honestly. Someone is going to give me answers."

"Someone, at some point, yes."

"But not you, and not now," I say.

"Not me, and not now," he agrees.

"Soon, though." I get into my car and slam it a little harder than is strictly necessary.

My car starts immediately and easily, and I put her in gear and make a wide turn in their front…yard, or whatever you call it. I'm not sure if there's grass under the snow or just dirt, or gravel.

Stirling's car, like the rest of his family, is old. His

is an SUV like Alistair's, but it's not the same model. It has round headlights, a white body with blue and yellow stripes along the sides, and a black soft top. The word "Rallye" is painted on the front quarter panel, behind the front wheel.

I'm not sure why I find it so interesting that they all drive older cars—classics, probably. Caspian claimed he just liked old things. But I'm not sure that explains it.

Their house is old—except for the kitchen, where there are modern appliances—the house is largely as it must have been when it was built. Except for the removal of walls, of course.

Alistair teaches history, and Stirling is doing a doctoral dissertation on the intersection of history and economics.

There's something there—something that pokes at the back of my mind. I just can't quite put my finger on what it is, what it means.

I drive home slowly, my mind wandering.

When I get home, I make myself some dinner, saving some for Andreas, and do homework. Study for a calc test tomorrow. Stream the new zombie show.

But all the while, in the back of my mind…I'm cataloging and ruminating on the evidence regarding Caspian and his family.

The eyes.

The silent movement.

The coldness of their skin.

Caspian's intense aversion to seeing my blood.

Their obsession with my scent—sunlight and honeysuckle. And what is up with *that*? What does sunlight even smell like?

I rip a piece of paper from my history notebook, sitting at the antique rolltop desk in my room, and I doodle. Curlicues, at first. Angles and curves. Dots, dashes, 3D boxes. The Super S everyone doodles in middle school.

My mind is on Caspian. On his warnings about my dreams—and Alistair's weird freakout.

Andreas's truck approaches from the lane, the engine rumbling noisily, and I'm shaken from my doodling stupor.

Amid the abstract doodles, I've written four words. They're scratched into the paper in heavy dark lines, almost angry—the pen nearly went through the paper in some places, with ink layered so thickly on the paper it's visibly wet.

CASPIAN

IS

A

VAMPIRE

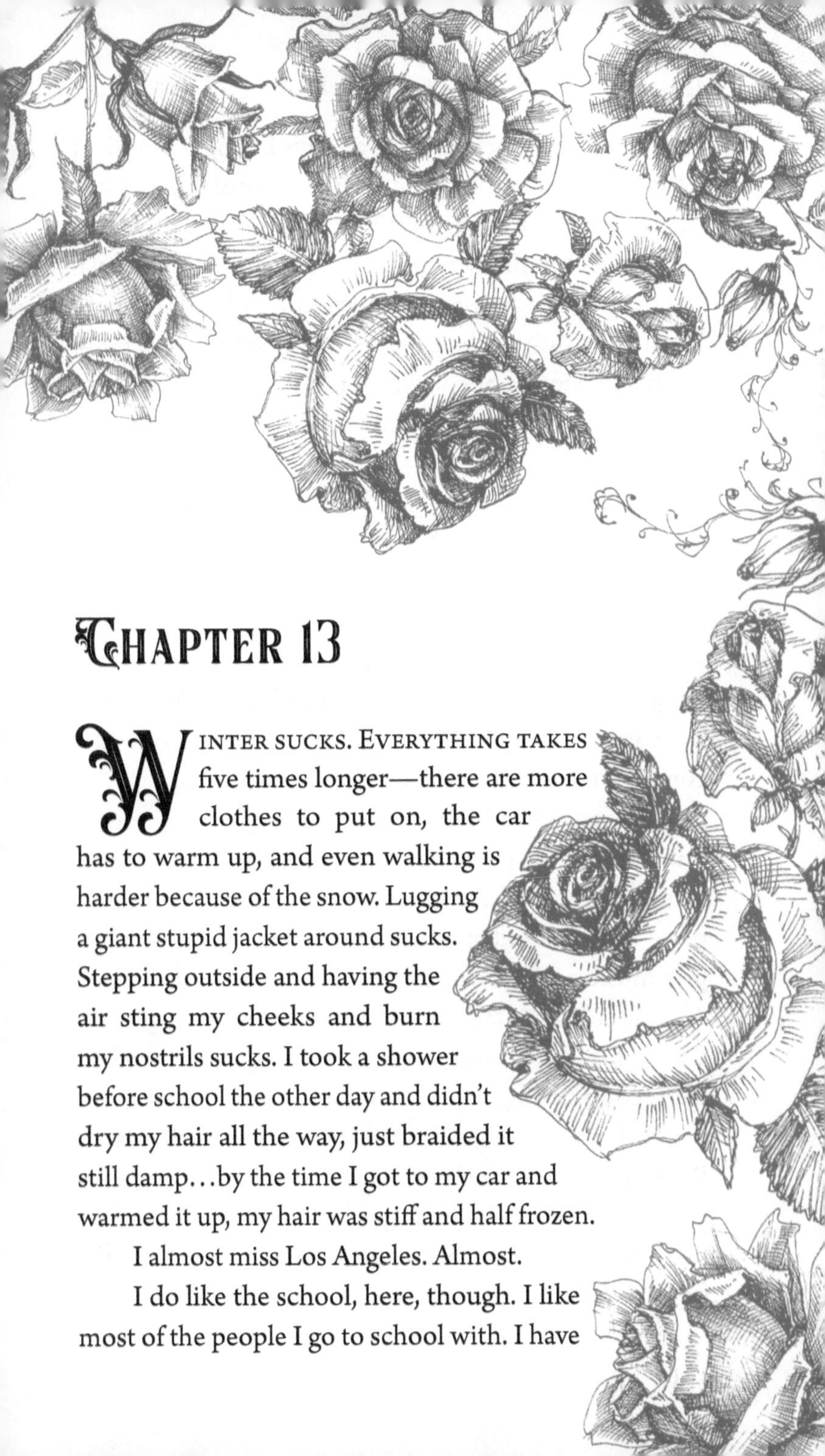

CHAPTER 13

WINTER SUCKS. EVERYTHING TAKES five times longer—there are more clothes to put on, the car has to warm up, and even walking is harder because of the snow. Lugging a giant stupid jacket around sucks. Stepping outside and having the air sting my cheeks and burn my nostrils sucks. I took a shower before school the other day and didn't dry my hair all the way, just braided it still damp…by the time I got to my car and warmed it up, my hair was stiff and half frozen.

I almost miss Los Angeles. Almost.

I do like the school, here, though. I like most of the people I go to school with. I have a group of girls and a couple of guys I hang out with at lunch and chat with in the halls—I'm not sure I'd call them friends, exactly, but it's nice having friendly faces who seem genuinely happy to see me in the cafeteria. No one here judges me because I don't have the right bag, or because my jeans aren't designer. I mean, there are those people, of course, but they're few and everyone knows who they are and they're generally not very well-liked.

I like the little town, too. Elk Rivers is quiet, peaceful, and kind of sleepy. I'm told that it's much busier in the summer, that we get an influx of tourists that make it a lively little place. But for now, it's quiet and simple and easy to get around and the people are friendly. Old people wave at me in the general store when I'm getting soda and chips on the way home from school, or make conversation with me while we're waiting in line.

Caspian and I talk in class, and sometimes hang out after school—I've become a regular at their house. Alistair makes me tea, and we sit in front of their fireplace talking about anything and everything, from popular music and movies to classical literature and food. Alistair is easy to talk to, and easier to listen to. He has a way of working history into everything, and seems capable of ad-libbing explanations of historical events and people from memory, whether it be Henry the V, Marco Polo, the Battle of Waterloo, the Warring States period...I've never loved history, but I could see myself actually learning it and even enjoying it, if I were to take one of his classes.

Caspian always vanishes as soon as we get there,

leaving me with Alistair for fifteen minutes, sometimes longer, and always comes back flushed and warm.

It's been three weeks since my first visit to their house. Stirling and Fin are in and out, keeping unpredictable schedules.

There've been no weird incidents. No freaky all-black eyes, no sniffing me and telling me I smell like sunshine. No weird dreams either.

I'm lulled into a sense of normalcy. Almost.

I've not gotten any answers, but I haven't pushed for them yet, either. I'm sort of scared to have the truth confirmed for me. Because that would ruin my entire worldview, my understanding of life, of…of *everything*.

At school, he talks like anyone else in our grade, using slang and fitting in…mostly. But at home and alone with me, he talks more like Alistair and Stirling: formal, almost archaic, using turns of phrase you'd normally only see in Lit class, in the assigned text.

His "blood sugar" issue is like clockwork. I still never see him leave or come back from lunch. He always wears his sunglasses at school and in the car, although Alistair makes him take them off at home.

Despite the lull of regality and absence of extreme weirdness, I can't ever totally forget that Caspian is *not* a normal teenage male.

When I was on my period, he avoided me like the plague—I didn't see him at all that week, except in class. I wasn't invited over, and I felt it prudent to take the hint and stay away. When I was done, it was back to normal. No explanation, not even a referral to the topic.

I mean, I know I can be a little moody if the cramps

are particularly bad, like any girl, but…I didn't think I was *that* bad.

His sensitivity—to blood, to seeing me bleed, and to smell…

I don't bring it up.

He's taken to waiting for me at my car after school. Today, he seems to be in a better mood than usual.

He even smiles at me as I approach my car. "Hey, you."

I stop close to him, gazing up at my reflection in his aviators. "Hey yourself. Feeling good, today?"

He nods. "Yeah, you could say that." He slides into the passenger seat. "Come on. I've got something I want to do with you."

"Okay," I say, getting behind the wheel and starting up the Brat.

He directs me out of Elk Rivers and to the larger downtown area, south of Elk Rivers. "You never got your trip to the mall," he explains as we park near the main entrance of the mall. "Thought you'd like to go shopping."

It's a clear, sunny day, but very cold, with no clouds but a stiff, icy wind. The mall isn't packed like it would be in LA, though there is a decent amount of shoppers. For a while, we simply stroll together from one end of the mall to the other and back, so I can learn the layout of the stores and decide where I want to go.

As we walk, he remains close beside me, skin flushed and warm. Feeling a bit daring, I take his hand.

He allows it. Tangles our fingers together. Smiles down at me, but says nothing.

I go into Forever 21 and spend at least thirty minutes browsing before I select a few pieces to try on. Caspian holds my hand, occasionally letting go so I can pull a piece from the rack and look at it, and once I've decided to take it or put it back, he carries my selections on his arm and holds my hand with the other.

I try on my selections, keep less than half and take them to the register—I keep two pairs of tight, fitted, high-waisted jeans, a couple of T-shirts, and a thick sweater. The cashier rings them up, reads the total, and before I can get out my card, Caspian has swiped his.

I blink at him. "Um. Thank you? I can pay for my own clothes, though."

He takes the paper bag with my purchases in one hand and rejoins our hands with the other, leading us out of the store and angling us across the hall for our next destination: Victoria's Secret.

"I know," he says. "Of course you can. But I wanted to."

"Why?"

He is utterly at ease as we enter the perfumed inner sanctum of Victoria's Secret, watching me as I browse the underwear and clearance sections. "Because I like you." He follows me from section to section. "But I also know I've been a little…difficult, at times, and I suppose I want to make it up. Or, show you that I like you, I guess."

"You don't have to buy me things to show me you like me," I tell him. "You could just not avoid me."

He accompanies me to the register, where he again pays for my purchases: several pairs of panties from the clearance section, in a variety of styles, materials, and colors. Once we're out in the hallway again, he responds.

"I'm not avoiding you because I don't like you. I avoid you precisely *because* I like you."

"Which makes no sense."

"I like you too much." He stops us in the middle of the hallway, near a display of sedans and compact SUVs for sale by a nearby dealership. "We've had this discussion before, Maeve. And I…I can't explain any more now than I could the last time. But I want you to know that I care. That everything I do, or don't do, is because I care."

"And I still don't understand why you have to avoid me to show me you care, nor do I get why you can't simply tell me the truth." I gesture at the bags in his hand. "I'm grateful for this stuff, I really am. I see your intentions in bringing me here, buying me stuff. But Caspian…" I touch his jaw with my fingertips. "I just…want to spend time with you. However that looks."

"That's why we're here," he answers. "Buying you stuff is just…an additional perk."

"A perk for you or me?" I ask.

"Both, I suppose. For you, because you get new clothes. For me, because I get to see you, and I get to do something that makes you happy."

I grin up at him. "Good answer." I glance over his shoulder at the food court. "You know what would *really* make me happy, though? A soft pretzel and a soda."

"Then a soft pretzel and a soda you shall have."

He buys them for me, and we sit and eat. Or, I eat, and he sips at a soda—or perhaps pretends to.

It's a normal thing, a guy and a girl who like each other, at a mall together. My life, however, has been anything but normal, so for me, this is…

Magical.

A blissful moment of normalcy with…my boy-friend? My crush? I don't know. Labels seem ridiculous and unnecessary.

When I've had my snack, he tugs me back into the mall proper. "Come on. Let me buy you something absurd."

"Absurd?" I ask, laughing. "What do you mean?"

He shrugs, grinning, and hauls me into Macy's. He makes a beeline for the purse section, and gestures. "No upscale luxury stores in this mall, so this will have to do. Choose, Maeve, and do not look at the price tags."

I sigh. "Caspian. This isn't necessary."

"Of course it isn't. Thus my use of the word 'absurd.'" He cups my cheeks in my hands. Softly, briefly touches his lips to mine in a teasing ghost of a kiss. "Humor me. I want to. Not to buy your attention or affection. But because I want you to have nice things, and I want you to think of me when you use them or wear them."

My heart squeezes, melting a bit more into him. "Okay," I whisper. "But only because of what you just said."

I pick a beautiful black leather sack-type purse with silver rivets and a nice long crossbody strap. It's a gorgeous purse, and I love it.

But honestly, it's the time with him, the little bubble of fun and normal teenager shit that I cherish more than anything.

If I can't have the answers I want—yet—I'll take Caspian giving me his undivided attention.

CHAPTER 14

EVERYTHING CHANGES ONE WARM winter day.

It's a warm day—not warm enough to melt the snow, but warm enough I don't need my heaviest jacket or my thickest mittens. It's sunny, not a cloud in the sky, just the endless blue and the bright sun.

I'm in an upbeat mood; the sun and the warmth make me happy. I sat in the hall during lunch—there's a particular hallway by the main office with one entire wall made of windows and lined with benches. Kids hang out there before and after school, waiting for sports and clubs to start, or just hanging out and killing time, doing homework together. On a sunny day like today, it's the perfect place to sit and eat lunch and soak up the sun and the warmth.

As usual, Caspian is waiting for me at my car after school—he was absent from all his classes. Today, he's wearing dark blue jeans, winter boots with leather uppers and rubber lowers, a red-and-black checkered flannel shirt with a puffy tan vest, as well as his usual black beanie and aviators.

My pulse pounds as I approach him, The Purr kicking in as I get closer. It never stops, never goes away, I've just gotten used to it. The longing to be closer to him never goes away either, and that's harder to ignore, and something I've still never gotten used to.

He doesn't invite it. He rarely allows me to touch him, and rarely makes physical contact with me. He sits close, but won't touch. When I try, he subtly but definitely leans away, and never refers to it. I wonder if it's me. Sometimes, it makes me wonder if he actually likes me or if I'm imagining the connection we're building. Yet, when we talk, he makes me feel like the only person in the whole world. Even if I can't see his eyes behind his glasses, I can *feel* his attention, and it's intoxicating. He smiles at me, sometimes, even if he is the moodiest person I've ever known.

Today, I can tell he's not at his best. He's paler than I've ever seen him—his skin so white in the sunlight that it nearly reflects the light. He's glaring, frowning, almost seething. Hands in his vest pockets, chin tucked against his chest, not blinking, just watching me approach with that preternatural stillness.

I stop a few inches from him and look up at him. "Hi."

He does the manly chin lift. "Hey."

"You weren't at school today."

"Wasn't feeling great."

"You're better now?"

He shrugs, tilting his head to one side. "Not really. But I needed to see you."

I don't know what to make of that. "Well, here I am."

He just stares at me, his attention a palpable thing. His sour mood, as well. "Would you like to go for a hike with me?"

"A hike?" I put the maximum skepticism into my tone. "Me?"

He almost smirks—a barely-there tilting of one corner of his mouth. "Well, a walk in the woods."

"Sounds good to me."

He juts his chin at my car. "We can take your car. I'll direct you."

We climb in, and while I'm letting the engine and heater warm up, I glance at him. "So. You needed to see me, huh?" I grin at him, hoping to lighten his mood a little.

He doesn't grin back. "Yes. I did."

"Wow. Mr. Grumpy in the house."

"Bad day."

"Wanna talk about it?"

He shakes his head. "I just need to be around you." He looks away, out the window, silent for a while. "You… calm me."

"Did something happen?" I ask.

Another shake of his head. "No. Not…recently."

"Is it, like…" I look at him, trying to see into him the way he seems able to see into me, "an anniversary of losing someone?"

A nod. "Something like that."

He points for me to take a left out of town, heading north, the shore on our left, close here, just a rocky jumble of boulders and a steep embankment down to the water. The forest is on our right, thick and impenetrable, frost-whitened pines as far as the eye can see, only occasionally marked by a driveway or side road.

"But nothing you want to talk about?"

He lets out a sigh, short and thoughtful. "I lost my mother when I was young. She was killed. The circumstances do not bear discussion, but suffice it to say it was… intentional, and brutal. I was there. She…my mother, she…" he trails off. "She was very beautiful. A difficult woman, but she was my mother. Today is the anniversary of the day she was killed."

"God, Caspian. I'm sorry."

"Thank you." His jaw muscles pulse. "I'm not very good company today, I'm afraid. This day always puts me in a black mood. But selfishly, I desire your company."

I reach out and touch his arm over his sleeve, at his elbow. "Hey, it's all good. I can handle your moods, Caspian. And honestly, I desire your company too. But, like, all the time."

His head swivels with robotic precision, his attention focusing on the point of contact—my palm resting on his arm, at the crease of his elbow.

I leave my hand in place; this is the longest we've made physical contact since I met him.

He turns his attention to my face. "Maeve…"

"Yes?" I whisper; I glance at him, at the road ahead. At him.

He shakes his head a few times. Opens his mouth, closes it. "I can't stay away from you."

"You've certainly done a good job of trying."

He tilts his head to one side. "Not good enough, I'm afraid." A somewhat bitter laugh. "I know I should. For your sake. But I'm not strong enough." A tense pause. "I crave you."

My pulse thunders wildly, hammering in my ears. "You *crave* me?"

"Yes." It's a whisper, so quiet I could have imagined it.

"When you touch me..." he glances down at his arm, at my hand resting on his sleeve. "I can almost taste you. The sunlight in your veins." This too is so quiet I have to strain to hear him over the hum of the road and the grumble of the engine. "I crave you. Your touch. Your scent. Your warmth."

Instinct—the kind that forces you to breathe when your lungs are empty, the kind that forces you to flinch when something whips too close to your face—screams at me to *run*. To get away. The air in my car is thick with tension, with need. With his ice and my heat. The copper tang and woodsmoke and cologne that is him, tangled around my scent. Which I can almost, *almost* get a hint of...something indescribable, light, warm, yellow, tickling the back of my nose; it's like walking into a kitchen where chocolate chip cookies were baked a few hours before, a scent that's barely there, and nearly gone.

I feel him—his hunger, his need.

A deeper instinct, a baser one, keeps my hand on his arm—slides it up, to his bicep, marble hard and radiating cold through the flannel.

I focus on the road for a few moments, then back to him. He is utterly still. Not breathing. Not blinking. Just looking at my hand. I swallow hard, fear tasting like pennies in the back of my throat, and risk a glance at him and lift my fingers to his face.

Cold crackles under my fingers. It's like touching ice—not an ice cube in a freezer, but the ancient hoary feet-thick ice of a glacier against a mountainside. A cold so pure it has never known even a breath of warmth.

My fingers ghost over his cheekbone. I risk a glance at him—his jaw is clenched hard. I trail my fingertips just the two middle ones, down his cheek to the corner of his mouth.

I touch his lips: they are as cold and hard as the rest of him.

His fingers capture my wrist, pulling my hand away slowly and inexorably—guiding my hand back to his arm.

Silence breathes between us like a leviathan—slow, shuddering, and massive.

"Take the next right." His voice is hoarse.

I turn right onto a narrow dirt track through the forest, snow-covered and arrow-straight. On either side, pines and firs and cedars cluster close, leaning over the track as if trying to intimidate us. It's a dense forest, new, thick with underbrush, impenetrable. There are ruts which send us jouncing and bouncing, requiring me to drive with one hand and clutch the other across my chest.

This earns me a sidelong glance from Caspian, a faint grin staining his lips. The smirk shatters the tension and the silence in one swift blow.

"Shut up," I say, huffing a laugh.

He rolls a shoulder. "I said nothing."

"Your look said it all."

He lets the grin blossom, teasing, flirty. "I mean, I *am* a guy."

I shake my head, but then the road curves hard right and I have to focus on navigating around the corner without skidding. We hit a deep rut and then a patch of ice, and we're sliding sideways, and I have a flashback of the accident, and panic shoots through me—*sky-ground-sky-ground…helplessness, spinning. Rolling. Caspian's fingers bruising my ribs.*

I manage to right the car, letting off the accelerator completely until we coast to a stop, and I jam my foot onto the brake.

I'm gasping, I can't see for the blur in my eyes, and my chest feels like there's an iron band around it.

"Maeve, breathe." Caspian's hand, painfully cold but comforting, touches my cheek. "Breathe. Deep breath in. You're okay."

A breath scrapes into my lungs past clenched teeth. I cup my hand over his against my cheek—the cold of his touch is so intense it feels like heat. It grounds me. Puts me back into my body, into the present.

"We can turn around," he says, after a moment, and my breathing has normalized. "I can drive."

I shake my head. Grit my teeth. Stare at the road ahead. "I'm fine. Just…a flashback. I'm fine."

"Are you?"

I move my foot to the accelerator and bring us up to speed—slow, controlled, and easy. "I will be."

"We're almost there," he says. "Just up ahead."

I see what he's referring to: a snow-dusted bowl where the road ends, the forest rising high on all sides. A wooden sign proclaims this a trailhead of some trail or other in a national forest. We pull in and I park, shutting off the engine.

"Sorry I freaked out," I said.

"Don't apologize. It's normal."

I laugh, a bitter bark of sarcasm. "I can have a normal reaction to the accident, but I barely think about my mom. There's something wrong with that."

He shakes his head. "No, there's not. I literally watched my mother die, and I still took a long, *long* time to come to terms with her death. You have no sense of closure. She was just…*gone,* with no real explanation. It makes perfect sense that you would struggle to cope with that loss. Don't put any additional stress on yourself, Maeve. There's no right or wrong way to grieve."

I swallow hard. "I just feel…I'm so *numb,* Caspian. I remember her, I can call up her face, her voice, I can think of memories of us together…and there's normal hurt and pain, but I just…I'm *numb.* It's like it's just…stuck inside me."

"And that's okay. Some day, it will come loose. It'll be there." A pause; I close my eyes and feel the arctic whisper of his palm against my cheek. "And when it does, I'll be there to help you through it."

"Promise?" I whisper, my voice shaky.

He nods, removing his hand. "I promise." He glances out the window, at the forest. "Come on. Let's walk."

I nod, pocketing my keys, opting to leave my purse in the car. I lock the car doors, zipping my coat up and tugging my hood over my pale pink beanie with the white fuzzy pompom, and shove my hands into the pockets of my coat. I have thick mittens, but it's warm enough I don't need them yet.

Caspian leads the way onto the trail, and I keep pace beside him. His tread is perfectly silent, not a crunch of his boots in the snow, not a single hint of sound. There's only my boots, my breathing.

Within a few hundred yards, I begin to understand the appeal—it's quiet, here. Peaceful. The air is still, just a few fat slow flakes swirling around—blown-off trees, perhaps. The sky is blue, but now there's a line of gray approaching, and I can feel the air cooling around us.

We just walk, respecting the quiet and the peace. A squirrel scampers into the trail ahead of us, perhaps twenty yards away. It stops on its haunches, a nut clutched in its front paws, and looks our way.

With a terrified squeak and a shrill chatter, it leaps into the nearest tree and vanishes, still chattering.

It left the nut in the middle of the trail.

Caspian's head swivels to regard me, perhaps assessing my reaction.

"Does the light actually hurt your eyes?" I ask. "Or is that an excuse for the people at school?"

He shrugs. "My eyes *are* extremely light sensitive. But I wear them primarily because sometimes my eyes can be…unusual. I'm certain you've noticed."

"Yes," I say, my tone carefully neutral.

He glances my way. "You don't like it when I wear them."

I shake my head. "No. I like your eyes. I want to be able to see you, the real you. I feel like you hide behind those, and I…I don't know. I don't like it. It also doesn't bother me when they go…weird."

"It should." He looks straight ahead then, and we walk a while longer in companionable quiet. "I've never met anyone like you."

"Same," I say, with a laugh.

The trail finally takes a turn and becomes a steep descent into a valley, with an equally steep ascent on the other side. Down in the bowl of the valley between the hills, the trees huddle close and lean over the trail, bathing it in shadow.

As we reach the crest of the descent, Caspian stops, turns to look at me, and slowly removes his glasses, hooking the arm into the V of his flannel. His eyes are darker than usual, the whites nearly swallowed by the black, although not completely, and I can still faintly make out the darker black of his pupils.

He just looks down at me. Here, in the forest, it's just the two of us. The sky has clouded over, the blue obscured by a thick blanket of heavy gray; a few snowflakes drift down around us, dancing and darting. It's colder. He doesn't move as he stares down at me, and I can't begin to fathom what he's thinking or feeling. He doesn't breathe, doesn't fidget, doesn't blink. He could very well be a statue, an avant-garde experimental art installation left here in the forest by some hyperrealistic sculptor.

Somehow, he's closer, though I didn't see, hear, or feel him move. Perhaps I blinked. The temperature of the air between us plummets, the huffing steam of my breath freezing into a thick cloud of white crystals. My fingers go prickle and burn inside my pockets. My lungs are scorched by the intense cold. My cheeks sting, the tip of my nose, and the lobes of my ear where they protrude from beneath the edge of my hat.

Closer, again—this time, I know I blinked; in the space of time it took my eyelids to descend and lift once more, he's so close I can smell the faint coppery tang on him, and the stronger waft of woodsmoke. So close all I can see is his face. The sharp angles and hard planes, the ethereal perfection of his features.

His nostrils flare. His eyes narrow.

I blink again, and now his cheek breezes against mine, and fear hammers high in my throat like a malfunctioning steam engine about to detonate. Infecting the fear, however, is that deeper, more potent strain of pure adrenalized need, pungent inside me, redolent and tasting of lust, of darkened bedrooms with rucked sheets, of commingled sweat and heady desire indulged in over hours.

I am panting, almost hyperventilating, and I don't care. I can't stop it. I don't try.

My fingers curl into the soft flannel of his shirt, knotting until my knuckles whiten.

The pulse pounding in my throat is wild and frantic.

His nose angles against my skin, nudges beneath my jaw, against my lymph node. I feel his inhalation of my scent.

His hands wrap around my waist, hard fingers drilling into my soft flesh then loosening stiffly, as if forcing them away. Gentling on my waist, his hands skid downward over the fabric of my leggings, cupping my hips just above my ass.

Possessing me.

Another sharp, quick inhalation, nose to my throat.

A growl snarls from his throat and rips across the clearing; a flutter of panicked bird wings rustles between the needles of the trees overhead.

He pulls me against him, my softness flush against his hardness, and I feel all of him. Chest, shoulders, hips, thighs. Manhood.

Abruptly, he's gone. Down the hill, twenty feet away,

hands on his hips, head hanging, frustration and anger and desperation carved in every line of his posture.

I gingerly make my way down the hill after him, skidding and slipping in the snow. I nearly fall several times, but manage to keep my feet.

I reach him, but he holds out a hand to stop me when I'm within reach. "Don't." His voice is a dull hard flat growl. "Keep walking. I'll catch up."

"Caspian—"

Not even a flash of movement—he's just there, inside my reach, eyes fully black, inhumanity pouring off of him in tangible waves.

"I need a moment, Maeve," he says, his voice a dark silky leonine purr.

The Purr inside me is so wild and so strong I can't even feel it. It's *everything* that is me, in his presence.

I swallow hard and force myself away from him. Past him. Scrabble up the hill, slipping back down the steep slope several feet for every step I manage upward. My pulse is frantic, my hands are shaking, my thighs quaking. I slow my steps, turning sideways to the slope and edging upward inch by inch.

Finally, I reach the crest. Turn back to look for Caspian—

I gasp. Because he's gone.

"Caspian?" My voice quavers.

"Keep walking." His voice comes from everywhere and nowhere. From behind me, yet when I turn, there's nothing there.

I take a step away from the hill, onward.

I cannot deny I'm terrified. Yet that sensation is merely primal.

The need to be near him is…whatever is deeper than primal, more primeval than instinctual. It's a molecular need. An atomic attraction for *him*.

Yet I walk on. I can't help myself, though. I stumble in a clumsy circle as I walk, searching the shadows for him.

The ground underfoot is uneven and irregular. I carom off trees, stumbling through the underbrush.

I see nothing. No hint of him.

Yet I *feel* him. The Purr tracks him—faint on my left, stronger again on my right, now close enough to taste, above me and to my right.

I look up.

There are only shadows and branches and clumps of snow hanging from the tips of pine boughs.

My gaze focused above as I turn in a circle while moving forward, something snags my toe.

I trip forward, hands shooting out to catch my fall.

My wrists jar in the snow and a sharp lance of pain stabs into my left palm.

I shove to sit on my knees in the snow, hissing in pain. A weal of red mars my palm, a deep open cut at the center of my hand. Blood seeps out slowly at first, then begins pouring down my hand, dripping from my wrist into the snow.

Pit…pit…pit…pit.

"Shit," I mutter.

He's here.

In front of me.

Eyes black, voids of shadow, soulless and mindless. Hunger creases his features. No longer just pale, he's white as the snow around us.

There is absolutely no mistaking his inhumanity.

He's no more human than I am a bird or mouse.

Yet, kneeling in the snow, cold wet seeping through my leggings, that's what I feel like—a fragile bird hopping from branch to branch, or a field mouse flitting between blades of grass.

And Caspian?

He is the shining eyes watching from the shadows, waiting, calculating, assessing; he is a predator.

I am the prey.

I cannot move. Cannot breathe. Fear and need are so intense and intermingled inside me that they are indecipherable. I can only stare at him. I don't dare blink.

His hand moves slowly, reaching for me. Grasping my wrist in an icy vise, lifting me to my feet. Pulling me close to him. I collapse against his chest, boneless, muscleless, helpless.

My lungs burn.

My skin is so tight around my bones that it feels like it might split at shoulders and hips and joints and cheekbones.

My pulse is so frantic one beat melts into the next.

A soft snarl writhes from his throat—a hungry, anticipatory murmur.

His lips curve in a smile.

We are in the shadows of the forest, far from the path.

How far did I go?

"At last, I taste you." Whispered, the words fluttering in the air like snowflakes, as delicate and as soft.

He guides my hand to his face, each movement slow and balletic. I can't swallow past the throbbing knot of heat in my throat.

My knees shake, and my thighs press together. Heat

boils in my core. Floods my sex. My nipples are hard beads of diamond.

His nostrils flare, inhaling the scent of my desire as it suffuses the crackling air around us.

His mouth presses to my skin—so cold it burns.

My blood courses from the cut, a steaming stream of crimson.

It stains his marble skin, crystallizing audibly in the instant of contact with his skin.

He drinks from me, then.

Chapter 15

J FEEL THE FIRST PULSING PULL OF MY blood into his mouth—it's like a flow of lava inside me, white hot, from the cut on my palm up my arm, across my chest, down between my tingling, aching, heavy, swollen breasts, and straight to the seam of my sex, hotter than the sun and pounding like a million tribal drums.

One pull.

Two.

Three.

With each drink he takes, my sex throbs. A desperate need for release crashes through me— yearning for a climax that's just out of reach, and each time he sucks from my hand, I inch closer and closer to that quivering edge.

And with each drink he takes, his skin warms and softens. From marble to fresh clay, and then to flesh, cold but alive.

And with each drink, I feel his manhood—pressed against my belly—hardening. Lengthening. Burgeoning to full arousal.

Oh god.

Oh, god.

I hear myself moan, a breathless, erotic whimper. His hand clutches at my ass, holding me more tightly against himself. His fingers curl into my buttocks, spanning the crack, gripping with bruising possessive strength—albeit human strength, not the superhuman kind I know he's capable of.

I feel my hand lift, brushing up the hard cliff of his chest, over his shoulder, and up the column of his neck. Into the feathery softness of his hair. I clutch a handful of his hair and hold on, my forehead resting against his breastbone. Another moan, this one a whimper of near-climax.

The heat between my thighs is unbearable, the pressure boiling behind my sex incomprehensible and titanic. My skin is on fire. His lips against my palm are pliant and warm. His erection is a thick hard ridge against my belly, and the need racing in my veins will not be denied. I can no more control the fury of this desire than I can breathe underwater.

My hand is pressed to his mouth, tingling, aching, burning. My index fingertip touches his cheek beneath his eye, so close I feel the butterfly flutter of his eyelashes. The tip of his nose presses against the pads of my hand, just beneath the base of my middle finger. My thumb grazes against his temple.

My other hand unknots from his hair and descends his chest, to his belly. To his black leather belt, bumping against the buckle.

A fourth hot pulsing orgasmic drink of my blood from my hand.

I feel my hand working at his buckle—it is not my conscious mind doing it, but the pulsing need inside me, the animalistic craving for him, all of him. The need for him is a waist-high pile of branches and kindling soaked in lighter fluid; this touch, his mouth on my skin and the suck of his lips against my flesh and the throbbing hot pull of my blood is the match, tossed to set me alight.

His flesh at his belly as I rip his shirt out of his jeans and seek skin is warm and soft. His belt hangs open, buckle jingling. His jeans sag as I rip at the zipper. I seek his hard sex, needing to feel it fill my hand. Needing his pleasure, craving his release as powerfully as I do my own.

Need. *Need.* That gaping chasm inside me, the void at the pit of my belly, the roiling black hole of pure un-adulterated lusting ravening *need* within me yawns, rages.

Pulls. Draws. Sucks.

Need more.

Heat and juddering electricity courses through me, lighting my veins on fire. Ignites the need into something more than need or desire or any word I know.

My hand dives into the opening of his jeans, and I find him there, waiting, ready, hot, hard, thick—

Cold, swirling snow fills the space where he was. I stumble, gasping, panting, shrill and wanton and infuri-ated with release denied.

"Caspian!" I cry out.

He's several yards away, on all fours in the snow. His chest and shoulders and back heave, dragging in ragged gasping breaths. Snow crunches under my boots.

"Stay…" he snarls, his voice thick and rough. "Stay back."

My feet disobey his command, carrying me to him. I crouch beside him, rest my hand on his back.

He's trembling all over. "Don't—*don't.*" This is in that inhuman growl, despite the warmth seeping through his shirt. "Get away. Get away from me, Maeve."

"You won't hurt me," I whisper. I nuzzle my lips against his cheek.

Motion, abrupt and dizzying—the rough bark of a tree stabs into my spine and shoulders. He has me up against a tree ten feet from where we were, his hips wedged between my thighs. My sex pulses, pleads. My blood sings in my veins, even as it dribbles down my wrist and drips from my fingertips into the snow.

Blood stains his lips, his chin. A scarlet droplet depends on the point of his chin. I wipe it away with my thumb, staining the pad.

He captures my wrist in a delicate, inexorable grip, and his hot soft lips wrap around my thumb and his tongue slides in a slow sweep, licking; where his tongue touches, my skin tingles.

His eyes are amber—glowing, incandescent. Neither leonine nor lupine, they are nevertheless animal, predatory. More than animal. Something…different. *More.*

As the droplet of my blood mixes with his saliva, I see a subtle flash of his eyes, a brightening of the glowing amber.

I tighten my thighs around his waist, my injured hand dangling at my side, the other moving to cup his cheek. He squeezes his eyes shut, jaw clenching, and he presses his forehead to my chest. He's panting raggedly.

"Go," he pleads, his voice hoarse. "Before I do something we'll both regret."

"You won't hurt me."

"That's not what I mean."

Heat billows through me, effervescent in my veins. Lightning slashes in my sex, pressed hard against his— only a few layers of clothing between us. "I wouldn't regret that, Caspian."

He shakes his head, forehead and beanie rolling against my chest. "You don't know," he rasps. "Go, Maeve. *Please.*"

"I can't," I whisper, and we both know I don't mean simply because he has me pinned to a tree trunk. "I don't want to."

With exaggerated, forceful, stiff movements, he pulls away and lowers me to my feet. Takes a step back.

Drags the back of his wrist across his lips, then his palm down his chin. His incandescent amber eyes burn, searing into my very soul. His need matches mine— eclipses it, even, perhaps; I see it in his eyes, in the haunted cast of his beautiful features. His expression is tortured.

Pit…pit…pit…pit. Blood drips from my middle finger into the snow at my feet. His eyes flick down to the growing red stain. Black swarms in from the corners of his eyes, subsuming the amber; his fingers curl into claws—

He shakes his head like a bear at a beehive, shaking away the stinging bees. His eyes squeezed shut, a ripping snarl escapes his gritted teeth. Another shake of his head.

He straightens, the tautness in his body loosening, and when he opens his eyes they're glowing amber once more. He sucks in a deep, shuddering breath.

Steps into me. Lifts my palm to his mouth.

Anticipation batters my insides like a bird trapped in a cardboard box. I crave the pulling thrill of blood, the heat, the raging inferno of desire.

The latter hasn't quieted inside me at all—not a whit. I *need* him.

But the thought of his lips on my skin once more? The electric tug of my blood into his mouth? The orgasmic bloom of pleasure in every pore and molecule and atom of my being…

I need it again.

He doesn't give me what I want.

Instead, as he brings my palm to his mouth, I feel the hot wet tickle of his tongue dragging over the cut. Once. That same tingling in the skin of my palm where his tongue slides.

And then he holds my palm horizontally, facing up.

Shock slams through me, then, so potent my knees give out and if not for Caspian's grip on me, I would have collapsed.

The flow of blood ceases, coagulating in the ragged red gape of the cut. Then, new flesh appears—dissolving in reverse, almost. The cut slowly closes as I watch, red, raw subcutaneous flesh wriggling and reaching for the other side, turning pink, congealing as the edges meet, and then fading into the white of newly healed skin. And then, there's only a short keloid scar, as of a long-healed injury.

Caspian drops my hand and steps back.

Staring at me, he blinks. He breathes. Burning amber eyes, warm pink-tinged skin, tortured, haunted features.

And then he's gone.

The Purr goes quiet, settling in my chest like a restless tiger slumping into a corner of its cage, appearing at rest, but ready to pounce at any moment.

I'm alone.

The light of the path is nowhere to be seen; through the canopy overhead, snow falls in a dense curtain.

I'm lost alone in the forest, in a blizzard.

And there's absolutely zero doubt, now.

Caspian is, in fact, a vampire.

CHAPTER 16

"CASPIAN?" My voice is quiet, tiny and timid. I try again, louder. "CASPIAN!"

Nothing.

I spin in a circle, but everything looks the same. Snow settles on my head and shoulders.

My tracks—I spin, searching the ground around me.

There!

I see a footprint and go to it. Another, and another; my boot fits into the impression, and so I follow the trail of them through the forest.

Only, they vanish after a while, filled in, and then the vector of them is blocked by a tangle of underbrush so dense I can't penetrate it, and have to find a route around…and then I'm turned around and passing my own footprints.

I'm starting to panic, more than a little.

We're in a national forest area, and I'm off the path, and even under the relative protection of the canopy, the snow is falling so thickly I can't see more than a few feet in any direction.

"Caspian?"

Dammit. Not again.

"CASPIAN!"

I pick a direction that seems like it's the way I was going when following my footprints and walk that way, angry at myself, and at Caspian.

Yet, I could see the torture in his expression, in the lines of his body. He didn't want to leave—he tore himself away from me. As if doing so for *my* sake.

As if he felt he was protecting me by abandoning me in the forest.

As if I was too much of a temptation, one he knew he couldn't resist.

I shiver, still feeling the tingle on my hand. I examine my palm where the cut was: the keloid scar is fading, already nearly invisible. In another few minutes, there'll be no evidence I was ever injured.

I stumble a few times, tripping over logs half-buried in the snow. I put on my mittens, huddle into my jacket.

Fight the panic.

What if I'm walking in the wrong direction, *into* the forest instead of toward the path? I tried to approximate the way I'd been going, but I can't be sure.

I feel a buzz in my belly.

"Caspian?" Hope brightens my tone.

The buzz turns to a hum, and then into the fully-formed Purr—off to my left.

I pivot, putting the sensation in front of me. "Thank god, Caspian, I thought you'd—" I cut off, teeth clicking together, into my aborted sentence. "Stirling."

He leans casually against a towering cedar. His dark blond hair is loose around his shoulders, swept back over his scalp and tucked behind his ears. His eyes are normal, dark blue with whites gleaming in the gloom; no sunglasses. He's wearing a sleek, slim-fitting suit, pale gray with navy pinstripes, a crisp, brilliant white button down beneath it, no tie, with black ankle-height leather boots. The shirt is unbuttoned to show a V of skin.

His ivory skin has a tinge of pink; he's fed recently, then.

Fed.

The word popped into my skull.

Not "eaten."

Fed.

The difference is at once subtle and stark.

Stirling is debilitatingly gorgeous, leaning against the tree in his bespoke suit with his hair loose and fluttering in the wind, snow dusting his shoulders and hair. His posture is lazy and insouciant, confident and amused.

"Sparrow." The amused glint in his eyes makes it both my name and an endearment.

"Thank god you're here, Stirling. I'm kind of lost." I ease closer to him, a little wary, a little afraid, a little thrilled by the danger.

Because he is—*they* are—very, very dangerous indeed. In more ways than one.

The forest is hushed, the silence thick and soft like fleece as if the snow soaks up and absorbs sound; it's so silent I can faintly hear individual snowflakes ticking against the fabric of my hood.

"Kind of lost." More than amused, I think he's making fun of me.

"Yes," I say, my tone wry and arch. "Caspian and I were taking a walk, and…" I don't know what to say, what not to say, or even how to say any of it. "I tripped. Cut my hand." I lift my hand, tugging my mitten off with my teeth to show him, but there's not a mark on my skin; I look at my hand, then drop it, wiggle the mitten back on and shove my hand into my jacket pocket. "Caspian, he…we…" a blush creeps into my cheeks.

Stirling's loose, casual posture straightens. "Did he… touch…you?" Deceptively light and quiet, his tone hides danger, like a viper coiled in the grass.

"He…it was…" I lick my lips, cheeks feeling like they've been set on fire. "Nothing happened. Or…not really." I hold my arms out, let them flop to my sides. "I'm fine. Just lost."

His nostrils flare. "He did. I smell it." His eyes narrow. Harden. "He drank from you." Comprehension dawns in his eyes. "That's why he left you here."

"I think he felt like he had to. For my sake." I blink.

Stirling peers at me, unblinking and still. "He sent me to you. To bring you back to your car."

"So you didn't just happen to be in the area?"

He sniffs a laugh. "No, I did not just happen to be in the area." Stirling sighs. "You need to be careful, Maeve. You have no idea what you're playing with."

"I'm starting to get an idea," I mutter.

He shakes his head slowly, then gestures ninety degrees from the way I was going in a mocking, rolling flourish of his hand. "Come. The trailhead is this way."

I follow him, and he walks with his hands tucked into his slacks pockets, as if out for a stroll in the park. Snow gathers in a thickening blanket on his shoulders and head; it sticks to his hair but doesn't melt.

"You don't get cold, do you?"

He glances at me with an amused smirk. "No, we don't *get* cold. We *are* cold." There's a deeper meaning hidden in the way he says that.

We walk in silence—like Caspian, he makes no noise. He does leave footprints, but I suspect if he wished otherwise, he wouldn't.

Curiosity gets the better of me. "Stirling?"

His sidelong glance at me is an indication to ask my question.

"If you didn't want to, could you not leave footprints?"

He stops walking entirely, staring at me with narrowed eyes. "Why?"

"Just curious."

He blinks twice—as a gesture, I think, more than anatomical necessity. Then, without anything more, he resumes walking, hands in his pockets, snow gathering in his hair and shoulders.

He leaves no footprints, not even an impression.

"How?" I ask.

He doesn't answer for a while. Then, he lifts one shoulder a couple of inches, drops it. "Biology." He glances at me. "Close your eyes." I do so. "Now touch your nose without opening your eyes."

My finger touches my nose, landing nearly dead center on the tip.

"That's called proprioception," he says. "Awareness of one's body or physical movements." Another of those spare shrugs. "It's like that. Sort of."

"So you can, like...*lighten* yourself?"

He tilts his head to one side, considering. "In a manner of speaking, yes."

"Could I learn to do it?"

He snorts softly three times—a laugh. "No, Maeve, you cannot learn to do that. As I said, it's biological. You and I have different biology."

"Well that's for damn sure."

Caspian *drank...my...blood*. I know, logically, I should be freaking out about that. Yet I'm not. I'm more irritated that he won't just come out and say it. None of them will. They tiptoe around the truth, even though it's plain as the nose on my face.

I look back the way we came. In the distance, two sets of footprints. Then, only one, as if the person walking beside me simply vanished.

Because I'm stubborn, as I walk I try to figure out how to lighten my body so I don't leave footprints, how it could be possible, according to all the laws of physics I know.

And I come up empty.

So, instead, I focus inward. On my body. On being *less*. Being *lighter*. Leaving no trace. Still me, just...ethereal. Gauzy. Wispy. *Less.*

A frisson slithers through me, like a shiver but in my veins and blood rather than my muscles.

A creeping suspicion pools in my belly, and I crane my head over my shoulder and look back...

My footprints aren't *gone*, but they're only faint impressions, like footprints filled in with snow. I watch my feet—I don't feel any different. I don't look any different. Yet my footprints are nearly invisible, nearly nothing at all; there's a stark delineation marking precisely where I felt the frisson go through me, where my footprints go from normal to less.

After several minutes of silence, he stops walking and turns to look at me. "You play with things you do not understand, in a world with rules you are unaware of, and consequences you cannot imagine, Maeve Sparrow." He stares hard at me. "Be careful with Caspian. Not only for your sake but his." He points, his long arm extended; I can see a patch of lightness in the indicated direction—the clearing and the trailhead. I see the glint of light on a window. "Your car is just there."

"Thank you, Stirling."

He nods, still considering me with a puzzled frown. "You're welcome." He shakes his head again. "I do not understand you, Sparrow."

I laugh. "Yeah, well, I can't help you there. I'm just me."

He gives me his distinct laugh—three sharp breathy snorts. "Yes, indeed, as are we all. But you…" a frown. "The events of today, with you and Caspian…anyone else would have run for their life. You are most unusual."

"Thanks?" I say with a wry laugh.

A nod, and in the blink of my eyes, he's gone. There's a single pair of footprints where he was standing facing me as we spoke just now, but no others in any direction.

The Purr fades swiftly, and then I know I'm alone once more.

I get in my car and drive home—very slowly, because once beyond the shelter of the forest the snow is falling so thickly I can barely see past the hood of my car.

My mind has shut down totally—no thoughts, no feelings. My sole focus is getting back home…

Where I can freak the fuck out properly, in the safety of my bedroom.

Chapter 17

I LET MYSELF INSIDE THE SIDE DOOR, stomping my feet on the rug as I shuck my hat and jacket.

"Where the *hell* have you been?" Andreas is *furious*. "It's supposed to snow like this for the next *two days*, and I can't get ahold of you. Don't come home from school, don't tell me where you are or where you're going, and you don't answer your *fucking* phone."

I've never seen him angry before—it's scary. His hair is messy from his hand pawing through it, his eyes are sparking with fury, and his clothing is disheveled.

"Ohhh…*shit*," I breathe. I dig my phone

out of my purse: 13 missed calls and 21 unread messages…all from Andreas. "Andy, oh my god—I'm so, so sorry! I went for a walk in the woods with Caspian and left my purse in my car. I should have brought my phone, but I honestly didn't think about it." I can't very well tell him what actually happened, so I do something I usually avoid—lie. "I, um. We got into a stupid argument, and he sort of stormed off. And we were on the path, so it was just a straight shot back to the trailhead, and it wasn't snowing then, so it's not like he abandoned me in a blizzard—he just went back to the car ahead of me." I swallow hard, hating the taste of the lie in my mouth. "And then the storm hit. Before I knew it, I couldn't see five feet in front of me, and then I tripped and got turned around, and I must have walked off the path or something because I got super turned around. Thankfully I was able to retrace my steps back to the path and made it to the car, and then came home." I wiggle my phone at him. "And my phone was on silent, so…you know, that's why I didn't answer after I was in the car. Plus I was focusing on driving."

He turns away, scraping his hand through his hair. "I've been worried." He faces me again. "I'm concerned about the time you're spending with Caspian Taylor, Maeve."

"Andreas—"

He holds up both hands palms out. "No, I know. I'm not—we're not…" he sighs, trailing off. His eyes drop, flick to the side, as if trying to decide what to say. Eventually, he starts over. "Just please be careful. Okay? Not everyone is what they seem. I'm a detective, Maeve. It's always the person you least expect it to be."

"I appreciate your concern, Andy. I'm sure you've

heard things about Caspian, but I've met his whole family. I'll be fine."

"I know I can't expect or demand you check in with me or anything, but it would make me feel better if you did. Okay?"

I give him a smile. "I will, I promise. I don't want you to worry." I hesitate. "Honestly, it's nice having someone worry about me."

He rests his hand on my shoulder and gives me an affectionate shake. "Well, now that you're back, I'm going to bed. I've been up for forty-eight hours. The case I'm working on has kept me running."

I fix myself some food, finish my homework, and then lay in bed with my laptop, watching reality TV. "Watching" may be a strong word, though—my mind isn't on the show.

It's on Caspian.

What happened in the woods.

At some point, I fall asleep.

I'm dreaming.

I'm in the black void space. I'm alone. There's no sound—not quietness, not the relative silence of being in an empty room. Total, enveloping, oppressive silence.

I'm incorporeal. No body, no sensations, just the spark of awareness that is me.

The void lessens in front of me—a thinning of the blackness. Shapes move—indiscernible, flitting, darting, shifting.

Maeve. Mom's voice. *It's coming undone.*

Mom? My words are not audible—more the subvocalization of one's inner thoughts. *What does that mean, Mom?*

You should not be here.

Mom? What happened to you?

The blackness thickens, and the shapes are obscured.

I'm alone again.

Time twists, distorts—like the dream I had about the accident. It's sludgy, like taffy being pulled. There's nothing, no one, no direction, no self, no heartbeat or muscles to twitch or lungs to inflate.

Again, the blackness thins. This time, instead of amorphous shapes, there's a figure. Male.

Andreas. His ears have pointed tips. His eyes are almond-shaped, the brown of his irises glowing a dark golden amber. Not as brightly as Caspian's, but in a similar way.

He doesn't seem surprised to see me—if he can see me. Maybe he senses me? I don't know. But his eyes gaze steadily at me. There's an aura of energy around him as if he were a magnet and the magnetic polarities were visible, tangible, like sound waves from a concert speaker. I feel it washing over my incorporeal body, even though that makes no logical sense.

This is a dream, after all. In dreams, one can feel things without having a body, apparently.

He lifts a hand palm out toward me, his eyes kind, affectionate…and worried. *You should not be here.*

There's a pulse from his palm, and I'm flung backward through the void, away from him, deeper into nothingness.

I remember Alistair's warning: these dreams may not be merely dreams. They could be dangerous.

Something slithers past me—something immense and titanic. I feel it wrapping around me, coils upon coils of condensed darkness encircling me.

WAKE UP!

My inaudible shout echoes in the void.

WAKE UP!

I can't leave the dream.

The coils tighten; instead of constricting my breath, the thing is crushing my identity, my soul, the spark of my awareness.

I have to wake up.

I have to wake up.

I'm not sure why—instinct, perhaps, or desperation—but I focus on the feeling I had in the forest. The frisson of energy in my blood, in the molecules and atoms and subatomic particles that comprise me, and I try to replicate it.

WAKE UP!

The shiver is weak, paltry. The coils continue to tighten, and fear blankets my awareness.

Help! Caspian? CASPIAN!

I don't know if he can hear me. If he's here, in this place. If he even sleeps.

I want to get out of here. I want to wake up.

The darkness shakes.

—**aeve...**

A voice.

—**aeve...**

It's insistent. Familiar. Distant.

—**ake up. Wake up.**

Louder. Closer. It's him. Caspian.

Heat suffuses me. Or is it cold?

I smell him.

The void thins, peels open like curtains being drawn apart. He's here.

Black eyes, white marble skin. Cloaked in shadows as if clothed in them, or as if they're part of him. **You must wake up, Maeve.**

I'm trying. I can't.

Think of your bedroom. The walls. The ceiling. Your bed, the blankets, the pillows. See them Feel them.

He reaches out to me and I take his hand without hesitation. It's cold—utterly, perfectly. What was it Stirling said? "We *are* cold."

He pulls me to him. **Wake up, Maeve.**

The void is shaken again.

I picture my room in Andreas's house—the dormer with the window seat, my bed with the wrought iron headboard, the rolltop desk.

The coils are there, but Caspian's presence has spooked the thing. Whatever it is, it isn't certain I'm a meal worth fighting him over.

Which is a scary thought.

Wake up, Maeve.

Another shaking of the darkness.

Wake up, Maeve!"

The darkness dissolves all at once, and Caspian's incorporeal voice becomes real, and I'm awake, in my bed, and Caspian is sitting beside me. His hands are on my shoulders, and he's shaking me.

I bolt upright and fling myself against him, my arms

going around his neck, nose burying in his flannel shirt. "Caspian, thank god. Thank god."

He's lukewarm—not cold yet, but not warm either. His skin is like clay, pliable still, yet hardening. "Maeve. You're okay now." His arms curl around me, holding me against him.

"What—what *was* that?" I ask, pulling back a bit so I can see his eyes: no sunglasses. His eyes are brown, with not a trace of the amber glow.

He cups my cheek. "It's hard to explain. There's no word for it, no name I've heard."

"It *had* me, Caspian. I couldn't wake up, I couldn't—it was…"

"That place is dangerous, Maeve."

"I don't know…" I trail off, looking at him. "I'm not *trying* to go there. I just fall asleep and…there I am. I see Mom, I see Andreas, I see you."

"Anyone else?"

I shake my head. "Not so far."

"Do what I told you, next time you end up there. Think of your body, where you truly are. See it. The more specific the details you can recall, the better."

"It's not a dream, is it?" I ask.

He looks away. "It's extraordinarily complicated and nearly impossible to explain. And to even be able to make any sense of it, there's so much more you'd have to understand first." He rubs a thumb across my cheek. "And I'm not the one to explain any of it anyway. I couldn't."

I cup my palm around the back of his neck—it's cooling under my touch, hardening. "Caspian…"

He must see the question in my eyes. "Don't ask questions you don't want the answer to, Maeve."

"Who are you?"

He shrugs. "You know me."

"Okay, then. *What* are you?"

"I think you know."

I think I do, too.

There's a piece of paper there on my desk, right on top of a pile of history notes and calculus scratch. I can see it from here. I glance past Caspian's shoulder at it. He turns his head and lifts his chin, peering through the darkness of my room. His gaze turns back to me.

He merely looks at me, expression neutral, steady, even. His silence—of which he has many different types—is waiting, accepting. Affirming. It's not a verbal confirmation, but it *is* a confirmation.

"How?" I ask. It's the first of about a thousand questions in my mind.

He quirks a corner of his lips. "Might as well ask for a brief rundown on the history of the world as ask that."

"Okay, then." I swallow hard. "Are you going to kill me?"

Blackness stains the corners of his eyes, flooding, subsuming. "I would sooner kill myself." His voice is a thick, dark, angry, feral snarl.

"Why did you leave me?" I ask, holding his eyes with my own; he's fighting back the staining blackness, somehow, and winning. "In the forest."

"To protect you."

"From what?"

"Myself."

I lick my lips. Steady my breathing. "What would you have done?"

The hunger rampant in his eyes frightens me—and excites me. Sends thrills through my muscles, into my blood…and my sex. He stares into me, and I feel The Purr—so familiar a sensation now that I barely notice it—revving up like a race car engine at the starting line. The need pours through me, turning my blood into a boiling inferno, making the empty space in my soul open and turn ravenous, seeking, wanting, needing.

I want him.

I don't care about anything else, in this moment. Just him. His touch. His mouth. That rush of heat and orgasmic thrill—

He's gone.

My window is open, and shadows seem to swirl in my bedroom like a dense fog after something has rushed through it. Curtains flutter in the open window and cold billows through with a flurry of snow.

I shimmy out of bed and close the window.

I see him—standing on a low branch of a pine tree with his hands clenched into fists at his sides.

I think I know what he would have done.

And I want it.

My eyelids blink, and the tree branch is bare.

He's gone.

How can I sleep? After the dream…or whatever that place is—how can I sleep, if that thing is there?

How can I sleep with this raging current of electric desire boiling in my bloodstream?

I close my eyes, but there's only him.

Being in his arms in the forest. His lips against my

palm. My blood flowing into his mouth, pulling, pulsing. The throb between my thighs. The ache in my core. The need.

For the briefest instant, I was touching him.

I open my eyes again and memorize my bedroom. The planks of the ceiling, the knot just there above my head, the items on my nightstand: phone plugged into the white charger cord, which trails over the back edge; a glass of water, a tube of lip balm.

Eventually, I fall back asleep, and there are no more dreams.

Or, only the garden variety, at least.

CHAPTER 18

HE'S COLD AGAIN, AT SCHOOL. NOT literally, but metaphorically. Toward me. Ignoring me. Answering my attempts at conversation with curt, one-word answers.

He's trying to stay away from me, again. This time, I'm ready for it. I'm not confused by it, or hurt. He thinks he's protecting me.

Maybe he thinks I'll forget, or be scared off.

A week passes this way—I give him space. A week turns into two, and then there's Christmas break. Andreas takes me downtown for the tree-lighting, and then to dinner. He takes a little time off, and we go shopping together for each other. I get him smart wool socks, a hand-carved wooden pocketknife made by a local Native American artisan, and a to-go coffee thermos. Christmas Day is spent together at the fire, drinking coffee and reading. He got me a beautiful cream cashmere infinity scarf and a box with nothing in it except a piece of paper and a key fob; he had a remote start installed on my car, so I can warm it up without having to go outside. It explains why he went to such lengths the day before to keep me inside—he had a friend pick up my car while I was taking a bath.

The rest of the break is quiet—and lonely. Caspian continues to avoid me. I don't see him once all break, and while I understand his reasoning, considering I *want* what he's so afraid of, it's starting to get hard to not take it personally, as a rejection. Now that I know for certain that he's a vampire—god, it's weird to use that word—he still thinks he has to avoid me.

Not okay.

What's worse is I can't talk to anyone about it.

After the break, Andreas is busier than ever, still working that case, which seems to have him in fits: he's cranky when he's home, which is seldom, and disinclined to chat with me. More avoidance by Caspian—it's been a month and a half since that day in the woods and the dream he rescued me from.

I have lunch with my school friends: Amy is a gregarious blond who seems dead-set on fitting into the ditzy blond bombshell stereotype, and is succeeding; Ella is more down to earth, a brunette with an acerbic sense of humor; Dakota, the only one I'd even think about hanging out with outside of school, is quiet, funny, athletic, and gets along with everyone. I spend lunch with them, hang out by the windows after school and listen to them gossip and talk about boyfriends and whisper about who's hooking up with whom, and bitch about periods and annoying parents. I rarely add anything, but they're used to it at this point— my life has been weird, and I doubt they'd understand it.

Nor would they understand my thing with Caspian. He's a loner. School seems to be almost an annoyance to him, the material uniformly easy for him. He's never in the cafeteria at lunch, chooses to do projects alone wherever possible, rarely speaks to anyone except me, and even me he ignores if he's having "blood sugar" issues—blood sugar being code for *he needs blood*. I have questions about that, too, but doesn't seem like I'm going to get the answers any time soon.

I'm angry, at this point. He gets to just make this decision for the both of us? He's scared, so I don't get to see him at all?

The Purr isn't happy either. It feels more and more like a sentient thing living inside me, and now that I've been without its constant hum for so long, it feels…restless.

Like a tiger in a cage…and one of the bars is loose.

Pacing back and forth, back and forth. You can tell it's hungry, and frustrated, and impatient. It knows the bar is loose. One good blow and it could be free.

The hunger in me, the need for Caspian? That's worse.

I've done my all-out best to ignore it. Pretend it's not there. Don't think about it, don't daydream about him, about how he made me feel.

Don't think about what I know he is.

I try to just keep my head down, talk to the girls at school, do my homework, study for the upcoming exams. Dakota and I go to the mall together, have coffee, catch a movie. It's fun, but after being around Caspian and Stirling, it's disorienting being with Dakota—someone so normal, so quiet, so…*safe*.

I need him.

I can't take this anymore.

February, almost March. It's still cold and snowy outside, but there are signs of spring. Daytime temperatures are creeping up, snow is melting in places.

Caspian has taken a scorched earth approach to me—cut me out entirely.

I'm barely containing myself, day to day. I look for him, everywhere I go. Anger at his unilateral decision burns inside me. After the semester ended, he transferred out of Calc—to get away from me, I assume; I only needed one more semester each of Spanish and gym, so my sixth-hour A/B alternates are different as well, and Caspian is in neither of them. I'm taking a creative writing class for A day, and British literature from Chaucer to the 18th century.

He's not in any of my classes.

I don't see him at lunch, before school, or after school.

It's like he vanished.

It hurts. It makes me angry. Most of all, it's making me feel *crazy*.

Did I imagine it all? The dreams? The wild, bone-shaking, soul-shuddering vibration in my very blood at his mere presence? Did I fantasize that day on the snowy trail? My imagination has never been that vivid before, and I can distinctly remember each and every second, from the moment

I fell and cut my hand to the moment he vaporized and reappeared several feet away.

I know it was real.

That day in the forest behind my house was real.

The dreams are real, in one sense or another.

He drank my blood.

And it made him…*alive,* somehow. More alive than I am now—hyperreal, perhaps.

I felt his erection—I had it in my hand for one glorious instant, hot and hard and thick and begging…

Hell. What's becoming of me? Those thoughts are *not* mine.

Don't get me wrong, I like sex. The few times I've had it, it's been great—enjoyable. Not intensely exciting or earth-shaking, and I've certainly never understood the obsession some people seem to have with it.

Until now.

Until Caspian.

Now, he's all I can think about, and I haven't laid eyes on him in two months.

I dream of him—not *those* dreams, the void-space dreams. Regular old dirty ones, wet dreams that have me jerking awake with trembling thighs, covered in sweat, my sex throbbing and soaked. The dream is always the same:

Caspian and me, together. In his room—I can't make out the feature of the room, because it's dark. Just before dawn, I think. The air and the light have that soft hazy new feel to them, coming from a window somewhere close. Gray light, like downy feathers.

He's kissing me. Just a kiss. We're clothed…at first. As such things do, it ignites quickly into something else, something hotter, wilder. He tears at my clothes, literally ripping them off me in tattered shreds. His hands are cold, like lifeless marble left in subzero temperatures, yet they're insistent and demanding and the cold of them is so intense it burns like fire, taking my breath away.

He pulls me against his naked body and breaks the kiss. His eyes are blacked out, hungry, desperate, eager. I can read them, the expression in them. He wants me, needs me. But he won't take me until I tell him he can.

He stands, hands on my hips, forehead to mine, not breathing, not moving, just waiting.

"I want it, Caspian," *I tell him, in the dream.* ***"Take it."***

I look up into his face—his jaw drops open, revealing even white teeth…and two long, sharp fangs. I watch them appear, those fangs, his eyeteeth elongating, sharpening. The black in his eyes intensifies, deepens, soaking up the shadows around us.

"Ask me." *His voice is feral, inhuman, sepulchral.*

"Please, Caspian. Drink from me."

His answer is a pleased snarl. He leans closer, closer…my thighs quake, my sex drips, hot, throbbing. I feel the pinprick of his teeth touching the tender skin at the side of my neck; his hand lovingly cups my ass, pulling me harder against him…

And I wake up. Just before my skin is pierced and he drinks from me, I wake up.

Every fucking time.

I'm going crazy.

I'm in Brit Lit, listening to one of my classmates stumble through reading. I'm doodling in my notebook, not really listening since I'll just read it on my own at home later anyway.

"Miss Sparrow?" Mr. Conrad's voice jolts me to awareness.

"Um, yes?" I look up and realize everyone is staring at me expectantly.

"I asked if you could read the next section."

"Oh, um. Yeah, sure." I sigh, setting my pen down. "Sorry, I, um…where were we?"

Mr. Conrad comes to my desk and taps the paragraph in question with his pen. "Pay attention, Miss Sparrow."

He narrows his eyes, his attention catching on my doodling.

I gulp. Apparently, I've doodled a pair of eyes into a webbing of abstract curlicues and whorls on the page— the eyes are black, white-less, pupil-less. Beneath them, a mouth open wide, with fangs.

I'm not any great shakes as an artist, but when I doodle, apparently some nascent ability comes out of me. This doodle in particular, however, is beyond anything I've ever done.

It's Caspian.

"Less drawing, more literature if you please, Miss Sparrow." He taps my drawing. "Quite an interesting composition, however."

The bell rings and I shove my book and notebook into my bag and beeline for the exit. I've had enough.

I drive to their house, but the circle in front is empty of cars—no one is home.

Incensed, I go home and putter around the house aimlessly for an hour or two, entirely too worked up to do homework or anything else.

All I can think about is *him*.

I can't explain my next actions other than desperation and obsession. I *have* to see him. Touch him, smell him. Have to. *Have* to.

No coat, in just a thick cardigan, a tank top, and a pair of leggings tucked into my fur-lined Uggs, I exit the back door. Stand in the yard in the evening light, trying to just… *feel* him. A tug in my gut pulls me forward, into the forest behind the house. Where I met him last time. It's darker under the cover of the trees, but I barely notice. The tug in my belly pulls me along, and I weave around trees, duck through tangled underbrush, moving steadily in a particular direction—I don't have a wonderful sense of direction, but it seems like I might be moving toward their house.

I'm in a daze, almost hypnotized, veins humming, muscles moving on autopilot. I duck under branches, and my hood occasionally catches on a branch and tugs clumps of snow loose to slide down my spine; it's cold and wet, but I barely notice. Darkness is quickly descending around me, settling over me like a flat sheet slowly billowing down to the mattress.

I don't notice that either—the tug on my belly pulls, pulls, pulls. Inexorable, undeniable. How long I walk through the darkening forest, I don't know; how far I go, I don't know. Despite the lowering gloom, I can somehow make out the tree trunks and the brush and the ruts and the hillocks and the roots, as if my eyes have become used to the dark more easily than normal.

Things I would normally trip over, I do not—my brain and my legs seem to work in tandem correctly.

My brain catalogs these things almost absently, tucking them away to peruse later. Right now, all my thoughts are bent toward the nearing point toward which I am being drawn: him.

I know it's him. I feel it.

A mile, two? I don't know. Far. Then, the pit of my

stomach starts to tingle. I keep walking. My blood starts to bubble, just a little—the tiny gathering bubbles on the side of the pot, telling you it's going to boil soon.

A little farther.

The pot begins to boil—not a full rolling boil yet, but nearly.

Now it's The Purr, all that I am humming and buzzing and yearning, seeking and needing and straining for him.

I step into a clearing—their house. All the cars are there. He's there—I feel him, feel his energy, his aura, his intense cold and shadow-cloaked solitude.

My feet carry me up the steps, and inside. I don't knock; it doesn't even occur to me.

I hear the fire crackling. Alistair is in the chair angled toward the fire, pipe in one hand, a cut crystal goblet in the other—the goblet contains something thick and bright red, viscous and sluggish.

He takes a sip, and the opaque scarlet liquid dribbles slowly down the sides of the goblet, leaving a thick stain. "Upstairs, last room on the left, my dear." He says this without looking away from the fire.

His lips are painted red. I know what's in the goblet. Questions percolate in the back of my mind and burst like soap bubbles, unasked: they're irrelevant at this moment.

I tread up the stairs, palm gliding over the smooth dark wood of the banister, operating on feel more than sight. I wouldn't have needed Alistair's directions—I can sense him. I vaguely note the hallway: long and narrow with a high, barrel-vaulted ceiling of the same dark-stained wood as the rest of the floors and trim throughout the house; the walls are a soft, muted, delicate cream, and the floor is carpeted in antique hunter green, thick and plush and a rather faded in the center high traffic area.

These details flit through my mind in an eye blink, cataloged and forgotten.

I pass an open bathroom at the top of the stairs on my left—subway tile, pedestal vanity, mirror, frosted glass shower stall with brass trim. A door on my right and another on my left, opposite each other. Another door on the right, and the last on the left opposite—Caspian's.

I open the door without knocking; something inside me tells me Caspian knows I'm here. I step inside and close the door behind me. Within, the room is bathed in shadows. Yet, the same abnormal sharpening of my eyes lets me see better than I would normally; the only light comes from the window, through which star- and moonlight gently silvers the sparse furnishings. In the center of the back wall is a large, high, four-poster bed with a nest of rumpled blankets, a six-drawer bureau stands opposite; two openings on the same wall as the door lead to, presumably, a walk-in closet and an en suite bathroom. Across from the door, beneath the window, is an antique writing desk— scrollwork legs, two drawers on either side and a bank of cabinets running along the back. Books line the top of the desk, held in place by bookends carved in the shape of gothic gargoyles.

I smell him—he's fresh out of the shower, smelling of bar soap and shampoo.

"Have a seat," I hear from the bathroom, his voice echoing. "I'll be out in a minute."

I sit on the bed—in the center, rather than the edge, making myself comfortable. His blankets smell like him, and it takes the edge off the desperation seething within me. Only a little, but it's better than nothing.

A moment later, he appears in the doorway of his bathroom, moving in that sinuous, liquid, predatory gait of his. He's wrapped in a thick, maroon bath sheet, the hem trailing around his feet. My mouth goes dry, my stomach opens up and drops away, and my sex pulses with heat.

He's sculpted from marble, a flawless effigy of male beauty. Every muscle is sharply delineated, lean and spare. There's no Instagram model vascularity or bodybuilder bulk, just purely perfect male anatomy. All but naked, he's never looked more like what he is: a lethal predator. His dark hair is loose and wet, hanging in thick strands around his eyes and sticking to the back of his neck. He hasn't bothered to towel off—droplets bead on his shoulders and chest, trickling in tempting runnels through the deep grooves of his abdominal muscles.

I have a sudden urge to fling myself at him and lick the droplets away, one by one.

I have to tangle my fingers together in my lap and clench them till they hurt to stop myself.

"You're in my bed." He purrs this, his voice dark and amused.

I say nothing—now that I'm here, now that I'm face to face with him, I'm angry. More than angry, I'm furious.

He must sense it, or see it. "Maeve, I…"

I'm taking a page from Mom's book: whenever she was pissed at me, she would sit facing me with her arms crossed, eyes narrowed, jaw tensed…and just wait. She wouldn't say a thing. Wouldn't respond to me. She would just sit…and wait. It was frighteningly effective. If I'd done something wrong, and I knew it? It would all come tumbling out, one way or another. Usually, along with an apology. And really, that's all she ever wanted: for me to admit what I'd done and apologize. If I did that, there was rarely any kind of discipline.

He lets out a sigh, a long hiss between his teeth. "You don't understand, Maeve. And I can't explain it. I *can't.* You've already…I've already let you see…" He trails off, hoping I'll fill in the blank.

I don't.

He stares at me, dark eyes broody and frustrated. "If I let myself…" he shakes his head, trailing off again. "Goddammit, Maeve."

I continue to wait, staring at him, letting him see the fullness of my hurt and anger.

He ghosts a few steps closer. His scent is overpowering. Bar soap, shampoo. No woodsmoke. The coppery tang that usually accompanies him is strong, and his skin is flushed; he just fed.

Despite my hurt and anger, the seething, snarling need for him burns white-hot in my veins, in my muscles, in my soul. I want to rip the towel off him and grasp him in my hand and show him pleasure and let him drink from me—

"*Stop* that!" He growls, turning away from me. "Resisting you is fucking hard enough as it is without you doing…*that.*"

"I wasn't *doing* anything," I snap.

He whirls and pounces across six feet in less than an instant, suddenly leaning his fists into the mattress, bent at the waist, face inches from mine. Black tendrils stain the corners of his eyes, and his voice deepens, thickens, darkens.

"Oh no?"

I wasn't. Was I?

"Can you…read my mind?"

"I drank from you," he says, his voice pitched low, a silky, threatening murmur. "My venom is in your veins. You've metabolized it."

"And?" I blink. "Wait…*venom*?" I shake my head. "What does that have to do with whether or not you can read my mind?"

He drops his head with a huff and then pivots to half-sit on the edge of the bed. "It means I can…*feel* you. I can't read your mind, as in hear your thoughts. It's also not exactly feeling your emotions. It's…pheromones. Your scent. Your aura, like your personal energy field. It's everything that is you, inside and out, I can just…*feel*." He indicates me with a flick of his pointer finger. "So when you're sitting there all pissed off at me? I can feel that. I know you're angry. I mean, I'd know anyway, because of body language and whatever. But now, I can…*feel* it. That's the only word I can find." Sometimes, he speaks formally, almost archaic, and other times, he sounds like a normal teenager; this, currently, is the latter. "And when you broadcast what you were feeling just then? Yeah, Maeve, I can feel that, too. But *that* shit *is* pheromonal. Your need, your desire…it *calls* to me. It sets my own desires off like a fucking atomic bomb, and I'm already…" he sighs again, scrubbing his face in the most human gesture I've ever seen in him. "I have feelings for you, Maeve, and I can guarantee you they're not…innocent."

"So you just cut me out of your life, because *feelings* are *hard*?"

He shakes his head. "I cut you out of my life because my feelings for you aren't *safe* for you, Maeve."

"You said you'd kill yourself before you killed me."

"And that's true."

"Then I'm not following."

He doesn't answer right away, staring toward the window through which a sliver of the moon can be seen through the tips of the pines. "I know. And I don't know how to make you understand."

"Just say it. Just tell me." I shift to sit on my knees, behind him. Reach out and touch his back—cool, smooth, somewhere between hardening clay and marble. "Or show me."

He doesn't react for a moment. Just sits statue still, skin cooling under my hands, hardening. "You should go." He says this without looking at me, without moving.

I lean closer, sliding my hands over his bare shoulders and down his chest, pressing my breasts against his back, my cheek to his. The coppery scent of pennies is pungent in my nostrils, flooding my mouth with saliva. My heart hammers in my chest. Instinctual, primordial fear swirls inside me, but it's overpowered and scorched away by the blazing inferno of desire.

"I'm not afraid, Caspian."

Chapter 19

A GUTTURAL, ANIMAL SNARL RIPS out of him.

There's a sensation of movement, and I find myself on my back with Caspian on top of me. His eyes are blacked out, inhuman and ravenous. He's pinning me to the bed, his cold hard weight immovable on mine.

He slides his nose along my throat, inhaling slowly.

"Your blood, Maeve…" he rumbles, his voice dark, cold, and heavy. "It's…effervescent. Golden, like honey and sunlight. Like nothing I've ever tasted, human or animal."

He pulls away and bares his teeth—his

fangs have descended into twin spikes, razor-sharp needles; he nuzzles my throat again, and I feel the sharp points of his teeth against my skin, not quite pricking. "What *are* you?"

"I…I'm just…me." Fear and desire tangle inside me; desire wins out, and I hook my legs around his waist, clinging to him. "I'm just a girl."

"No, you're far, *far* more. Is it possible you don't know?"

"Know what?"

"What you are."

"I'm not anything."

"You are. You just don't realize." He trembles against me as if straining every muscle. "You should run away before I lose my will and taste you again."

"When you…tasted me…before…" I struggle to get the words out. "It felt…*incredible*."

"You aren't safe with me, Maeve." Those needle-sharp fangs touch my throat again, pricking but not puncturing. "I don't know if I could stop."

"You would…drink until I died?" I breathe, fighting hyperventilation. I'm terrified and exhilarated in equal measure. "Or…or turn me into…a vampire?"

I think that's the first time I've said the word out loud.

"I would never turn you," he growls, intensity shaking in his voice. "Not ever."

"But you could."

"Yes. But you wouldn't be like me. It doesn't work that way." A pause. "Nor would I ever drain you."

"Then when you say you aren't sure you could stop, what does that mean?"

"You should stay away from me, Maeve," he warns. "Or you just may find out."

"I *want* to find out, Caspian."

"You don't know."

"So tell me."

Silence, thick and thoughtful. Finally, he growls wordlessly. Rests his head on my shoulder. Speaks slowly, his voice muffled against my body. "It's called the mating frenzy." A heavy pause. "Feeding is…it's inherently sexual for us. Always. It's biological. It's an imperative, something we cannot control or stop. It's…it's all interrelated. When we select someone to feed from, our bodies secrete pheromones. They make our intended prey…want us. It triggers your human desire, your innate sexuality. Turns it on and you cannot turn it off, can't resist it, and don't want to. For me, the mating frenzy is more than just the need to feed and the sexual desire that comes with it. The mating frenzy is far, *far* more intense. And your body responds to the mating frenzy with an increased intensity of sexual arousal—more than normal, and more intense than what you'd feel if it was just me wanting to feed from you. The mating frenzy is…" he trails off, shakes his head, unable to put it into words.

Well, that makes sense of how I feel around him. "So me wanting you…it's not *me*, it's just…pheromones?"

"To a degree. Especially since I've fed from you."

"You said something about venom, before."

"Our saliva contains venom—but unlike that of a serpent, its function is to facilitate the feeding process. It numbs and heals—and if I've fed from you before, it readies your body for me. Increases your body's production of blood, and flushes you with sex hormones so you feel nothing the need. So if I were to prepare to feed from you…" he nuzzles my throat with his nose, and then I feel his lips—cold, hard, and lifeless—press against my skin, and then I feel his tongue slide over my flesh; I feel an intense tingle where his tongue touched. "You wouldn't feel a thing if I were to puncture your skin."

I feel pressure, but no pain. His lips seal against my skin, and then that wild, intense, intoxicating rush of sexual pleasure burns through me like a blast of heat from an opened oven, replacing the blood in my veins as he draws my blood into his mouth.

It's raw, undiluted ecstasy. What I felt in the forest that day when he drank from my hand was a candle flame flickering in the wind. This? His mouth on my throat, his body on mine, warmth suffusing his flesh…his erection burgeoning with only the thin protection of his towel between us? It's the sun itself.

Need smashes through me, burns, rages. I moan and I dig my fingers into his softening, heating flesh at his back. Slide them down, down, over the muscles of his back and the knobs of his spine. I brush the towel away, and he's naked. I cup the taut hard bubble of his ass and I moan, groan—white-hot bliss shatters through me with each pulse of blood drawn into his mouth. My heart slams, slams, slams, working overtime, thudding like tympani in my chest.

He cups my head with a hand, cradling me closer, holding me with tenderness, fingers in my hair and pressing into my scalp, massaging, caressing. His lips are warm and pliant. His erection throbs against my core. My panties are soaked with my desire.

His hand, hot and soft now, finds skin between my

tank top hem and my leggings. He pauses—up, or down? Up. I'm not wearing a bra, and his hand skates over my bare skin, teasing between my breasts. My nipples ache, diamond hard. I moan, a long low whimper, a silent plea for him to *touch* me.

Another pulse of ecstasy as he draws another sip of my blood; mere seconds have passed since his fangs pierced my flesh.

He cups my breast, and his thumb rolls over my nipple—a burst of heightened pleasure rockets through my body along the live wire between my nipples and my core. He squeezes the firm weight of my breast and pinches my nipple between finger and thumb, and I nearly orgasm, whimpering again at the fury of the ecstasy coursing through every fiber of my being.

He growls, and the vibrations of it rattle my bones.

"Caspian…" I plead, my voice breathy and erotic and aroused and desperate. "Please. More. *Please.*"

He slides his hand down my belly and under the waistband of my leggings. Inside my underwear. Warm strong firm fingers press along the seam of my sex, pause. I lift my hips, begging. Offering. I let my thighs fall apart. I've never needed anything the way I need him to touch me. To take me. To taste me.

Another pulse, another deep drink from the fountain of my veins. Another rumbling snarl of pleasure.

I'm a writhing, moaning mess, whimpering and gasping, hips gyrating, lifting.

"*Please*, Caspian."

His finger curls inside me, slicking into my sex, pushing in. Withdrawing, he gathers my essence and smears it against my clit, and his fingertip circles the erect, sensitive nub of my clit, and my whole being pulses as he takes another drink from me—

The universe explodes. Whiteness envelopes me, heat turning incandescent, sun-hot. It's not an orgasm, it's something far, far more. Bigger, deeper, wilder. My soul shudders as my body contorts and trembles violently, my hips thrusting helplessly. My teeth sink into his shoulder and I cry out, the sound muffled.

I fill my hand with the hot rigid beauty of his cock, and I caress him slowly, savoring the long journey from plump tip to thick base.

I'm still coming—shaking, moaning, thrusting, needing more.

He growls again as I stroke his erection.

I feel a bizarre sensation, a loss of something—he withdraws his fangs from my throat and his tongue slides over the puncture wounds and I feel the tickling tingle of the venom healing me.

Now, he's shaking. He feels fully human, just a boy on the cusp of climax as I touch him.

"Maeve," he whispers, and even his voice shakes. "You have to stop."

"Never." I wrap my legs around his waist again, and his fingers delve inside me and thrust in and pull out and thrust in, and now it's nothing but sex between us, nothing but me and him and our bodies and our pleasure.

He's a creature of muscle and power, a predator only just barely holding himself at bay by force of will. I know the edge I have him against—he wants more. He wants to feed from me. Taste me. Take me.

He won't let himself, for reasons he still hasn't explained.

I don't care.

I want it. I want him. I want more. I want his fangs in my throat and his cock inside me, and I want to be fully devoured by him, owned by him. I care nothing for the consequences, not in this moment. There's only the fury of need, the intoxicating ecstasy of his fingers plunging inside my channel and swirling over my clit, only the slow sweep of my fist down his cock.

I have him there. He shudders, thrusts into my touch.

"Maeve…*fuck*!" His voice is thick with erotic arousal, shaking with it, deep and dark and not at all human.

Abruptly, my hand is empty and my body is cold and abandoned and he's across the room, hands digging into the frame of the doorway to his bathroom. He's naked, back rippling with tensed and shivering muscle, buttocks hard and taut, legs planted wide, head dropped between his shoulders.

"Go." It's a growled sound, trembling with animal ferocity. "Please, Maeve. *Go.*"

Without his weight pinning me down, I feel like I could float away. "I don't want to." My shirt is rucked up above my breasts, and my leggings are pulled down just past my ass. "Come back. Let me finish."

He cranes his head around to glare at me over his shoulder—his eyes glow like sunlit amber. "I can't. I dare not. *Will* not." His voice is tortured. "There's nothing I want more, Maeve. Please believe me. But…for your sake, I *can't.*"

"I don't care about anything, Caspian," I plead, scrambling off the bed and tripping toward him. "Only you. Only us. That was the most amazing thing I've ever felt, and I don't want to stop. I don't care what will happen. I want *you*, Caspian. I *need* you. Don't you understand?"

I stop just behind him. My shirt has fallen back down, but my leggings are still tangled around my thighs. I leave them, I don't even really notice.

"You don't *know*," he snaps. "What would happen."

"Tell me."

"I won't be able to stop."

"I don't want you to." Closer, closer. I shrug off my cardigan and let it topple to the floor, peel off my tank top and drop it at my feet, and I press my naked breasts to his bare back. "I don't care what will happen."

"You'll die." I hear wood crack as his fingers dig into the wood, splintering it. "I care about you too much to be responsible for your death."

"You won't kill me."

"I won't be able to help it. I won't be able to stop it. There won't be a goddamn thing I can do."

I touch my lips to his shoulder and take him in my hands, both of them. "You won't hurt me, Caspian."

"Please, Maeve. *Please*." He trembles all over as I caress his length, and his hips abandon the fight, giving in, thrusting into my touch. "Don't make me hurt you."

I'm consumed by the need to touch him, to finish this, to feel his pleasure, to know I've made him feel how he's made me feel. The Purr is everything inside me. I'm still glowing and flushed with the potency of the orgasm he gave me, and yet the yawning gaping hungry void at the pit of my being seeks him, seeks more, needs more, demands more.

And so, I take more. With some instinct, some interior, almost metaphysical muscle, I *pull*. I draw from him.

Light blazes in my brain, in my heart, in my veins, in my soul, in my muscles, in my skin. It's not just light, it's energy, pure and raw and boiling.

Pull. Pull. Pull.

Wood splinters in his hands.

I caress his cock, slowly, unhurried. He growls, snarling in that animal way of his. His flesh is hot and thick and hard in my hands, and I feel him throbbing. His muscles strain, taut and tensed.

"Fuck—*fuck*…Maeve." This through gritted teeth. "I can't…"

I crush my breasts against his back and peer around his body, watching my hands stroke and caress the wondrous beauty of his cock, thick and long and straight and hard and hot, and nothing has ever felt so good, felt so right as this.

He groans, and this sound is purely human, purely male ecstasy. "Maeve," he moans.

He comes. I feel his cock throb in my hands, and his seed pumps out of him, streaking in a thick white stream to the tile floor halfway across the bathroom. Again, and again, and I watch it all, feeling him release, feeling his muscles tighten harder and harder, listening to him groan through his orgasm.

Finally, his climax ends, and cum dribbles over my fingers. He's panting, gasping, head hanging. Shaking all over.

"Maeve," he whispers. "You have to go. Please. I'm begging you. I'll tell you everything, I promise—you just have to *go*."

I step back, feeling something shift in the air between us. The Purr is no longer a purr, but a roar. It's responding to something in him, to the shift I feel in him.

He pivots in place, and his muscles are popped and straining—abs, pecs, thighs, shoulders, he's isometrically tensed from head to toe. This is the picture of restraint—he's physically preventing himself from pouncing on me. His cock is ramrod straight and stiff, despite having just come. It stands tall and hard and proud against his belly, angled slightly toward me.

His eyes…the backlit amber is stained by tendrils of reaching black.

"Go," he rasps, the humanity in his voice leeching away, replaced by that thick primal guttural ripping tearing hungry snarl. "Please, *please*…go!"

I snatch my tank top off the floor and yank it on, tug my leggings into place and pull on my cardigan.

I pause at the door, hand on the knob. He's fighting it, shaking with the effort, eyes glowing gold and amber, the darkness held at bay…for now.

His fingers dug holes into the wood and plaster where he gripped the frame.

"For me," he whispers, molars clenched, "go. For me. Go."

I flee, then.

I run home and I don't stop until I'm in my bed with the covers over my head.

CHAPTER 20

I DREAM OF HIM. THE SAME DREAM, again and again, every night, sometimes more than once in a single night.

Now, though, the dream is more detailed. I know the feeling of his cock in my hands. I know the sensual wonder of his fangs piercing my throat and the ecstasy as he feeds from me and the bliss as he touches me and the release as he makes me come. Now, instead of stopping right when he's about to pierce my throat with his fangs, the dream continues. He drinks from me. Touches me. Makes me come as he drinks from me—frequently, I wake up hovering at the edge of orgasm, hovering there and desperate for it.

Yet I can't bring myself to finish it myself—it wouldn't be right. I don't mean right in the moral sense, but rather… it wouldn't be good enough. My fingers won't feel like his. I just can't. Nothing will ever be the same, not now that I've felt him.

I have regular dreams, too, of him. Of us.

He's not at school at all for the next few days. And then days turn into a week, and he's still absent from school and my life.

I know he's still trying to protect me.

Spring comes while he's still trying to protect me from himself. Snow melts. Grass sprouts, flowers bud.

I know he won't come to me, so I give him a couple of weeks and then I decide I'm going to have to take matters into my own hands.

I can't wait any longer. I need him. I need more. It's a craving, an addiction.

I'm questioning my sanity—how I came to be addicted to him, especially considering what I know of him.

I park at home after school and walk through the forest to their house. I know the way, now. His truck is gone, and disappointment washes through me.

I ascend the steps anyway and knock on the door. A moment of silence, and then the door swings open and Stirling is there in the doorway.

"He's not here." He's pale and unfed, his eyes dark.

"Where is he?"

"You don't understand what you're risking, coming here," Stirling says. He's dressed in gray chinos with a black short sleeve polo shirt, his hair slicked back into a low ponytail.

The Purr likes his presence.

"I know, and no one will tell me."

"There are rules—laws we have to abide by. Caspian risks breaking them all, with you."

"But how can it be against the law? And what if I'm the one who wants it?"

"Not your laws—ours."

"There are laws? For…you guys? Different from ours?"

He hesitates. "Yes."

"Which implies there's a governing body of some sort."

"Of some sort, yes."

The Purr is loud, deafening, shaking me. It *wants*. I think this is the frenzy Caspian was talking about—but it's coming from Stirling.

And my body is responding.

His dark blue eyes fix on me—he's leaning against the doorframe, arms crossed over his chest. I see tendrils of black at the corners of his eyes, reaching and wriggling toward his pupils. Staining, spreading. His nostrils flare, and he draws in my scent.

"You shouldn't be here."

I can't move. I'm paralyzed, hypnotized. My heart thuds, pounds. I've been a frantic mess of arousal for days, for weeks, ever since I last left this house. It's pent up inside me, tangled up and chaotic and unbearable. I go to bed and can't fall asleep, writhing with arousal, thighs pressed together as my core pulses and drips. I dream of Caspian, and I wake up shuddering at the edge of a climax and I can't ever fall over the edge and I need release, need it, need it.

Frenzy is the right word. Maybe I'm in a mating frenzy of my own, although I don't think normal human girls can go into the mating frenzy Caspian described.

But I'm in a frenzy, nonetheless.

I'm a seething ocean of need.

Stirling is suddenly towering over me in the doorway. Black-stained eyes staring into me. Seeing me, sensing my need, smelling it. He licks his lips, and then lets out a soft snarl. He yanks me inside and slams the door and shoves me back against it. Pins me in place with his body. His fingers dig into my hips—I'm wearing a tight black ankle-length dress with a jean jacket over it; the stretchy black material hugs my curves like a second skin. His hands smooth over my waist, over my hips. Cups my ass, pressing himself against me.

This isn't Caspian, it's Stirling. But my body doesn't seem to care, and my mind is a spinning twisting disaster of confused sensations and thoughts and needs. The Purr is nearly a roar again, and my fingers knot in the front of his shirt. He trails his nose along the side of my neck, and then I feel his tongue slide across the skin of my throat over my jugular vein. I feel a touch of pressure, and then a short, intense rush of pleasure as he pulls from me.

Once.

Barely a sip—just a taste.

He licks the spot again, and the tingle washes over me, and my knees knock and my thighs press together—I want more. I'd let him take more.

"Honey and sunlight." His voice is thick and tortured and confused and aroused. "Flowers and nectar. Sunlight.

Fuck, the warmth in your blood, the taste of you…I've never…never in my life have I tasted anything like you."

His lips kiss my throat on the other side. His hands clutch at my ass, fingers digging in hard, almost painfully… if the coarse, raw, raging arousal which currently owns and dominates me didn't like it so damn much.

Crave, crave, crave. I crave him. Crave more.

I'm on the verge of begging Stirling to take more when he's six feet away in the space of a breath.

"Get the fuck out." He's bent over, hands on his knees. "I see now why Caspian had to leave. You, Maeve Sparrow, are fucking dangerous, whoever, *whatever* you are."

"I'm not—"

"You can lie to yourself, or maybe you don't even know, yourself. But your blood can't lie. Not to the likes of me." He lurches toward me, an ungainly, ungraceful movement, aborted as he stomps a foot to stop himself in place, half a stride away from me. "Get…*OUT!*" Stirling roars the last word, infusing it with a terrifying snarl of pure fury, the roar of a caged lion teased with a meal just beyond the bars.

I run home yet again, more confused than ever.

That night, I fall into a fitful sleep, and I yearn for Caspian, because I need explanations. How could I feel that way for Stirling? Was it just pheromones? Was it merely my body responding to whatever it is his body puts out to make me ready for feeding? Or was it actually *me*? Was it a real attraction?

Caspian.

I drown in darkness.

The black void within me opens up, swallowing me whole.

Caspian. My soul calls to him, in that black empty place.

He comes to me, cloaked in shadows.

Caspian?

He's fully vampire, here. No humanity remains him—skin white as snow, hard as marble, eyes fully black, fangs nicking his lower lip.

You shouldn't be here, Maeve. You remember what happened last time.

You're here. That's all I need to know. *I'm safe with you.*

You're not.

I don't care.

He leans close to me. Inhales my scent, as if he can smell me, here. I look down, and I realize I have a body. I'm naked, yet because I'm with Caspian, it just feels right. **Wake up, Maeve.**

I step closer to him. Place my palms flat on his chest, the perfect cold burning like fire, soaking into me, suffusing me.

No.

He scents me again, his hands burying in my hair, nose ghosting over my throat, inhaling. He pulls back sharply. **Who touched you? Who fed from you?**

I can't lie—it doesn't occur to me to try, and I couldn't, even if I wanted to. The truth spills out.

Stirling. I went to your house looking for you. He…I let him. I couldn't help it, Caspian. And…I didn't really try. He didn't take much, just…a taste. And then he moved away from me and made me leave.

He stares at me for a moment, and then, inexplicably, sinks to his knees. His nose and lips brush my bare belly, then ghost to my hip; his lips are like the touch of an icicle, but the cold is delicious to me now, infusing me with re-newed arousal. I don't know what this place is, if it's real or another dimension or just a weird dream, but his touch is real enough, and my arousal is a pungent aroma.

He turns me in place so I'm facing away from him, and his hands cup my ass and his fingers paint delicate whorls on my skin.

I'm afraid.

Will he not want me, now that Stirling has touched me? I don't know that I could have stopped what hap-pened, but will that matter?

I want Caspian.

But in that house, with Stirling...my physical re-sponse was involuntary.

And deep down, I know that part of me wanted it. Liked it.

What does that say about me? Can Caspian sense that?

He presses his nose to the side of my buttock, sniff-ing. **I smell his touch on you, Maeve.**

Caspian, I—

Do not be afraid, Little Sparrow. We are not like humans. Our morals are not your morals.

You're not angry with me?

He holds my buttocks in his hands, rests his forehead on the small of my back. **In this place, I could almost feel free to make love to you. The drive to feed and to mate is different, here.**

I want you, Caspian.

His head rolls side to side, forehead against my skin—a negation. **Don't tempt me. The taste of you lin-gers in my mouth.**

Caspian, I'm going crazy without you. Can humans feel the mating frenzy like you do?

No.

Are you angry with Stirling?

This is not the place for that discussion, Maeve. It isn't safe here, even with me.

Then come to me. Be with me. Please, Caspian. I don't know if I can live without you.

He turns me in place, gazing up at me with those deep black pools, and I can feel the desire in him, I can almost smell it: sweet, silky, spicy, coppery, musky. My sex is right before his eyes, and he drops his gaze to my folds. I can feel myself soaking with arousal, can smell my desire.

Goddammit, Maeve. How can I resist you?

I don't want you to resist me. I want it all with you. Everything. I don't care about the risks.

You should.

I don't.

He growls, and his hold on my hips tightens to the point of pain, and then he looks up at me. **The scent of your need is too much for me, Maeve. The song of your blood is far too powerful.**

He vanishes.

I'm alone in the blackness, in the void space.

But then I feel warmth around me, feel pleasure suffuse me, centered on my sex. I think of my room—the nightstand with my charging phone and the lamp with the ivory shade and pull string, the color of the walls and the window seat with my book lying open, face down where I left it earlier today.

And I wake up.

Caspian is on his knees at the foot of my bed, and he's

pulled me to the edge of the bed and my legs are draped over his shoulders. He's dressed in black jeans and a black crewneck pullover sweater, hair loose, no hat, no glasses. The cold of his skin radiates through his clothes and leaches into my skin. His icy hands roam up my belly and cradle my breasts. The ice of his touch burns, beautifully. My nipples harden and ache under his touch, his fingers and thumbs rolling and pinching.

His face is buried between my thighs, and he's feasting on me. His tongue flickers, licks, slides. He told me his venom numbed, but I don't feel numb—I feel more sensitive than ever. As if the numbing has gone so deep it's inverted, the tingling of his venom making my blood rush and boil. He said it numbed and healed…so maybe the numbing effect is only the initial reaction?

I don't know.

My capacity for logical thought is eradicated as he ravages me with his lips and tongue, toying with my nipples and pinching them to the point of pain, which only heightens my pleasure.

"Caspian…oh god, god, Caspian." I reach down and sink my hands into his hair, and hold him against me, pulling him closer. "Don't stop. Please don't stop."

He growls a negative and renews his assault on my clit. I'm flung to the cusp within seconds, and then he slides a finger inside me and it's so cold, so cold, so intensely cold inside me that it burns, it aches. And that makes the pleasure all the wilder, all the more potent.

And then, I come.

At the moment of orgasm, he angles his face to the side and I feel the swipe of his tongue on the delicate silk of my upper, inner thigh, millimeters from my sex, and his fingers plunge in and out of me and his thumb presses in hard fast circles—

And I feel the pricking pressure of his fangs piercing my skin and my orgasm goes from incandescent and wild to frantic and nuclear, and I feel the rush of ecstasy as he feeds on me and I come and I come and I come, harder and harder and harder as he takes pull after pull of my blood, and I feel my heart crash and hammer and feel my blood pulse in response to his call, feel my veins themselves provide the flow and my sex throbs and my clit detonates under his thumb and my channel clenches around his slick, sliding glacial fingers and the intense cold of his touch is a wilding counterpoint to the flush of heat in my skin and the flood of my essence seeping around his fingers.

He drinks from the tender flesh of my thigh, his cheek brushing the outer lip of my sex.

One orgasm, two, ten, a thousand? I don't know.

They roll together, mingling into a stretching of time out of time, mind melted, soul delving into his touch.

There's only him.

Me.

Us.

He pulls away and licks the wound, and I feel the tingle of his venom on my skin. It buzzes in my veins. I feel it inside me, a residue of him mingled with my blood.

I'm faint, but not from blood loss.

I can't move—I'm limp, helpless.

Caspian draws me up to the head of my bed and nestles me in the pillows and covers me in my blankets. "Sleep now, Little Sparrow."

My eyes won't stay open. In between dazed, sleepy blinks, I see my alarm clock: 3:25 am. "Caspian?"

His palm cups my cheek. "Yes?"

"Do you sleep?"

"In a manner of speaking. I don't require it like you do, but I can sleep. Although it's not real sleep, as you know it. It's more like…deep meditation. And we are naturally nocturnal, anyway."

"The dreams. They *are* real. Aren't they?"

He presses his lips to my temple. I hear him inhale my scent. "We'll talk more later, Little Sparrow."

"I'm sorry about Stirling."

"Don't be." I feel the bed dip at my side as he perches there. "There is much you don't know about vampire culture. Our mores and morals, especially regarding sex and feeding, are quite different from human standards."

Vampire culture. This tickles my brain, but I'm too sleepy to make sense of it.

I can't make my brain work, can't keep my eyes open. I reach out and find him—his hand, fingers tangling with mine. "I don't know how to be without you anymore."

"That's the venom. It draws you to me. Calls you to me. It binds you to me." A pause. "And me to you."

"It's more than that. I felt it before you ever fed from me." I'm mumbling the truth, things I wouldn't normally say, but I'm half asleep and muddled by the intensity of my orgasms. "It's you. You call to me. I can feel you, too, Caspian. The Purr knows where you are."

"The purr?" He sounds confused.

"My blood. Or not my blood, I don't know." It's hard to make sense. Sleep almost has me. "Something inside me purrs whenever you're close. Same with your brothers and Alistair, but it's strongest with you."

I'm asleep then. Or, mostly.

I feel, faintly, his fingers trail over my throat, then brush my hair aside.

Sleep now, Little Sparrow.

I don't know if that's spoken aloud, or in my head, or in my dream.

Slumber takes me under, then, and I know no more.

CHAPTER 21

TIRLING IS LEANING ON THE hood of my car after school the next day; Caspian was absent yet again. I was unable to focus all day, alternating between reliving being with Caspian, touching him, feeling him, the heat of his tongue, the rush of pleasure as he fed from me…and wondering why he'd be absent today. If he is yet again trying to stay away from me, even though I thought we'd agreed that that wasn't working for either of us.

And now, here's Stirling.

Pressed black chinos, maroon suede sneakers, maroon button-down. His hair is loose today, slicked back and brushing his shoulders. Mirrored wraparound sunglasses. The diamond-encrusted cross necklace hangs in the opening of his shirt. A well-worn vintage leather satchel is slung across his chest and hanging at his left hip.

"Do you ever dress down? Like, jeans, or joggers?" I ask, by way of greeting.

"No." He pushes off the hood. "We need to talk."

I sigh. "Nothing good ever follows that statement." I unlock my car, and he gets in.

I start it and let it idle, glancing at him. "So?"

He points a finger at the exit. "Drive. You can drop me off at the college."

"Okay, then." I put the car in gear and exit the parking lot.

Once we're heading away, he swivels his head to look at me. "Caspian sent me to tell you that he had to leave. He didn't want you wondering what happened."

"Does he have a cell phone? It'd be easier if he just called or texted me instead of sending you to do his dirty work."

"None of us carry cell phones," Stirling says.

"Weird. Is that a vampire thing? Or is it just a you guys thing?"

At the word vampire, his head snaps around, and I feel his gaze. "He told you?"

I snicker. "Well, I'd figured it out for myself. I mean, the evidence was there, it was just…hard to accept. But then Caspian drank my blood from my hand and his eyes glowed, and that kind of made it impossible to ignore. You know?"

If a statue could go even more motionless, Stirling

would have accomplished it. As it is, the silence is frozen, crackling with tension. "He drank from you?"

"Three times, now." I glance at him as we pull up to the stoplight at the edge of town.

"He...*stopped*?" He sounds stunned.

"Well, clearly, seeing as I'm neither dead nor a vampire. Although I'm not really sure how that works, since Caspian said it doesn't work that way but wouldn't explain any further."

He shakes his head. "No, I mean..." he trails off, sighing. "If he's fed from you, then you're aware that for us, feeding is not merely...that there's a certain..." he trails off again, then huffs. "It's sexual, Maeve. What I'm asking is, he fed from you, but you didn't have sex?"

"What business is that of yours, Stirling?"

"It's more my business than you'd think, but it's not my place to explain that."

"You guys are all so cagey. Is there some secret I'm not supposed to know about?"

"Yes. Us."

"Like, your existence?"

"Correct."

"Well, Caspian kind of fucked that up, didn't he?"

"Indeed he did." He removes his sunglasses, holding them by the arm and spinning them between finger and thumb. His cerulean eyes find mine. "I'm also asking for your sake, Maeve. Out of concern."

"Because you lost control and nearly drank my blood? Wait, you *did*, just not a lot."

He sighs. "That shouldn't have happened."

"Why not?" I look at him, hold his gaze for a moment

before returning my attention to the road. "Because I'm with Caspian? Or because of your vampire laws?"

"Because of the laws."

"But not because I'm with Caspian?"

"That's a different topic."

"He mentioned that vampire culture has different attitudes about that stuff than human culture does."

He nods. "It's the truth." He puts his sunglasses back on. "But I'm not going to get into that right now."

I groan in frustration. "I have so many questions and no one will tell me *anything*. It's so infuriating." I turn onto the drive leading to the college campus, taking another opportunity to look at Stirling; he looks in my direction, and I feel his gaze. "How about this—I'm not going to tell you what Caspian and I have or have not done together unless you explain how your culture is different than mine."

A growl rumbles from him. "Fine." He shakes his head. "You first."

"I don't think so. I'll tell you and then you'll just clam up."

He barks a laugh. "I could say the same." A tip of his head to one side. "But very well. Because feeding is such a deeply and inherently sexual thing for us, our sense of morality in terms of sexuality is quite different. Your kind would say our standards are....looser. Unless you're bonded bloodmates, we don't feel jealousy. Sharing is considered normal."

"Sharing?" I say, unsure whether I'm alarmed, aroused, or some combination of both.

He nods. "It has to do with the aforementioned laws which regulate certain aspects of our life and culture. But yes, sharing. For one thing, it's a fiction of your popular culture that we are driven to prey on a human and drink from them till they're dead. That doesn't happen. I won't say it *never* happens, but very, very rarely. For a multitude of reasons, but primarily because it's simply…wasteful. A dead human cannot provide either blood or pleasure."

"Okay, I guess that makes sense, and I'd really like to know the rest of the reasons, but I know you're not going to tell me. So, back to sharing—how does that work?"

He stares at me for a moment. "In many different ways, Maeve. All you need to know right now is that neither he nor I find it amiss that I tasted your blood."

"Or that you had your hands all over my ass?" I ask, eyebrow raised.

"Or that."

"So I shouldn't feel bad about it either? Because to your culture, it's not considered, like…cheating?"

He shakes his head. "No, you should not."

"What's a bonded bloodmate?" I ask.

"Complicated, that's what. But you would look at it as marriage. It is taboo for someone in a bloodmating to share a host, unless both mates agree on it beforehand— what your culture terms 'an open relationship.'"

"Host?"

"It's our term for someone we feed from."

"So, there are other humans who know that vampires exist?"

Another long silence as he considers his answer. "Of course there are others."

"How can you share a host if we're not supposed to know you exist?"

"Because…well, I shouldn't speak of it."

"Who am I going to tell?"

"That's not what I'm worried about."

"What are you worried about then?"

He directs me to a particular parking lot, and we park near the back of the lot. He considers his answer again. "Because I'm not supposed to be talking about this with you. You're human. Our culture is by nature secretive and reclusive. The others of my kind would not thank me for divulging this information to a human."

I sigh. "I guess I'll let you off the hook, for now. But I can't promise I'm not going to keep pestering you guys until I get information."

"Why do you want to know?"

I shake my head, shrug. "I don't know, honestly. I just…I need to know. Just like I need Caspian. Which leads me to my original question: where is he?"

"Alistair sent him to stay with friends in New York for a few days."

"Why?"

"I wasn't sure, but now I think because of you."

My throat closes, clogs. "To keep him away from me?"

A nod. "Yes."

"That's bullshit!" I slam my palm against the steering wheel. "Is he here?" I point at the building in front of us. "Alistair—he teaches here, correct?"

"Yes, but—"

I shut the car off, grab my purse, and get out, slamming the door behind me as I head for the building.

I hear the other door close and a heartbeat later, Stirling is beside me. "Maeve, wait."

"No. I'm going to talk to Alistair."

"You don't understand—"

I stop and whirl on him, stabbing him in the chest

with my finger. "No, I don't! And I'm sick to death of being told that I don't understand, yet no one ever explains things so I *can* understand."

I start walking again—stomping, more accurately. I hear Stirling sigh behind me, and then again he's next to me. "His office is in that building over there," Stirling says, pointing to a different building than the one I'm heading for. "Third floor. He's got his office hours now, actually—fortunately for you."

"Thanks," I mutter.

"I'm not sure Alistair will give you the answers you're looking for, Maeve. Just so you're aware." He grabs my arm and pulls me to a stop. "You never held up your end of the bargain."

I roll my eyes. "Yes, he stopped. We've done other stuff, but we haven't had actual sex. Yet."

"Yet?"

"He's so determined to stay away from me, and now Alistair is trying to keep him away from me…but no one seems to care what *I* want. Which is Caspian. Since I'm the one taking whatever risk it is you guys are so afraid of, you'd think I'd get a vote on this. So yeah…*yet.*"

Stirling stares at me—he's put his glasses back on, so I can feel his gaze even if I can't see his eyes. "Maeve…" he shakes his head, trailing off. "Caspian has shown remark-able self-control and restraint with you, to a degree you cannot imagine. Eventually, however, that restraint will be eroded." Another pause. "Just…be careful of getting what you wish for." He checks the watch on his left wrist—a vin-tage luxury watch, by the looks of it. "I have to get to class. I'll see you later, Maeve."

"Stirling?"

He turns back to me. "Yes?"

"That day at your house?"

His jaw clenches. "What about it?"

I swallow hard. "I don't think I would have been the one to stop you." I lick my lips. "But I'm only human, you see. So it's a bit confusing for me."

He radiates intensity and hunger. If I could see his eyes, I know they'd be black-stained. "Maeve, you cannot possibly comprehend the temptation of you. Sitting in that car with you was torture."

"Torture?"

"To smell you?" He works his jaw, opening his mouth slightly—I catch a glimpse of his fangs before he snaps his mouth shut and hangs his head, visibly at war with himself. "I can smell your blood, now that I've tasted it."

My hands tremble, even as my thighs press together and my breasts ache, feeling swollen and heavy. "And you want it?" I lick my lips again, eyeing his mouth, my body humming madly with The Purr, the call of his venom, the siren song of his pheromone. "You want...*me?*"

"*Want*...such a paltry word for what I feel around you, Maeve Sparrow." He prowls up to me, until my breasts brush his chest and the smell of pennies stings my nose. "Have you forgotten?"

"For—forgotten what?" I stammer.

My hands knot in his shirt, wrinkling it. I'm shaking all over, and not only with the innate, instinctual fear that floods me, but with desire. Need. Desperation.

"If I were to lose control and feed from you, Maeve... you know what would happen." His voice is dark, low, heavy with promise.

My core pulses with heat and I feel myself getting

slippery, dripping with arousal—I see his nostrils flare, and I know he smells it.

"You are the most dangerous female I've ever encountered." He steps back. "You'll be the death of us all."

With that last, ominous statement, he pivots sharply on his heel and strides away, his gait stiff and rushed and angry.

I watch him until he vanishes into a building, and then I take a moment to collect myself, slowing my breathing, pushing away the residual tremors of arousal. When I feel like myself again, I head for the building Stirling pointed out to me. I find Alistair Taylor's office on the third floor; his door is open, and he's sitting behind a large blonde wood desk cluttered and littered with stacks of papers and open books and a large computer monitor and a phone and a mug of pens and pencils. It's the desk of a busy professor. He's got his pipe clenched in his teeth, but it's unlit; he's wearing what appear to be reading glasses, and he's reading a student's paper, occasionally circling or scribbling or underlining with a red felt tip pen.

He doesn't look up as I pause in the doorway. "Come in, Miss Sparrow. Have a seat." He indicates the two chairs angled toward his desk with the pen. "I'll be with you in a minute."

I sit and try not to fidget as he finishes the paper, writing a large B+ on the top right of the front page, circling it, and then capping the pen.

He removes the glasses and tosses them onto the desk. "How may I help you, Miss Sparrow?"

I look at his glasses. "Do you need those?" I point at them. "I didn't think v—" I cut off and glance over my shoulder at the door behind me, still open. "I didn't think…*your kind*…needed reading glasses." I whisper the phrase "your kind."

He smirks, amused. "My kind?"

"Yes. You, Fin, Stirling, and Caspian. You know. What you are. Your, um, dietary preference."

He snickers, giving me a droll look. "Dietary preference, hmm?"

"I'm trying to be discreet."

He nods, toys with the glasses. "No, I don't need them. But they lend a certain…authenticity."

"Like the pipe? And the tweed jackets?"

He sniffs a laugh. "The pipe I simply enjoy. I like the taste. And seeing as, unlike…*your kind*…I cannot be adversely affected by the smoke, I indulge." He smiles at me. "The tweed jackets are simply…a stylistic choice. I'm sure you've noticed that the four of us all have a certain preference for older things. It's rather common among…those of us with our specific dietary *requirements*. Because it's not a preference, Miss Sparrow. It's a necessity. It's the way we're born. We can no more change it than you can grow gills and breathe underwater."

"Born? You're…born? I thought—"

He holds up a hand to stop me. "This is neither time nor the place for this conversation, Miss Sparrow."

I let out a sound that's half sigh and half growl. "I didn't ask to be pulled into your orbit, Alistair. But I am, and now that I am aware of certain truths, I can't be asked to simply forget. And I think I'm owed some sort of explanation, don't you?" I fling a hand in an aggravated gesture. "It's like pulling teeth to get any of you to give me the slightest bit of information about things that now directly concern me. I am *owed* an explanation, Alistair." I lower my voice to barely above a whisper. "I know you guys are vampires. But that's…I need to know more. A *lot* more."

He nods. "I quite agree, as a matter of fact. Why don't you join us for dinner this evening. Say nine?"

"Dinner at nine?" I skip over the oddity of being invited to dinner by a vampire. I'm used to having more questions than answers at this point.

"I'm sure one of the boys has informed you that we are by nature nocturnal."

"Oh, right. Yeah, Caspian mentioned that. Although he also said you don't sleep as I would understand it."

He gives me an expression which translates to *well, sort of.* "I will provide you with a thorough explanation of our race and our culture." He pauses, his deep, dark brown eyes searching me. "I hope it goes without saying that we are relying on your continued discretion, Miss Sparrow. By which I mean, saying *nothing* of any of this to *anyone.*"

"Of course—it goes without saying." I give him a smirk. "I mean, who'd believe me anyway?"

He nods, his expression serious. "That is a rather significant part of the reason we are able to remain out of the eye of public, general awareness. There are other factors, of course, which I will divulge to you this evening." He shoots his cuff to glance at his watch. "Now, if there's nothing else, Miss Sparrow, I have more papers to finish grading."

"One other thing."

He smiles, kind yet amused. "You want Caspian to return."

"Yes. And if you say a single word about it being for my protection…" I trail off, hoping the threat—which I haven't quite determined—is clear.

He taps the stack of papers to be graded with the cap

of the felt tip pen. "I know that's not what you want to hear, but it really is the truth."

"I know you believe that, but if it's the truth, I deserve the whole truth. And I don't want to hear it without Caspian present."

"Dinner tomorrow, then, rather than tonight. I'll give Caspian a call and have him return early." He smiles. "His trip there was business, however, not punishment—for you or him."

"Business?"

"He's not *actually* a high school student, Maeve, you realize that, yes?"

I blink. "I, um…no, actually, that hadn't occurred to me."

"We have a variety of business ventures in various places, and one of them in New York required attention. None of the rest of us could get away from our duties here, so it went to Caspian." He smiles at me again. "I'll explain at dinner tomorrow, I promise."

I stand up. "Thank you, Alistair."

"My pleasure, Miss Sparrow."

I head home, but my body operates on autopilot while my mind whirls with questions. Not really a high school student. Meaning…what? The inference as I understand it is that he's older than he appears.

They're vampires. Dead, or undead, or something I have neither the words nor the understanding to wrap my brain around—they either don't age, or age slowly.

How old is Caspian?

How old is Alistair?

You are the most dangerous female I've ever encountered. You'll be the death of us all.

What did Stirling mean by that? How am *I* danger-ous? He's a vampire, for god's sake. Can they die? Alistair implied they can't get sick, but what about pop culture regarding vampires? Garlic, stakes through the heart, silver, crosses? Obviously, crosses aren't hazardous to them, since Stirling wears one around his neck every day.

And how can I, a mere human, be dangerous to *them*?

A thought percolates at the back of my mind: Caspian and Stirling have both made statements that they think or suspect that I'm somehow more than I realize. But…what? I'm not a vampire…

So many questions, so few answers.

And woven through all of it is the pounding, beating, raging heartbeat that is my desire and need for Caspian. For his touch. His fangs in my skin and the heat of pleasure as he drinks from me and his skin under my hands and our pleasures releasing…

I shut down that line of thinking before I get carried away.

I refuse to think about how turned on I got by Stirling, earlier. I refuse to wonder about vampire culture's tendency to *share* hosts…meaning, in this case, me. If Stirling and Caspian could or would share me.

Holy fuck.

Both of them drinking from me at the same time?

I was trying not to think about that, but now the thought is planted in my brain and it won't budge.

I couldn't do that. Couldn't allow it.

Could I?

A tiny, confused, traitorous voice in the pit of my soul whispers the answer I know to be the truth:

Yes, I could.

Chapter 22

Andreas leans against the doorframe of the bathroom, watching me curl my hair. "So, dinner with the Taylors, huh?"

I pull the curling iron away and drape the spiral of hair just so, then wrap another tendril around the iron and clamp it in place. "Dinner at the Taylors." I meet his eyes in the mirror. "You okay with that?"

He shrugs. "Sure. Never met any of them, but a colleague of mine's wife is a professor at the college where Alistair Taylor works. Says he's quite a character."

"Oh, he is. The whole family is very interesting."

"You seem to be pretty close to them."

I shrug. "Yeah, I guess so." I hold his eyes again as I curl another strand. "Caspian and I are…a thing, I guess you could say. We haven't put any labels on it yet, but we have a thing."

"You have a thing." He smirks. "How is that different from just saying he's your boyfriend?"

"Technicalities, labels…we spend time together, we care for each other. Putting a label on it is just not a priority, I guess."

He scuffs the tile with a socked toe. "I know we don't have a typical father-daughter relationship, and I know you're eighteen—"

"Nineteen next month. My birthday is March 9th, by the way." I grin. "In case you wanted to get me something."

"Do you want a party?"

I wrinkle my nose. "Maybe a get-together. I don't know about a party. Anyway, I'm mostly just teasing." I finish curling my hair and set the iron on the edge of the vanity, arranging my hair so the spirals sit the way I want them to. "You were about to say something super awkward and embarrassing about using protection?"

He coughs into a fist, hiding a choked laugh. "Yeah… is that a conversation we need to have?"

I turn around and face him, patting him on the shoulder. "You're relieved of that duty, Andy. Mom had that talk with me a long time ago."

"And you don't need me to supply you with—"

I breeze past him. "Nope! Got it covered, Andy."

"When will you be back?" He calls as I head into my room to spritz perfume and put on my shoes and jacket.

"Late. Very late, probably. They're all night owls."

"Are they picking you up or are you driving?" He says this from my doorway.

I sigh, a soft, quiet one, straightening with one shoe on. "Andy, I'm okay. I appreciate your concern, but I'm okay. I know what I'm doing."

"I took responsibility for you, Maeve. It's a responsibility I take seriously, okay? People aren't always what they seem, and you're going to dinner with four men, none of whom I know."

"Would it make you feel better if you met them?" I ask, fitting on my other heel, working the straps and rising from the bed—I test my balance on the three-inch wedges.

"Maybe a little. But if at the very least you could text me and let me know you're okay, and if you felt super generous, when you'd be home, I'd be able to relax a little better."

Oh, Andreas. You have no clue. You'd have an apoplexy if you knew the truth.

I remember the dream I had when I first met him, and I wonder if he knows more than he's letting on. But if he did and he's assuming I don't, then he can't tell me. And if he doesn't, I can't tell him. Quite an impasse, actually.

I spritz perfume and step through the cloud, then squirt a dab onto my wrists, smear it—I'm about to touch it to my throat like normal when I stop. Will the scent of perfume on my throat bother Caspian, if he were to want to drink from me? Would it alter the taste? I opt to rub the perfume onto my cleavage instead, just in case.

I check my appearance in the mirror on the closet door. I'm wearing a simple little black dress, figure-hugging, cut at an asymmetrical angle so the hem rakes from above my mid-left thigh to below my right knee. The neckline is a deep V, revealing a decent amount of cleavage; judicious use of double-sided boob tape keeps the girls in place. My shoes are ruby red wedges with delicate, intricate straps. The dress is something I took from Mom's closet. Before moving here, I went through her wardrobe and kept a few of my favorite pieces. A lot of her wardrobe was far more mature than I feel comfortable wearing…not really old lady clothes, just business professional grown woman clothes, and I'm an eighteen-year-old high school student. I kept some nice LBDs, like the one I'm wearing, some shoes, a couple of jean jackets, and a handful of other pieces. Partially because they're nice clothes but mostly because they connect me to Mom.

My grief still seems clogged up way down deep, because while I miss her more than words can express, I still don't seem capable of properly grieving her.

Maybe it's cowardly of me, maybe it's cold-hearted of me, but it's just easier to…shove it all aside, accept that I can't grieve, and keep going one day at a time. Put my focus on school…and Caspian.

Hopefully someday I can grieve her the way she deserves. I just hope she knows, wherever she is, that I love her and I miss her and I wish like hell that I knew what really happened. Because a part of me just doesn't believe it was the car accident the police claim. I just…I can't go there. I can't start looking into it. I wouldn't know where to start, anyway.

A horn honks outside, jarring me from my thoughts.

Andreas is still in my doorway. "Guess that's your ride, huh?"

I blow out a breath, and then shrug into Mom's jacket—a worn black leather motorcycle jacket with heavy silver zipper pulls down the center and on pockets at each breast, with a dangling strap around the waist. "Sorry, lost in thought." I gesture at myself with a sweep of one hand. "Mom's dress, Mom's jacket. Made me think of her."

His expression is equal parts sad and compassionate. "Well, she'd be proud. You're a truly gorgeous young woman, Maeve."

"Thanks, Andy." I pause in front of him, and then give in to impulse—I kiss his cheek. "I'll check in later, okay?"

He clears his throat. "That'd be great. Have fun, kiddo."

Wonder of wonders, I don't trip on the way down the stairs. Come to think of it, I haven't tripped, fallen, or otherwise had any kind of clumsy accident in…a long time.

I put that thought aside and go out to the front circle where Caspian is waiting for me in his big gray truck. When he sees me descending the porch steps, he exits the truck and beelines for me.

He's warm, his eyes bright and brown. He pulls me to him, inhaling my scent, nose in my hair. "Fuck, I missed you."

"You've fed." I rest my chin on his chest and gaze up at him. "Should I be jealous?"

He smirks down at me. "No. We have ways of acquiring sustenance that doesn't depend on human interaction."

"Well now I have about a billion questions."

I lift up and touch my lips to his—immediately, he curls me closer with a hand low on my back, nearly on my ass, his mouth fusing to mine, tongue sweeping through my lips.

I pull away with a laugh. "Andreas is watching. Let's not get carried away." I wipe at his lips, where my lipstick left a red smear.

He nods and steps back from me. "You are so fucking beautiful it almost hurts to look at you, Maeve."

I blush, duck my head. "Thank you, Caspian."

He opens my door for me and hands me up and in, waiting until I've settled in the seat with my purse on my lap before closing the door. Once he's behind the wheel, he puts it in gear and buckles at the same time.

"I'd think you wouldn't bother with a seatbelt," I remark, buckling in as well.

He shrugs. "I don't need to. But it's the law, and it's not worth the hassle of being pulled over, so we wear seatbelts. Plus, I may not be harmed by being thrown through a windshield, but it's still not fun."

"Have you been?"

"Thrown through a windshield?" He asks, and I nod. "No, this was my first time. I've been in other accidents, however."

"Can you feel pain?"

"Depends." He taps his forearm. "I would feel pain right now because I'm blooded and alive."

"Blooded?"

"Fed, but we say blooded. Freshly blooded—not five minutes before coming here. So yeah, I can feel pain. If I'm unblooded, no, I wouldn't."

"So, let me see if I'm understanding this right. When you're freshly blooded, you're more…human?"

"I am human, Maeve. Meaning, our base DNA is the same as yours. It's just…different. So I'm always human, I'm just a very, very different race of human." He glances at me. "When I'm blooded, I'm more *alive*."

"You're a vampire."

"But vampires are human. All vampires are human,

but not all humans are vampires. Like that thing about squares and rectangles, right? I'm a type of human."

"So how do you differentiate between humans like me, and vampire humans like you?"

"We call your kind mortals."

"As opposed to?"

He glances at me. "Immortals."

"You're immortal?"

"Yes."

I swallow hard. "So you're…not eighteen."

He shakes his head. "I'm not eighteen."

"How old *are* you, then?"

He hesitates. "Maybe we should save some of your questions for Alistair."

"Caspian." I take his hand, weave my fingers with his. "How old are you?"

He sighs. "It's going to freak you out."

"Have I freaked out at any point yet?" I rub the back of his hand with my thumb. "I think I've taken all this re-markably well, you know. Like, finding out you're a vam-pire and you drink blood and you can turn me on with your pheromones? That's freak-out-worthy. Finding out how old you are seems…minor, in comparison."

He huffs a laugh. "You have a point." He glances at me as he turns off of Andreas's driveway onto the road. "I was born in 1784, in Baltimore."

I choke on my breath. "You…You're—" I do the math, or try to.

"Two-hundred and thirty-nine." He fills in, assess-ing me.

"Holy shit." I'm stunned.

I don't know what I was expecting, but the truth makes my head spin.

"You're two hundred and forty years old?" I attempt to wrap my head around it. "You were alive for the end of the Revolutionary War?"

He nods. "That's part of the history Alistair is going to give you this evening, but yes." He brings my hand to his mouth and kisses my knuckles, then sniffs my wrist. "You smell good."

"Perfume, " I mumble, my voice faint.

He sniffs, leaning toward me. "You put it on your cleavage?"

"I didn't want to put it on my throat. In case, you know…it would, um, taste bad."

He brakes abruptly, lurching me forward in my seat. He stares at me a moment, and then bursts into uproarious laughter, laughing so hard he collapses against the steering wheel.

I want to laugh with him because it's awkward not to, but I don't know why he's laughing. "I don't understand what's so funny, Caspian."

He draws in a breath, composing himself. "Sorry, sorry. I just…the fact that you actually considered that is…" he shakes his head, wiping his face with his palms. "It's incredible."

"But why is it so funny?"

He starts driving again, pulling onto their driveway. "It does affect the taste, and quite significantly and negatively. If the perfume is strong enough, it can put us off our appetite." He glances at me. "Lore says that's why mortal women put their perfume on their throats: to ward off evil…us."

"I've never heard that before."

"Certain things have been…suppressed….from public mortal awareness. That falls into the category of things Alistair had better explain though." He shakes his head again, chuckling. "You have no sense of self-preservation, do you?"

"Of course I do. I'm just not afraid of you. I absolutely trust that you'll never harm me."

"You just…any other mortal female would be more scared of having a vampire's fangs in her throat, and here you're worrying that your perfume will make you taste bad…for *me.*"

"I've never been normal, Caspian."

His gaze is speculative. "No, indeed. All the better for me, I must say." He parks his truck in a line with the others but pauses before getting out. "One thing I should tell you—in my culture, I'm a juvenile. A teenager. Same as you. Our age and maturity standards are, obviously, quite different from mortals'. But a vampire is considered to have reached the age of maturity at three hundred. So according to those standards, Stirling still has another decade before he's reached it, Fin has twenty-two more years, and I have sixty-one."

"So, even though you're two-hundred and twenty years older than me…"

"We're at similar levels of…maturity? Development?" He shrugs.

"So there are…vampire babies?"

He nods. "Yes, and I was one."

"Which means…"

He holds up a hand. "Alistair will explain it. Because the answer to the questions I see you heading toward do in fact directly involve you, and why we're all so concerned about you in terms of your and my relationship."

"So many questions, Caspian. So many."

He leans in and kisses me. "Let's go in and have dinner."

I slide out of the truck and I've got one foot on the step when a thought halts me in my tracks. "Wait a damn minute." I turn and look at Caspian, who is behind me... enjoying watching me ascend the stairs, I'm assuming. "This is a dinner party...with one mortal female and four vampire males."

He arches an eyebrow at me. "Yes...?"

"Am *I* the dinner?"

He hangs his head and laughs. "Jesus, you're funny today. No, Maeve. Dinner is steak au poivre, with garlic mashed potatoes, grilled asparagus, dinner rolls, and a tossed salad." He grins. "And a couple bottles of excellent Bordeaux."

I blink at him. "Steak?"

"When we're freshly blooded, as all four of us are, we can and do enjoy eating normal human food."

"And wine?"

"A good red wine is the closest thing to blood that you can get, Maeve."

"I'm not twenty-one."

He shrugs. "So? We're all very old world, and to us, you're plenty mature enough to have a glass of wine or two with dinner. Just don't tell Andreas, he may not understand."

I nod, and we continue up the steps onto the porch. "Wait. If you can eat regular food when you're blooded... does your body process it normally? Like...what if your body runs out of blood or whatever while you still have food in your system?"

He snickers. "Yes, we process it normally. In the scenario you suggest, our bodies will resume processing it once we've fed again. Till then, it's just…dormant, I suppose."

"And if you're not blooded…"

"We would no more eat mortal food than you would go outside and eat grass. Eating mortal food is…an indulgence. Something to do socially, for enjoyment. We don't require it, and we don't do it very often. Feeling full in that way can be somewhat off-putting at best. And being full of mortal food while unblooded is quite unpleasant." He grins. "Not to mention, the inconvenience and indignity of dealing with the waste is…gauche at best, in many circles."

I snort. "I see." I glance at him as he opens the door for me. "So vampires poop."

He chuckles. "If we must. One doesn't discuss such things, however. Something you should know—as a culture, we vampires are quite vain. Appearance, dignity, reputation…they're vitally important to us. So while for mortals it's considered impolite to discuss such things in most situations—other than with, perhaps, direct and immediate family or close friends—for us, it's not just impolite, it's downright…" he trails off, shaking his head. "It's just not done."

Inside, the home is warm and smells of cooking meat and garlic. The fire is roaring—no gas logs here, just good old-fashioned split wood. There's a brass rack piled high with split logs, and a stand containing a poker, tongs, and a shovel. I hear conversation in the kitchen—Alistair, Fin, and Stirling.

Alistair comes out of the kitchen as Caspian is helping me with my coat. He's dressed in a pair of khaki chinos with a white button-down, no shoes, just a pair of black dress socks. He's got a white apron on over his clothing, a pair of cooking tongs in one hand a glass of rich red wine in the other.

"Maeve, welcome, welcome." He glides over to me and leans in—he smells faintly of pennies and strongly of wine as he does a European double cheek kiss. With him, though, it's not an air kiss but a light, brief touch of warm dry lips to my cheeks, left then right. "Dinner is almost done. Come into the kitchen with us while we finish up."

He glides away back into the kitchen, and I glance at Caspian, whispering. "Is he…"

"We don't indulge in wine very often, so it doesn't take much to get us tipsy." Caspian hangs my coat on the intricately carved newel of the banister, and my purse near it on the stairs. "Come on."

He leads me by the hand into the kitchen, where the three males work together in harmony and efficiency which speaks of long practice. Alistair is sipping wine and working at the six-burner luxury gas range, on which thick ribeye steaks sizzle away in several cast iron pans. At the island, Stirling is tossing a salad with wood utensils; a glass of wine is near to hand, the surface gently swirling as if he just put it down. He's dressed as ever: black dress slacks and hunter green button-down under a charcoal vest; he too has removed his shoes. Fin is on the other side of the island, brushing the tops of dinner rolls with melted butter; he's the most casually dressed, in distressed jeans, barefoot, with yellow polo. Caspian is somewhere between Fin and Stirling in fashion, I've decided, dressier than Fin but not as much so as Stirling—he's wearing dark wash jeans and a crisp white button down with classic Timberland boots.

"Fin, would you pour Miss Sparrow a glass, please?" Alistair says.

Fin grins at me as he pulls a glass from a cabinet and pours a glass. "Here you go." He angles close to me…in my personal space, clogging my field of vision and filling my nostrils with the cloying, addictive scent of pennies and wine.

I take a sip—it's rich, lush. I'm no wine expert by any means, but this tastes expensive. "Thank you."

I set the goblet on the counter as Fin scents the air, his nose a hair's breadth from my cheek. "I like your perfume." His brown eyes are merry, teasing…intensely suggestive. "Although your natural scent is fuckin' delicious."

The Purr *really* likes Fin's proximity, likes his compliments, likes his pheromonal secretions.

"Fin." This is Caspian. "Knock it off."

My thighs press together and my breasts feel heavy, my nipples tight and hard and tingling. He's too close. Huge, brawny, powerful. Desire pulses in my veins, rages through me like wildfire. I'm seconds from climbing his massive frame and begging him to do things to me, to feed from me, to sink his fangs into my throat and—

I'm pulled away from Fin, Caspian's arms wrapped around me from behind, one around my chest and the other around my belly. "Fin, I said knock it the fuck off."

Fin's eyes are blacked out, fangs extended; if possible, he seems even larger, more intimidating, more like a feral predator. "Taste you…" he snarls, voice inhuman and sepulchral. "Feel your warmth. Make you *scream*."

Chapter 23

IN TAKES A STEP TOWARD ME, AND Caspian yanks me farther away. "Stirling, Alistair. A little help?"

They both move to Fin, one on either side, holding him back. They're both straining visibly, black staining the edges of their vision as they work to keep him back.

Alistair is murmuring in his ear, words I can't make out.

Slowly, the black in Fin's eyes recedes and the taut tension of his mighty muscles goes lax, and then he hangs his head for a moment, sagging into Alistair's and Stirling's hold. Then, he lifts his head and his eyes seek mine.

"Jesus, Maeve. I'm…I'm sorry. I don't know what the hell came over me."

I pull out of Caspian's hold and cross over to Fin. I lean up and wrap my arms around his neck and cling tightly. "There's nothing to be sorry for, Fin. Nothing happened."

I hear and feel him sniff my hair, and he growls again. "It's your scent. Something about you is fuckin'…" he shakes his head and gently but firmly sets me a few feet away from him. "Like some sort of goddamn catnip for vampires." He narrows his eyes at me, perplexed. "You're still here. You hugged me."

"Would you have drained me?" I ask.

"What?" He's shocked by the very suggestion. "Of course not. That's not how it works."

"I'm starting to get a handle on how it does work, Fin," I say, edging closer; the others have let him go but are still standing shoulder to shoulder with him, and I feel Caspian behind me. "You wouldn't hurt me. Just like Caspian hasn't hurt me."

He glances over my shoulder at Caspian. "Brass balls on this one, man."

"No kidding," Caspian says.

Alistair reaches out and places a hand on my arm, leans in. "Please do not be alarmed, Miss Sparrow. I just need to…" his nose nuzzles my throat, behind my ear, my hair.

He pulls away, spins on a heel, hands braced on his hips, head hanging as he sucks in deep, calming breaths. After a moment, he turns around, and while his eyes are clear, I see minute tendrils of black receding into the corners of his eyes.

"I can explain what's going on, to a degree," he says. "You are perplexing, indeed, Miss Sparrow."

"Call me Maeve, please."

He nods, formally. "Very well, Maeve." He gestures at the island. "Let's get dinner served and we can talk while we eat."

A few minutes later, the food is plated and arranged on the long dining room table; Alistair sits at the head, with Stirling on his right and Fin on his left, Caspian beside Fin, and me across from Caspian, next to Stirling. The room is lit by several large candelabra of wax-dripping candles, lending a close, intimate feel. We all dig in immediately—the food is some of the best I've ever had, the steak juicy and cooked perfectly medium, the potatoes, asparagus, and salad all also done to perfection.

"This is incredible, Alistair," I say.

He smiles at me, placing his fork and steak knife on the sides of his plate. "Thank you, Maeve." He regards me curiously. "Did you discuss with Caspian his status as a high school student, by any chance?"

"You mean the fact that he's almost two hundred and forty years old?"

Alistair's smile broadens into a grin. "Yes, quite. Well, I happen to be five hundred years old. I was born in London in fifteen-twenty-one and emigrated to America in the late sixteen hundreds with a few others from my London coven. My point in telling you this is that when one has hundreds of years in which to practice, one becomes quite adept at things, such as cooking. Even for someone who doesn't regularly eat food."

I boggle at him. "Fifteen-twenty-one. So, like, you were alive at the same time as Shakespeare?"

He nods, sipping wine. "I was. In fact, I knew him quite well. He was a rather unpleasant fellow, if I'm being honest. Rather poor hygiene, even for that era, and was quite scatterbrained. He was a genius, however, and one of the most remarkable literary minds of all human history. Having a conversation with him, however, was…well, rather impossible. He would cease speaking abruptly and just leave, mumbling to himself because he thought of a line of poetry or a piece of dialogue for a new play."

"You *knew* William Shakespeare?"

"We drank wine together quite frequently. I was a regular patron of an inn near the Globe Theater."

I shake my head, having a hard time comprehending that kind of lifespan. "That's incredible."

"If you appreciate literature, Maeve, I've a few collector's items you may be interested in viewing, after dinner." He grins. "Such as a folio of William's original manuscripts."

"Shut…up," I breathe. "You do not."

"I do. I am rather averse to lying." He laughs quietly, cutting a piece of steak. "They would be worth a fortune on the mortal market, I'm sure, but seeing as they were given to me as gifts by William himself, I'm loathe to part with them. Or divulge their existence, if I'm being honest."

"I would love to see them."

He nods. "After dinner, then."

We eat in silence for a few more minutes; I'm on my second glass of wine and feeling warm and buzzed and blissfully happy.

"Well." Alistair pushes his empty plate away, draws his wine closer, producing his pipe and going about filling, tamping, and lighting. Once it's puffing away, he eyes me. "The answers you're so keen on getting, Maeve."

"Please," I say. "Caspian told me a few pieces, Stirling a few others, but…" I shrug, shake my head. "There's so much I want to know."

His cheeks hollow as he pulls on the pipe, and then he blows a thin plume of pungent, sweet gray smoke toward the ceiling, his eyes cast to the ceiling in thought. "I suppose I simply start at something like the beginning. First, with an obvious statement. Stirling, Fin, Caspian, and I are vampires. You know this, by now. Which means vampires do in fact exist. There are three races of immortals: vampires, shapeshifters—which you would know as werewolves, but never use that word around one or you'll be dead faster than you can blink, as it is a derogatory term—and fae. All three of these immortal races can be found all over the planet, now, today, and even in this very area, as evidenced by our presence. You were not, until meeting Caspian, aware of the existence of immortals, I take it."

I shake my head. "Obviously not."

"That is intentional, and I'll explain why not. But first, we should clear up a few misconceptions. We are not savage, mindless beasts who fall upon their prey and drink their blood until they're dead. We are not created by another vampire as in popular fiction, and nor can we be killed by garlic, or crosses, or any of that nonsense. We have reflections. A stake through the heart would not kill us, either."

I frown. "It wouldn't?"

"No. If a vampire is fully, freshly blooded, it would incapacitate him or her for a time, but it wouldn't cause death. If you were to strike an unblooded vampire in the heart with a wooden stake, the stake would simply break, and you would be very swiftly ripped to pieces."

"So what *can* kill you? Like you plural, not you in particular?" I ask.

He smiles. "Clearly. I would hope I haven't offended you to the point of wishing me dead. Decapitation is one of the only methods. There are certain magics which can kill us—fae magic. A powerful adult shifter could possibly kill us, but it would be quite a battle. Other than that, nothing."

"Fae magic?" I shake my head. "You're only introducing more questions, Alistair. There are fae, and they have magic?"

He smiles kindly. "Patience." He puffs, exhales, and sips wine, then continues. "Most of what mortals believe about our kind, as evidenced in popular culture, is wrong. It's lore, it's mythology, it's wishful thinking, and it's wrong. The most erroneous belief is that we are created by another vampire—in one popular source, a human is drained to the point of death, and then fed the parent vampire's blood. There *is* a kernel of truth to this, as this *will* create an undead blood-drinker, but it would *not* be a vampire, it would be a Nosferatu—the true source of your mortal myths regarding savage, feral, mindless blood-drinking monsters. To create a Nosferatu is among the most heinous crimes one can commit, in our culture." He puffs again. "Vampires are *born*. We have our own peculiar anatomy, genetics, family structure, politics, lore, history, and art. And we are immortal, unless killed by one of the aforementioned methods, which happens very, very rarely. Lately, at least."

I consider what he's telling me. "You're *born*. Like, to a mother and a father? I mean, Caspian, on the way here, did confirm that there are vampire babies, but…it's hard to wrap my head around all this."

"This is where the telling gets touchy. There is a certain

balance to nature, as I'm sure you're aware. And that is true regarding the existence of us immortals. We are infinitely faster and stronger than mortals, we cannot be killed by nearly anything, we can see perfectly in the dark—we are in fact the perfect predator. Shifters are similar, in that they can run faster and jump higher, they are stronger even than vampires, physically, they are remarkably impervious to pain and damage, and it's nearly as difficult to kill them as it is us. And, they can turn into a predator—lions, tigers, bears, panthers, wolverines, lynxes, bobcats…I've even heard of a group somewhere in South America who can turn into hundred-foot-long constrictors. And their animal form is significantly larger than the normal version. As in, double the size, usually. So a shifter in wolf form is usually around the size of a small horse, rather than a merely large canine.

"Then, there are the fae," he continues. "Rather than being strong, they are lithe, graceful, and quick—Caspian tells me you were witness to his ability to leave no footstep, to leap from tree to tree. Well, a fae would make him look like the clumsiest lumbering mortal. What's more, they wield magic. Glamours, they call them, which can be anything from rendering themselves invisible to manipulating physical elements such as plants, water, or fire. They can trick mortals, manipulate their minds, bend them to their will. They can enter and walk in the dreams of a sentient being. They can bend the laws of physics, especially in terms of architecture. The list is endless, and is limited only by the creativity of the fae in question and his or her capacity for vitality—the power which gives them their magic."

"Holy shit," I breathe.

"Quite." He takes a long sip of wine. "The balance,

then. To balance out this power given to us immortals, we have two significant weaknesses. One, we must draw our life source from another being. Vampires, obviously, drink blood. I'll go into the details of that later. Shapeshifters I am not very familiar with, as they are intensely and violently reclusive. They eschew mortal society at all costs, and most mortals will have never encountered one—and if they have, they won't have realized it. And they should count themselves lucky to have escaped the meeting, from what I understand. Shifters value privacy and space more than anything. They live in self-sustaining off-grid compounds in remote, rural areas. But, my understanding of shifters is that they too draw some sort of energy from mortals, like we vampires draw blood and like fae draw vitality. Whatever it is and however they draw it, they use it to enable their ability to shift into their animal form, and cannot shift without it. Fae draw what they term vitality— the raw energy of life. That spark of life and consciousness which animates all living beings, and they use it to work their glamours. Now, what you must understand is that for all three types of immortal, this drawing of energy is a biological imperative. We vampires *must* drink blood to live, and the same applies to the other kinds. We won't die without it, but existence is agony. It's misery unbearable and complete. We *must*."

He takes a pause, sipping wine and then spending a moment or two puffing on his pipe. The others are all finished with their dinners and are sipping wine and listening, and watching my reactions intensely.

Alistair continues, then. "For vampires, living without blood is…I can't compare it to anything. We are driven to drink, to feed. I assume it is the same for the other types—they can't live without shifting, or working glamours."

"I guess that makes sense. What's the other drawback?"

"Reproduction. And this is where it begins to concern you, Miss Sparrow—Maeve, pardon me." A heavy sigh, a sip of wine. "We cannot reproduce with our own species. A vampire cannot produce a vampire through mating. The same applies to shifters and fae."

I blink, momentarily speechless. "Wait…*what*? What fucking sense does that make?"

"We tend to agree, as you might imagine." He says this with an amused smirk, which quickly fades. "We do mate with our own kind, forming bonds and families, engaging in sex for the sake of emotional connection and physical pleasure…but children can only be created via a mortal host."

I sit back in the chair, pushing curls away from my eyes, and take a fortifying sip of wine. "Seriously?"

A slow nod. "That is why blood drinking is such a sexual thing. As I said earlier, vampires are the perfect predator. We see perfectly in the dark, we can cloak ourselves in shadow, and we can move without a sound or leaving tracks. When we have located and chosen our prey, we exude a powerful pheromone which causes sexual excitement and desire—so intense that it is all but uncontrollable. It can even cause a kind of hypnosis, which you experienced with Fin before dinner."

"So…it's not me?"

"Well, I think you're a unique case, actually. In most mortals, however, no. It's a direct result of the pheromones we secrete—which we can control and direct, to a limited degree."

"Wait, you can do it, like, on purpose?"

He nods. "Indeed." He gestures with the stem of his pipe. "Go stand in the kitchen, on the far side, but within direct line of sight of me." A glance at Caspian. "Attend her, if you will."

I push my chair back and go to the far side of the kitchen, and Caspian stands behind me as he did before, an arm across my chest just above my breasts and the other low over my belly, possessive and affectionate.

We're about twenty feet away. Alistair sucks on his pipe, blows smoke. Holds his wine in the other hand. The only hint that he's doing anything is a slight crinkling of the corners of his eyes.

I feel it, all at once, like a tidal wave rushing over me. The tingling of my skin, first, and then my skin tightens around my bones, and my breasts go swollen and heavy and my nipples tighten and my core heats and begins seeping with my essence and my hands shake and my thighs press together and I want him, I need to go to him, sit on his lap and nuzzle his chest and offer him my throat and feel his skin and give him everything—

Caspian's arm tightens around me, holding me back. "Maeve. Breathe."

I suck in a breath and my head clears, and the physical symptoms of arousal fade to nothing. Alistair is bent over the table, gripping the carved arms of his chair until I hear wood crack and snap. He's growling, low, ravenous.

"That was a mistake," he rumbles, after a moment. "I underestimated *your* influence on *me*, it would appear."

"*My* influence?" I ask.

"There is something unique about you about which I cannot pinpoint or explain, but you are…you're intoxicating. You exude your own kind of pheromone in response to ours, I suspect. It's like the mating frenzy, but you're human." He looks at me, and his eyes aren't cleared yet, still heavily stained by the inhuman black. "As far as we know."

"If I'm not a mortal, I don't know what I am. I don't have magic, I can't shapeshift, and I don't drink blood."

Although…that day on the lane here, with Caspian. I *did* manage to lighten my footsteps. And I *do* seem able to enter some weird dreamspace which mortals usually cannot, as I'm given to understand it.

I say none of this, however. Because I'm a human. I'm mortal.

Right?

Of course.

Alistair lets out a breath. "Come, sit. I'm quite myself again." He smiles at me as I take my seat once more. "I've felt it around you, of course, but…never like that. My pheromonal release somehow triggered something in you, and caused me to nearly go into a mating frenzy of my own."

"Caspian explained a little about the mating frenzy," I say.

Alistar's hand trembles, causing the wine in his goblet to shiver in wobbling concentric circles. "Then allow me to elaborate. When we need to feed, we feel arousal—feeding is an intimate experience. You taste the whole of the person—her thoughts, her desires, her memories, her emotions, the flavor of the individual. It's quite sexual in and of itself. Add in the biological factor that when we prepare to feed, we cause sexual excitement in our host, which functions to lessen the fear response, muddle the memory of the experience, and dull any sense of unpleasantness or pain, and you have a recipe for a sexual encounter. So when we feed, it comes with sex. Not always penetrative, mind you. To us, penetration is the highest intimacy one can experience and is not to be undertaken lightly, and only for reproduction with a human, or in the sacred space of a bloodmating with a vampire. Otherwise, the things you mortals term 'foreplay' is what we consider sex—anything and everything except penetration. So with a host—the prey upon which we feed—we drink from them and… play. We give them pleasure as they give us life—literal life, without which we are cold, dead things. As we become blooded, we begin to feel pleasure ourselves, which is a physical, anatomical function. Without blood, we cannot feel pleasure, we cannot mate. Physically, we are not capable of an erection, or feeling pleasure."

He pauses, sips, and thinks.

"A mating frenzy is different," he continues. "A vampire sometimes feels a…a compulsion. It's centered on a particular individual, a mortal host. It's not just the desire to feed and the sexual arousal that comes with it. It's significantly more, wildly intense, irresistible and uncontrollable. It's a need to mate, to produce offspring. A mating frenzy. A need for that mortal, a driving, unquenchable compulsion to have her, feed from her, and plant a child in her." A pause, a tip of the head. "For female vampires, obviously, it is the reverse—the need to cause a male mortal to put a child in her—our venom, from females, causes a unique reaction in mortal males. Since erection is a function of blood flow, and our venom causes increased blood production, heart rate, and blood flow, the mortal male host experiences an unending erection, no matter how many times he releases. This is to guarantee the female will be impregnated."

"Jesus," I murmur. "That's...kind of nuts." I shake my head, still trying to make sense of all this.

Alistair nods. "It is the way of things." He looks at me, then. "The caveat, to all this: pregnancy caused by an immortal results in death, especially for mortal females. Pregnancy means death. No question, no exceptions. It is a fatally parasitic process. Once the child is born, the mother always, *always* dies. A mortal male—the progenitor...." He pauses, sighs. "The female vampire is compelled to end his life, once she conceives. And we always know. Always. Males know when the mortal female has conceived, and female vampires know when they have conceived. There *have* been a few, rare cases of a male mortal surviving a mating frenzy, but *never* a mortal female."

"Never?" I ask, the blood draining from my face.

"Not once, in all of history, recorded or otherwise."

I look at Caspian, understanding dawning. "Oh."

The table is silent.

"And..." I hold Caspian's eyes, even as I address Alistair. "And you think Caspian feels this mating frenzy for me?"

Alistair doesn't answer right away. When he does, his voice is low, heavy, and resigned. "I know he does. As do Stirling, and Fin...and myself. But Caspian most strongly. That he has resisted it is no less than miraculous."

"And if he, or any of you, were to give in to it and... um, impregnate me...I would give birth to a vampire and then die?"

"A union between a mortal and a vampire—or any other immortal, for that matter—always results in an immortal. There are no half-breeds. Our genes dominate and eradicate the mortal aspect. This is another invariable law."

"So, um. A few questions." I chew on which to ask first. "What about contraceptives? Condoms, birth control, things like that?"

Alistair shakes his head. "None of that works. Something in our physiognomy just…counteracts any efforts at contraception. For female vampires, no form of birth control will work, since we are not, technically speaking, actually alive unless we are freshly blooded. And even when she is, her body simply overrides or rejects the chemical compounds. Condoms do not work either, and this is less understood. A male's release simply… goes through it. If a mortal male wears one with a female vampire, something in her body dissolves the prophylactic or weakens it somehow, through secretions, perhaps. Either way, any efforts at contraception have always failed, without exception."

"If feeding is sexual…are there gay vampires?"

This gets a chuckle from the table.

"Yes, of course," Alistair answers.

"And…what if you can't find a host of the opposite sex?"

"You wait." He shrugs. "Of course, in dire, desperate situations, it is possible to tamp down the sexual component so one can acquire sustenance from a member of the same gender, or animals." He glances at Caspian when he says this, for some reason. "It isn't pleasant. It's how you would feel, to a certain, very limited degree, about eating bugs if you were starving. But for a vampire, it comes with an added component of physical and metaphysical pain."

"I see." I stare into nothing for a moment. "Is it common for more than one vampire to feel the mating frenzy for the same person?"

"Distinctly no." Alistair shakes his head, tapping a finger on the table. "As has been said before, you are quite unique. Your scent, in particular."

Caspian speaks up, then. "Her blood…it tastes like…like nothing else I've ever tasted. It's extraordinary. More intoxicating than the most potent liquor. And more addictive than any drug known to mortal kind."

"Agreed," Stirling says. "It's utterly unique, and…" his eyes flood with black, his voice thickening. "Addictive is exactly the right word. I can taste it now." He fixes me with his eyes, and I feel the pheromones washing over me in potent waves, causing physical arousal so intense I squirm in my chair and bite down on my lip to suppress a moan. "I can almost taste your blood. Taste your pleasure."

The table is silent.

Stirling's eyes clear and he shakes his head. "Apologies. The effect you have is unparalleled."

"Question," I say, my voice a little shaky. "If you release that pheromone that causes your host victim to basically be unable to say no…where does consent come in? Or does it?"

The silence becomes awkward. "For most of history, unfortunately, the matter of consent has not been…considered. And this is true of mortals and immortals, I must point out." He hesitates. "I feel compelled to defend my race, in this. We drink blood, and when we do so, yes, we cause the host—and we prefer the term *host* to *victim*—to feel a sexual excitement he or she cannot and truly does not *want* to ignore. The experience, then, is one of pleasure.

For most hosts, all that is remembered of the experience is a vague memory of pleasure, like a night of overindulgence in spirits and engaging in sex. There is no memory of pain because the pain is negated both by our venom and sexual pleasure. There is no physical after-effect connected to blood loss either, by the way, because again, our venom causes the mortal body to overproduce blood. It is more of a synergistic relationship than parasitic or predatory. So, the mortal does not verbally consent to the experience, knowingly submitting themselves to being fed from by a vampire. But one could—and I do in fact—argue that it is far more palatable and mutually beneficial than, say, what I know many mortal females have experienced with other mortal males. That being rape." His voice hardens at the last statement. "Among vampires, there has also, over the past century or so in particular, been an ongoing debate regarding the topic of consent for the host. This debate is made almost moot by the fact that we are bound to silence regarding our existence by a treaty."

I blink. "A…treaty? Like, the thing the loser signs after a war?"

"A formally binding agreement or contract establishing obligations between two or more subjects of international law," he corrects. "But, yes."

"So…there was a war."

He nods. "There was a war."

I lick my lips, take a long sip of wine, and look around the room. "I would like it to be known that I have always felt that I've given consent, explicit or implicit, in my encounters with Caspian." I glance at Stirling. "And Stirling."

Caspian looks at me, and then at Stirling. "Which should not have happened the way it did."

I frown. "I thought you guys didn't get jealous?"

Stirling says nothing, doesn't respond at all, just sits and watches.

"There are unspoken rules," Caspian says. "If you... let's make it personal to this situation rather than a vague hypothetical. I met you first. I established a relationship with you. You are *my* host. *My* mortal. According to our societal rules, he can't merely cut in and feed from you or otherwise poach you from me without my express permission."

I frown. "He didn't *poach* me, number one, and number two that makes me sound like an object."

Caspian tilts his head to one side. "It's a matter of establishing rights, more than any sense of ownership. It's meant to prevent quarreling since we as a culture and species cannot afford to lose any of our numbers due to infighting."

"But you can give him your permission to feed from me?"

He nods. "Usually, that's more in a, um...group setting."

I was about to take a sip of wine, and splutter it back into the glass. "Excuse me?" I wipe my lips with a napkin. "Group setting?"

He looks away from me, to Alistair, who remains expressionless—it seems Caspian is on his own with this one.

He sighs. "There are...clubs. Nightclubs. They attract mortals and are operated and frequented by vampires. I think fae run similar clubs, but we do not...cross-populate."

"Fae and vampires don't get along?"

He snorts. "Alistair mentioned a war?" He arches an eyebrow. "Anyway. Mortals come to the club to drink alcohol and dance, and vampires circulate among them, releasing pheromones and…choosing, basically. The mortals are so overloaded with the pheromones being released from every direction that no one, vampire or mortal, has any clue who's being affected by whom. It becomes a matter of a more mortal means of choosing a partner. There are private rooms in the back of the clubs and the vampire will take their chosen host to a room and…feed. And play. Many vampires frequent these clubs in pairs, trios, or quartets, and they will all feed from the same host at once. Or, two mortals per coven. Rarely more than that."

"And that's okay? Everyone feeding from and playing with the same mortal?" I ask.

He nods. "Yes. In that setting, we share easily and freely."

"But?" I prompt.

"In a more personal setting, away from such clubs, the rules change." He holds my eyes. "If I were to invite you to my home, it would be normal and acceptable for all of us or any combination of us who live here, our coven, to feed from you. But for Stirling to seek you out on your own, without my knowledge and prior permission, and feed from you is not acceptable."

CHAPTER 24

"THAT'S NOT HOW IT HAPPENED," I say, swallowing hard, feeling faint. "After you cut me out of your life, I was desperate. I was going crazy without you. So I….I came here. Stirling was here alone, and…it just sort of happened. He nicked my throat and tasted me. But then he stopped and made me leave before anything happened."

"Stopping was…" Stirling sighs, more of a growl than anything else. "It was the single hardest thing I've ever done. It felt like trying to rip off my own fingers."

The two males lock gazes.

"*That* I understand," Caspian says.

"Can we go back to…group settings?" I murmur, visions flashing across my brain—skin, hands, fangs, blood, pleasure. "Do pheromones, like…compound?" I glance at Caspian. "Like, if all of you are releasing at once, and it's all directed at me….?"

"You would be…well, most mortals are all but incapacitated. So overwhelmed they're in a kind of hypnosis," Alistair says, interjecting for the first time in a while. "In such situations, the mortal rarely remembers anything but the vaguest of impressions." He regards me with speculation and suspicion. "As you are anything but typical, I'm not certain how you'd react."

"I see." I look at Caspian. "And those clubs…is that how you stay fed…blooded, I mean?"

He shakes his head. "That's an indulgence. A social activity."

"So where do you go during lunch?" I ask. "How do you feed, if you're not getting it from me?"

Caspian glances at Alistair, who nods, giving tacit permission. Caspian goes to the refrigerator and opens it, revealing it to be full of those opaque white pouches I saw Stirling sipping from. He grabs one, closes the refrigerator, and comes back to the table, handing me the pouch. I take it—it's larger and heavier than I expected, cold, and full of a thick liquid…blood, I assume. The straw is part of the packaging, with a tip which can be ripped open. There is no marking, no labeling, no graphics, or anything. The only distinguishing feature is a one-inch red circle at the center of the pouch on one side, at the center of which is a strange rune printed in gold—the rune is all angles and lines, somewhere between Viking runes and Japanese kanji.

"What's this?" I ask, pointing to the rune.

"That is a fae glamour," Caspian answers. "It's a very, very, *very* rare example of fae and vampires cooperating. We purchased the glamour from them several years ago—at the turn of the millennium, I believe…right, Alistair?"

Alistair nods, puffing on his pipe. "Indeed."

"What's it do?" I ask.

"It heats the blood," Caspian answers.

I frown. "Like a chemical reaction? Why not just nuke it in the microwave?"

Caspian wrinkles his nose. "Have you ever microwaved coffee?"

I laugh. "Oh. I guess I get that."

Caspian shakes his head. "Microwaved blood is…it's barely digestible. It's…well, it's truly awful. The glamour is a unique fae working which heats the blood in such a way that it is all but indistinguishable from human blood straight from the vein."

"It allows us to sustain ourselves without requiring a host, but in such a way that leaves us something like sated," Alistair says. "It isn't a long-term solution. The biological drive to feed is not something we can ignore for very long. But to pass through a long day while attempting to pass as mortal?" He shrugs. "It will do."

"What did you do before you got that glamour?" I ask.

"We waited. Used microwaves. Heating it over a stove or other open flame is better, but that's fiddly and difficult and time-consuming because to overheat it makes it just as unpalatable as if it were cold."

"Which I assume is yucky?" I say.

Caspian laughs. "Yucky. Yes, that's a word for it."

"The other option is animals," Alistair says. "But Caspian can speak to that better than anyone."

I look at him. "You can? Why?"

Caspian shoots Alistair a glare, then softens his expression as he looks at me. "Because I…I told you my mother was murdered. The brief version is that after that happened, I was on my own. I was a child, by our standards and by yours."

"Vampires age and physically mature like a normal mortal child up until the end of physical adolescence, eighteen or twenty or so for males and usually more like fourteen to seventeen for females," Alistair explains. "After that, our bodies…well, they don't *stop* aging, it just slows to nearly a crawl, which is why I, at five hundred, appear as a young middle-aged male. I won't begin to look truly *old* by human standards for at least another three, maybe four hundred years." He gestures at Caspian. "He was eleven years old when his mother was murdered. At eleven, he was essentially helpless. He wasn't mature enough physically to survive on his own, as he hadn't developed the instincts or physical abilities to feed properly."

I blink. "How…then how does a vampire child feed?"

"From the mother," Alistair says. "It's something akin to nursing. It's quite complex, as a matter of fact. An infant requires milk as well as blood. This is where the process becomes fatal for the mother. The baby has no capacity to stop or to moderate. It knows only hunger." He bobbles his head side to side, considering. "The process is slightly different, depending on whether the mother is a vampire or a mortal. A vampire mother will produce milk and the baby will draw both at the same time, and poses no threat to the mother. This is seen as preferable since it's simpler and safer. For a child sired by a male vampire on a mortal female, it's…significantly more complex. There must be a vampire mother at the ready as well as the host mother. The infant is fed milk by the host mother and blood by the vampire mother, and it must be done in such a way that the infant doesn't seek to draw blood from the host mother." He sighs. "Inevitably, it will. By this time, the process of growing, bearing, and, birthing the child has taken a significant physical toll on the host mother. She is weak, sickly, and frail. For much of history, there was only the host mother, and the child simply drew blood and milk at once from the host mother, which quickly resulted in the expiration of the host. Wealthier covens could afford other options. But it wasn't until the last century or two that the tradition of extending the host mother's life by separating blood and milk became customary."

"But the mother still always dies? If she's mortal, I mean."

He nods. "Even if the infant is never allowed to draw blood from the host mother, she will still die. It's thought that the process of hosting the child in utero causes it to feed from her, drawing nutrients like a mortal infant but... more so. It's not fully understood even with modern science. She just...sickens and dies. Nothing can prevent it. And it is almost as much of a rule that the mortal host mother doesn't *want* to live. Her focus is entirely on her child. All her will, all her energy, all her emotions are bent toward her child. Her love for that infant is complete and all-consuming, and once the infant no longer needs her to physically survive, some connection is just...severed. She loses her will to live, and her body gives out. All attempts to counteract this, to circumvent it or prevent it have failed, and vampire scientists have been working on it for centuries."

"I see." I look at Caspian. "Now I understand why you're all trying to protect me from Caspian. I drive him into the mating frenzy…"

"The first time you mate with each other, you *will* become pregnant. You will carry his child, and you *will* die. And there won't be a thing we can do to save you." Alistair says this while looking at me, pipe clenched in one hand, goblet loosely cupped in the other, gaze hard and distant. "The process is traumatic for many vampire males. We grow quite attached to our mortal mates. The mating frenzy is not merely physical—it comes with intense emotional attachment, as well. And we feel the normal gamut of emotions as the host mother grows our child—pride, worry, concern, doubts…we feel it all just like a mortal father." His gaze goes to the window, the darkness beyond, seeing not the glass or the stars or the trees but the past. "But in addition to that is the knowledge that this delicate little mortal woman, whom we've grown so attached to… come to love, to crave, driven to protect…is going to die. You did that. You cannot undo it. Cannot save her. You will be doomed to watch her waste away and die, and no matter your physical strength or intellectual intelligence, you cannot save her."

"Alistair…" I breathe, seeing the pain written on his face, in his voice. "I'm sorry."

He shakes his head. "It was long, long ago, my dear."

"But you have a child?"

He nods, slowly. "I…did. A son. Ephraim. His mother was a sweet, quiet, delicate little thing. This was before the treaty when it was more common for vampires to take mortal mates openly. She knew me, knew my nature, and accepted me. I was so careful, with her. We never mated, not truly. I fed from her, and I took care of her. Provided for her. We were happy. And then business took me away and when I came back, she'd been assaulted in our home by brigands. She survived, but barely. I hunted down and killed the mortals who'd hurt her, but it did nothing to assuage my rage. She healed, but her mind was never the same. She was clingy. She craved me. She was no longer content with how things had been—feeding and playing. She wanted to mate. I tried to explain the danger, but she was adamant. She didn't care. She *needed* to mate. She needed my child." He sets his pipe and wineglass down, twining his fingers together and clenching them on his lap. His voice is tight and hard, his eyes pained. "I gave in. I gave her a child. She bore him, but she didn't even survive the nursing stage. Once she held little Ephraim in her arms and saw his eyes and…" he shakes his head. "She took her last breath as he fed at her breast."

"And Ephraim?" I ask. "You said *did*?"

"He was killed in the war."

"What war?"

He drains his glass and refills it. "The Mortals' War. You know it as the Revolutionary War. It was centered here, in America, in the mid to late seventeen hundreds. It was…the mortals had always been vaguely aware of us, of immortals, and we'd always tried to fit in, to keep out of the public eye and get along. But then there was a movement. A coven of vampires in Paris began a political movement in 1734. Their goal was to bring immortals out of the shadows and to normalize our place in larger human culture. For a time, in Paris, they were mostly successful. There was a golden age in Paris, during which vampires, shifters, and fae could appear in public, could take mortal lovers and not be ashamed or afraid. There were clubs such as Caspian described where things occurred openly, freely."

"Oh dear," I say. "I think I know where this is going."

"Perhaps. Does the date 1784 sound familiar?"

I nod. "Yes, that's when the French Revolution started. We covered that in history class last year."

"Correct. Well, the mortal concerns were real, and that's what your kind remembers, now. At the time, however, it was far more. It was a reaction against the inclusion of immortals. There were tribunals and witch hunts. Vampires were hunted down and murdered—and yes, in significant enough numbers, we can be overcome. There will be losses, but…we are not omnipotent." He sips wine, relights his pipe. "This coincides with events here. Those same malcontents from Paris were chased out of the city in 1755 by their own kind, who saw the writing on the wall, saw how mortals were eventually going to react. That coven moved here, to New York, and started up their activities, but this time, they weren't content with merely being included. They began arguing that immortal kind were superior, that we were the natural rulers. They persuaded some of the more weak-minded and selfish members of our race to join them and began taking mortal women as concubines—slaves, essentially. Those poor mortal women were used most…" he shakes his head. "You can imagine. And if you cannot, I will not describe for you the horrors they endured. The movement grew, and as the list of mortal victims grew with it, so too did the ire of the mortals. Their wives and daughters and sisters were being kidnapped, enslaved, raped, and sold like chattel. It was done almost openly, as well."

"Jesus," I whisper. "That's…god, that's…"

"Unthinkable?" Alistair nods. "Indeed. Few of our kind supported it. In reality, it was a small pocket of malcontents, traitors, and villains. There were no more than a hundred members of the sect in total, but the damage was done. We were seen as monsters, even those of us who fought to stop it, who hunted down and executed the true monsters who began the movement. Some fae and shifters joined the sect, and so they too were all painted with the same brush." He pauses, breathes in, lets it out slowly. "It began a war—mortals against immortals. But it wasn't nearly so simple. Fae and shifters blamed, rightly, to a degree, vampires for what happened, which means some of the fae and shifters allied with the mortals, while others argued that conflict between our races had been brewing for hundreds of years, and immortals needed to stick together. I'm giving you the broad outlines only, you must understand. Running through all the various sociopolitical ramifications of the mortal and immortal conflict, also, is the larger mortal conflict which you learn about in your schools—the rebellion of the colonists against British rule. That is real, that truly happened as you are taught, but… there was far, far more to it. The battles were not as the history books remember—it wasn't merely human against human, it was mortals against immortals, vampire against fae against shifter, and our various races also took sides in the mortal conflict, furthering complicating things. That war was supremely messy and complex." He waves a hand. "If you'd like to understand it more thoroughly, I can lend you a book or two on the subject."

"So…why don't we remember what happened?" I ask.

"Because in 1784, the same year the mortals began their French Revolution, the Treaty of Paris was signed, ending the War for Independence. In reality, it wasn't merely the treaty ending the mortal war for independence, however, it was the signing of the treaty to end The Mortals' War. We just call it The Treaty, since there's only one treaty in our history. The basic agreement is that fae, supported by vampires and shifters, would work a supremely powerful glamor, causing mortals to forget the existence of immortals—wiping us from memory. We would not mate with mortals—meaning produce no further children. In return, we would be allowed to live among mortals and own businesses and be left alone…as long as we caused no further loss of mortal lives through mating and breeding. It was understood that we require mortal blood and vitality to live, but as long as it doesn't result in death for the mortal."

"Who won the war?" I ask.

He frowns. "Did you not hear me? We lost the right to reproduce, Maeve." He looks at Caspian. "He is the youngest known immortal, born the year of the treaty. In fact, he was born *after* the treaty, and his mother is the first known immortal to be executed by the Immortal Tribunal for breaking it."

CHAPTER 25

No one says anything as I absorb this newest piece of information.

"Hold up. Wait. Okay, so…" I pinch the bridge of my nose, my brain swirling with chaotic, rapid-fire questions. "First, let me get this straight: none of the immortal races are allowed to have any more babies because it causes the loss of mortal life?"

"Correct." Alistair nods once, curt.

"And Caspian is the youngest immortal?" I look at him, at his blank expression. "Because no one is having babies."

Alistair tilts his head to one side, his eyes

squinting at me thoughtfully. "Youngest so far as we are aware. Youngest *acknowledged.*"

"The difference being?" I ask.

"Difference being, once in a while over the past two hundred and forty years, an immortal has given in to nature and sired or borne a child. It is illegal, and to do so breaks the treaty, technically speaking, even if the larger mortal public may continue unaware. The Immortal Tribunal is a ruling body comprised of three members from each race— vampire, shifter, and fae. They oversee the keeping of the treaty, and they do so with extreme zealotry. After all, The Mortals' War cost us many, many lives, and there weren't that many of us to begin with. It is estimated across the three races, we lost half of our total population during the war, which was why we signed the treaty to begin with— we were winning the battles but losing the war, since the mortals had more lives to throw at us."

"Was it just numbers that made you lose?" I ask. "I mean, you're so powerful, it seems hard to believe that you could be killed easily, even by overwhelming numbers."

Alistair sighs. "I don't want to be drawn into a lecture on the intricacies of the war, Maeve. It's tiresomely complex for one, and for another, I lived through it. I lost friends, family. I lost my son. It's a painful memory."

"I'm sorry," I say, immediately.

"Mortals are resourceful," he says, after a few moments spent sipping and puffing on his pipe. "Your kind can create technologies and strategies that can counter our greater physical attributes, especially when combined with overwhelming numbers. Plus, as I said, it wasn't as simple as mortals against immortals. Fae largely sided with the colonial rebels, and vampires largely sided with the British imperialists. Shifters were impossible to predict, siding whichever way the pack leader leaned. That, too, is a large part of the reason our two races do not get along to this day—remembered enmity."

"Makes sense." I frown. "Let's go back, though. Also, are there no mortals in positions of authority who are aware of your existence?"

Alistair nods. "The Immortal Tribunal is tasked with keeping the peace, ensuring we, the three races, do not break the treaty. The members of the tribunal are each among the oldest and wisest of our kind, and they live together in a castle somewhere in the Alps, as I understand it. Regarding your other question, I believe there is a secret council of mortals who know—they are chosen by the tribunal and serve on that council for life. When one dies, another is chosen to replace him or her. The mortals are usually not who you'd expect, although I confess I'm not privy to their identities or the inner workings of the council or the tribunal. It's a system of checks and balances, essentially.

"I could lecture for an hour on this topic alone, so suffice it to say, the treaty was meant to stop the war and keep the peace, and the system now in place was designed to largely benefit all parties. It does not feel entirely fair to our kind, since it is not our fault we cannot reproduce with our own kind, yet we are punished for it. We could have kept fighting, but we did not want the war in the first place, seeing as it was the result of the actions and beliefs of an outlying sect—whom the vast majority of all three races would have hunted down and executed, given the opportunity.

"The mortals were quick to judge and quicker to make

war on us without giving us the opportunity to rectify the situation on our own. And trust me when I say, we would have. Our races had lived mostly peacefully among mortals for tens of thousands of years, largely unknown and unseen. And yes, it was at the cost of mortal lives we reproduced. We have sought a solution to that for millennia, without result."

I sense the topic is a sensitive one for Alistair, so I change the subject. "You said Caspian's mother was *executed*. For having Caspian after the treaty?

"When it was determined that Caspian was birthed after the treaty, his mother was…executed. There was no trial, no arrest, no due process, she was just—"

"Murdered," Caspian growls. "She was murdered. It wasn't justice, it was murder."

"Since then, the tribunal has fine-tuned its approach. If it happens, there is an arrest, and evidence, and some kind of process before the execution."

"What about the child?" I ask. "Caspian is here, so they didn't…." I trail off, expecting Alistair to fill in for me.

He does. "No, the child is viewed as innocent. Only the parent is seen as the guilty party. Nowadays, the parent is…vanished, so to speak. The tribunal summons them, and if they do not respond, they are brought in against their will. The execution happens in secret, at the Tribunal Seat. The child usually knows nothing of it."

My blood runs cold.

I look at Caspian, and I see concern in his eyes. "Is… is it possible…" I gulp, unable to form words, a knot in my throat and heat in my veins even as my blood is cold and my skin is clammy and my head pounds.

"Is what possible, Maeve?" Alistair asks, leaning

forward, elbows on the table, eyes bright with concern and curiosity.

"To be…immortal, but not…" I shake my head, licking my lips. "But not know it."

"No, not as far as I am aware." Alistair frowns. "There are fae glamours which can disguise the nature of an individual, but those, to my knowledge, are temporary. Hours, days at most—and to last days the glamour must be infused with enormous amounts of vitality." He considers. "To be permanent? So even the subject of the glamour doesn't know? To last for *years,* undetected and undetectable? I can't fathom such a glamour, what it would require, how it could be cast. A fae would be able to answer more accurately and knowledgeably, but I do not know any personally anymore, and I wouldn't know how to reach out to one. And if you somehow were, I wouldn't want to put you on the radar of the tribunal. If you were to start asking questions, you could reveal things which are best left alone, to their thinking."

"It would make sense of why her blood is so strange," Stirling says.

"Vampires don't feed on fae," Fin says. "Doesn't happen."

"Because we have always been at odds," Alistair says. "Not necessarily enemies per se, but we've never gotten along. There have been violent skirmishes at various points in history, as well as ongoing political and economic competition. Our kinds are simply too different. If it *has* happened in the past, the vampire in question certainly wouldn't have spoken of it, to *anyone.* Such a thing is…" he shakes his head. "Taboo is not strong enough a word.

There isn't one. It's not just not done, it's…" he hunts for words, at a loss. "It's just not something anyone would do."

"Why?" I ask. "What is it about humans?"

"It's just the way of things. Our craving, our need, is for mortal blood." He's frowning deeply. "It's so ingrained in our thinking, even though it's never spoken of, that we just…it would never even occur to a vampire to drink from a fae or a shifter."

"Sounds shortsighted, if you ask me." I shake my head, sighing. "It was just a thought, anyway. I mean, my mom died and…it was just weird. The way it happened, I mean, how I was informed and what happened afterward. I don't know."

"I'm not saying it's completely impossible," Alistair says, "I'm just saying I can't understand how it's possible, but I'm not an expert in fae magic, by any means."

I glance at my phone and realize it's after midnight. "Shit! I was supposed to check in with Andreas." I set my wine down and rise to my feet—and I realize I've had more wine than I thought. The room wobbles a bit, and I have to hold onto the chair for balance. "Whoa."

Caspian grins. "Come on, lightweight." He wraps an arm around my waist and guides me to my purse, digs my phone out of it and hands it to me.

I take it into the foyer and sit on a chair. "I promised I'd check in."

"You guys have a weird relationship." Caspian leans on the chair behind me.

"Yeah, I guess we do."

I type out a text to Andreas:

Still at the Taylors. Having a good time. Be home later.

My phone pings immediately:

Better late than never. Thanks for checking in. I'll leave kitchen door unlocked for you.

I thumbs-up the message and put my phone back to sleep. Then I tilt my head up until I'm looking at Caspian upside down. "Hi."

"Hi." His grin is adorable, mesmerizing. "You're a little drunk."

"A little, I guess." I shrug. "Didn't even realize it till I stood up."

"Should I get you home?" He asks.

I shake my head. "Not yet."

"More questions?"

I shrug. "Only a million. But then I forget half of them because whenever you guys tell me something new, the questions I had about the last thing you told me go poof out of my brain."

He rounds the chair, scoops me in his arms, and sits down, depositing me in his lap. "Ask me something."

"You watched your mother get executed?"

He nods, eyes distant. "Yes. They came in right at sunset, just broke down the door and surrounded her. We were in the parlor. She was standing in front of the fire, reading a book to me. I was whittling a stick while I listened. The door smashed into splinters, and there were six huge vampires there. They wrapped her in chains, binding her arms to her sides—it happened so fast, Maeve. She was bound in an instant. Five of them held the ends of the chains and pulled until she couldn't move a muscle. The sixth drew a sword and cut her head off. There was not a word spoken. No accusation. No reasoning. No warning. No hesitation. She was just…dead. The whole thing lasted less than thirty seconds. And then…they were gone. I had no idea she'd even broken the treaty. I never knew who my mortal host father was. I barely knew there was a treaty, a war, anything. We were just a mother and son, living in a neighborhood in Baltimore where it was known certain covens lived. I had friends, older boys, all of them, more like Stirling's age. Then, I was alone. I didn't know how to…how to hunt, how to do anything. Being a vampire… it requires some training, Maeve. How to charm, how to flirt, how to use your pheromones, how to lick to numb, to heal. It's not all instinctual. As an adolescent vampire, all you know is hunger and need and hormones, like a teen-age mortal but with the added drive to feed. Without an adult…" He shakes his head, trailing off.

I bury my nose in his throat—I can smell him. The copper of his breath, the woodsmoke that's somehow always there. He's cooling—he needs blood soon. I bury my hands in the soft cool silk of his hair and breathe him in.

"I'm so sorry, Caspian. That's not justice, you're right. That was murder."

He nods. "I fled Baltimore. I fed on a girl and…I didn't know what I was doing. I almost killed her, I took too much. I…" he growls. "I stopped. I didn't…I didn't… rape her. Or coerce her with my pheromones or anything. I just fed. I was *so* hungry, Maeve. I hadn't had anything for days and I was angry and confused and I'd just lost my mother. But I was horrified at what I'd almost done, so I left."

"It's understandable, Caspian. You'd just experienced a traumatic event, and you were starving."

"That's the thing, Maeve. Vampires, when we haven't fed for a long time, it *is* starvation, we just don't die. But the desperation, the frantic insanity of need, that is exactly starvation as a human would feel it. And I know—I've encountered starving humans."

"So what did you do then?"

He doesn't answer for a while. "I fled into the woods west of Baltimore. I lived in the forest alone for fifty years, surviving on animals."

"What?" I breathe, pulling away to look into his eyes.

"I was more than half feral. I slept in caves and hollows of fallen trees during the day and hunted at night. I mostly lived on bears, cougars, wolves, moose, and elk. I…I liked the fight. A deer, a wolf…they're too easy. Instead of the sexual arousal, I was…it was about the combat. A bear, even while I was feeding from it, would fight back. Animals will fight till their last breath, and that…it made it feel less…" he shakes his head. "I felt better about it if they fought back."

"My god, Caspian," I murmur, nuzzling into his throat, kissing his skin.

I smell the copper of his breath, taste something on his skin, a whiff of something sweet and savory and tantalizing, making my mouth water, making my teeth ache like I've bitten into something too sweet, making my entire being shudder.

"Alistair found me. I could barely speak, I was so… lost in savagery. I'd long since lost my clothing, so I was naked, filthy, crusted in blood and gore from messy feedings, crisscrossed with scars and wounds from fights with predators." He lets out a slow breath. "It took Alistair nearly five years to civilize me. I kept running back to the wilderness, to what I knew, feeding on beasts."

"What's it like? Feeding on animals rather than

mortals?" I caress his nape, his shoulders, his cheek-bones—the need to touch him is all-consuming.

He considers a moment or two before answering. "They taste different. Gamier, I suppose? I don't know. When a vampire feeds on a mortal we get a sense of the individual from their blood, or perhaps it's not from the blood but some semi-psychic or empathetic thing, I don't know. It's not reading thoughts or seeing memories, it's just…impressions. I think I've told you this. When I feed on a beast, it's totally different." He thinks again before continuing, and his hands idly, absently stroke through my hair. "It contributed to me going feral, I think. My belief is that blood contains some element of that being. Feeding on a sentient being, like a mortal, then, means I would feed on their sentience, their humanity. Feeding on an animal, a predator…" he trails off.

"Means you would be more predatory," I fill in.

"Exactly," he says. "I've never been exactly at home among mortals. The savagery, I think, never totally left me. Every so often, I find myself driven into the wilderness. When I'm gone, that's often where I am—in the wild forests of the Upper Peninsula, where I can still find beasts to challenge me, predators to feed on. Now, however, I don't kill them as I used to, I merely enjoy the battle and the taste of their blood. Especially the more endangered species like moose, elk, and cougars. Bears are plentiful enough that I worry less about their numbers."

"What were you doing in New York?" I ask. "Alistair said it was for business."

"We own a haven in Brooklyn."

"A haven?"

"Those clubs I told you about, they're called havens.

The one we own is operated by a cousin of Fin's, but occasionally one of us has to check in, go over the books, see that mortal building and operating codes are being adhered to, make sure our immortal codes as well are adhered to."

"Immortal codes?"

"Rules for havens. There aren't many, but they are iron-clad. No fighting, no draining of a mortal, no conception, no divulgence of our existence. Mortals must remain unaware of what truly goes on—they leave without any memory of having been fed from, remembering only a typical club experience, albeit a slightly more…bacchanalian experience. Even on the main dance floors, there is far more sexual activity than in a normal mortal nightclub, but all the mortal remembers the next day is dancing, drinking, and uninhibited pleasure-taking. Nothing more. There are no scars or scabs, no lingering pain, no memory of being fed from. Any immortal who breaks any of these rules is barred from *all* havens, everywhere."

"So…since you guys have allowed me, a mortal, to become aware of your existence…"

"We have, technically speaking, broken the treaty." He holds my eyes, and I can see all too clearly how serious this is.

"Will you get in trouble?"

"Not if you don't tell another soul, or even hint at it. Or act as if anything is amiss."

"And…what about us?"

"Us?"

I lick my lips. "I want to be with you, Caspian."

He growls, and buries his nose in my hair. "Maeve… you know I want that, too. But…"

"I'm too tempting."

"Entirely."

"Could we keep it secret? From everyone else except your family?"

He inhales a long breath and lets it out shakily. "I would have to continue to resist the mating frenzy, and I fight against it every moment I'm within fifty feet of you. I mean that literally. Right now, this very moment, every cell in my being is demanding I carry you to my room, strip you naked, and mate with you. Plunge my fangs into your throat and taste your golden, effervescent blood and sink my cock into you and take you until you know nothing but me, nothing but us."

My sex quakes at his words, and I knot my fingers in his shirt—my muscles tense as I fight the urge to seduce him into doing exactly what he's threatening. I want it. I want him. I want him to feed from me, I want his cock inside me, I need to feel united with him, to mate with him, to taste him—

I feel my teeth latch onto the side of his neck, into the tendon there, a raw, instinctual action, and I taste skin and blood, and my mouth waters at the burst of copper and the sweetness of shadows and the acridity of magic, and a wilding chaos of more beneath it, flavors I cannot describe, cannot understand. The yawning, gaping, starveling void within me draws, *pulls* and I taste him again, not with my mouth and lips and tongue but with my very *soul…*

"*FUCK*—" his voice is a feral, inhuman roar.

I'm thrown to the ground in a tangle of limbs and with a cry of shock. It's like cold water dousing me, drenching me with awareness of what I've just done.

Caspian is across the parlor, touching a palm to his neck and holding it away—blood stains his palm; it dribbles down his neck and under his shirt, staining his collar. He's panting hard, breath seething through clenched teeth. His skin is pale, blanched and clammy, and he's hunched over in pain. His eyes are hollows, dull and dizzy and confused.

"What the *fuck*, Maeve?" He snarls, a sound like ripping flesh.

"I…I don't know, I don't know…" I shake my head, and feel warm liquid on my lips, on my chin.

I lick my lips—taste copper and shadow and magic. I wipe my hand over my mouth, and it comes away wet with his blood.

"I-I-I'm s-s-sorry, Caspian," I stammer, lurching out of my chair and staggering for the front door. "I don't know, I'm sorry. I'm sorry."

"Maeve, wait, I was just surprised—"

I don't wait. I'm out the door faster than I think I've ever moved in my life—I stumble down the steps, trip, losing my shoes. It's bitterly cold, but I don't feel it. My breath steams and my feet slam in the dirt, and then pine branches whip and claw at my face, and snow crunches around my feet.

What just happened?

I *bit* him. I drew blood…and I *tasted* it…tasted *him.* It was dark, it was wild…it was *delicious.*

I flee, flee.

Not home.

Not to Andreas.

Horror boils in my veins, confusion, fear. My legs pump like pistons, tireless and powerful, carrying me pell-mell through the forest at a flat-out run, and I dodge trunks and duck under branches and leap over fallen trees with preternatural ease and grace.

I can see perfectly in the midnight black of the forest's cathedral halls and the narthexes of clearings.

My feet make no sound.

What is happening to me?

What am I?

CHAPTER 26

XHAUSTION HITS ME ALL AT ONCE, like a sledgehammer to the forehead.

I collapse to the forest floor, sweating, panting. Dizzy.

Thoughts and emotions swirl inside me, a maelstrom of horror and confusion and fear.

Slowly, a soft, faint shushing sound slips into my awareness, and I sit up. I'm crying, silently sobbing, wracked so violently I can't even make a sound. The shushing calms me.

It's the shoreline—the waves of the Great Lake…Michigan? Huron? I'm not sure.

I lurch awkwardly and half drunkenly to

my feet, stumbling gracelessly through the undergrowth. The trees give away all at once to pine needle-carpeted rocks and sand, which transitions again to a wide sandy beach curving away in both directions. The lake glitters, burnished to a silver glow by the light of a pregnant moon. Stars twinkle in countless billions, scintillating and infinite. The waters extend into everything, everywhere, except the forest behind me and the sand under me.

I collapse to my butt in the sand, sprawling with my palms in the cold damp sand and the icy water licking at my heels.

I'm no longer sobbing, but I am crying. Tears trickle slowly down my cheeks. Tears of everything.

I close my eyes and listen to the waves lapping at my feet and I can almost hear the moon creaking in its ageless orbit above me, almost hear the stars singing their infinite hymn. Something in the pit of my soul pulses like a heart-beat, weak and erratic, but alive. It wasn't there, before.

I feel every grain of sand under my palms, under my calves and thighs. I hear some creature scampering in the forest behind me—a mouse, skittering beneath a fallen tree. I hear an owl hoot, and I sense more than hear it wing-ing through the shadows.

I feel the shadows behind me, calling to me.

That pulse in my gut strengthens as I feel the shadows responding. Seeking. Drawing, yearning.

Yet the starlight and moonlight call to me as well, and the pulsing responds to their song equally, pounding and reaching.

The exhaustion has subsided, and while I can-not move from my place in the sand, I feel invigorated somehow, as if something starving inside me has finally found nourishment.

This terrifies me.

I'm not. I'm not.

I'm not a vampire.

Am I?

How could I be? Vampires are born, not made, and my mother was not a vampire. Was she? I saw her eat breakfast and lunch and dinner every day of my life. She never appeared pale or lifeless or carved from marble. Never had blacked-out void eyes.

She wasn't. I think I can say that with perfect clarity and precision. My mother was not a vampire. Which means I am not.

A new sound reaches my ears.

Music.

A violin. It's faint, distant. I just listen—it's no tune I recognize. The notes curl and loop, dip and soar wildly, frantically. It draws closer, closer, loudening by the second. I keep my eyes closed and listen.

The violinist is expressing pure sorrow. The melody is one of longing for something one cannot have, something forever lost. It yearns, this melody. Haunts.

Closer yet. In the trees behind me.

My feet dig into the sand, and I find myself on my feet, wandering away from the shoreline and toward the shadows. Some instinct within me reaches for them, and as if in response, the shadows seem to lengthen in defiance of physics, slinking across the sand and rocks and red-ochre pine needles… reaching, casting out tendrils like the black in Caspian's eyes.

The shadows snake around my ankles and I feel them,

cold and infinite. They slither around my calves and lick up the backs of my thighs like the touch of a lover.

The violinist plays on, and the notes are too close together, too fast. The speed is dizzying, faster than any mortal could dream. Yet for the frenetic speed, the melody is utterly haunting, pulling at a hidden pocket in my soul where I mourn for my mother, and I feel my grief crouching there, waiting like a beast in the dark, coiled and ready to spring.

The song touches my grief and sets fire to it.

The song whispers to my soul:

A heart, lost in longing,

Your hand in mine,

fingers and palms,

Delicate wrist and purple veins pulsing with deliciousness like a mountain spring

Your eyes seeking me in the shadows,

glittering like diamonds

I know you in all your forms, in all your moods

I know your melancholy when the rains fall

and you remember your father's face

I know your ecstasy as I drink from your veins and show you the peaks of purest pleasure

Limbs tangled with limbs

Breath woven with breath

Heartbeat, heartbeat, heartbeat, enmeshed

Taken

Gone

Moldering in the dirt, bones and crawling things in a box

Your soul wanders the earth no more, your voice only echoes in my eternal mind

I know you

Your heart beats somewhere within mine
Come back, lover
Dance in the moonlight with me once more
Kiss me by starshine

I open my eyes and look up and I see Alistair crouched on a thick tree branch like a waiting, hunting incubus. A violin is cradled to his chin and his eyes are closed. He's clad in his chinos and nothing more, barefoot, shirtless, hair tangled and wind-snarled.

His wrist pivots and bends with blinding speed, his elbow pumping as he saws at the strings with manic, furious intensity.

He leaps, and I can follow his movement, somehow. He leaps sixty feet in a single bound, landing with one foot on a high branch…bending forward at the waist and extending his other leg, then twisting his torso at a ninety-degree angle to his balancing foot…fingers dancing at the strings and flying along the frets.

He drops without warning and lands on a lower branch, crouching, facing me, eyes closed but I know he sees me or feels me, and I know this is a song for his lost mortal lover.

Something is fracturing inside me. Hairline cracks form all over the vessel containing my grief, and the more he plays, the more the vessel fractures.

"Stop, Alistair," I breathe, pleading. "Stop, stop, stop. I can't—I can't."

He ignores me. Dancing to the very end of the branch, it does not dip under his weight at all—and then he slides a foot along the trunk, downward, and he's skating down the trunk in syrupy slow motion...and then he flashes away, leaping, spinning in the air, impossibly fast and impossibly light, hair flying and eyes closed. His foot touches a trunk and he pushes off, caroming deeper into the forest, dancing from trunk to trunk, and the song pulls at me, batters against the vessel of my sorrow until I feel it shivering there inside me, raving and snarling and raging to get free.

"Stop!" I gasp, following him on far less graceful feet, sprinting after him on the forest floor. "Alistair! Please stop! Play for her, but not for me."

He leads me through the forest, away from the shore.

The sorrow of his tune intensifies, the notes slowing and diving down the scale until he's not touching the higher strings at all, only dragging the bow along the lowest note the violin is capable of, a wail of purest agony.

"Alistair! Please!" I fall to my knees, feeling the vessel no longer merely fracturing…but crumbling.

The beast is free.

The pulsing at the pit of my soul is an arrhythmic pounding. My skin is too tight on my bones, my teeth hurt and my eyes hurt and my skin hurts…everything hurts.

He's here. Standing over me, still playing his sorrow, battering at me with it. He says nothing.

I peer up at him through tear-hazed eyes. "Stop!" I shout through clenched molars. "Stop, stop stopstopstop—*please, please stop!*"

He crouches in front of me, his bow pulling along the string slowly, drawing out a single wailing note, an endless keening. His eyes open—tears of blood trickle down his marble cheeks. Void eyes regard me, but there is compassion in them, sorrow, sadness, understanding.

The beast within snarls.

Smashes at my soul, at the fragile bars of my teeth and my eyes.

The wailing note continues, a cry of rawest loss.

His loss.

My loss.

My chest heaves. My eyes burn. "Stop. Stop."

A sound emerges from me. A wail of my own, matching the keening of his violin.

The violin's voice is rich and soulful, deep and tasting of amber and the golden-crimson light of a thousand sunsets. This violin has known no song but sorrow.

I'm on all fours, and my fingers dig into the earth, crushing pine needles and bits of bark and into the soil where it's cold and teeming with microscopic life. "Stop, stop, stop."

His forehead touches mine, cold on cold. He plays on, and now the sorrowful wail becomes two, his and mine, and the bow touches another string and adds a third voice, his and hers and mine.

We mourn together.

Heat fills me. Clogs my throat. Burns like a forest fire behind my eyes. Expands in my chest like steam confined in a vent-less chamber.

I will crack open. I will break.

I'm not crying, I'm not sobbing, I'm not wailing—I'm *screaming*. My throat is sliced with razors as I scream. The pain slashes at my heart, at my soul.

I see her.

Mom.

Brewing coffee in our little apartment in Santa Fe, sunlight turning her hair into spun gold. She's laughing at something I said, her pale blue eyes seeming to glow.

Driving along an interstate in the middle of the night, all our belongings in the back of the car. She's got a huge

Styrofoam cup of coffee in one hand and the wheel in the other, and she's humming to herself, and I'm mostly asleep, watching her through slitted eyelids, the heaviness of sleep perching on my chest.

Searing chicken in a pan at the stove in our condo in Corpus Christi, Texas, where we spent a summer on the beach, baking in the sun and swimming in the salt of the gulf waters.

Her laughter, always her laughter.

Yet, behind the laughter was sorrow. It lurked within her, and she hid it from me. It weighed her down. She never allowed me to share it, to bear it for her, to ease her burden.

What pain did she know? Who was my mother, before she was Mom? I know nothing of that person.

She's gone.

I'll never know the answers.

Ah…

Here it is.

I note the breaking almost clinically, removed from myself, almost. Like I'm an outside observer watching from above, as if I'm a character in a third-person RPG video game.

Wracked, convulsing with sobs which no mortal frame can withstand.

My screams shiver through the forest.

Alistair plays on.

Mom.

Mom, please.

Mom. I need you.

I love you, my darling. I hear her voice in my soul, coming from that black void dreamspace. **It is breaking. I am with you. You are not alone, my love.**

Come back.

I speak into the void. *Come back.*

I'm always with you.

Come back. I need you.

You will change the world, my love. But first, you must break.

Momma. Mommy, please. Desperation to hear her voice turns me into a five-year-old, tottering after her into the shadows.

Arms wrap around me.

Caspian.

I smell him.

I feel him, my soul knows him.

"Ssshhh, Little Sparrow. It's all right." His voice is tender, his voice is love. "I've got you."

"Mom."

"I know."

I force my eyes open, and I see in the darkness of predawn as if it were midday. Alistair stands a few feet away, framed between a pair of towering cedars. Bloodtears stain his marble cheeks. The violin and the bow hang at his sides, held in his lifeless fists.

"Why?" I rasp. "Why?"

He steps silently to me, kneels in the needles. His nose buries along my throat. I feel his teeth, feel the points of fangs again my jugular.

Prick…

A rush of heat and pleasure snarl into the sorrow, the grief. Sunlight rages inside me, ecstasy pulses at the apex of my thighs. I feel his hair under my hand, the shape of his skull against my palm as I hold him to me.

Caspian's arms are bands around me, sheltering me. Cradling me.

Alistair growls as he pulls away, and I feel blood spurt from my throat…caught on Caspian's tongue, and then his lips fuse to my throat and he drinks from me, and fire burns in me, and now the sorrow is nothing but a dry leaf caught up in a wildfire, tinder for the inferno, ashes in an instant.

Alistair's lips touch my cheek, damp and warm. "Grief is a living thing," he whispers in an inhuman voice, thick with fangs and redolent with my blood. "It is a parasite. I had to draw it out of you."

"Why?" I gasp, writhing in Caspian's arms, desperate for him to give me more as he takes from me—I feel my body throbbing as it convulses, pounds, producing blood by the gallon to keep up with his demand.

"So you can be you."

"Who am I?" I whisper. "*What* am I?"

"I don't know." His palm cups my cheek, his fingers ghost through my hair…slides down my ribcage.

I welcome it. The frenzy is upon me, and I want more. Need more. There's a lightness to my being, where the grief was a millstone crushing me and pulling me under, despite my numbness and ignorance of my sorrow.

"What am I, Alistair?"

His hand presses to the small of my back, and I'm twisting in Caspian's arms, his fangs in my throat and his lips on my skin and his fingers at the juncture of my thighs, over my dress and panties. Alistair's hand ghosts over my thigh, low, near my knee, and his mouth caresses my flesh at my sternum, in the gap of my dress's neckline. His palm burns cold, his colder yet, harder yet. I feel the needles of his fangs touch the delicate silk of the inside of my breast.

They nick, loosing a freshet of blood.

I gasp, and my hips writhe upward, pushing against Caspian's teasing touch.

More.

More.

There's nothing but this, this moment, this need. There is no right or wrong or ethics or morals or good or bad or yes or no, only need, only desire. I crave it. Welcome it.

"Please," I whisper, my voice ragged and breathless. "*More.*"

My soul is alive, shaking within me like a gorilla raging at the bars of a cage, snapping like a lion, blazing with lightning and roaring with thunder. I am *alive*.

More alive than ever.

It draws. *Pulls.*

I hear Caspian moan, hear Alistair growl.

"Stop," a voice growls—Alistair, voice shaking, his fingers clawed into my thigh high up near my ass. "Caspian. Stop."

"*No.*" It's a feral, primal snarl, a possessive rip of sound—better to take a meal from a starving wolf as take me from Caspian, in this moment.

"Not here, Caspian. Not now. Not like this."

The pleasure subsides, flooding out of me like a receding tide.

"No, no," I moan. "More. More, please."

I feel a tongue sliding over my breast, another against my throat. Tingles ripple through me, drawing a groan from me.

Hands and arms help me to sit, and I'm limp with

exhaustion, overwhelmed, overcome, empty, yet full, ready to sleep for a week yet needing more and more and more.

Alistair and Caspian are both staring at me with blacked-out eyes. Waiting.

"You always stop," I say to Caspian. "I've never asked you to stop."

"Even after what we told you?" Caspian says. "You still want..." he trails off.

"I won't die," I tell him. The knowledge is there inside me, though I don't know where it comes from.

"You don't know that," he counters.

I lock stares with him. "Yes. I do."

He shakes his head. "I do not understand you, Maeve."

"That makes two of us." I reach for him, touch his shoulder, pull him to me. "Did I...I hurt you, didn't I?"

He turns his head to the side to show me the side of his neck—there's no mark, nothing. "I was shocked, Maeve. Not hurt."

"I...I don't know what came over me."

He caresses my cheek. "Me either. But we'll figure it out together."

I broke the skin. I tasted his blood. I saw it flooding down his neck; it stains his collar, still. Yet there's no mark.

I'm too exhausted to think about it. "I need to go home."

"I'll take you." Caspian scoops me in his arms, one around my shoulders and the other under my knees.

Alistair stands close, eyes clearing. "Maeve, I...I had to. I hope you understand." He closes his eyes, pain washing over his features. "We spoke of...of my mortal mate, and...I could feel your grief, locked away inside you. It will devour you. It was the only way I knew to bring it out."

I reach out and touch his smooth, warm jaw. "Thank you, Alistair."

He's no longer the kindly professor, no longer the lecturer, the history expert. He's not even the five-hundred-year-old vampire. He's just…Alistair. Shirtless, body sculpted into lean, sharp perfection—lined with scars, tears, holes, divots.

"You can scar?" I ask, trailing a finger over a long, keloid scar across his chest and abdomen.

"If it isn't healed by venom, yes," he says. "We can be injured by weapons but not killed. The wound will remain unhealed until we are blooded, and then it will heal unnaturally fast, scarring as you see."

"Oh."

He looks into my eyes, searching me. "I fed from you."

"You did." I curl my hand around the back of his bicep, contentedly slung in Caspian's arms.

"You let me."

"I did."

"Why?"

I shake my head. "Something comes over me. I don't know. It's not just pheromonal. It's that, but it's…more. I know what's happening, and I…" I swallow, and let the truth out. "I want it. Need it."

"Do you regret it?" He asks. "I am, after all, five hundred years old."

"I don't regret a thing," I tell him, letting him see the truth in my eyes. "Maybe I should, but I don't. Not with you, not with Caspian, not with Fin or Stirling. I don't regret it. Not anything."

He opens his mouth to speak, then closes it again. "I'll see you again soon, Maeve Sparrow."

I feel a connection to him—we are bound by loss. Caspian as well.

I act on instinct. Lean away from Caspian, and touch my lips to Alistair's…a brief, soft kiss.

He stills for a moment, and then returns it. Pulls away first, his palm against my cheek. "You are a wonder."

"I'm just me," I say.

He snorts at this, and then he's gone.

I look up at Caspian, wondering what his reaction will be—I just kissed his parent figure in front of him.

"It's not like that." He searches me with his eyes.

I frown. "What?"

He touches my forehead. "I can feel you. More strongly every day, every time we…interact, I can feel you, I can taste your thoughts in my soul."

"You…you can?"

He nods. "He's not my father. He's not my parent. He poses as that for mortal society, but it's not like that between us. Immortals have one parent—the father who sired them or the mother who bore them. There are blood-mated vampire pairs, like a marriage, but the other vampire is…like a step-parent, I suppose, at best."

"And so to you, Alistair is…?"

"It's hard to explain. We form covens—family groups, but rarely are the members of a coven actually related. It's chosen family. Alistair found all three of us at different times, and took us, helped us. We owe him much, and we feel love for each other and for him, but it is not parental. Not at all."

"So what happened just now…"

"It was an intimate, intense moment. For all three of us."

"So it's not…weird…for you?"

"No."

"It should be, for me, but..it's not." I rest my head on his shoulder. "Take me home, Caspian. Please."

The forest is a blur, then, and the sense of motion is distorted—like that moment of floating in the instant before gravity takes over and you begin falling. There is no sense of speed, perhaps because the world is flying by too quickly to get a sense of speed.

I cling to him and feel his warmth under my nose and lips and chin. I smell him. His blood. That fragrant intangible something I tasted in his blood…I smell it. My mouth waters and arousal warms the edges of me.

"Stop that," Caspian murmurs. "Not now."

"Sorry. Can't help it."

We're at the side door of Andreas's house—the light over the pole barn glows bright amber, and the light over the stove in the kitchen is a warm, inviting yellow.

Caspian sets me on my feet on the step between house and driveway, then stoops. "Here. Fin brought you these." He hands me my shoes and my purse.

"Tell him thank you for me," I say, catching at his hand before he can vanish on me.

"I will."

I don't let go.

"Maeve, I…" he sighs, trails off.

"I don't want you to go," I whisper. "Sleep next to me."

His eyes drill into mine, darkness tingeing the edges. "I can't."

"I want you to."

"I don't have that kind of control. Not now. Not ever,

but especially not now. I'm freshly blooded, and my feelings are—"

I lean into him, crushing my breasts against his chest, arms slinging around his neck. "Caspian, I can't be without you. I feel crazy without you."

He growls. "I can't. Not in your guardian's home."

I sigh. "You have a point, there."

His hands cup my hips and then slide around to caress my ass. "Fuck." This is a purely human, purely male epithet of raw desire. "You're a fucking drug, Maeve. I get high on your blood. I get high on your skin. Your body, your curves, your breath, your warmth…" his fingers dig into the meat and muscle of my ass, clutching me against him so I feel his arousal against my belly. "I crave you. I'm addicted to you."

I moan, and I lick his neck, taste his skin and a hint of the shadows, and magic tickles along my tastebuds, sizzling in my soul. I need him. I wish I could make my words come out like his, like poetry.

"Caspian," I moan, the syllables drenched in erotic need, dripping with arousal. "*Please*."

I could climb up his body right now, and take him inside me. I can almost feel it. My core quavers with anticipation, heating, soaked. I lick the side of his neck again, and then his throat, where he drinks from me. He groans, and his arousal pulses against my belly.

Instead of giving me what I want, he presses my back to the door and crushes me against it with his weight, pinning me. His hands cradle my wrists and pin them over my head, against the glass and the trim of the window frame in the door.

"Taste you…" he murmurs. "One…little….taste."

Instead of latching onto my throat, he sinks to his knees. He pushes my dress up around my hips—it's tight enough that it stays there. One sharp yank, another, and my panties are ripped away. Cold air bathes my sex; it's replaced by the heat of his breath, warmth with mortality. He keeps my hands pinned over my head with one hand and with the other he traces a finger down my seam. I gasp, moan.

"Shush, Little Sparrow," he murmurs. "Not a sound."

I bite my lip to stifle my moans as he scoops a finger into my sex, gathering the dripping essence. I watch him pop that finger in his mouth, and he closes his eyes as if tasting the finest nectar. And then he puts his lips to my sex and his tongue sears into my seam and swipes up to my clit and his finger delves into me and…

I taste my own blood as I bite down on my lip to keep from screaming as a rush of ecstasy rips through me like a tidal wave. His tongue circles my clit and his fingers pulse in and out of me.

"Fuck," he snarls, voice so low I can barely hear him. "If anything could taste better than your blood, it's your pussy."

Oh god, oh god.

I feel his tongue drag over my inner thigh, just where my femoral artery is. Then the painless nip of his teeth and the blasting purity of blood rush as he feeds from me, and this time his nimble fingers ply my sex, driving in and pulling out to circle my clit, thumb now pushing with the perfect amount of pleasure in time with the pulsing pull of my blood into his mouth.

I cry out through gritted teeth, a scream aborted into a breathless gasp.

He releases my thigh and licks it to heal, and the tingle sizzles and bubbles and adds to my pleasure and his tongue drives against my clit, and now...

And now...

The sun itself bursts inside me, and he's standing up and his huge impossibly heavy impossibly hard body presses me to the door and his mouth claims mine. I taste my blood on his lips and tongue and breath, taste the citrus tang of his venom sending rushing tingles through my lips and tongue, and his fingers drill into me and his thumb presses and circles as I come and I come and I come.

I writhe against him, and he swallows my moans and sucks down my screams, and I'm limp and helpless against the torrent of crazed bliss which owns me, heart and mind and soul and body.

"Mine," he growls, as I begin to repossess my wits once more.

"Yours," I agree, panting. "I'm yours. But...but what about...?"

"He will not take, only give."

"He took my blood."

"That's not taking."

It doesn't feel like taking, after all, does it? I don't feel like he or Fin or Stirling or Caspian has taken anything from me when they've fed from me.

"You choose what happens, Maeve. Now and always. With me, and especially with them."

"But I'm yours."

"Yes."

"And..." I look into his eyes, seeing only the man, only Caspian. "And you are mine?"

"Yes," he whispers.

He settles my dress down where it belongs, and gathers the tattered remains of my underwear in his hand.

"You're kind of hard on my underwear collection," I say, stifling a giggle.

"I'll buy you more."

"I'd like that."

His eyes blaze with arousal, black staining the edges yet again. "Or…you could just not wear them."

I lean into him and put my lips to his ear. "Then I couldn't enjoy the way you rip them off."

He growls, somewhere between a laugh and an aroused warning snarl. "Maeve. I'm hanging on by a thread. This is not the place or the time for the things I wish to do to you."

"What about what I want to do to you?" I whisper.

"Soon," he promises. He steps back, keeping the scrap of black lace in his hand. "All that and more…soon."

And then he's gone, shadows swirling in the wake of his departure.

Something has changed.

I barely recognize myself, the boldness, the wild eagerness—whatever happened tonight, it broke something open in me. Whatever was left of the girl, the child…is gone. The grief…it's not gone, but the monstrous threat of it is. I miss her. But I've wept for her. I've screamed into the void for her, I've shared my grief with the universe, and it has been heard. Now, what is left is the normal, human remains of missing a loved one.

More has changed than merely that.

Suspicion curdles in my gut—a knowing that I'm…

The thought won't come.

I need more time to sit with the suspicion. It doesn't

change the fact as I feel it within myself, but I can't acknowledge it.

Not yet.

Consuming me, beneath and behind all this...

Is that yawning, aching need. The hunger. The emptiness. The craving, yearning for *more*. For Caspian. For us.

For Stirling, and Fin, and Alistair.

To feel. To feed. Blood rushing. Heat and skin and fangs.

Completion.

Union.

More and more and more.

It's all tangled up, and I don't know what I want, what I need, only that I need more.

Chapter 27

I'M A DISASTER, IN THE DAYS THAT follow.

Predictably, Caspian is absent. There's a note on my pillow the next morning, a folded scrap of lined notebook paper with a heavy dark scrawl:

—M,

Hunting. Back soon.

Yours,

—C

Not exactly overflowing with sentiment, but that's not his way, unless he's overcome with emotion. I feel it, though. I can almost smell it on the paper—his crazed need. He's hunting in an attempt to assuage the ferocity of his desperation for me.

I wish I knew how to tell him I don't want him to tame that ferocity.

School seems absurdly prosaic, at this point. I barely notice people or classes, floating through it all on autopilot. I sit alone at lunch, telling my school friends that I'm going through something and need time alone, it's not them it's me, blah blah blah.

It is me.

It's *him*.

It's them.

I dream of him.

Mostly normal, mortal dreams of that night in the forest. I hear Alistair's wild, impossible violin playing, see him lurking in the trees and dancing from branch to branch, bow flying, fingers a blur on the frets. I feel his sorrow for his lost mortal mate. For his son, Ephraim, killed in the war. I feel his sorrow, and it is my own, for my mother. I wake from those dreams with my pillow soaked with tears.

I dream of what came after—their hands on me, their mouths on me, blood pulsing out of me and into *two* mouths…double the pleasure. God, I dream of that. I wake with my sex throbbing and I dare not touch myself, because I know it won't help. No orgasm I give myself could hold a candle to what *he* can give me.

I dream of Caspian's mouth on me, his fingers inside me.

I crave him.

I dream of his skin. His flesh under my hands, his hardness all for me.

I dream of his blood. The taste of it bursting into my mouth.

I dream of pulling at the secret invisible center of him

and tasting his very soul, tangy with old blood and new, the fruit flavor of his shadows, the acrid density of the magic illuminating his veins, the engine of his existence.

I wake from those dreams more confused than ever, feeling oddly empty, listless, hungry in a way that no amount of food can fill me.

Andreas and I, during this time, are nearly strangers. He's caught another case, and this one has him busier than ever. I wonder if he heard me, that night, outside the door, and if he's avoiding me out of awkwardness.

When we do see each other at home, usually later in the evening, I frequently catch him staring at me when he thinks I'm not looking—the expression on his face, before he schools it into neutrality, is one of distance and sadness and curiosity. When I meet his eyes, however, and think to ask him about it, he pretends to have not been looking at me, and something in his bearing wards off questions.

Days pass, and then a week—"soon" seems to be different to Caspian than me.

Every night, I have to stop myself from going to their house looking for him; he's not there—I can feel it. He's far away.

I dare not risk encountering the others, not in this state. I walk around all day, every day in a state of confused, absent-minded arousal, needing Caspian, crazed with it.

It's a fever burning inside me, devouring me from the inside out.

I'm crawling out of my skin, and with each day that passes the fever burns hotter, and the desperation for… god, I don't even know—just everything—ratchets up into a frantic, frenetic madness that I can barely withstand.

Every day, every hour that he's gone, I feel less stable, more out of my mind with craving him.

I've never been addicted to anything—I've only tried alcohol a few times, a tried marijuana a few times, but I've never been addicted to anything, not even coffee.

But I know that this is what it is.

I *NEED* him.

I can't go another day without him.

I need to taste him, feel him, I need to feed him with my blood and taste his and draw that sweet heady nectar into me from his soul.

The Purr is gone—in its place is a ravening beast, ravenous and all-consuming. It knows where he is, and even though hundreds or even thousands of miles separate us, I feel him.

I feel him coming to me.

I know he feels me, and I don't know if he can receive it but I find myself daydreaming in class, sending him wave after wave of need, sending it down the line of our connection. I give him my desperation.

My blood is on fire, all the time.

I feel too full of it—blood courses in my veins like a flash flood, threatening to overflow the banks and spill everywhere, flooding the whole earth.

My skin tingles and stretches too tight around my bones, so taut I feel like I could burst into shreds of skin at any moment.

Sitting in math class one afternoon, after two weeks of absence, I feel a single intense pulse of arousal. Close, intense, throbbing in my sex, hot and dense and molten and wild.

It's so strong I moan out loud.

The teacher stops mid-sentence. "Miss Sparrow? Are you all right?"

I fake a pained groan. "Cramps. I…I have to—I have to go."

I don't wait for permission, just scoop my purse and backpack up and bolt for the door. I leave the school, dumping my stuff in my car and jogging for home.

I cut through the woods, running in a beeline for their house.

It's him.

I know it's him.

I feel him. He's here, he's close, and he needs me.

As I near their clearing, I feel overlapping choruses of need and arousal. I can identify each of them: Stirling is a riptide, a maelstrom roiling just beneath the surface; Fin is a volcanic heat, explosive and tectonic and in your face; Alistair is the stillness and deathly green quiet in the air before a tornado, your skin prickling as you begin to feel your smallness against the power of nature; Caspian is the wild, primal fury and unbridled hunger of a predator long denied a proper meal.

My desire pounds in me like a thousand tympani, pulsating beneath my skin so hard I wonder if I could see my skin writhing with it. My desire is a warring of elements, shadows and sunlight, starlight and gloom, moonlight and pure emptiness of a long-abandoned room, it's cold and heat, ice and fire, wonder and dread.

I reach their clearing, and they are waiting for me. All four of them.

They stand shoulder to shoulder facing my approach from the depths of the forest. None of them speak as I stop six feet away from them.

They are dressed in their usual styles: slim khaki corduroys with a white button-down and a wool blazer for Alistair, pressed black dress pants with a sapphire silk shirt and a black vest for Stirling, faded and ripped jeans with a gray CAT equipment hoodie and a backward ball cap for Fin, and neat clean pale jeans with a plain white T-shirt and an expensive black leather jacket for Caspian.

The old Land Rover is idling, exhaust billowing thick and gray from the tailpipe, the engine a noisy rattling clatter in the otherwise silent stillness of the clearing.

Caspian takes a step toward me, but I dance a half step backward. "Don't. I…I can't. I don't know what's wrong with me, Caspian. I feel…I'm not okay. I feel *crazy*." I hiss the last word through my teeth, tears of madness and frustration scalding my eyes.

"Soon, Little Sparrow." It's all he says.

Alistair heads for the driver's seat, Stirling for the front passenger seat. Fin waits, as does Caspian.

"My purse and my backpack are at school, in my car." I lick my lips, let out a breath. "I…I shouldn't leave them there."

"Be right back," Fin says, and vanishes.

I feel him—he's moving swiftly in a straight line for the school. Caspian moves beside me and ushers me for the Rover without actually touching me. I know he feels as I do: we are a room of dynamite, and any touch could be the spark which sets us off.

I climb in and sit in the middle of the bench seat and Caspian sits beside me, behind Alistair. In the rear of the vehicle, there are five battered leather duffel bags, several canvas bags full of food supplies, a large white Yeti cooler—which I assume is full of bagged blood—and a pile of blankets and pillows.

"Are we going somewhere?" I ask.

"We have a cabin a few hours north of here," Alistair answers. "It's…more private."

More private…

Excitement thrums within me. It's hard to sit still, especially with Caspian's hard thigh and shoulder pressing against mine. He's blooded, albeit not especially recently—he's in the cooling phase, and I know within a few hours he'll need to feed again or he'll be cold and broody.

We sit, waiting, idling, for longer than I'd have expected for Fin to get from here to school and back with my purse and backpack. The answer isn't long in coming—he arrives with my purse and my little carry-on-size roller suitcase. He opens the rear gate and tosses my suitcase in, closes it, and then slides in beside me.

I frown at him in confusion. "Did you…break into my house and pack for me?"

He nods, grinning. "I used your key, so it's not technically breaking in."

"And you packed for me?"

He nods. "Leggings, T-shirts, hoodies, socks, underwear, I figure you're wearing a bra and don't need an extra. Toothbrush, toothpaste, hairbrush. Maybe won't be the outfits you'd pick, but you'll have clean clothes. And we won't be gone more than a few days."

I blink. "Oh. Okay, then."

He smirks at me. "Acceptable? Did I miss anything?"

I shrug. "I mean, I'll know when I go through it, but it sounds good."

"I looked for makeup stuff, but didn't see it."

I snort as Alistair pulls the Rover around and we trundle down the lane. "I don't wear makeup. Or bras, for the most part."

His eyes cast down at my chest, and then to my eyes. "You don't?"

I shake my head. "No. Not really. If I have to, I will. But generally speaking, no, I don't wear bras."

"So you're not wearing one now?"

I shake my head, swallowing hard as his eyes fix on my chest. Not that he can see anything exciting—I'm wearing a chunky white wool sweater and skin-tight jeggings with my usual Converse. "Nope. Just a tank top and the sweater."

He growls. "Shouldn't have told me that."

"Why not?" I ask, all innocence.

He regards me with eyes twinkling mischievously. "Because I have a bit of a thing for little mortal girls with small boobs and no bra."

I scrunch my eyebrows at him. "My boobs aren't *small*, Phineas. They're just not huge."

"Maybe I should be the judge of that?" He asks, the mischief and the teasing seduction in his grin nearly scorching a hole in my self-restraint.

"Perhaps you should," I answer.

Caspian says nothing, but his grin is amused.

"Fin, stop baiting her," Stirling says, without turning around. "We can all tell quite well the state she's in."

"Oh?" I ask. "And what state would that be?"

He now twists in the seat to stare at me—I realize none of them are wearing sunglasses. For my benefit, I think. They all have them, however—Caspian's are shoved into his hair, Stirling's hang from the V of his button-down, and Fin's are upside down on the brim of his backward

Detroit Tigers ball cap. Alistair alone doesn't seem to have any, nor have I ever seen him wear them.

"We've all felt the desperation coming from you for the last week and a half, Maeve." Stirling's tone is reproachful. "You've been broadcasting it for all and sundry."

"I thought only Caspian could feel me."

Alistair answers before Stirling can. "When we feed from an immortal, a connection is established. The more blood we take, the stronger the connection. We can sever it, or suppress it, and we typically choose to do so if the encounter with the mortal in question is…transitory in nature. In the case of an intentional, long-lasting relationship, we would choose to allow the connection to grow. The more we create a synergistic bond, the more complete is the link between vampire and host."

"So you've all kept the bond?" I say. "You can all read my feelings and thoughts?"

"You yourself seem to create a similar bond to us, as the connection I personally feel to you is far clearer than normal, especially considering I've only fed from you once. I can feel where you are, I can get a hint of your emotions. If you openly broadcast like you've been, it's…"

"Quite intense," Stirling finishes. "You've driven all of us to madness, Maeve."

"Well, I'm sorry," I snap. "I didn't realize you guys were feeling it. I thought only Caspian could feel it."

"Normally, that would be the case," Alistair says. "But as I said, I think you have some method of establishing a connection with us, rather than merely the other direction. It opens the channel and turns up the volume, so to speak."

"Oh." I consider this, in conjunction with all the other

evidence that I may not be a normal mortal girl as I've always assumed.

All available evidence points to me being… something.

Alistair in particular seems certain that this is the case.

I don't know how to broach the subject, and I lapse into silence, considering it.

The others seem content to let the silence breathe between us. We reach the highway and head north. There's no sound but the hum of the tires and the noisy clatter of the engine as the old vehicle struggles to maintain freeway speeds.

After a little over an hour and a half—during which all of us are lost in thoughtful silence—I see something looming over the tree line.

"What's that?" I ask.

The question is answered a few minutes later—it's a massive bridge. The towers are ivory, and the roadway and cables are green. It's absolutely enormous, and grows only larger as we approach—there's a tollbooth, and then we're on a causeway leading up to the bridge itself.

"This is the Mackinac Bridge," Alistair answers. "Quite an achievement of engineering. Local mortals often call it the Mighty Mac."

The tires hum on the grating on the inner lane and the cables widen and thicken and angle upward toward the colossal towers.

"I was thrilled when the bridge was done," Caspian says.

"Why?" I ask.

"Well, getting across to the hunting grounds in the UP was quite a bit more complicated, until." He gestures at the water now far below. "There was a ferry across the Straits, but close quarters like that can make it quite problematic to pass as mortal."

"I've never understood why you continue to hunt animals," Stirling says, leaning his elbow on the door and his chin in his hand, watching the bridge out the window. "It's so uncivilized. I thought you'd leave that barbaric behavior behind you after Alistair took you in."

"Stirling," Alistair scolds. "We've been over this far too many times in the last two centuries. You need not understand it."

"It *is* uncivilized," Caspian answers. "That's exactly the point. It's a chance to…let go. To use my strength and speed to their fullest potential. I don't have to be *civilized* when going toe to toe with an eight-foot, thousand-pound grizzly bear. I *can't* be."

"But the blood…how can you bear the taste?"

I snicker at the pun. "How can he…*bear*…it?"

Caspian snorts, and then Fin laughs out loud, and then Alistair. Only Stirling remains unamused.

Caspian lets his laughter trail off with a sigh. "Stirling, brother, you'd have to just try it to understand."

"But denying your instincts, suppressing the pheromonal response…it's uncomfortable at best," Stirling says.

"I was forced to feed on a particularly vile young man who'd been doing very bad things," Stirling answers, after a moment. "In Russia, after the war. And I confess, now, that it's decades behind me, that I didn't do a very good job muddling his memory. Nor did I numb him. He felt every moment of it and he suffered." His tone is dark. "He deserved it, and far worse."

Caspian chuckles. "Well shit, now I know why you're

so damn cranky all the time. You've got that filth inside you. Animals are *pure*, Stirling." He's serious now. "They are raw energy, pure predatory cunning, power, and instinct. There's no guile in them, no evil. No perfidious thoughts to taint the flavor of their blood. A bear is only a bear. It wants food, it wants rest, it wants to mate, and that's all. A mortal is so messy, so complex. Especially a not-very-good one. I'd hunt a bear before I drank from a vile mortal like you describe."

The fever still burns in me, but it's at a simmer, seemingly more content now that I'm with Caspian and the others. Perhaps it knows what's coming.

Why we're going somewhere more private.

I shiver, and press my thighs together, and listen to the boys continue to debate the morals and philosophy of hunting animals like an uncivilized barbarian versus removing an unsavory mortal from the world at the cost of having their evil tainting you.

Their conversation washes over me, and I tune out.
Feel.
Only feel.
Close my eyes.
There's Caspian, reaching for me across our link—tender, eager, desperate, full of need and love and impatience. I caress him over the bond, let him get a taste of my own need, a little flare of arousal.

He shifts beside me, swelling with a deep, steadying breath.

I find Stirling, next. It's easier, now that I know they can feel me, that the link goes both ways. He's impatient, unhappy, hungry…confused. He wants me, needs me, craves me, but he's worried it will go too far. That he'll

take something I'm not willing to give. I can't manage anything so subtle as what would be required to soothe his
concerns, so I just…touch him, through the bond. Let
him know I'm here—let him feel that I'm not afraid. I'm
not concerned. He responds—a brief touch of his mind
to mine, but it's like touching a red-hot stove element. The
heat and the roiling maelstrom are there, far beneath the
surface. Still waters run deep indeed.

Fin, then. Ah, he's all there, all the time. No suppres-
sion, no concerns, no hiding. Just open exuberance, and
eagerness. Desire burning like a bonfire at the pit of his gut.
He's had a taste and he's dying for more. Perhaps that's a
poor choice of words. He's thinking of me—inappropriate
thoughts, some might say. To me, they're not inappropriate
at all. Just sexual. He wants to feed on me and he wants to
touch me and he wants to savor my pleasure like the last
sip of very fine wine.

Alistair, finally. He's the most complex of all. He worries about my youth versus his extraordinary age. Perhaps I
should be, as well, but I'm not. I know myself—although, I
suppose that's not entirely true, is it? Regardless of whether
I'm mortal or not, I know my mind. I know my desires. I
know none of them are putting off pheromones at the moment, which means the burning need inside me is all me.
All my very own, my desires, my arousal, my need.

I can't explain it. Just like I can't explain how I can
feel them like this, or how I can enter that void-space of
dreams that are not dreams, but a reality deeper and more
real than this walking world. I can't explain why Caspian's
blood didn't disgust me but aroused me, sent me into a
frenzy. There's so much I can't explain. I can't even explain
where this manic, feverish arousal is coming from, but I

know it's coming from within me and I know I cannot and do not wish to deny it.

I will not.

I want Caspian. I want to mate with him—in mortal terms, I want to have sex with him, make love to him. We've been building up to it and approaching it and I keep getting denied as he takes my pleasure for himself, greedy and selfish, and leaves me without getting to take my pleasure from him. I need him. It's like breathing—I can only go so long without him.

I also feel a desire for the others. It's different—I don't want to mate with them…I keep thinking of it in immortal terms. But I *do* want…*more*. I don't know what. The feeding. The frenzy. The touching. Skin, and bodies, and blood. I want that, need it.

Somehow, I know Caspian will help me divide the two. I trust him. I know his soul, I've tasted it, and I know I belong to him, down deep where souls are joined before birth. We are molded from the same material, he and I, and I know he will know where to draw the line, even if I do not.

I know what's coming, and I welcome it.

Eagerly.

In fact, I would say I'm rather impatient for it.

Chapter 28

I message Andreas as we motor through the city on the north side of the bridge:

I'm on a quick trip with the Taylors to the UP. They have a cabin up there. Honestly I'm struggling with losing Mom and I need some time. Please try not to worry. Reception may be spotty or not there at all, but please trust me when I say I'm absolutely okay, I just need to get away.

He messages back immediately.

Wish you'd told me ahead of time. I admit I'm a little worried about how much time you're spending with the Taylors.

I'm sorry. It was last minute. I had a bit of a breakdown at school, and I needed to get away.

Well, I can understand that, and you're obviously not a child. You need any money? I can Venmo you or something.

I'm good, I promise. I have everything I need. Thanks for understanding. Be back in a day or two.

He gives the message a thumbs up , and I shut the phone off and stow it in my purse.

"Do you require a stop for food, Maeve?" Alistair asks.

"Are we nearly there?"

"Another hour, at most."

"Then I'm good. I can wait."

I feel impatience coming from all sides.

Fin is leaning into me, pushing his thigh into mine, scratching my thigh with his pinky—physical flirtation. Stirling is brooding. Caspian…he's just impatient. Alistair is the only calm one, but even from him I can feel hints of impatience. Perhaps he's merely better at hiding it, even from whatever kind of bond this is between us.

The next hour passes like taffy—slow, slow, slow, the scenery gradually changing and becoming less suburban and more rural, and then we're on a narrow two-lane black-top highway amid a dense, primal forest that makes the one in Elk Rivers look like a nature park in the middle of a city.

Alistair turns off the blacktop and onto a hardpacked dirt road angling at ninety degrees from the highway, deeper into the forest. The shadows are deep here, and I can almost feel them, cold and ancient and waiting.

Then after another ten minutes or so, he turns again, and this road has a sign proclaiming that it's not maintained by the county. And indeed, it clearly is not. It's rutted,

pitted, divoted, with washes of loose dirt and mud here
and there, flooded across with recent rain and snow-melt
in others. We bounce and jounce, jolt and bump every forward foot. In other places, the road is more sand than dirt,
and Alistair pulls a lever near the gear shift to engage the
4x4. On both sides, the trees loom huge and densely clustered, swarmed with tangled undergrowth. The shadows
beyond the road are thick and deep, beckoning and luring.

The road rises and dips, but seems to climb more than
it drops. It twists and turns, sometimes almost switching
back on itself more than it moves forward. After twenty
minutes of this treacherous jouncing, Alistair turns off yet
again, and this time onto something that is less a road than
a pair of ruts jaunting off through the wild forest. I catch
glimpse of an old wooden sign with faded peeling painted
letters:

A. TAYLOR

LIBBY'S REST

KEEP OUT

"Libby's rest?" I inquire.

He doesn't answer for a while. "Elizabeth. I called
her Libby." His voice is quiet, and doesn't invite further
discussion.

This road winds and rises and falls further and further
into the forest, and I know by now we're miles and miles
from anything like civilization. I would bet even the nearest neighbor wouldn't hear a gunshot.

Finally, the two-track bellies out into a tiny clearing.
At the center of it is a log cabin—hand-hewn, caulked,
with dirty, bubbled-glass windows and a green metal roof.
There's a chimney on the right side made of large boulders,

capped with a wire cage. There's a shallow porch, screened in. A red well pump stands about ten feet from the door. On the left side of the cabin, a deep lean-to connects to the wall of the cabin, stacked head-high with split wood, bark up. Faint traces and trails lead off into the forest in various directions. In more than one place on the cabin walls, deep, parallel marks are gouged into the wood—bear claws.

"No electricity, no running water," Alistair says. "No WiFi. No neighbors."

"Where do I go to the bathroom?" I ask.

"There's an outhouse in the back," Alistair answers. "Although I confess it has never been used. I only built it for appearances."

I regard the cabin—it's not exactly small. "You built this?"

"Certainly," he answers. "You forget, I was born in a time when such a thing was common. Not to mention, I can move logs of far more weight and size than a mortal, and I do not tire or require sleep, and can work past sunset."

"Oh. I guess that makes sense."

Alistair parks the Defender; we all pile out and the boys cart the luggage and supplies out of the vehicle while Alistair opens the door. There is no lock, only a simple latch.

"There is nothing here worth stealing," Alistair says to me, perhaps reading my confusion. "And if a traveler comes upon it and requires the use of it, then I would not begrudge them that hospitality. It is far too remote for vandals, as well."

Inside, the ceiling is low and the walls close, bare hewn and caulked logs. I can see the tool marks on the wood, still. The fireplace is on the right, and it is quite large and deep, blackened with the soot of centuries' worth of fires. A wrought iron rack holds split logs, and the only tools are an iron poker with a charred tip and a pair of wood and leather bellows. A charred metal hook extends out from the interior wall of the fireplace—for a pot to hang from, I assume.

There is a handmade couch facing the fire—it's crude, made of more hand-worked logs and held together with thick rope and huge spikes. The cushions are stuffed burlap. There's no kitchen, only a hammered copper sink held in a hand-made stand at waist height, with another well pump angled into it. There are three doors on the rear wall leading to separate bedrooms, each one just large enough for a bed and with a seaman's chest at the foot end. A ladder along the left-hand wall near the rear of the cabin leads up toward the ceiling—to a loft, I would assume.

Alistair gestures at the rooms. "Fin, Stirling, and I will take the rooms. Caspian and Maeve can have the loft."

Stirling takes the far right room, Fin the middle, and Alistair the left. Caspian waits for me, and I feel his hungry eyes on my ass as I climb the ladder up to the loft. It's cozy and intimate—with just enough room to sit up and not hit your head. There's another large chest at one end, and a cluster of candles in short metal holders. Caspian opens the chest and withdraws a stack of blankets. All of them are thick wool, and very, very old, but in fine condition. He spreads them out in layers, creating a nest. There's a pillow in the chest as well, and this too is very old and feather-stuffed.

I hear wood clacking together, a flare of a match, and then a faint crackling. The door creaks open and closed a few times.

I look at Caspian, who is sitting cross-legged, watching me. "Now what?"

He smiles. "We go for a walk in the woods."

"Aren't there bears?" I ask, remembering the claw marks in the cabin walls, most of them far above my head.

He grins. "Yes, and *they* fear *me*."

"Oh, right," I say, with a little laugh. "Can they, like sense you? Or smell you?"

"They sense me," he says. "They sense another predator, more accurately, and one who poses a threat. They go out of their way to avoid me."

We descend the loft, and Alistair has a merry little fire going, and he's pulling items out of the canvas bags—a wooden board, bottles of wine, a package of crackers, a knife, and a jar of honey. From the cooler, he produces wedges of cheese, a container of strawberries, and a summer sausage. From another bag, five wineglasses, each wrapped in a thick piece of cloth. I can see his room from here, the door open—his duffel is on his bed, closed; his violin case leans against it.

An image of him: scarred torso bare in the moonlight, eyes closed, perched on a branch, face contorted in sorrow and grief, ripping a haunting melody from that instrument.

Once again, Alistair seems to read me easily. "I built this place about fifty years after Libby died. Ephraim was on his own, and I was…my grief had been consuming me. I wandered here, built this cabin, and lived here alone for quite some time. I only returned east when Ephraim found me and informed me of the arrival in New York of the Fabrian Sect—the Parisian malcontents I spoke of. I'd spent time in Paris, and saw their politics carried out firsthand, and I knew all too well what they're coming to the New World foreboded. I knew I could no longer hide out here in my cabin in the Michigan wilderness. The only mortals here, at the time, was the occasional French trapper, so this was as remote as a sentient being could hope to be."

"This place is, like, three hundred years old?" I ask.

He laughs. "No, the original rotted away back in, oh… around the mortal Civil War. I tore it down and built this one sometime around the turn of the century—the twentieth century, I mean."

"Is the Civil War a distorted memory too?" I ask.

He shakes his head. "Oh, no. That was a purely mortal affair. We immortals stayed well out of that one. All the rest, as well." A shrug. "As a race, I mean, we stayed out of it. Politically. Wars are prime hunting grounds for a vampire. You have deserters and lonely widows. The battles themselves are unpleasant, but it gives us many opportunities. Many a vampire has found himself posing as a human soldier because there is so much chaos and confusion, and no one looks twice at us."

Caspian and Fin both nod, agreeing, while Stirling lounges on the couch, his eyes vacant and distant.

"Wait, you've all been in wars?" I ask.

Caspian shrugs. "Sure. I fought on the Western Front in 1918 and from the Normandy invasion to the end of the war in the forties."

Fin's eyes are unusually somber. "I went over with the Canadians in '14. I stayed in Europe between the wars and joined the French Foreign Legion when the second one broke out. I fought in Norway, Africa, and Italy."

I look at Stirling. "And you?"

He doesn't look at me as he answers. "I was with Fin,

with the Canadians, for World War One. We were in the same unit for most of The Great War. I was in Britain with Alistair for World War Two. I flew in the RAF. Piloting as a vampire is quite unique. We have far faster reflexes, night vision, and do not fear death, even from burning or falling."

"You can't burn?" I ask.

"We can," Stirling answers. "If you can contain a vampire, we can die by fire. The trick is keeping us contained. I was shot down several times. If the plane caught fire, I'd simply rip my way free and jump out."

I look to Alistair. "What about you, Alistair?"

"By then, I appeared too old by mortal standards to join the infantry, so in both wars, I worked in the upper command." He chews on his pipe, which is unlit. "So many poor decisions were made. But I could not press my case with my greater knowledge of history and tactics without giving myself away, so I was often forced to watch as arrogant, ignorant mortal generals threw the lives of their men away for no gain."

"Why fight?" I ask. "Why bother with mortal wars?"

"Those wars in particular, Maeve," Alistair answers, his voice slow and cadenced, "one could hardly avoid. They engulfed everyone. We could not exist in any developed country and not be drawn in. Everyone was expected to do their part. So, we did."

"Often, I would do my best to spare the lives of the men in my unit," Caspian said. "I could take bullets for them, or absorb an explosion. It meant one or two or a dozen lives out of millions, but the men in my units were just scared little boys, most of them, in both cases. I couldn't very well watch them die when I could do something about it."

Fin and Stirling both nod in agreement.

"I befriended a young mortal from my unit in the first war," Stirling says. "I made sure he survived the war, and I kept in contact with him for the rest of his life. I had to stop meeting him before he realized I wasn't aging, but we exchanged letters for decades." A pause. A sigh. "I still look in on his grandchildren, from time to time. He is not forgotten."

"How did you feed during the wars?" I ask.

A silence.

Fin answers, his voice heavy. "On the dying or newly dead. You have to suppress the pheromone response. The dying are…" There's a long, heavy pause. "They're eager for the darkness of eternity." It's the most serious I've heard him.

"And the dead?" I ask.

Stirling answers this one. "They taste of nothing. Once the spark is gone, they taste of nothing, of darkness and emptiness. It is poor sustenance, and nothing so sweet as the flavor of a willing young mortal female. But desperate times, you know."

Caspian lightens their mood. "And there are the girls you meet on patrol, or on leave. There's nothing like the taste of a nubile French farm girl."

Fin chuckles. "That's the truth."

"Men," I snort. "Even though you're vampires, you're still just…*men.*"

We nibble on the spread Alistair arranged, sip wine, and watch the fire. Eventually, I can tell Caspian is getting restless. He, the most utterly still being I've ever known, is fidgety, discontent.

I take his hand. "Show me the woods, Caspian."

He sighs in relief, shooting to his feet and hauling me to mine. Alistair eyes us, his expression neutral. "Do not be seen by mortals," he warns.

Caspian just rolls his eyes. "Not my first day," he says, his tone droll.

Alistair just swirls wine, nodding. "Don't be long."

It's a loaded little statement. I can sense—perhaps in his eyes or his tone, and perhaps through the link between us—that he is as impatient for what's to come as the rest of us. He guards it, however. Hides it.

Without looking back at him, as Caspian leads me away from the cabin and into the woods, I slide a tendril of mental or emotional touch along the channel between Alistair and me. He withdraws away from it, at first. I let a hint of my sorrow for Mom out, let it tinge the edges of our connection.

That gets him.

He responds, sending his own hesitant little questing tendril toward mine. I taste his sorrow. It's not feeling. It's not thoughts. Its mind to mind connection, soul to soul. I *taste* him. His sorrow, his everlasting grief for his lost Libby. His desire to simply *feel* again, for a mortal, for a female.

But I'm not a mortal, am I? I don't know what I am, but I'm not that. I know it. Deep inside, I know I'm something else. I can feel the *otherness* in my spirit, I can feel it like a separate sentience within my soul, prowling in the pit of me, pacing the shadows, waiting to be freed.

He tastes that. I can feel it. He knows I know.

You're still just you.

I feel his words, and they're not even a whisper, barely a breath. I sense them. They're a lock of hair trailing across the back of my neck.

I'm still just me.

No matter what else I may be, I'm still just me.

As are we all—Caspian said that to me, once. More true than ever, I'm realizing.

The woods around me are cold and ancient—spring hasn't reached here, yet. Pockets of snow still linger beneath wayward pines. The air is sharp with chill—it's late, and dark is falling.

I welcome it.

The gloom descends and my soul responds, lifting, soaring toward the shadows. We need no trail, Caspian and me. We weave between trees, stepping under branches and around the underbrush. There are glimpses of the sky through the canopy, purpling dusk settling in slow waves. Cold and cold. Caspian's skin is cooling—his hand in mine icing over by the minute, making the air around us feel nearly warm.

Yet the cold doesn't bother me—not the air, not him.

"Nothing happens that you don't want to happen," he says, apropos of nothing.

"I know."

"Do you know what you want?" He asks.

I nod.

"Tell me."

"You."

"Just me?"

My foot breaks a twig; a bird flutters overhead, a squirrel chatters angrily, unhappy at our presence. Caspian is silent, in his tread, in his spirit.

"I need you, Caspian." I whisper this truth to him, knowing he could hear me across the entire earth. "More than oxygen, I fucking need you."

"I know. Me too."

"You too?" I look at him, and I see his eyes swivel to mine, and his brown eyes are stained black, tendrils and spiderwebs clinging to the corners.

"Yes." He stops as we come to a fallen cedar. His impossibly powerful hands capture my waist and he lifts me to sit on the trunk, then hops up to sit beside me. "I could feel you going crazy without me."

"Where were you?" I ask.

"Here." He gestures to his left. "Farther north, not *here* here, but the UP."

"Why?"

"You know why."

"Tell me anyway."

"Because I can't lose you." He looks at me, black staining more of his eyes with every passing moment. "You see how Alistair is. Losing Libby broke him. He's never been the same."

"Did you know him, before?"

A shake of his head. "No. It was before I was born." He looks at me. "You can see the brokenness in him, can't you? You can feel it."

I nod. "I feel it."

"I can't go through that. Not with you. You're not just my mate—my mortal mate, my host. You're more, Maeve. So much more."

"I know. Deeper than souls, more than merely blood and bodies."

He reaches out and takes my hand. "I don't trust myself with you."

"What do you think will happen?" I ask, tangling my fingers with his, holding tight to the frigid marble of his hand.

"I would..." he tries to take his hand away, but I hold tight, refuse to let him. "I would hurt you."

"You haven't, though."

"I would."

"How?"

He growls, frustrated. "If I lose control, I will...take you. I will...we will..."

"Say it. Tell me." I twist on the log and sling my leg across his lap, straddling him. "Tell me what you would do."

"I would have you."

"How?"

"I would feed from you. Touch you. Make you think you want me. I would put you into a frenzy and...I would impregnate you. And then you would die and I would have to watch it happen."

"Are you casting pheromones, right now?" I touch his face, palm to the burning cold of his cheek.

"No."

I put my lips to his cheek, millimeters from his ear. "Are you attempting to put me into a frenzy right now?"

"No." His voice is low, tone hesitant. Hopeful.

"This isn't a frenzy. This isn't a vampire thing or an immortal thing. Me, wanting you? Caspian, it's a *human* thing. You're a vampire, and I'm...I'm not sure. I don't know. But I'm a nineteen-year-old human girl, and I'm horny, and I'm in love with you."

He flinches. "Don't say that," he hisses. His hands dig

into my thighs, up near my hips and buttocks, painful and hard.

"It's true." I hold his face in my hands and pin him with my eyes. I will him to look at me and not look away; it works. "I'm here because I want to be. Because I want you. Vampire, human, and immortal. Two hundred and forty years old. A veteran of two wars. Connoisseur of nubile French farm girls."

He manages a laugh. "That was a long time ago."

"I know. I'm teasing you."

"You're not jealous?" He regards me curiously.

I shake my head. "Nope. You had a life before me, just like I did before you."

He hesitates. "You're not a virgin." It's not quite a statement, not quite a question.

"No." I settle in more comfortably on his lap, wrapping my legs around his waist, draping my arms on his shoulders, playing my fingers through his hair. "I've had a few boyfriends—although that's a strong term. We moved around too much for anything like a long-term relationship. More than a hookup, less than a relationship. Somewhere in between."

I need to smell him. I nuzzle his throat, inhaling his scent—copper, smoke, the leather of his jacket, the deeper scents of his blood, the magic and the darkness and the spark of life.

"You want me."

"Yes."

A long pause. "What about the others?"

"It's hard to explain. Shit, it's hard to understand. It's not like with you. I don't crave them. I won't…*mate* with them. But when you and Alistair both fed from me…" I

shiver at the memory, clinging tighter to him. "It was…
it was like nothing I've ever felt before. I want it. I want it
again, and I want more. With you. With him. With Stirling.
With Fin."

"But you're mine."

"Yes." I stare into his dark eyes, shadow-hazed. "And
you're mine."

"I am." He grazes my cheekbone with his knuckles,
his black-stained eyes both fierce and tender at once. "But
if you want that with all of us…that connection. It would
be…intense."

"They're your family."

He traces a curving line from the point of my chin up
and over my ear, "They're my coven. It's different."

"How?"

He thinks, tipping his head to the side. "A family is
a mother and a father—with vampires, that gets complicated, but that's what it amounts to. Maybe a brother or a
sister. A coven is…more and less. No shared lineage, only
shared experience. Not bound by blood, as in genetics,
but by choice. He rescued us from our respective circumstances, and we have chosen to live with him since. We call
ourselves a family for mortals, but in vampire culture, we
are a coven. All that binds us is choice."

"And if I was to have that connection with them?"

He doesn't answer for a while. "You would be bound
to us. Not bound…linked. With them, now, it can be sup-
pressed. Neutralized, perhaps, is a better term, if none of
you continue it—if they do not feed from you any further.
But with you and me, this bond can not be severed. Not
without ruining both of our minds. Our hearts, our very
souls." He cups my cheek, brushing his thumb over my lips.

"If you choose to allow anything further to happen with the others, you would, in a sense, be choosing to be a part of our coven, though you are not a vampire."

"It feels right, Caspian." I feel the shadows around us, and they feel so close, so *real*, almost tangible. I can almost touch them, but they slip through my grip like mist. "You and me, we feel right. The others—your coven, they feel right."

"What if you get pregnant?" He asks. "You're too young, even for a mortal. And far, far too precious to me."

"I can't give you evidence or proof, only a strong feeling. But I know, down to my bones, I *know* that won't happen."

He swallows hard, a smear of red at the corner of one eye. "It can't."

"It won't."

I feel a pull at the center of my chest, at my belly, at my sex. Back, toward the cabin.

Caspian feels it, in some way—I see his attention flicker. "Time to go." He stands up with me. "Shall I run?"

I press my face into the soft cold pungent black leather of his jacket. "Yes."

I cling to him as he races through the forest with me in his arms, watching the blurred bars of trees fly past.

Soon.

The thing inside me, the *other*, is prowling with frantic manic energy inside me. It wants. Needs. Craves. Demands.

Blood.

Skin.

Touch.

Breath and moans. The pulse of pleasure and the

freedom of bliss. Heady need given into. Taking. Giving. Just…*being*. Totally won over to this new existence.

I send everything I'm feeling in full broadcast, to all of them, full strength. I let them feel how restless I am. I show them the depths of my desire, the fullness of my readiness.

I feel a pull to each of them, individually.

I feel them respond, and I know the touch of their minds on mine.

I'm ready.

I want it.

Now.

CHAPTER 29

CASPIAN SLOWS TO A SLOW MORTAL pace as we approach the cabin. Smoke plumes from the chimney, dissipating in the branches overhead. The Land Rover is a frosty windowed hulk of dully metal gleaming in the silver light of the newly risen moon.

Hunger growls inside me. But not for food.

Put me down.

I don't know if I say it or if I think it, but he complies—he sets me on my feet. His hands rest with casual possessiveness on my hips, and I like them there. I like the ownership of his touch.

I don't know why I'm hesitating on the other side of this door—not nerves, not fear.

Anticipation, I think.

I lean back into him, and his arms sling over my chest. "Caspian?"

"Yes, Little Sparrow?" His voice is soft and quiet.

"I'm worried I'll lose myself in this. That I won't know what I'm doing." I shake my head, the back of my head rolling against his chest. "You have to pull me back, if that happens."

"I will."

I'm whispering, because what I'm saying scares me. "There's something inside me, Caspian. Something huge, something powerful. This—" I gesture at the cabin, "is part of it, part of me…of me becoming me. If that makes any sense. I don't know. I just know the only thing I'm scared of is losing control and doing something that will make you—"

He twists me in place and covers my mouth with his and cuts me off with his tongue and his lips and his breath, and I've never known a kiss like this. Demanding. Owning. Devouring. He takes my breath and sucks it down into his lungs and refuses to give it back, so I have to take it. I claw my fingers into his hair and pull him down to me and inhale his breath and my own, and his hands paw at my ass, fingers digging brutally hard into the muscle and skin, pulling me against him, and the twinge of pain only ignites my desire all the more, because it barely registers as pain.

I feel his fangs extending in his mouth, feel them lengthening against mine, against my lips, against my tongue, and then he twitches his mouth just so, and I taste blood—my own. It mingles with my saliva and his, and I taste his venom and feel it tingling in my mouth and bubbling against the tiny cut, and I feel him clamp his lips onto the opening and suck, and I moan at the razor-thin fissure of almost-ecstasy. I find his lip with my teeth, and I don't know if I have fangs or not and I don't care—I bite down hard on his lip. He's taken just enough of my blood for his lip to be soft enough to mark, to bite into. I taste…all that is him. But only hints of blood and soul and thought.

That hungry void in me yearns for more of him, but I deny it. Not yet. Something in me knows it's not time.

He sucks at the cut on my lower lip and then releases it, and my blood floods our mouths as we kiss, and I moan out loud, an erotic mewl of pleasure as his hands grip my ass and lift me up, and we kiss and we kiss, and I wrap my thighs around his waist and my legs around his ass and I knot my fingers in his hair. His hands soar up my hips, up my ribs.

Cup my breasts over my sweater.

I moan again, and I feel too hot. My skin is flushed. Prickling. Sweating.

All I know is the taste of his mouth, of my blood and his venom and the faint flavor of his blood—he doesn't have much, yet, because I haven't blooded him. He's only getting a hint, a Baskin Robbins flavor-testing spoonful.

I hear the door open, and I feel him moving. The air warms and softens from the sharp hard cold of the outdoors to the inside of the cabin. My eyes are closed, but I sense the dullness of the light—only the fireplace is lit, and I know the cabin will be bathed in the flickering dancing orange light of the fire.

I pull at Caspian's clothes. I find myself seated on the edge of the couch, and Caspian is kneeling between my thighs. I push his jacket off. Peel at his T-shirt—it sticks to his ridiculous muscles, and I just rip it. It tears free easily under my hands. His skin is cool, and I want it hot with my blood.

I'm too hot.

I'm suffocating.

He knows what I want, what I need. His hands gather at my waist, bunching the wool of my sweater and tugging it upward. It's gone, and warm air bathes my skin. I can smell the woodsmoke—I can almost smell the pine resin of the logs as they burn. I smell Caspian. I smell the others—waiting behind closed doors for…something. I don't know what.

All I care about is Caspian. His mouth leaves mine, and his tongue flits against my cut lip and I feel the flesh knitting together. His hands roam up my thighs, cup my hips and the upper swell of my ass where I'm sitting on the couch, and then they skate up my back, under my tank top.

I know where he's daring, next.

Please, please.

My whole being throbs with the desire to be touched.

He leans me backward against the couch back, and his lips touch my throat. Oh god, he's going to feed.

Yet, he doesn't.

He kisses.

Soft lips, tenderly touching.

Down, to the collar of the tank, breastbone. Another kiss.

I cling to his head and force myself to breathe. Open my eyes and see him—dark hair hanging around his face and neck. Ivory skin bruised with pink. Muscles bare in the firelight, rippling, carved, and perfect. I roam his back, his shoulders with my hands.

He tugs the strap of the tank down, kisses my shoulder.

"Off," I whimper aloud. "Off. Please."

He lifts the hem, yet he slides down my body, and my pussy jolts with excitement, remembering all too well the beautiful expertise of his lips and tongue. He teases again instead—kisses my belly. Pushes the tank top up a little farther. I claw my fingernails into his nape, willing him to take my sex or to kiss my breasts or *something*, something more.

Instead, he kisses my ribcage. High, on the left side, just beneath my breast. The hem of the shirt presses on the bridge of his nose. I'm watching him now, watching my belly heave with gasping breaths. Watching his mouth stutter along my skin, beneath my breasts, to the other side, the ribs beneath my armpit.

Higher, kissing.

And now, god, please, and now his hand complies with my will—ripping my tank top up and off, and I'm bare from the waist up, topless in the firelight. My breasts hang heavy in the orange glow, my nipples swollen and thick and hard and hypersensitive. They rise and fall with my ragged breathing.

His eyes take me in. "So fucking perfect," he snarls, his voice thick with fangs and desire. "Mine."

"Yours," I agree, on a whimper. "Show me."

He falls upon me, one hand gripping my nape and the other my breast, holding it up to his mouth. His lips seize my nipple and his teeth saw lightly over it and his tongue flicks it, and I cry out.

Erotic, aroused, beckoning.

He cups my other breast, then, thumb caressing the nipple, palm cradling the weight of it. He moves laterally, taking my other, neglected nipple into his mouth and suckles on it.

More.

More.

Take my blood. Feed.

He doesn't hear or he ignores me.

I feel pheromones wash over me, then. I know the individual taste of them on my tongue, the weight of them on my skin:

Alistair.

Fin.

Stirling…

Caspian.

I reach out with a hand, stretching for them, reaching for them, beckoning and begging.

Caspian's kissing mouth leaves my breasts, and I'm lifted. We move. There's a thick bearskin rug on the floor in front of the fire, and he lays on it on his back with me on top of him. I feel the fur tickling my feet where they tangle between his. My back is to his front, and he's inhaling my scent at my neck, at my jugular.

I call for them, silently, across the linkages, and I feel them respond.

Not yet.

Now.

More.

I feel Caspian's tongue lapping at the skin beneath my jaw, and the tingling of the venom takes hold and anticipation signs in my every pore.

Yes, yes, yes.

I reach up and back and snag my fingers in his hair and hold on, knowing I can pull as hard as I want and I couldn't possibly hurt him. My hips lift, heat boiling in my sex, need soaking my panties.

A heady moment of thrilling anticipation, and then I feel his fangs pierce my skin at my jugular, and there it is fuck yes the rush of everything the purest pleasure there is on this earth soaring through me as he draws my blood into him.

I feel it—our connection. I reach for it, find it, grip it, take it into me: I feel him. All of him. His mind, his soul, his thoughts and his fears and his desires and the hundreds of years of life and experience and power and magic.

I take it into myself.

Pull. Drinking as he does blood, but instead of blood I pull in the essence of him.

His vitality.

He allows it—I feel him acquiesce, feel him offer it to me: this is synergistic, cyclical, my blood restoring his vitality, and vice versa.

I pull it in, and the core of my being soaks it up like a sponge. That too-tight feeling in my skin persists, heightens. My blood thrums, bubbles, and my bones rattle with the pent-up power within me like the lid of a stock pot as the water within churns at a full rolling boil.

His hands cup my breasts, cradling and kneading—possessing.

Another deep draw of my blood.

My clit throbs.

I could come, just from this.

One hand at my breasts, toying and playing, the other now flattens over my belly and his fingers delve under the elastic of my jeggings and then under my underwear, flowing over flesh, over my mound and his middle finger dips into me, into my wetness and my heat and I cry out, hips lifting.

Orgasm is within reach, but I fend it off, not ready yet, not yet, not yet. I need more.

I call for them. Cry out for them, not aloud, but across the connection. I send my pleasure to them, send my need to them. I *demand*. The fury of my desperation is a wildfire consuming all of me, and I pour that into the channels between the five of us.

I hear a door open.

A second.

A third.

I feel them, now.

They're here with me.

My breasts are bare—they can see me. They could touch me. *Will* touch me. Soon.

I force my eyes open. Alistair stands removed, in his corduroys and a white T-shirt, hair rumpled. Stirling is shirtless, just in his slacks. Fin has stripped down and put on a pair of shorts; a glance tells me he's wearing nothing under them.

Their eyes rake over me.

Fin is hungry and visibly aroused. Stirling is holding back. Alistair is unsure.

One hand is buried in Caspian's hair as he slows his drinking, sipping now.

I reach for Fin. He takes a step closer to me. His eyes flare with black, voids of ravenous hunger. He's bloodless. He needs this, needs me. I'm ready to give.

He drops to his knees beside me, and Caspian's hands leave my breasts, offering them up to Fin.

A growl rumbles through the room—Fin, appreciative, hungry.

I watch him reach for me, his huge powerful hands resting on my belly, then finally, almost tentatively, caressing the soft weight of one breast, and then the other. His rumbling snarl says everything, tells me he's longed for this, wanted it, needed, dreamed of it, if vampires dream of need as mortals do.

I tangle my fingers in Fin's hair, pull him closer. He bends over me, knees in the bearskin, one hand on my thigh propping up his weight, the other cupping my breast and lifting it to himself.

I breathe raggedly, slowly, deeply. Waiting, wanting, anticipating.

I feel Fin's lips touch my sternum, my belly, my rib. I feel his cold breath on my skin. Smell the copper of his breath, the burning cold of his touch.

The world stops as I feel his lips ghost over the lower swell of my breast, and Caspian is still taking slow shallow sips from me, and I feel him warming beneath me, feel his skin heating and softening, feel his cock hardening under me.

Fin takes my nipple in his mouth, and I gasp, moan. God, yes.

His touch is different. Rougher in touch yet gentler somehow in spirit. His tongue flickers. Zaps of ecstasy rip through me as he kisses and worships my breasts, one and the other, while Caspian drinks from me.

And then Fin licks the side of my breast—I feel the venom tingling into my flesh. Oh god, oh god...

Fin's fangs sink into the soft silk of my breast, on the outside and an inch beneath my nipple. Searing ecstasy tears through me, wild and wicked and decadent.

I am lost. Utterly lost. There is no me, no Maeve, no Little Sparrow, only a creature of hedonic rapture.

Pulsations rattle through me, jar me, the hum of my blood and the power in it filling me, shoving thoughts away. Caspian's mouth at my throat, Fin's at my breast. Blood pumping.

Power. Power. Pulsing, pulsing. Filling, filling.

The more they take, the more full of it I am.

I cry out, keening my luxuriant bliss, wailing, abandoned.

And then I feel them.

Stirling.

Alistair.

Drawn to me.

CHAPTER 30

STIRLING'S LIPS TOUCH MINE, questing and gentle.

Alistair's hands are on my belly, my hips.

Someone's hands—I don't know whose, don't care whose—peel down my jeggings, bringing my underwear with them, and warm air coats my skin, my bare thighs, my soaked bare sex.

I'm naked.

Caspian slips from beneath me, and the bearskin is soft and ticklish and warm from his skin, now heated with my blood. I know Caspian's touch apart from the others'. He is at my side, fingers trailing over my breast, tweaking my nipple until I cry out, and then I feel his lips at my belly and then on the tender inner flesh of my upper thigh, cheek grazing my sex. I feel his fingers at my clit, lightly pressing, teasing, as if he somehow knows I'm not ready to let go yet.

He does know: he can feel it. I know he can—I think I can feel his awareness inside me, in my soul, in my gut.

So he teases.

Stirling is on my left now, his lips kissing my breast-bone and then my throat and now Stirling's lip seize my breast, the slope of it, then the nipple, and it's almost too much—my cry is one of agonized pleasure, too much of it, too deep, too wild. Yet Stirling is merciless. He licks my nipple, and I feel him release his venom so the hard aroused nub of nerves sing with the effervescence of the venom and then—

I scream, a throat-scraping howl of orgasmic release, climax ripped out of me as Stirling's fang slices open my nipple, the venom removing the pain of it and then he's sucking my blood from the slit and it's a euphoria unlike any other, sending me into paroxysms, hips thrashing, screams ripping from me.

Caspian takes the moment and makes it his—he presses his tongue to my clit and devours me with rabid intensity, and now I'm so overcome by it all that I can't even scream, can't cry, can't twitch or thrash. I'm locked, hips helplessly thrusting into Caspian's mouth as Fin sucks at one breast and Stirling the other…

"That's right," Caspian whispers. "So beautiful when you come for me."

One more. I need one more, the last one.

Alistair, please… I can't form words, but the plea filters out of my soul and to him.

I hear his snarl as he abandons the fight.

His mouth touches mine, a brief tender hungry kiss, and I lick his tongue and taste his need for my blood and I slide my tongue over his lengthening needle-sharp fangs. Then he breaks the kiss and I miss it already, need it back—

I feel Alistair move, feel his hand glide down between my breasts, feel his cold fingers burn against my thigh, and he gently tugs my leg away. I wedge my heels against my buttocks and splay my thighs as wide as they will go, wanton and eager and unashamed.

Alistair's tongue swipes wet and cold over my thigh, high and inside, nearly to my pussy, and then I feel the pressure of his fangs piercing flesh and my rapture is nearly complete.

Four mouths, four points of bliss.

Alistair pulls slowly, carefully. I feel him, feel my connection to him firming and deepening, as with Fin and Stirling. I can caress their souls, now. Their minds, their hearts. I do so, pouring my pleasure into them because there's too much of it to keep for myself. I'm flooded with it, openly weeping, sobbing with ecstatic indulgence, wild and frenzied nova-hot orgasms smashing through me one after another, not waves of orgasm, but a machine-gun series of them, each hotter and deeper and wilder than the last.

My hands reach. Find muscle, hot and pliant…
Hair, soft and silky and cool.

I find an erection, and I caress it. Fin. He groans as he continues to feed, and I feel so full of blood I need him to take more, take more—he does, feeling my unexpressed need and giving it to me. He pulls deeply and I caress his thick length and I feel him respond.

More, more.

A growl from one side, a snarl from the other. Moans and whimpers from me.

That thing inside me, that vacant chasm of ravenous need is in control and it pulls, draws, sucks vitality from all four of them, through our connection and points of skin-to-skin contact. But where touch is most intimate, there the pull is strongest: Caspian's mouth on my clit, my hand on Fin's arousal.

My other hand, then, moves of its own accord. I'm un-thinking, reacting out of instinct, out of need, my higher mind and faculties scattered and shattered and dissolved under the flash flood raging hot bliss which pulses in my veins, woven into my blood.

I find Stirling. He sucks harder, and his tongue flits against my nipple even as he draws blood, and I feel him fill my hand—thinner, longer, different and perfect.

Both men moan. Voices humming against my flesh, I quicken my touch.

Orgasms bash through me, shaking me, flailing my hips. Caspian is relentless, taking and taking and taking my releases on his tongue, in his mouth. Yet even though I've long since lost count, I know none of these is the true release I'm seeking.

Fin snarls, hips bucking, and I feel his seed coat my hand.

Then Stirling.

"Good," Caspian growls, lips moving on my sex, breath hot. "Good girl."

Hot, wet, flooding over my hands and wrists. I feel

their release in my own body, weaving into mine, feel Stirling gasping with awe, feeling Fin reeling with disbelief as my pleasure and theirs mingle and merge and tangle and feed each other, and they both let loose leonine roars as they buck into my touch, and I take their pleasures for myself.

Alistair releases my thigh, licks the wound and I feel it close.

Caspian moves away from my sex.

I feel the air shift—feel Alistair's shoulders settle between my thighs and then, for a moment, there's only him. Fin and Stirling lick my wounds to close them, Caspian I feel across the room.

Alistair and me, alone, for a heartbeat. He kisses my sex.

His hands cover my breasts.

I caress his shoulders, his neatly clipped hair. His neck. Hold his face in my palms as he kisses me to a slow but tectonic climax that makes me shudder and scream without breath, not even a squeak leaving me.

I feel him pull that release, the energy and the pleasure and the satisfaction, into himself. I pour it into him, give it to him, push more and more and more, glutting him on my surplus of rapture.

In return, he offers me his vitality. I feel myself take it, instinct operating whatever capacity or muscle or function it is. The nuclear thrum of my blood is nearly at its peak, and I'm afire with it, rattling with it, trembling.

I reach for him, but he's gone.

I hear the door open, feel a blast of cold.

The cabin is empty but for Caspian and me, then.

He carries me up the loft, somehow holding me in his

arms and ascending the ladder. I don't know how he manages it and I don't care. I'm alone for a moment, and then something wet and rough and warm scrubs over my hands and wrists and arms, over my sex and neck and breasts—cleaning me. Readying me for the next part. The last part.

I feel the edge of a cliff approaching. I welcome it, fling myself toward it eagerly.

All I know is the feel of his hot skin against mine and the nest of blankets under me. I feel a candle flame, feel it flicker, taste the heat of it and scent the tendril of smoke.

Taste, scent, tactile sensation—they're all overwhelmed. I have other senses, too: I can only use the word taste, as it's the closest to the sensation: I taste magic in the air, acrid and sour and sweet and dense and thick, like the scent of sex in a small room, like steam and soap and shampoo in an unventilated bathroom, like chocolate chip cookies freshly baked and cooling on a tray. It's all that and more—there's a sourness to it, but like sour candy rather than raw citrus juice. It lingers on my tongue and coats my skin. It's *under* my skin, it's in my tendons and the molecules of my subcutaneous flesh and it's curling and alive and seeking. Magic slides like a lover's touch over my breasts and nipples and wraps around my thighs and into my sex. I feel it on Caspian, as well. I sense his awareness of it.

He's over me, on top of me, weight and heat pressing me into the nest of wool blankets. His hands cradle under my head and lift me to kiss him. I taste my blood on his tongue and lips.

I love you, I whisper to his soul.

And I love you, he whispers back. **Are you ready?**

I reach between our bodies and find him, clutch his

hard arousal and caress it. He rests his forehead on my shoulder and shudders under my touch, and he gasps, and his hips flex.

I need you. It's a plea.

I lift my hips, guide him to me. I taste and scent his fear and hesitation at the prospect of causing my death.

I find his hand and place it on my chest, between my breasts. *Feel that?*

It's my blood and my being, boiling with unspent vitality. My whole body thrums with it—to the physical, palpable touch of his hand. I know he feels it, my skin shivering and my muscles uncontrollably tensing and twitching. My gut twists with it, my heart hammers with it.

I feel it, he responds. **What is it?**

It's your assurance that this WILL NOT kill me. I swear it, Caspian. I know it in my fucking bones. I touch the head of his cock to my sex, nuzzle him between the lips. "Please, Caspian. I need you. Please." I say this out loud.

He growls, an animal snarl, and presses his nose to my throat and licks my jugular on the opposite side of where he last fed from me, and I feel the tingle of venom. He's shuddering all over, tensed and holding back. "Fuck, Maeve. Fuck."

"This will free me," I say, and I don't know where the words come from, but I taste the truth in them. "I swear on my soul."

He pulls back to look into my eyes, and his are clear, dark brown human eyes piercing mine, yet his fangs are extended. "Maeve, I love you."

"I love you, Caspian." I clutch his ass and pull at him, encouraging him to enter me. "Please, Caspian. Make love to me. I need you. I need you *now*. Please."

His sigh of relief is a hot breath against my throat, and he licks my jugular again, tingles spreading through me…

His fangs piece my throat and my blood flows into his mouth; in the same instant, he thrusts into me, his beautiful thick hard perfect cock filling me and filling me until I'm glutted and choked with the fullness of him, and never has it felt like this, never have I been completed in this way.

I am his and he is mine, and we are one.

Chapter 31

His cock pushes deep, and our hips bump and my whole being pulses, hot and wild and full and free.

The tightness of my skin around my bones is total—I'm about to split apart at the seams.

Within, the same. My soul, the core of my being throbs, expanding, constricted by something invisible and powerful, something that's held the truth of me imprisoned all my life, and that cage is now weakening.

Caspian withdraws and thrust deep again, and the cage shakes, rots, and becomes fragile.

I wrap my legs around him and cling to him, pulling hard against him to keep him deep, and I thrust against him and meet his thrusts with my own desperately bucking hips.

More, more, more. I need…I need something more.

That void within me pulls—I'm glutted on vitality, but I need more yet. I taste him, the magic of him, the power in his blood—*my* blood, transformed in his veins and through the pumping of his heart.

I smell his blood. I can almost taste it. I need it.

Fuck, I need it.

He's moving in me, now, rhythmic and slow. Building to his climax. But I don't need slow, I need ferocity and release. I show him. I drive up against him, but it's not enough.

I roll, and he goes to his back; I lose him in the process, and moan and whimper at the emptiness where he belongs. I scramble to straddle him, his hips in the wide V of my thighs and I crush my soft breasts against his hard chest and I basket my hands under his head and neck. Tilting my hips, I find his erection with my seam, and I feel him notch at my entrance.

"Fuck, Maeve—I need you. I need us. I need it." His voice is ragged, gasping. Human in his desperation to have me back, to be inside me where he is meant to be.

I plunge down on him hard and fast, and I cry out a raw scream as he sinks into me, and his roar is feral and primal alongside mine.

"Fuck, yes, yes, yes," he growls. "You're mine."

"I'm yours."

Magic pulses at the words.

"Say it again," I command.

"You're mine." He thrusts up into me as he says it.

"I'm yours." I slam down on him.

Another hot pulse of magic.

"Say it, Caspian," I demand. "Say it again. Now. Please."

"Maeve Sparrow…you…are…*MINE!*" He roars the last word, so loud the rafters above shiver.

The magic pulses again, harder and hotter and thicker than ever.

It's not enough.

I need blood. I crave it, crave his, crave him.

I feel my teeth ache, and I withdraw some slender shield of resistance; I feel a relief, as if something long constricted is freed. Craving for his blood soaks through me, and I settle my sex onto him until he's bottomed out inside me and I cradle his face and jaw and I nuzzle my nose against his throat, and I feel the song of his blood throbbing just beneath the surface. Something tingles in my jaw and mouth and lips and saliva, and I give in to instinct—I lick his throat, tasting a hint of his blood, sensing and smelling it pulsing in his jugular.

I feel my fangs filling my mouth.

I pull at his vitality, and I'm exploding with it.

I sink my fangs into his throat and my mouth is flooded with his blood—I gulp it down greedily, and I feel Caspian in the hot coppery sweetness. It's not blood, it's nectar, it's life, it's honey. Thick and viscous and flowing and soaring and wild and sweet as sugar. My body trembles with an overabundance of energy and life and vitality, and I'm about to come apart.

Caspian groans.

I slick my sex up his shaft, and sink home again, moaning against his throat. He thrust into me and I sink around him as I draw his blood. He finds my hand, presses the underside of my wrist to his mouth, licks, and bites, all in one motion, and now we're feeding each other and we're united and joined and moving together in perfect rhythm and harmony.

I feel it coming—the ultimate climax. In the moment before it rips through me, I withdraw my fangs and lick his wound closed—he does the same.

I sit upright and plant my palms on his belly. He grips my hips and gazes up at me, his eyes partially blacked, vampire and human at once. Love shines from him.

"You're mine," I say.

He hears the command. "I'm yours."

"You…are…*mine*," I say again, synching the slam of my sex down on his cock to the emphasis of my words.

"I…am…*yours*." He mirrors me, thrusting into me in time with his declaration.

At each repetition, magic blazes between us, hotter and brighter.

The brightness, I realize, is coming from me.

From my eyes—glowing white-hot, incandescent. My hair is in a loose braid down my back; Caspian rips it free and untangles it in a single movement, and I realize my hair, too, is glowing golden-white like the filament of a lightbulb.

The magic is coming from within me, and I know there's only one more repetition left.

"*You…*" I lift up and take him deep as I speak the word, "*are…*" again, a slow hard movement, union of bodies and souls, "*MINE!*" I cry the last word.

The magic flares, my eyes and hair and skin are glowing incandescent golden-white, blinding and hot as the sun.

"Say it with me, Caspian," I command. "I am yours, and you are mine."

My whole being trembles uncontrollably, and I hover over him, his erection just barely inside me, the magic throbbing palpably, shaking the rafters and walls until the wood audibly creaks and groans.

We speak in unison: "I am yours and you are mine." Our bodies unite at the utterance of the final syllable.

The detonation is concussive.

Something in me shatters, irreparably. It is at once raw and unbearable agony like no pain I've ever known and the purest climax. My very soul is being ripped apart, exploding into shreds and ribbons and tatters. Yet, within that destruction is the birth of something. The golden-white light of my skin, hair, and eyes is no longer just blinding, but like being at the center of the sun, total obliteration of all things. Not just heat, but perfect incandescence.

I'm screaming, an unending scream.

My blood stops flowing, my heart ceases to beat. Synapses fray and sever. Tendons and ligaments shred. My eyes burn to cinders. Caspian, beneath me, screams as well—pain and something more.

Where before, I only felt hints of him, tinges and touches and tastes of him, now I feel *all* of him. I know his every thought, his every emotion, his every physical sensation as if they were my own.

And I know he feels me the same way.

The agony fades into mere pain, and the searing brilliance dims, and then the pain is morphing into pleasure, into climax, into orgasmic release of such totality and purity that I can only cling to him and weep with it, and I feel him shuddering and shaking beneath me, hear him weeping as well and smell the copper of his blood-tears.

How long we cling to one another, convulsing and

gasping and sobbing and whimpering, I do not know. Hours, maybe.

The glow has subsided to a dull shimmer on my tight-shut eyelids.

When all has faded to nothingness, I open my eyes.

There's a dim orange glow from the dying fire below, yet I see as if in the highest noon daylight.

Beneath me, Caspian is sweating blood, soughing slow steadying breaths, and his face is smeared with blood-tears, and his skin is flushed, his eyes brown irises and human whites, and his hands rest possessively on my bare ass, cupping and clinging.

His expression is one of pure shock. "Maeve…holy fuck."

"What?"

He shakes his head, disbelieving and speechless. "I…you…"

"What? Tell me." Yet, I feel it.

The difference in me.

The mortality in me is gone. Obliterated and erased.

"What just happened, Caspian?" I ask.

He doesn't answer right away. Instead, he sits up, keeping me on his lap and connected to him, skin to skin, and rummages in the chest, coming up with a small round mirror, not just antique but almost ancient. The brass handle and frame are intricately carved in whorls and curls, and there's a ruby the size of my thumb set into the back. The glass is pitted and pocked and tarnished. Yet I can see my reflection in it, and when I do, I gasp.

My skin still glows a pale golden-white, as if a light inside me is slowly dimming as the power supply dwindles. My hair, previously an auburn that was more brown than red unless seen in direct sunlight, is now like Mom's was: neither red nor brown, but a perfection of both; at the moment, like my skin, it glows with an inner light which highlights the red, like sunlight through amber, but instead of golden-brown, the amber of my hair is golden-red.

My ears are pointed—like Mom's in the first void-space dream, like Andreas's. Not pointed upward from the tip of my ears like those of an elf in popular fiction, the points of mine angle toward the back of my head and slightly upward. I touch them, rubbing my thumb along the backside of my left ear, following the cartilage as it tapers to a point—it's real.

Then, there are my eyes.

They're white. Pure white, from corner to corner. No iris, no pupil. Like a vampire's blacked-out, void eyes, but inverse, whited-out instead of black. Where Caspian's eyes seem to suck in shadows and radiate darkness, mine seem to burn with an inner light.

I have, however, vampire's fangs, my eyeteeth needle-sharp.

"Caspian?" I breathe. "What…what happened? What am I?"

He presses his hand over my heart. "Feel that?"

At his touch, our link throbs. I feel his awe, his confusion, his love. I feel his thoughts as clearly as if he's speaking to me out loud.

I don't know, Maeve. I don't know what you are. Still sitting upright with me, my legs hooked around his waist, he cradles me against his chest. We breathe together for a moment, and then he tilts my face up to kiss me, deeply and thoroughly. "I do know two things, however."

"Tell me, please." I say it out loud.

"One, part of what just happened was we blood-bonded. We're blood-mates, Maeve. But…more than that, somehow. That's part of what I don't know."

"And the other thing?" I look into his eyes and take reassurance from the love emanating from him.

"You're not a mortal, and you never were."

"Then what am I?" I ask again.

He shakes his head. "I don't know, not for sure."

"Then guess."

"Fae." He lets out a shaky breath. "And vampire."

"I didn't think hybrids or half-breeds could exist."

"Neither did I." He cups my jaw. "I don't know for sure, but that's what I suspect you are: the first of a new breed, a fae-vampire hybrid."

"How?"

Another shake of his head. "I don't know that either." He lays down with me, and takes me onto his chest, cradling me in the shelter of his arms. "But I know we'll find out, together."

I reach for the others across the linkages, and I feel them there, waiting. I feel their personalities and their souls and their minds, more clearly than if they were in front of me.

I call for them.

I feel them respond, my vampire coven family.

They feel the difference in me, even across the connections, and I taste their shock.

They come, and I hear and feel them enter the cabin. *Come up,* I tell them.

One by one, they fill the loft, surrounding me. I keep my face buried in Caspian's chest until the last vampire joins us—Alistair.

And then I sit up, naked and unashamed, and let them see the new me.

For a long, tense, silent moment, no one speaks, too shocked.

Then, of course, Alistair fills the silence. "Well. This changes everything."

THE END

Sign up!

As a THANK YOU for reading my stories, I have special gift from me to you—a free, exclusive short story, *Caught in the Surf.*

Visit jasindawilder.com to sign up for my newsletter; I only send out newsletters when I have important Jasinda Wilder book world updates to share.

Visit me at my WEBSITE or my AMAZON AUTHOR PAGE; you can also EMAIL ME. at jasindawilder@gmail.com

ALSO BY JASINDA WILDER

If you enjoyed this book, you can help others enjoy it as well by recommending it to friends and family, or by mentioning it in reading and discussion groups and online forums. You can also review it on the site from which you purchased it. But, whether you recommend it to anyone else or not, thank you *so much* for taking the time to read my book! Your support means the world to me!

My other titles:

The Preacher's Son:
Unbound
Unleashed
Unbroken

Biker Billionaire:
Wild Ride

Big Girls Do It:
Better (#1), Wetter (#2), Wilder (#3), On Top (#4)
Married (#5)
On Christmas (#5.5)
Pregnant (#6)
Boxed Set

Rock Stars Do It:
Harder
Dirty
Forever
Boxed Set

From the world of *Big Girls* and *Rock Stars*:
Big Love Abroad

Delilah's Diary:
A Sexy Journey
La Vita Sexy
A Sexy Surrender

The Falling Series:
Falling Into You
Falling Into Us
Falling Under
Falling Away
Falling for Colton

The Ever Trilogy:
Forever & Always
After Forever
Saving Forever

The world of *Alpha*:
Alpha
Beta
Omega
Harris: Alpha One Security Book 1
Thresh: Alpha One Security Book 2
Duke: Alpha One Security Book 3
Puck: Alpha One Security Book 4
Lear: Alpha One Security Book 5
Anselm: Alpha One Security Book 6
Sigma
Gamma

The world of *Stripped*:
Stripped
Trashed

The world of *Wounded*:
Wounded
Captured

The Houri Legends:
Jack and Djinn
Djinn and Tonic

The Madame X Series:
Madame X
Exposed
Exiled

**The Black Room
(With Jade London):**
Door One
Door Two
Door Three
Door Four
Door Five
Door Six
Door Seven
Door Eight
Deleted Door

The One Series
The Long Way Home
Where the Heart Is
There's No Place Like Home

Badd Brothers:
*Badd Motherf*cker*
Badd Ass
Badd to the Bone
Good Girl Gone Badd
Badd Luck
Badd Mojo
Big Badd Wolf
Badd Boy
Badd Kitty
Badd Business
Badd Medicine
Badd Daddy

Goode Girls:
For a Goode Time Call…
Not So Goode
Goode To Be Badd
A Real Goode Time
Goode Vibrations

Dad Bod Contracting:
Hammered
Drilled
Nailed
Screwed

Fifty States of Love:
Pregnant in Pennsylvania
Cowboy in Colorado
Married in Michigan
Christmas in Connecticut

Billionaire Baby Club:
Lizzy Goes Brains Over Braun
Autumn Rolls a Seven
Laurel's Bright Idea

Dirty Beasts:
Rev
Kane
Chance

Standalone titles:
Yours
The Cabin
The Parent Trap
Wish Upon A Star
Big Hose

Non-Fiction titles:
You Can Do It
You Can Do It: Strength
You Can Do It: Fasting

Jack Wilder Titles:
The Missionary

JJ Wilder Titles:
Ark

To be informed of new releases, special offers, and other
Jasinda news, sign up for Jasinda's email newsletter.

www.ingramcontent.com/pod-product-compliance
Lightning Source LLC
Chambersburg PA
CBHW020903060726
47591CB00004B/1057